The Carbon Cult

Oliver B. Williams

Oliver B. Williams

First Edition 2014
First Printing 2014

Second Edition 2020
Second Printing 2020

Zeitgeist Publishers
Oxnard, CA
www.zeitgeistpublisher.com

Jacket Design by Oliver B. Williams

Proofreading by Irmgard Williams

ISBN: 978-0-578-82914-2

Fiction

Published in the United States of America

10 9 8 7 6 5 4 3 2

ACKNOWLEDGEMENTS

The Carbon Cult is my third full length novel. A thought—a cognitive tickle—nagged at me, now, and in the past. I asked my wife, Irmgard, "What if our history, instead of being 'God's plan,' is a 'human plan?' What if the major events—the trajectory of history—had been written, enacted, and manipulated like a screenplay? Or more troubling, as a ritual?" Considering this epitome of all conspiracy theories, I continued with this query. I asked my friend Dr. Gary Emery (who I trust to be very forthright with me) the same question. He encouraged me to follow that thread.

I'm grateful to Irmgard Williams for reading each completed chapter, and providing continued encouragement. I'm a forest person; she's a tree person. We complement one another well; she sees errors and details invisible to me. Gary Emery read several chapters at a time as I completed them. He didn't sigh in total exasperation at the completion of each reading, so I felt encouraged even further.

DEDICATION

To my wonderful children: Oliver, Christopher, Adrian, and Avery. I cherish every second of my life without regrets, because any change in my life's path means they may not have existed.

Chapter 1

Kristoph Éclair

Paris, 1978

He contemplated how they would kill him, probably with a sniper's bullet to the brain. *I am the boogeyman, the unseen prime mover. They do not know me, yet I am in their lives—and I, too, must die.*

Kristoph Éclair deliberated his status: Few were aware—at forty-four years of age, he was the most powerful person on earth. He mulled over the end: The world as most knew it would end in forty-five years—except for those tucked away in remote rainforests and mountain crevasses. He and his brood had engendered the end, nurtured it, and carefully constructed its scaffolding for decades. From childhood he had been groomed and reared to function in his capacity—the conspiracy theorist's nirvana. He existed in a complex web where history's outcome had been made to look like fate, but the design had been scribed and determined long ago.

He meditated, reflecting on his life's purpose: Some children grow up going to Sunday school, some to temple, and some go on family picnics or gatherings every Sunday. His religion—to enact the fate of the world as determined by his father and other members of their invisible, surreptitious and covert society. His scriptures, written less than a century ago, prophesized current events, not by mysticism, nor channeling spirits, nor convulsing to oblivion in order to retrieve the dubious droppings of a passing spirit. His scriptures had been set forth at the dawn of technology, during a period still virgin from marketing, advertising and fads. And the scriptures had not been penned by blind prophets, smitten with drug-induced visions while roaming a desert; nor did they emanate from the incantations from a tribal wise man. The prophet was his father. The future had been seized by a few keen far-seers, standing at the brink of the technology revolution. They steered the course as they saw fit, as nothing opposed them.

He did not believe in accidents—all events occur with meaning and purpose, though the participants may be unaware of the mechanism they otherwise call fate. Hence, not knowing exactly when he would die rendered him distraught, uncomfortable for a man not accustomed to the challenges of not being in control—not aware of outcomes before they occur. Everyone agreed it would be better if he did not know. He might waver, or call it off, or change tactics, or delay the process. He often walked the city streets alone, examining faces, studying families, divining what his life would be—what he would be—if he were not who he was. *Royalty over the millennia—who among them yearned to be free of their rank by birth? I ache because I live at an extreme. What of those at my opposing extreme? Those who are mindless, powerless, impoverished and peasant-bred—do they yearn for my life? Or, do they simply wish better creature comforts? Or, have some individuals trained themselves to cope with existence, and, thus, live as each passing second prescribes?* He struggled to shrug off an impending despondency, a yearning to relive his lifelong past.

My torture spawns from comparison, yet I cannot compare myself to anybody, living or dead. Judged by comparative standards, I embody evil, yet I have no evil intent. I wish the best for all on a grand scale. Have I done evil? Most would say, "Yes, of course, you have done evil and continue to do it to this day, and to your dying day." Most derive the fabric of their moral code from the Ten Commandments. How many deaths of men, women and children have my plans and actions expedited? Should I sit down with pen, paper and calculator, recalling each deed, each action, each order? Wars, famine, religious strife, disease, economic failure, genocides—by deed, thought, or order—I've planned them—expedited them—and my predecessors for

7

generations have done the same. I'll settle on a number—a billion lives. "I am directly responsible for the deaths and suffering of a billion human beings," he muttered. *There, I said the words. Who else could say those words with veracity—with sanity? What's the difference between a billion and a million or ten billion or one trillion? Zeros are irrelevant to the universal conscience, or so I have been taught. They inoculated me against guilt in so many ways, yet my inner onslaught continues. The levies give way. I welcome the bullet.*

Sitting naked in a lotus position, he drifted into a state of self-tolerance. He refused to meditate on rugs or carpeted floors. He insisted on a cold, hard surface. This one was oak; he preferred marble. A sunny but cold December day in Paris, his apartment was more chilled from the night air, insulated by the three-foot thick medieval walls. In whichever city he resided, he lived in an ancient structure. In 1978 medieval houses were abundant in Europe—nonexistent in America. Born in the United States, he preferred his permanent domicile in Europe.

Frustrated with his thoughts and unable to find calm, he muttered impatiently, "My head is trying to kill me." His life's work was coming to fruition, and he did not rejoice. As a child traveling with caretakers and nannies, he anticipated the trips with glee and enthusiasm. Each reminder of the trip ahead of him, each new day, brought a spark of exhilaration. He'd absorb himself in the process, cloaking himself into each minute of the future as if it were happening now.

He remembered his childhood being an adventure. Whenever he travelled by car, he'd sit in the back seat, enthralled by the sensations: the billboards whizzing by, the telephone poles appearing and disappearing instantly, the warm night air in unknown towns, alien people going about doing what they do, variations in insect and bird sounds, even the texture of the air caressing his face. So, whenever a journey commenced, and the reality was upon him, he would slowly retreat into glum, knowing that it would soon be all over, and his destination will have already been reached. The journey was important; the destination was an unappreciated finale.

Suicide was not an option. He had to continue. Yet, after the following few days, his labyrinthine plan would crystallize, the web of events locked into place. Soon, Mohammad Reza Shah Pahlavi would be deposed, and the Ayatollah Ruhollah Khomeini would assume the role of the leader of Iran. He had accomplished another link in the grand scheme of events, the complex algorithm of the future devised decades ago.

His operations were clandestine, under the most severe, yet subtle, subterfuge. Few knew his name, what he did, or even that he existed. Yet he knew that he was the most powerful man in the world.

He focused his power, like pin-pointed sunlight through a magnifying glass. Power was not fortune, fame, freedom, nor sensual extravagance. It was as God, moving the apparently immovable without being seen. Humankind was unaware of his potency; he did not take credit for his accomplishments—personal aggrandizement was irrelevant.

Kristoph and his cohort had never left anything to chance, or even to partial oversight. Each detail, each minutia, had been scrutinized and planned. Some of the original schematics remained unchanged to this day, devised and activated by his father, François, more than seventy years ago. If only he could have met the man who progenated his life's work, religion, essence and death. His father had master-minded the death, misery and destruction of so many millions of others. But without him, the world of today could very well have remained Victorian, perhaps even regressing to feudalism, or remaining locked into the desperate little national cultural scraps plaguing Europe and the world at his time.

Kristoph had an important meeting to attend, reports to hear, and projects to approve. For him, linear progression was a fantasy, an imaginary construct created by a concrete brain to cope with an otherwise unperceivable universe. They had achieved success with their current project. It was ninety-nine-point-nine percent complete. He was too well aware the last tenth of a percent could bring the entire affair to a halt, crushing it instantly in a reversal of fortune, and capsizing his life's work. This truth he knew: *The future is not linear; time is not linear.*

Activated by his impending schedule, he sprang from the floor in an acrobatic jump. After showering and dressing, he stepped into the cobblestone alley, in earshot of the hectic Parisian pace only a few blocks away. He adored open solitude; he adored crowds and masses as well. This quiet, narrow, French alley reminded him of where his father had devised the Twentieth Century. He had never met the man.

Self-consciously, he scanned some nearby upper-story windows. Men with less power than he were surrounded by vigilant bodyguards. These men worried about wandering into open and public areas without verifiable protection—a show of power surrounding them. These men were often kidnapped, later to show up cowering and whimpering on a poorly produced 8mm film, kidnapper yelping demands, flailing about his hostage's severed finger or ear. Other times these men were simply cut down by a sniper's bullet.

Kristoph had a singular manifesto: Design, plan—plan for many levels and layers—tend to the details, then get out of the way. He believed the process was akin to cooking: Once the chef has assembled all the ingredients in the proper amounts and order, he should let the heat do the work. Whatever force that ushers outcomes into a final amalgam had disdain for outside influence once the system had taken on momentum. He believed one can only trip up what might otherwise be in one's favor.

He stayed to cobblestone alleys and side streets, preferring the claustrophobic density of opposing buildings squeezing his passage. After the two-mile journey, he paused across the street to face an unassuming building housing a Parisian neighborhood bakery. He scanned the building and surrounding area, nonchalantly noting a woman hanging her clothes on her balcony and another woman extended through her window, watering her potted plants.

The baker saw him crossing the alley through his store window and greeted him warmly, jolting out the door waving a freshly baked baguette. The baker loved Kristoph, and Kristoph reciprocated the affect. He identified, even empathized with the baker, yet he felt simultaneously as if he were stroking a friendly stray puppy. The dissociation disconcerted him—he had to remain focused. *How can the unfettered and naive feelings, attitudes, and expressions of this simple man represent humanity? The sum total of all bakers over time and space cannot be the grand scheme of my forbearers. We have festered, becoming this ugly, biological stain, which I shall wretch from evolution's grip.* He shook the baker's hand heartily, asked him about his family, then whispered into the baker's ear—a comment causing the baker to stir euphorically. He broke from the baker's embrace, walked the brief distance to the stairwell, and climbed to the third floor where he expected his meeting party awaited him.

The drab, paint-peeled, dark green wooden door wreaked of the experiences of its age. Even the tarnished, dull bronze number "6" decal affixed at eye level gave the impression of the room beyond as a domicile for the despondent and sensorially deprived. After inserting the key, he turned the lock carefully, listening for the latch mechanism to engage. He knew that improper access would have dire consequences.

The barren room sported a single, high-mounted, three-by-three window on the left wall, projecting some light through its shutter slats. A lonely clear light bulb swung slowly at the end of a wire from the high ceiling. Dilapidated lathe and plaster walls entreated the occupant to look away, lest your mood suffer the same despondency as past tenants. A door on the opposite wall—blending in with the water marks, chipped plaster and peeled paint—barely broke the monotony of abandonment. He strode the perimeter of the room circuitously, to the left and under the window in order to arrive at the door—to which he could have traversed directly across. Though he had ritualized the process by now, he recalled the safeguards he had designed and had directed their implementation in these rooms merely five years ago.

Another door blocked him, set only ten feet inside the wall from the first door. He opened this door with another key, turning it twice around while listening for sounds of the process. A latch clicked with a strident finality, and the door sprung open automatically.

He stood at the threshold of the second room, guardedly poised to avoid too hasty an entrance. Suddenly, blue and red horizontal lights scanned him, alternating from his feet up to his head twice. The room became immediately ablaze with warm colored lighting, inviting him to enter. Without fanfare or acclimation, he glided into a room in stark contrast with the first—alabaster ceramic floors, bright white walls interspersed with large paintings and statues, and a stark white tiled ceiling, scattered with one-foot diameter, dark semi spheres. The dynamic space sprawled at least two thousand square feet.

Several adjoining benches formed a circle twenty feet in diameter, dominating the center of the room. A single, low-back swivel chair defined the circle's center, surrounded by circumscribing benches. Twelve television monitors, each equidistant, were mounted on the bench, all aligned toward the center, vigilantly awaiting the chair's occupant's arrival. The lower part of each monitor had a label affixed, reading clockwise: Paris 1, Paris 2, Tehran 1, Tehran 2, New York, Washington, Tel Aviv, Munich, Bombay, Peking, Moscow, Cairo.

Kristoph shuffled unobtrusively into the center of the circle through a narrow gap in the benches' perimeter, sat without flair or circumstance, and adjusted the headphones hanging from the chair's back. He spun around in the chair several revolutions, seemingly mischievously, as a child might play on a spinning chair, assessing the presence and temperament of each face on each monitor. Isolated and surreptitious in life, he remained so among his associates as well. He looked at their faces on the monitor screens, but they could not see him. A wave of loneliness washed through him. They could hear him, but even his voice was electronically altered. They had all abided by these regulations for years, though some of the participants were his childhood comrades, and two were family members. Still, they could not risk any transmission of his face and voice, nor could they risk the content of their conferences escaping their private network. They had abandoned in-person conferences as soon as the technology had availed itself to remote conferencing. All of them together in one place jeopardized trillions of dollars, untold time, and the planet's most significant history.

He realized that the domino effect they had put into play through his organization's active, covert involvement in global affairs had gained steep momentum. Things were coming together too hastily, too successfully. He was not prepared for the quest to stop. He longed for a glitch—something to delay the inevitable. Any bad news would translate to prolonging the process, yet not terminating the story.

His gaze lingered on the woman on the Tehran 2 monitor, a flash of remorse glassed his eyes, and he switched to Cairo. "Sorry to keep you waiting. I can tell you're all upbeat on this occasion." He paused, smiling thoughtfully at the Cairo monitor. "Though you're a bit apprehensive, Cairo," Kristoph commented, "I believe I know the

13

reason," he uttered, pausing, to discuss later. "I would like to hear from you all, but let's get to the crux of the situation first. Our subject matter, as you're all aware, is our impending revolution in Iran."

He nudged the floor with his heel, spinning his chair toward the monitor labeled Tehran 1. As he peered toward the screen, his expression softened as he recalled the history behind the face on the monitor. He battled another wave of despair, then recovered. *Nasser. I miss you, my old friend.* When they were children, he and Nasser played soccer around the oilfields of Iraq, Iran and Saudi Arabia while Nasser's father conducted his oil and finance concerns. He tore off a piece of his baguette and took a big bite before speaking. "Tehran One. Where is the Shah currently? Has he left Tehran?" Kristoph asked his old friend, omitting a salutation.

"Concurrent with our ten-year staging, the resistance to the Shah has escalated to a critical mass. The Shah continues to make moves in our favor, as he antagonizes the very ones he should appease. As of December 12, strikes continue to paralyze the country. Basic services here in Tehran have been reduced to skeletal rationing, including basic utilities. Sanitation removal has been nonexistent for six weeks, and the stench from garbage and human waste taints certain neighborhoods. The state television broadcasts only two hours per day. This revolution is about to boil over. Though the Shah remains here in Tehran, I would venture to say that the current climate will force him out no later than next month, January." Nasser grimaced as if blocking a thought but hoping he would be asked to speak his mind. "I'd like to add some additional information—some security feedback that may be useful to us."

Under normal circumstances, Kristoph had known Nasser to be level-headed, patient and collected. His friend's need to garnish his report carried relevance that he knew the others would not sense. Its seriousness should be heeded. He considered asking him to go offline with his additional comments until they had an opportunity to meet, face to face, but he was not sure when that would be, and he valued Nasser's assessments, as impromptu as this one was. "Please, proceed," Kristoph replied, sounding as upbeat as possible.

"Though we never leave a footprint, the absence of one here is about as damning. There exists here—among the more erudite politicians and intellectuals—an undercurrent of questioning and curiosity," Nasser recited as if lecturing a classroom. "How is it that this revolution could occur? It lacks all the hallmarks of revolution—a discontent and uncontrolled military, chronic class struggle, years of costly and ineffective war or calamity. These factors are absent in Iran, so what fueled this revolution? Furthermore, it's occurring at remarkable speed; it's massively popular. It results in the defeat of a well-financed and internationally connected government. The revolutionaries are completely opposed to developed cultural gradients nurtured by western culture. This revolution replaces Western modernization with a religion-based dictatorship. So again, the question is being asked: What is behind this phenomenon? Our effect, and the void we have left, create a disparaging dichotomy."

Hoping Nasser's comments would forecast retardation of the deterioration of Iran's government, Kristoph's respite was momentary. The news was cautionary but not formidable. He grasped that he could not sound disappointed. "I understand the information and your accurate synopsis. Your recommendations?" Kristoph replied. He noticed Nasser started mouthing his response before he had finished his comment.

"Planting the footprints of frequently guilty and easily blamed entities, like the CIA, KGB, or MI-6," Nasser responded readily.

His temple twitched as he recalled past occasions his association had framed intelligence agencies, only to instill righteous indignation within the affected organizations, causing them to probe the source of their vilification. He knew the CIA was present in Iran, easily victimized by properly planted evidence. Yet, the Shah's departure was counter-productive to the CIA's objectives, and this kind of dirty trick ploy would draw unwanted attention. Here was an opportunity, he thought, to set back the Iranian program here and now. If he agreed with Nasser's recommendation, he would induce a greater probability for failure. Perhaps the timetable of his own demise would be prolonged—perhaps not—but at least he would ameliorate his burgeoning guilt. He could live and die in peace, knowing his bourgeois conscience had been appeased. *No! From wherever this insidious feeling of wrong-doing evolves, it's not me, and it is not real. Think Universe, Kristoph! You're disgusting, lamenting over nonexistent friends, the family you never had, playgrounds, and the laughter of children. Leave it and forge on with your work.*

As if his hesitation had not existed, he responded. "If we create an object, an explanation for the void, our footprint could become evident. Like the man who suspects the unknown witness to his crime, he ventures to terminate the witness, thus exposing himself as the heretofore unknown culprit in the process. Let the rumors and conspiracy theories fly. Indeed, rumors of an unknown cult, a secret organization planning the outcomes of global destinies—these anecdotes are our best camouflage." He spun around in his chair, assessing the other faces. All were blank, except for Cairo who continued to exude agitation. Then he turned back to Nasser, clinging to remnants of feelings he had just convinced himself to abandon. "Come to Paris—tomorrow. We'll discuss this situation further." He saw his old friend's face light up at these words as he nodded affirmatively.

"Tehran Two. Next, please." He rotated toward an olive complexioned, dark-haired, richly feminine face. Though he had trusted her for more than fifteen years, he had known her only as a Persian woman named Ravan. Her soft round, brown eyes would be soothing if it were not for her penetrating gaze. The reality of her forty-one years was shrouded, revealing instead a youthful woman in her mid-twenties. Privy to her actual age, he squinted toward the monitor, probing for the tell-tale signs of maturity—receding skin tautness below her chin, forehead revealing marks of stress, corners of eyes and mouth, replacing plasticity with crevice. She smiled perfunctorily, but looked relieved as if she were hoping she would be called upon next to speak, and she launched officiously into her commentary.

"I've monitored foreign concerns here, both in the cities and countryside. My sexual trysts continue with Fardis Mofatteh, former student of Khomeini and leader of the faction most antagonistic to the Shah. Here is what I have learned: US, British, and German companies had established bases of operations throughout Iran but especially in major cities, and the employees are in danger of detention if they do not vacate the country soon. American employees especially may be held as hostages."

He pressed his fingertips and thumbs together, inserted his nose into his joined hands as if he had formed a mask of prayer, simultaneously issuing the acknowledging grin of an unexpected windfall. He struggled against overconfidence, knowing that what seemed too good, probably was too good. Yet, the outcomes surrounding Iran's current turmoil could not have been better coordinated. "Yes," he whispered with a drawl, "That's a perk. Such an action would force the Carter administration into an impotent quandary, angering and frustrating the American people. And the longer a potential hostage crisis persists, the greater certainty the Carter administration will be voted out in 1980. We've groomed a candidate, one who'll deliver his lines like the faithful, fake cowboy he is." He paused, mulling over Tehran 2's report. "I think you should stoke the fire. We'll send you a list of American companies whose employees are

17

likely to continue to hold up in the city. You can pass this information on in your inimitable fashion—but let's try to make sure a hostage situation results. Given that the Carter administration botches a negotiated release of the hostages; our man will be elected next year."

A flurry of energy erupted from Cairo's monitor, startling Kristoph. The representative had lost patience and, without further reservation, emitted a comment. "I apologize for the interruption, but I may have some breaking intelligence to provide which may enhance the current topic."

Kristoph turned toward the intruding monitor, more engrossed in the motivation than interrupted by the message. Poised to hear Cairo's concerns, he was aware of what his colleague would warn—the foul precedence occurring in the Middle East with the establishment of a theocratic state, and the danger of allowing the resentment to the West's support of Israel to crystallize with a new Iranian regime. He recognized it, and he wanted it. His job was almost complete. "Please, Cairo, proceed. That is, if you have no objections, Tehran 2." He shot a furtive glance back to the monitor as if she could see him. She nodded politely, bemused that her warnings had been converted to blessings. Kristoph rotated to Cairo's monitor. The sun-glassed man appeared agitated, pressed to deliver his information.

"My sources are immersed in Baghdad. As you know, we have inside ties with Saddam Hussein's family and confidants. Even our contacts' children are friends with the sons of the dictator Hussein, fifteen-year-old Uday and thirteen-year-old Qusay. Had our organization calculated what I'm about to say into the algorithm of the Arab world? I can say with the greatest confidence that Saddam will seize Iran's transitory and unstable period during the post revolution and attack Iran, most likely within a year." Cairo blurted his expository in a single breath, depleted of air at the end of his remark.

Cairo caught him off guard, differing from Kristoph's expectations. He appreciated little surprises like that. They kept him entertained and away from the despondent boredom toward which he had recently gravitated. *Ahh, he caught on to that dynamic. I had not expected him to factor in the Iraqi component. He does not realize that over the next twenty-five years Iraq catalyzes our program.* "And attack he should," Kristoph blurted confidently. "The algorithm requires Hussein to alienate himself from his neighbors and, eventually, from the West. Khomeini's most likely reply will be a bloody and fruitless war, but it will take attention away from his theocratic Islamic republic. Indeed, given enough time, Khomeini would be the aggressor instead. As we are aware, he would like to replace Hussein's Sunni Arab state with an Islamic republic. Colleagues, my only superstition is the belief that gloating brings about a reversal of fortune, so I'll refrain from that self-indulgence." He noticed Cairo's stunned countenance, appalled Kristoph had all but discounted his anxious concerns and well-placed intelligence sources. *Perhaps I should have apportioned more core information to him. Yet his appall suggests he believed he acted independently, a factor making him less trustworthy for future operations.* He repressed his tenacious gloom, once again faced with the elimination of another familiar associate.

Oscillations of police sirens outside his window reminded him the room was not as sound-proof as he would like it. Too much development and construction in a short period of time invites curiosity and suspicion. So, unless they had constructed a building from the beginning, they could not construct internal facilities involving imported technology or anything looking out of the ordinary for the neighborhood. They chose their neighborhoods meticulously, then lived and worked from these social niches, establishing homes and innocuous businesses. Only after considerable consolidation periods did they discretely move in their technical hardware. He had learned his lessons well as these logistics had been handed down from François Éclair decades ago: He preferred to chose his base of operations in neighborhoods and towns supporting both commerce and tranquility. He had meticulously read his father's journals: Where one lives and works must support your public face, the face you want everyone to see and know. If you inhabit neighborhoods where occupants seek anonymity and shadow, then you are guilty by association. He did not want to disappear. But he did want to remain invisible. Yet, recently he felt it prudent to cultivate external security and eyes to keep watch. They were too close and had worked too hard for a careless and spurious slip to endanger their goals. Not that anybody outside the organization had the remotest idea of his business or intentions, but any snooping could bring about questions to which uncomfortable responses might result. Overcautious or paranoid—he did not care what label—he demanded all potential leaks be watched.

He had been uneasy with this meeting even before it had commenced. He knew the contents of the reports and had communicated with all his representatives and cohorts. The inertia from decades of planning and implementation would not shift on a whim or discrepancy. Had he his druthers, he would have remained in his apartment, meditating for another hour. Then he would have taken a stroll along the Seine and, perhaps, driven his Audi into the countryside.

Am I my mold? Am I merely the solidified polymer, having filled and conformed to the shapes and contours of the model into which I was poured? Or, do I have another essence? Another me? Would the viscous fluid that was me, before solidifying into this mold, have its own shape? Would it have formed autonomously had my predecessors not interceded on my development? My purpose divined from the beginning, knowing I have a purpose, higher than kings, more exalted than the pharaohs of Egypt. I know the future because we made it. I would not sire children to be branded and groomed into my lot. Sterilization was the best—my only real decision, created and made by me. It was the only action divined and executed by me. Yet, I must have offspring designed from my genes, and it must fill the mold of the my cult, no matter how much I have resisted the notion.

He recovered his composure, having drifted into a dissociation, catalyzed by the siren, but culminating from the finalizing events which the participants of the meeting had confirmed. He knew that though the others could not see him, they sensed his emotional departure. The end was close at hand, and he had no child, no successor, no protégé to follow in his footsteps.

He struggled to settle the churn from within. His reflection from an unlit monitor suggested repose and serenity. *Our ancient organization is not a religion, not a belief system, not a clandestine association into which one might join though fraternal machinations. Nor was it a profession, career or life's work. It is me. To betray it is to betray myself. It is unbetrayable. We have cultivated our roots throughout the world's governments, cultures, arts and technologies. To question it is to question my own existence.* Yet, as he ruminated and fretted his identity, he realized his defining characteristic was that of Descartes: He knew he was unique and different by his very thinking and imagining. He had to nurture a successor, quickly. And by the very nature of its immediacy, he realized he must traverse the boundaries outside his royal blood and recruit a commoner to carry the baton.

Even in his demise, his clandestine organization would continue, its momentum well entrenched into the fiber of history. Ravan knew what to do, as did Nasser. Events had fallen into place too readily, too naturally. The revolution over which they had planned, toiled, and germinated seeds would soon bear fruit. They had placed causal relationships so deeply under cover; the naturalness of the events could only be questioned by the most paranoid, the most suspicious, and the most willing to attract negative self-attention. He had to die soon, and he must have a successor. *How did my father postpone the inevitable?*

He emerged from his trance, barely apologetic. "I'm sorry for the disruption. Obviously, I was distracted. I have a question," he inserted with guarded hesitation. "Somewhat off-topic. The work we're doing on the autoimmune virus. That's complete, to my understanding. We're implementing it in Africa, am I correct?"

"Indeed, it's already underway," Zora Green, the Tel Aviv correspondent responded. "As you are aware, my scientists have worked diligently on this project in Zurich, Tel Aviv, Lagos, and some remote stations in the Congo."

Kristoph appreciated Dr. Green. She was officious, exuding the emotions of a department store automaton. He grinned inwardly, recalling the private sexual fantasies he had entertained about her. "To my understanding, your team discovered the virus through recombinant DNA sequencing, attempting to juxtapose the human genome, and instead created this rather whimsical plague—a virus spread only by blood-to-blood contact, and most likely transmitted sporadically during anal sexual intercourse." He paused thoughtfully, contemplating the potential outcome, meantime noting Zora Green had maintained her stone face.

"The affliction will first affect male homosexuals because of rectal membrane bleeding and semen contact. Then people who share needles, mostly street drug addicts. Eventually, it will diffuse into the general population, spreading through blood transfusions and heterosexual intercourse. We anticipate epidemic scales in third world nations, and in nations unable to bridle their populace's sexual behaviors. We plan to unleash it in Nigeria, Uganda, Sudan and the Congo," Dr. Green announced with dispassion.

He sensed the gloom returning, not from loss of interest in his idea, but from Zora Green's antiseptic, dissociated explanation of a new strain of a plague unleashed on billions. He contemplated her diligence—exemplary given the limited technology available to conduct this complex task. He had provided her with the organization's most sophisticated computers, yet he understood that she had merely scratched the surface at defining the human genome. *I need it, yet it's so far off. She's on target but missed the point. She's developed ten thousand A-bombs on Hiroshima, but in viral form, where nobody will recognize the culprit behind their demise. But does she really comprehend the underlying utility of her gene technology?*

He resisted putting forth his query as if asking a sexual favor in anticipation of rejection. "Here's my question—have you come close to replacing zygotic host nucleus DNA with an independent extraneous strand? In other words, cloning?" He scrutinized her expression at the end of his question, observing the first tinge of emotional reaction. He couldn't stop imagining what she would be like in bed—probably a super nova of pent up energy, he mused.

"We've cloned simple multi-celled phyla, including species of coelenterates, planaria and echinoderms," Dr. Green remarked monotonically. "The highest vertebrate attempted was a salamander—no success. And no mammals as of yet. I—"

Frustrated, she had not perceived the gist of his queries, he cut her off. "I'll be blunt. How soon could you clone a human?" Kristoph interjected.

Rather than react to the defensively to the question, her expression softened. "Given the proper resources and time, within two years. Our primary impediment is not knowledge—it's computational power. In order to fully complete the task, we would need on the order of ten terabytes of quickly retrievable memory capacity, and multiple operating CPU's with clock speeds approaching microwave frequencies, say two to three gigahertz—not to mention billions of bytes of random access memory. This computing technology is currently fledgling."

Overcome be a by a gush of emotion, he realized if he had ever loved anybody, it was Zora Green. Instantly he recalled the synchrony of their lives—thinking, feeling, doing—they shared the same life function. "Technology advances faster than the market can accept. Just like my father's automobiles; he had developed most of the automotive technology commonly taken for granted today, only before 1915. He released it very slowly and anonymously. Today's processing technology follows the same formula, allowing for slow market diffusion. I have schematics and micro lithographs for processor, storage and memory technology, the market won't assimilate for another twenty-five years."

Could I live forever? My father had delayed it well into his sixties. How? Perhaps, because of the more robust African genealogy. The idea seemed more ego-centered and detached than his own impending procreation demanded. The poles weighting two equally balanced opposites vexed him. Usually adept at decision-making, he was tormented by the ambiguity. He could not forsake the idea, nor could he grasp it, own it, and make it his to happen. Despising procrastination, he relented to himself, admitting he needed a more open forum—a closer encounter with Zora Green.

"Dr. Green, I must discuss matters with you offline, in one week, say, in Vienna. Meet me at Hotel Sacher in Vienna—one week."

Chapter 2

François Éclair

Bern, New Years Eve, 1903

François Éclair gloated inwardly, careful to not let his self-reflected success appear obvious to his hosts. He had manipulated being invited to this meeting of minds, a group of young scientists and mathematicians for whom he had an intuition—a feeling of great promise for a revolution in thinking and an evolution of science.

He wanted to stay through the night, discuss hours of science and philosophy with his associates, but he knew he had yet another, even more pressing engagement. Eager to stay, yet fixed on his later meeting, he had not yet tilled their discussions with his clandestine purpose for being there.

The three intellectuals with whom he met were brilliant in mathematics, philosophy and physics, but the physicist was the one who had attracted him to Bern. *Properly nourished, this man will innovate physics and enervate technology. But his path must be wide enough so that he does not notice the barriers along the edges. He is a pacifist, which does not fit the goals either. Yet, given enough motivation, he can be convinced to cast those limitations aside.*

"You've flattered me with your invitation, Herr Doktor Einstein," François Éclair remarked suddenly after exhaling his cigar smoke. "Your treatise on the equivalence of mass and energy will rock the academic world. Given, you are marginalized in the patent office, how do you think such far reaching concepts will affect your chances at tenure within an institution worthy of your brilliance?" His host, Albert Einstein, never seemed to conceal his reactions, much to François' delight. Einstein frowned.

"My essay on the photovoltaic effect will open the door for me. I will not release my paper on special relativity until after the relationship between light and electricity has been absorbed. But,

25

indeed, Herr Éclair—you are, yourself, brilliant; such a grasp of physics, mathematics and philosophy. Why is it that you are not an established, tenured professor?"

Éclair pondered his response by inhaling his cigar and slowly blowing out a narrow stream of smoke, attempting to make it coil snake-like. He needed to condense his remarks into foundations for the future, knowing that whatever he said would be cogitated and remembered. "I am a modest tinkerer, Herr Einstein. I am, I suppose, the clockmaker of the new age. The great ideas—ideas which you, Herr Habicht and Herr Solovine will propose—these ideas need physical manifestations." He paused, checking on his colleagues' attentiveness. "For example, your photovoltaic effect, do you not foresee an application in the future where this theoretical construct might have a material manifestation? Say, a device that turns sunlight directly into electricity?"

"That's a fanciful concept, Herr Éclair. But what is the relevance for now? Even our philosophical discussions this evening have focused on Spinoza, who proffered the empiricism of human emotions. Yet, we cannot measure them, nor certainly not construct devices that emulate nor moderate any human state," Conrad Habicht remarked, cutting in before Einstein could react.

"You are correct, Herr Habicht. But if you accept that I have a sensitivity to the future and the past, then let me propose a concept to you. And Herr Solovine, your mathematical counsel would certainly be helpful in this regard. Consider that mankind's evolution is not only ontological and phylogenetical, but it is also intellectual—not intellectual in terms of education but rather in terms of information about the universe. And I do not mean simply available information tucked away in a library, but information that will be available to everyone. Given this premise, one might ask the question: What is the mathematical function defining this evolution? Evolution may be random, but it is not without vector. Hence, if it were completely random, then there would be no evident direction. But there is—and we are Endstation thus far. This journey has taken millions—even billions—of years. What if the function were exponential and, though, it appears shallow and linear, is it about to take off? What if we are currently seated at the knee of an exponential spike—an explosion of advancement in science?

"I would say you state a compelling conjecture. But since mankind has not been in the business of data keeping for millions of years, we cannot substantiate your premise on measurement and empirical evidence," Maurice Solovine replied dryly.

"But evidence has been collected, nevertheless, Herr Solovine. He have a wealth of fossil evidence, and more is being unearthed even as we speak. And the explosion of civilizations starting just six thousand years ago—the existence of homo sapiens far preceding emerging civilizations—this fact alone must offer corroboration to my premise. Stone tools for millennia, followed by the advent of civilization a mere six thousand years ago, then printing presses four hundred years ago, and now we discuss atoms and the essence of matter as if casually making light banter. We are gods who have not yet taken our seats on Olympus, my friends." Éclair needed to impress Einstein, staking a claim below his morass of abstract symbols and staunch empiricism. He noticed Einstein solemnly reflecting; Habicht seemed enthralled; Solovine appeared dubious.

"So, you are suggesting that Darwin's theories of evolution apply to information and societies as well as basic morphology?" Habicht interjected with persuaded enthusiasm.

"I'm saying I do not believe the final chapter has been written regarding the underpinning philosophy of Darwinism." François paused, studying the others, waiting for a hint of approval. "Indeed, I do not believe even Darwin himself had completely perceived the implications of his discoveries. As we all agree, sciences are sparked from a system of philosophies, then expand or dissolve based on experimentation, usually to disprove or discredit dogma. Darwin did not proceed from such a framework. His discoveries were based upon phenomenological observation. His science, though, surely valid, has yet to be backfilled with a philosophy, other than to endorse the scientific process. I believe the zeitgeist over the last century supports its credibility and will continue to accelerate."

Éclair had a schematic for the future, requiring Europe—and the rest of the world—to change course based on the tributaries he planned to trench. The men leading his charge would spawn from young innovators and intellectuals like his current company. Yet, they needed to bend to his will, without knowing neither that it was his will, nor that they were bending. "My dear Herren—you clearly see from the color of my skin that I am a mulatto. Yet, I can see, you dote on my words and ideas with intellectual gusto, whether or not you agree. And, as familiar as you are with Frederick Nietzsche, you must also realize that he posited that 'the mongrel leads the pack' as well. Do you not think genetic variety is the keystone to mutation, and hence, evolution?"

"As greater variation provides a larger pool for random selection, I would certainly agree. But what does your racial blending have to do with the current theme? Forgive me. I do not understand your allusion," Einstein remarked with unabashed naïve sincerity.

He carefully formulated his thoughts. *These are intellectuals to whom you speak. They know nothing of the political and cultural strife to vex the world. My words must prime—not avert nor amuse.* "You offer a spark in the fabric of science which, in essence, is a mutation. It is that catalyst from which the next lineage of social and scientific evolution will spawn and proliferate." Éclair hesitated. He did not want to proceed too hastily, but he needed to germinate the process now. "Herr Doktor Einstein. You have honored me over the past few months, sharing your work and papers with me. And here is what captures me: Your unpublished paper regarding mass and energy—the duality of the two, defining an equation which delivers unfathomable amounts of energy from small amounts of matter. As we sit here in these comfortable surroundings, your den heated by your wood-burning furnace, you must ask yourself this question: From where and from what will energy be derived in one hundred years? From the oxidation of cellulose-containing plant material, or from a technology derived from your equation? And—you must ask yourself the following question in parallel: Will the governments of the world—leaders perhaps not yet born, or perhaps currently honing their political skills as we speak. Will the political leaders of this new century settle for gunpowder and bullets to decimate their enemies—or energy from your equation?" He watched Einstein stare blankly at him, not as if he did not comprehend, but rather that he had been caught unprepared. "You will make this science a gift to humanity. But who in humanity will take advantage of it? If the bullies should seize it, you must be prepared to provide balance."

"Herr Éclair! You speak not as if you speculate about the future, but rather, you actually can see the future. Please, forgive me, but the assuredness by which you claim such events detracts from the ideas themselves," the young Habicht inserted, though seemingly fascinated by what he had heard.

"What our friend speculates is rational, though; the reality he spins remains one possibility out of many," Einstein remarked, cutting off Habicht.

"One hones probability from zero to one, based upon dominant forces and patterns over time, my friends. You, of all people, should know that simple truth," Éclair replied. He turned, looking out the window, startled that it was already dark. "I'm afraid I must take my leave. As I mentioned at the beginning of our discourse, I am expecting business associates over for a meeting of minds. It is boring and business related, otherwise I would invite you to join us. My friends—and I feel such a bond strong enough to call you, friends—I look forward to our next meeting. You know how to find me as I shall continue to remain at my Bern quarters for the rest of the winter, and into spring."

Éclair shook each man's hand with an endearing clasp, not a perfunctory gesture of departure. His gaze met Einstein's, and, for that brief instant, he felt Einstein had imparted a textbook's volume of information.

As he strode toward the street, away from Einstein's flat, he flung the outside gate open, nearly colliding with two elderly female locals. He marveled at the similarities each sported as if they were relatives, even sisters. Yet, he knew they were not at all related. The women simply evinced the style and customs of this region of Switzerland—short, nearly man-cropped hair; dark, distrusting glances; hunched stances, and a dialect which, by all other descriptions, tainted the German language.

He marched with wide gait toward his residence six blocks away, a five-hundred-year-old house on a cobble-stone alley, wedged over the banks of the Aare River, bisecting the town. He had just enough time remaining in the day to tinker with his project, an automobile in his laboratory. It was the centerpiece for his grand analysis—his schematic of the future—months in preparation, years in concept. He had worked into the morning last night to finalize the presentation he would deliver to his group of esteemed friends—colleagues, partners and associates he had collected from around the world, from Oxford to Berlin to Bombay to Lagos to San Francisco to Buenos Aires. Each individual was special, unique in his or her own talent and genius. He would lay his vision before them on this New Year's eve, the last day of 1903.

He trampled his doorstep; his feet stung from stamping the snow from them. Impatient to get to his laboratory, he cursed his tight-fitting leather gloves as he peeled them off. The cold door handle relayed a message to his perpetual idea center: *no more keys in the future*. He fumbled with his keys, annoyed, having forgotten whether the key turned clockwise or counterclockwise.

To him, the essence of the future sat in his laboratory. Though still invigorated by his recent dialogues with Einstein and the others, his pragmatism responded to the mechanism beckoning him. *All things new will spring from the design, manufacture, pursuit and utilization of automobiles. The dawn of a new civilization is upon us, and I shall own it.*

Once in the foyer, he checked his pocket watch—7:30 PM. His friends would arrive soon. *Gershon will no doubt be first.* He grinned affectionately. *A perfect New Year's celebration*, he thought. *The future will be ours because the course is clear and predictable.* Nudged by an idea, he looked at his watch once more.

Digits instead of hands.

Chapter 3

The Gathering

François had dabbled in his lab for over an hour, waiting for his friends to arrive. He was primed, and he had become restless. So impatient, he yearned to know everyone's whereabouts at the moment. He figured the swirling blizzard that had just besieged the area had delayed them. He was preparing to deliver a message about owning the future through science and technology, yet atmospheric turbulence was hampering his efforts. He made a note: a *device for instant voice communication with anyone, from anywhere, to anywhere.*

He sizzled with the intensity of the times, fully aware that he stood at the focal point of the change of humanity—the culmination of evolution that would shift the long lasting tug between man and nature, to man. Just four years into the Twentieth Century, and the future seemed within his grasp—machines and energy would supplant animals and fire. Everywhere he looked, whatever he saw, an imminent change pounced back at him. Each brick, each tool, every book, building, carriage, man, woman and horse—all would be conveyed to a new frontier. Science would be the new religion, technology its evangelist. He presided over a gospel: He and his group of visionaries would mediate both.

Perhaps, he pondered, his feeling was mere intuition, or perhaps it was a sophisticated insight fueled by his keen comprehension of science and mathematics, all tempered by exhaustive studies of history, philosophy and economics. Whatever he felt, he viewed the future with a wizard's crystal ball. Voraciously, systematically, he read scientific treatises, inventions, proposals and discoveries. He stayed in close contact with contemporary marvels of discovery and insight. Warmth welled inside as he recalled his evening with Einstein, Solovine and Habicht. He languished that he could never meet Darwin and Marx personally. He sought the company of Freud, Planck and

Heisenberg. He knew that whatever resistance the old world conjured, the barriers would be swept away swiftly, relentlessly. He buzzed; the deluge of new information was escalating at an exhilarating rate, much faster than any century before. This floodgate of innovation meant something, and he intended to be in the middle of it. He intended to manipulate it as his childhood caretakers had predicted he would.

Yet, he realized that old methods, mores, beliefs, and time-honored values die slowly if they ever die at all. Though relics of the past may subside, and perhaps the current progeny play with new toys, the underlying fears and ignorance of humanity quickly gravitate to the charlatans of religious sanctimony and obstruction. The proselytizers continue to spout venom, ever hoping to spawn a reversal of rationale—a return to the old ways. François could help design and steer the course of the new momentum, but its self-perpetuation would die if the masses were not rewarded continually for simply not turning back. The beginning was now, but an unplanned ending could result in total regression rather than a phased and transitional advancement. As he carved the beginning and template for his evolution, he forged an ending as well. He awaited the arrival of his colleagues and contemplated the future as if it were history.

He tinkered in the cold of his laboratory, gripping his wrench with an artist's flair, constantly mulling over ideas. He mused at the sensual quality of the slick, glassy surface pressing against his palm— not a fleshy sensual quality, but a sparking intellectual stimulation. *Perhaps that's going too far*, he thought. *It's only a wrench.* With it cupped firmly in his hand, he tightened the last two bolts on the internal combustion engine which he had assembled, disassembled, re-juxtaposed and re-examined—part by part—for the past twelve weeks.

Irked by the shadows and yellow hue from his light, he repositioned his incandescent bulb hanging from the hood of the automobile. He recognized even this simple contraption was black magic to his yokel neighbors. *Yet, I believe—as brilliant as he is—even young Dr. Einstein would be amazed at this simple piece of machinery, and even more amazed at its power over the future.* He glanced back at the electric generator, annoyed by its incessant clamor, but confirming that its exhaust continued to belch to the outside as he did not want to die from carbon monoxide poisoning. *The noise from these internal combustion engines must be muffled.* He scribbled another note. "Better yet, the source of electricity should be distantly remote. Still, it's a far cry better than a gas lantern," he muttered. He made another note: "Community electric power distributed from a central station."

He straightened himself slowly, having been bent over the automobile for over an hour. His friends would arrive shortly. He had so much to show them, and much to discuss. The last thing he needed was a sore back. He rubbed his hands together, grimacing at the texture of the oil and grit accumulated on his skin and under his nails. The combination of the Swiss winter, the humidity of the nearby Aare river, and his motionless stance while scrutinizing the automobile's engine had rendered him agonizingly chilled. Cold agonized him more than being too hot. He had lit the portable coal stove, but its potency had yielded to the raging blizzard outside. *We need more efficient heaters. Burning wood and coal will be passé.* He passed his hand over the light bulb, absorbing its radiated warmth.

As if the heat from the bulb had transmitted a cutaneous message to him, he bolted across his garage to a workbench. After wiping his hands meticulously with a towel, he dashed toward his desk, moving aside the many mechanical drawings he had composed from observing the engine parts of his automobile. He felt consumed with power, energy, ideas. Images of the future flew at him, one after another, and the light bulb had just bestowed one more.

Hungry for information, he scanned his desk, looking for his material science reference book. "Damn, I wish I had information at my fingertips at all times," he cursed, leading to self-dialogue.

"Magic. Fantasy. I say what I'm looking for, the results appear before me. Appear on what? Paper? How would it get there? Another method to display information would be required. The information would have to take the form of light. Or a miniature printing press. That would work as well."

He tried recalling where he had seen the book last. Suddenly, he remembered—two days ago he was combing metal resistivity tables for a better filament material. The book was on his upstairs study desk, and he dashed upstairs, returning with the volume. He flipped through the pages, knowing the approximate location of his query. *Ohm's Law. Voltage. Current. Resistance. I need a length of wire with enough resistance to heat to red hot without oxidizing. It won't be contained or enveloped in an inert gas like the bulb filament. It can't be too long, or too short. Copper? No. Silver. Absolutely not. Nickel alloy. Yes. Nickel and chromium. Nichrome will do nicely. And I have a length of it around here. I hope it's enough.* He fidgeted with his slide rule, calculating the length of wire required based on the voltage output of his generator. Then he tore back downstairs, found the nichrome, measured it, and cut it to length. He wrapped the wire around a broom handle, making a six-foot long coil. He attached one end of the wire directly to a generator terminal. Then he connected a potentiometer between the second wire and the other generator terminal.

He turned the potentiometer dial slowly, vigilantly, while observing the nichrome coil for change. His eyes gleamed demonically as the wire started to glow. He shuffled his feet in place joyously, his whole demeanor charged with energy. The coil glowed orange, and he warmed his hands over it as one would over an open hearth.

He scribbled more notes at his workbench. "Convection. It needs moving air. An electric motor with a propeller to blow the hot air and distribute it about the room. With the electricity supplied from external central sources, central heating devices containing these coiled wires with pipes leading to the rooms of the house—efficient central heating."

Suddenly, he heard the tunnel door creaking. His satisfaction from the success of his electric heater intensified, guessing that his friend, Gershon, must be the first arrival. Gershon would witness the glowing nichrome wires first hand.

This meeting had been months in planning. He had telegraphed his friends frequently over the past year. For this meeting he had provided each with specific instructions on how to enter the house. His five-hundred-year old dwelling had been constructed next to a medieval bathhouse. The city now kept the dilapidated structure as an apologetic monument, but it was closed to the public. Unknown to all, except possibly some mundane architectural historian, tunnels connected François' house to the neighboring bathhouse. And the subterranean vaults of the bathhouse were connected by tunnels with entrances several hundred meters down the brook over which his house was constructed.

François was adamant about privacy. Locals had little else to do but spy on their neighbors. They considered conformity—not cleanliness—next to godliness, and they scoured their territories relentlessly, seeking violators. He had gathered this insight—not from being suspicious or paranoid—but from social experimentation. He had confirmed, through conversational maneuvers, that any given neighbor was watching him or his house at any time. He did not want to be categorized or gossiped about, especially since he was one of the few non-natives living in the eight-hundred-year old town. He'd rather maintain a benign appearing lifestyle than lie about his affairs. He expected, and it was natural, that he would be considered an eccentric—he was a non-white foreigner. But they did not deem him as a dangerous or subversively eccentric; such derision would be disruptive to his plans. This evening's meeting was important, and he did not want to later fend off uninvited curiosities about the number of visitors he received so late on a New Year's Eve. He had instructed each of his associates not to come to the front door, but rather enter the house via a path he had cleared from the bathhouse. The path's entry, hundreds of meters away, was concealed at night, and the entrance was not associated with his house.

He heard his first visitor arriving. The little-used shaft belched dust, and the rusty hinges groaned their disdain. *Gershon*, he mused, grinning. Of all his friends, he'd have to admit, he held the greatest fondness for Gershon Akerling. *No doubt, he'll offer a spontaneous-sounding racial slur in order to break the ice.* He paused in concern, worried that the current snow storm would delay, or even inhibit, the others' appearance. Brilliant as his friends were, some were incompetent in matters involving practical preparation and timing. Gershon was most important—he and his Russian family held significant influence in banking and mining throughout Europe. Gershon was the most likely to immediately appreciate the import of his discoveries. He fondly recalled the years as children they had spent fantasizing about a future emblazoned in change and promise. Even as boys they realized horses would not continue to be the mode of individual transportation, and clunky oversized steam engines powered by wood and coal would not serve as the primary mode of public transportation. Though all were committed to following François' plan, Gershon was most adept at slicing through to the message's essence.

The corners of his mouth tightened in amusement as he anticipated his friend's entrance. He remained fixed to his notes and calculations, pretending to be more absorbed than he was; his euphoria over his successful, albeit impromptu, electric heater continued to distract him. Not compelled to turn around, he knew Gershon's footsteps, his presence, how his body transferred its energy to its surroundings as he made his way toward his study.

"You loathsome half-breed! What odious perversions of nature will you spew into mankind's future today?" Gershon's Russian-accented voice bellowed behind him. François' restraint gave way to laughter. He gloated inwardly at the insult's accuracy. Not at all perturbed, François cherished being set off from the rest. After jousting with Einstein about both the merits and impoverished logic of Friedrich Nietzsche, he swelled, knowing his mongrel-ness was beyond question, and the pack of wolves would eventually be rendered sheep by him. "My Algerian father and French mother—neither of whom had the courtesy to return to investigate the fruit of their labor—had intercourse. Or at least, so I've been told. But my only consolation is that during the course of their passion, the product of the union would rile the likes of you, my friend," he responded, turning around to shake his friend's hand. "Unlike you, I don't have the genetic deficiencies that racial purity spawns, especially coming from that stagnant, incestuous Sumerian gene pool in which you place your ancestral origins."

"Indeed, I bow to your—as of yet broadly unaccepted—racial superiority," Gershon replied, bowing deeply with whimsical haughtiness. He gestured, holding back his pent up curiosity, to the glowing wire. "Performing more Satanism, I see."

"Indeed. The heat from these glowing coils emanates directly from Hell," Éclair replied with dead-pan sincerity. "Which is where you should proceed without delay."

Gershon raised an amused eyebrow, and the two friends laughed heartily. Immediately, Gershon turned intensely serious.

"Really, Éclair. What is this contraption?" Gershon asked with magnetic fascination, walking toward the makeshift heater.

François felt ambivalent. He wanted to explain his spur-of-the-moment invention, but at the same time he wanted to proceed to the highlight of the evening and discover the whereabouts of the others. "A flash of an idea I just got two hours ago while observing the heat emanating from an incandescent bulb. You know how they glow and give off heat? Well, what if one wanted less light, and more heat? Passing current through a sufficient length of wire with the proper resistance results in more efficient transfer of electrical energy to heat energy. I'd say the idea speaks to the future of the hearth." He paused to assess his friend's astonishment in the device. "But on this eve of the new year, we gathered for more than electric heaters, cabbages and kings, did we not?" Gershon was warming his hands over the coils, passing them back and forth in mesmerized focus.

"Two hours ago, you say? My god, man. You amaze me," Gershon responded genuinely astounded. "But, yes, quite so. The others. As I said, they may be delayed by the storm. I was in Basel, and the trains had little difficulty. Last I had heard, Marie was in Munich; Lester in Madrid; Adrian had arrived in London from New York a week ago, but his present whereabouts, I could not say. Suresh departed for Paris from Bombay over two weeks ago as you already are aware. Have you not gotten any word?"

Éclair grimaced, shaking his head slowly in frustration. He worried the others may not arrive. "Telegraph and mail service here are not reliable," he replied. "I should have chosen Basel, or even Zurich. But this house captivated me. And the young man around the corner— he works in a patent office, but he's at the cusp of a breakthrough." Gershon cocked his head in devious curiosity.

"Not getting interested in young men now, are we, my friend?" Gershon drawled with a broad, mischievous smirk.

François flashed a disapproving glance. His friend irritated him at times, finding humor and sarcasm in everything. "No, not this time. There's something about this young man. A brilliance—more than genius—like an apex in history. He wrote a treatise which will eventually uncover sources of infinite energy—the stuff of gods. I want to make sure he harnesses it correctly—if you know what I mean."

"I see. Well, since he has you as mentor, I'd say he's a very fortunate young fellow," Gershon paused, watching Éclair's reaction, realizing he had irritated him with his last comment. "Well, seeing the others may be delayed; if not here at all this evening, perhaps we should get on with it. After all, I represent half the funding, and Marie and Adrian the other."

A wave of air pulsed through the room. François and Gershon turned to one another, acknowledging silently another friend's arrival. François stepped to the wooden spiral staircase and looked down the four-story, tubular centerline trying to glean some identity without calling out. Knowing his friends, they would not be so gauche to yell out their arrival before being well inside. He detected a multiple presence.

Relieved more had arrived, he felt a sense of satisfaction. "Speak of the devil, I believe it's Marie and Adrian," he said as he stepped back to the foyer.

Gershon smiled with a sense of relief, then went back to fanning his hands over François' electric heater.

"We know you're standing at the top landing," a male voice said softly in English with an American dialect. "Please, don't shoot!" A woman laughed briefly at the comment.

"You're in civilized society now, and not in the American Wild West anymore. I don't even have a gun," François replied in feigned indignation.

Adrian Morgan and Marie Rothschild stepped from the staircase landing into the brightly lit foyer, smiling. He noticed they were both disheveled from the weather, sporting blizzard-reddened faces and deposits of snow on their overcoats. Marie's head remained lodged, turtle-style, inside her extended mink collar. Adrian appeared more resilient, but was frazzled nevertheless.

"What the hell is going on with the weather?" Adrian complained bitterly, shaking off his Russian chinchilla hat, a gift from Gershon.

Marie Rothschild seemed more emotionally distressed. "Yes. And what's going on with these Swiss customs officials? We came from Burgdorf. They had us wait in our cab for almost an hour. What the hell could they have been doing in that out-house-looking cabin of theirs? The telegraph service was down," Marie chimed in, brushing the snow from her collar. She suddenly looked self-conscious, peering at François meekly. "Oh. I hope you don't mind the snow on the floor. It's only water, you know," she added apologetically.

He looked at her impatiently, shrugging his shoulders. Irritated she had changed the subject, he considered the subject of the Austria-Hungary relation with its German neighbor more interesting than some water on the floor. "Frequently, Austria-Hungary becomes defensive or sensitive about some political issue, and naturally, postures at its border crossings. Have the Americans or British done anything recently for them to interpret being shunned?" François asked accusingly.

Adrian and Marie, now having shed their winter apparel, looked at one another with devilish expressions. "Always," they said in unison, chuckling.

Then they each caught sight of Gershon in the sitting room, dabbling with François' heater, turning the potentiometer back and forth to vary the glow. "Oh, my," Marie gasped, divided about where to direct her attention—Gershon or the glowing wires. She hugged

41

François quickly, kissed him on the cheek and dashed toward Gershon. Adrian squeezed him on the shoulder and followed behind her.

"We should not let his toy distract us from our business at hand," Gershon said in his thick Russian accent, acting unfazed by his friends' arrival, but still very pleased. "I'm glad you two could make it and did not get swept up in a wave of wintry or political gusts."

Marie rubbed Gershon's head, puppy-style while Adrian pinched his cheek. "If you don't react with more gusto to my arrival next time, I'll squeeze your balls mercilessly," Marie declared menacingly, but joking. "What's this? Never mind—don't tell me: The future of furnaces. Am I not mistaken, Franny?" she called, angling her head to direct her question remotely to François.

He withheld the reactionary guffaw to Marie's threat as if it had been directed to him, deciding to treat her comment, and their presence, with officious emotionlessness. "Impeccable insight, as usual, my dear," François replied. "My testicles are properly secured from your terrorist plots. But this contraption I whipped together an hour ago is a miniscule wisp compared to the future we shall fashion together. *Sans plus tarder*, we should commence our long-anticipated meeting," he made a sweeping motion toward the door. "Perhaps the others will arrive later. Be that as it may, we are all bound to our goals we shall set forth here, tonight. Follow me, please," François announced, walking while looking over his shoulder. "And we'll get to the heart of matters." They all filed behind him amenably and followed him down the spiral staircase.

Chapter 4

Fuel for the Future

Lingering gasoline vapors in his laboratory wafted into his nostrils. Euphoria, nostalgia. A sense of purpose. *Ahh!* Uncertain the others could identify the aroma, he paused at the threshold of the workroom housing his automobile. Then he turned and inhaled as if amidst a field of aromatic flowers while lifting his hands upward to conduct a symphony. "Anyone identify the odor?" he asked expectedly. He could tell from Marie's ubiquitous playful command of her surroundings that she recognized the scent.

"Smells like the chemical burned in the horseless carriages you're crazed about," Marie asserted. "Petrol? Benzene?"

Her voice. Her intelligence. He repressed a relentless but futile sentimentality, unrequited and forlorn. He kept it caged, but not destroyed.

Then Adrian answered abruptly. "It's refined petroleum. It's gasoline," he said. "How'd you come by it here?"

The odor which permeated his sinuses, François knew, would eventually permeate the globe. He lived in the future, but his existence was now, and the conflict between the two was sometimes disorienting. "These Swiss aren't so uncivilized—they do take advantage of farming technology," François replied with pedagogy. "Some use internal combustion engines instead of steam engines to power their grain mills. So I didn't purchase it here. I used a row boat to smuggle several liters across the Aare last fall, to avoid customs and unwanted curiosity." He turned to conduct his party to the central object of interest—his automobile—center-stage, now illuminated by the yellowish radiance from several incandescent bulbs.

François allowed his friends to acclimatize—adjust to the unique ambiance—before his presentation—a track on the future he was certain not one person in the room—not even Gershon—could

43

have, as of yet, possibly anticipated or conceived. He wished the rest had arrived, and that the late winter storm had been postponed or had occurred last week instead. Gershon impressed him, standing back relaxed, arms folded, smiling, confident, undauntedly awed by what he had mastered. Adrian and Marie approached the automobile on display, its engine exposed for inspection.

"My friend, Karl Benz, provided me with this automobile," François explained, subtly bragging about his pride's origin. "Well, to be accurate, he gave me the parts and schematics, and I put it together. I added a few modifications. For example, if you've heard horseless carriages before, they are excruciatingly noisy. I improvised a device that muffles the sound of the internal explosions. Hear for yourself."

He turned the crank on the front of the car, and the engine ignited with a small explosion. Uncharacteristic of Marie, she squeaked a scream, withdrawing it immediately, self-conscious and embarrassed about her squeamishness, but rattled nevertheless.

"My god! I thought one of you eccentric libertines brought a gun in here. Or maybe, the neighbors caught wind of what François is scheming in here and thought they'd put an end to the devil's work," Marie shouted, re-asserting an air of self-control.

François ignored her startle, choosing not to badger her about it. He pressed on with the business of the evening. As he stood next to the now rattling—but relatively noise-free—engine, readying himself to address his friends. He knew his next words were, what he believed to be, pronouncements for the future. "The odor of gasoline is the odor of what is to come. Gasoline—petrol—is the refined distillate of oil, my friends. It is our primary topic of discussion for this evening, so it's of no wonder that the air should not also be filled with its aroma. Automobiles will characterize the future; gasoline powers automobiles; gasoline is refined from crude oil; crude oil can be extracted from deposits under the surface of the earth. It will be more precious than gold and, infinitely, more practical."

He recognized his opening remark was abrupt and without transition. He had chosen these words as an opening comment, hoping to gauge the others' receptiveness through each person's reaction. Knowing him as they did, all remained expressionless and attentive. Indeed, the apparent absurdity of his statement intensified their resolution. He had opened with a promise of a winning bet with the highest odds—a fool's inducement. Yet, François offered insider information, and his veracity was impeccable. They understood: If he predicted it, then with little variation, it would come to pass.

He flashed an impish grin, knowing he had whet, not only their curiosity, but their hunger and thirst for power and effect as well. He motioned with his finger for all to follow, leaving the automobile engine running. As they marched away from the car, Adrian glanced back at it, troubled.

"The exhaust gases from the engine. Aren't they toxic?" Adrian inquired.

"Quite," François replied. "Mostly carbon monoxide, a gas which combines with hemoglobin more readily than oxygen. Hence, one suffocates." He pointed methodically to two hoses connected to the automobile. "Pipes leading away from the automobile exhaust the fumes to the outside—over the roof, to be more precise. I did the same with the fumes from the gasoline electric generator I assembled several months ago. The neighbors could never tolerate smelling odors such as these. They'd assail the front door with pitch forks and torches."

Adrian approached one of the hoses, extending his hand to touch.

"Careful! Very hot!" François warned. Adrian tapped his finger on the hose rapidly, then winced an acknowledging nod to François. "Automobile engines emit not only toxic fumes, but also a considerable amount of heat. Let's discuss everything in the room here next to the lab. I've set up a rather unique presentation for you all." He motioned enthusiastically, but impatiently, for everyone to follow through a narrow archway into another workroom, cleared for an audience, with cushioned chairs arranged facing a flat, white panel supported by a tripod.

"Please, my friends, be seated. I've prepared an experience for you—the future of lectures and presentations," he declared with gusto.

While his friends sat themselves reluctantly, preferring to know what he was up to behind them, François busied himself with a breadbox-sized contraption sitting on a small stand at the back of the room.

"I say, old man. I don't trust you behind me," Adrian announced, twisting around, half out of his seat. "Nor do I," Marie piped in. "One time I caught him playing with himself while I wasn't looking."

François looked away from his machine and smiled at her coyly. "That was you playing, not me. And you were too busy to look at me because of all the other young men keeping you occupied." Everyone laughed, including Marie, who gave credibility to his reply by not objecting to his assumed whimsical comment.

Suddenly the room turned dark. "I've switched off the electric lights in order for you to view the projection screen in front," François advised. "I'm sure you've seen a stereopticon. I've modified this one a bit to fit my purposes." He turned on the stereopticon, and a moving picture of him driving an automobile appeared on the screen, lasting for five seconds. The motion picture faded to a view of the planet earth as if one were standing on the moon, watching his home planet on the horizon. Realistic, still, blue with stars in the background, his sophisticated audience was not spared from gasping aloud.

"That motion picture of me driving an automobile and our blue planet floating in space—these are the topics of tonight; these are the topics of the future," he said so softly he almost whispered. He saw the others were so aroused by the moving picture, they had failed to question the realism of the likelihood of such a picture of earth. Adrian appeared the most excited, while Gershon and Marie remained patiently curious.

"How?!" Adrian jumped up, frantic, to see what François had done. "How did you make the picture move?"

"I'll tell you in due time. I'll tell you; it's not magic—it's technology—photographic manipulation. It's part of the future—our future. And that's what we're doing here tonight—discussing the future—and the inextricable roles we shall weave for ourselves. Now watch, listen and comprehend."

He inhaled a breath of exultation, but not grandiosity. For knowing what he knew, for preparing to present what he had prepared—he remained humble. However, he knew, no one—in the entire world, for all of history—had ever seen, or thought about, what he was about to show. He actuated a small lever at the rear of his stereopticon.

The image of the earth faded into the image of an automobile. Then the image of the automobile faded into a mechanical schematic of automobile components, transparent to the details. Juxtaposed scattered diagrams of engine pistons, gaskets, valves, and crank shafts filled the screen.

He marveled at the projection before he spoke. He caught his breath as the drawings and schematics excited him. "The automobile is the centerpiece of the future. The impetus for economies, commerce and technology will all be derived from auto-related ventures for the next century. If we fully understand this phenomenon and how it unfolds, if we superimpose our destinies over this tidal wave which will

47

drive all, then we can control the world." He paused, listening for gasps of disbelief, but silence prevailed—not a silence of apathy, but rather the awestruck stillness to not miss a word.

Assessing each friend's face, he quickly appraised his audience's interest. He sensed an energy exceeding enthusiasm—it felt closer to a silent fervor. "My prediction is not based on euphoric grandiosity, and it certainly is not delusional fantasy. One can extrapolate, as I have done, the future course of economies based on technology simply because many of these devices are yet to be invented, even though the science is freely available. I'll explain in broad, calculated strokes how I foresee the future unfolding, with the automobile and its life force—crude oil—as the prime mover for all. As clumsy and inconvenient as these "horseless carriages" appear today, they will replace horses completely within the next fifteen years. I have absolutely no doubt. Accept this premise about the future of automobile, and the rest falls into place." He flicked the stereopticon lever once more.

"Please observe the graph projected on the screen," François directed. "Note that the vertical left line of the frame is labelled Population, starting with '1B' on the lower part and progressing upward in equal intervals to '10B.' The lower horizontal line is labeled Time, progressing in equal intervals from 1900 to 2030.Notice that that the trend line advances with shallow ascent from the lower left corner. It abruptly rises to almost vertical from a sharp knee, and soars upward, two-thirds to the right of the figure. The mathematical formulas on the right of the graph define the trend line."

Clamor and slamming intruded upon the meeting from upstairs, though nary a head turned in curiosity. Like one who had finally found his wallet after searching frantically, François felt relieved, certain that his friend, Suresh Belani, had arrived. *Suresh. I knew he'd make it. He probably would hire a dog sled if necessary.*

Anyone who'd climb mountains in the Himalayas could get through a Swiss blizzard.

Suresh entered the room sheepishly, still brushing off the snow, nodding and bowing to his friends who turned after François had paused to allow Suresh his self-conscious and awkward entrance. Adrian and Marie smirked with haughty acknowledgement to one another as if each had predicted Suresh's tardy arrival with a seer's flair.

He had not visited with Suresh for several months. He wanted to rush up to him, hug him, shake his hand, and greet his lifelong friend, but he refrained. He glared at him through a smirk and then continued his talk. "The graph displayed before you represents change in global population over the next 120 years. It's an exponential curve extrapolating population growth. I've taken into account well over one hundred different variables. Most of these variables are premises and assumptions regarding advances in medical technology, reductions in infant mortality, communications, urban development, agricultural science and fresh water distribution," François explained methodically. "Of course, you all know I would love to indulge you in the details of these calculations. Indeed, if anyone wishes to engage me later, I'd be happy to go into further detail. But, since we have only a few hours, let me continue for the sake of those interested in the bigger picture," François commented while directing a saluatory nod at Suresh, who reciprocated with a grumble. It was François' mischievious intent to jokingly aggravate his friend who had just arrived. He knew Suresh was very detail oriented, as well as having been educated in mathematics. Much to the chagrin of the others, Suresh could extend meeting times to hours, even days, delving into rhetorical fringe themes of whatever the subject matter may be.

"That's unfair," Suresh blurted out. "Don't imply I have lost my enthusiasm. You know I've the highest regard for your discoveries and theories. We worked together for two years on the animal vaccine."

49

A side of François' teasing was really doling out punishment. Though he would never admonish Suresh for interrupting his presentation, he jabbed him with an anonymous-sounding, personally-pointed comment. Inwardly satisfied his missile hit its target, he said, "You and I will catch up later. Glad you could make it."

He used the shadow of a sharpened pencil to trace the line graph from left to right. "As you can see, global population is currently—essentially the first day of 1904—one billion, seven hundred million, increasing in this rather shallow linear fashion. However, as we move through the middle of the twentieth century, starting here circa 1950, we see a sharp upswing. By 2020 my calculations predict global population will have surged to over seven billion." He noticed Marie covering her mouth in astonishment; Gershon shook his head in silent desperation.

Adrian appeared stern, but alarmed, and swiveled about to face him. "You're saying there's to be a five-fold increase of human souls over little more than a century? I've the feeling the planet is over-crowded now. I've no doubt about your calculations—but seven billion!" Adrian erupted dramatically.

Éclair expected the population increase to perturb Adrian the most. Though they had been dearest friends for twenty years, he had always detected a void—an empty, infallible, irrational spot in their relationship. He sensed the racist beliefs festering at Adrian's core. François was tolerant, knowing Adrian was not the least bit conscious of these attitudes, but they existed nevertheless, and they percolated from his bosom whenever unconsciously titillated by non-Caucasian encroachments. His flare-up about the population increase had nothing to do with veracity, credibility, or accuracy. It had everything to do with which races would represent the greatest future growth. And François knew what troubled Adrian: This rampant growth would not be among Caucasians.

"If this population increase is due to advances in medical technology and food production, one would think the boon of these technologies would be contained within the nations which had sponsored the advancements to begin with," Adrian rebuked, arguing as if the counterpoint had already been explicitly stated.

François glanced at Suresh, noting he was particularly keen to the discussion. Although he was of Oriental extraction—and not white—his caste was very high, and he, too, had a certain disdain toward the seeming masses.

He knew that humanity's predilection toward social prejudices and parsing cultures, based on beliefs and ceremonies, was as ancient as homo sapiens. Reading Karl Marx and Friedrich Engels—as well as contemporaries like Werner Sombart and Max Weber— François had evolved not only a social awareness of society, culture, money and politics, but also an economic scrupulousness . The theater for global economic partitioning would occur between those who proffered sharing wealth among the masses, and those who clung to evolved feudalism—capitalism. As these two systems fermented with ongoing technologies, he recognized the mix would nurture his designs on the future. Advanced as his friends were, he applauded their gullible persuasion toward beliefs grounded in misguided cultural mythologies—men and supermen, angels and heathens, proletarians and aristocrats.

François understood the resulting social dilemmas with a keen and disparaging insight—as the world expanded in science, technology and economy, its seamy underbelly would burgeon as well. Bigotry, racial resentments, and ethnic intolerance would mushroom, probably outpacing the technology responsible for the underlying population's growth. This awareness made him prone to veer off his topic as he frustratingly attempted to resume his primary topic.

"Capitalism and corporate democracy spawn a need for ever expanding markets, my friends. The more people, the more consumers; the more consumers, the more robust the economies. Large, multi-national corporations will diffuse around the world, inundating every city, farm, and remote village. Communication technologies not yet available will broadcast globally. Containment within national borders will not exist. Just as we stand at the threshold of this revolution, you are already clamoring for restraint based on a false belief in racial superiority. This revolution will heed to little restraint. With these tremendous dynamics in populations, technologies, and pressure for corporate expansion, national boundaries will represent economic barriers, not cultural ones. Moderation, not fortification, of national divisions, will commence. The first marker to this forecast will be a war in which many nations of the world will participate: a world war." François grimaced, realizing he had diverged from his primary topic as he was too often prone to do. "Let's go back to the ultimate cause of this calamitous and tumultuous change—this horseless carriage, the automobile, and the changes accompanying it."

He actuated a lever on his stereopticon causing a different image to display. The projected image was in three equal horizontal parts: the top, a rendering of an automobile; the middle, the same globe he had shown before, but with a downward pointing arrow overlapping the middle and bottom image; on the bottom, from left to right in large, bold letters: OIL, RUBBER, STEEL, CONCRETE.

"The rapid expansion of the manufacture, marketing, and utilization of the automobile will cause reciprocal growth in oil, rubber, steel and concrete. BUT especially oil. Remember, with the planet's population expanding to over seven billion by 2020, economy and technology must facilitate the growth. Here's the simple premise: Automobiles will not be a luxury; they will be a necessity of life. The vast majority of individuals will own and utilize an automobile. And because of the colossal population, expect a largely disproportionate migration into urban areas where the distribution of goods and services becomes more efficient. Cities will swell to millions each, linked by paved roads designed for the swift transit of automobiles." He paused, sensing his audience's repressed distress at his proclamations—except for Gershon, who seemed pleased, even jubilant. As young men, he and Gershon had entertained such a future. "The future is their prophesy," they cajoled to others. But among themselves, they took their machinations in earnest. More than Yin and Yang, the two together comprised more than a whole. To others they exhibited a bond, the essence of which was not clear.

"With this information in hand, now, we stand to amass billions—trillions—of dollars given we act accordingly," Gershon remarked with subdued enthusiasm.

He rejoiced at his friend's acuminous comprehension. "Indeed, my friend, you are right on target. And more so, we aim to facilitate that which we foresee on the political horizon, allowing for a smoother course and eliminating impediments which will eventually yield to the tide anyway," François replied. He saw Marie scrunch her nose, confused by his comment about facilitation.

"So, you're saying, we will involve ourselves not only financially, but politically as well?" Marie inserted pensively.

He feared Marie would require the greatest convincing as she was influenced, as much by her family's conservatism as by her own unique and erudite autonomy. "It only stands to reason, but certainly not directly, and not even publicly. Deep and absolute anonymity, to the point you may not be certain who you are, will be the mode of operation from now on and through to our posterity. We are the progenitors of this movement, and it will mark history from henceforth," François replied. "But again, we careen off course once more!" He used his pencil to point its shadow at the word OIL.

"Obviously, children, the indigent and the poverty-stricken will not own an automobile. Given these limitations, I predict two billion operating motor cars by 2020. The machines will be icons of the family as well as the individual. They will represent freedom, prosperity, autonomy. They will change the landscape of the world." Suresh and Adrian rotated in their chairs at the same time, both almost delirious with a revelation—a common zeitgeist both seized simultaneously. François cut them off.

"Friends, if I read you correctly, you comprehend the possibilities," he uttered with a sensual flair. "All these motor cars— they burn fuel. And they are each disposable."

"Yes!" Suresh blurted. "Disposable. What happens to the metal and rubber from the disposed and spent vehicles? Think of the massive waste of metal and energy. Where will the populations of the future put it all? The oceans? The mountains? The deserts? You said vast cities will span the globe. Certainly the waste materials cannot go near these—how might one describe them—metropolises?"

"And the burned fuel? What about the emission of the waste gases? And the combined cumulative heat from the engines—like the one sitting in the other room?" Adrian added. "One single engine in the room next to us produces enough heat to warm the room to excess. What effect will two billion engines have—operating continuously—on local temperatures?"

His friends caught him off guard. He was well aware of the contamination; he counted on it. But he had underestimated his friends, expecting them to seize the profits before contemplating the liabilities. "All excellent comments!" François replied, reaching his hand behind his stereopticon. Another depiction of the earth projected on the screen, an isometric rendering with a slice removed exposing a hypothetical thin inner shell directly below the earth's surface, and a solid sphere exactly at the center. "Perhaps these calculations will speak to your objections—which are both valid and insightful."

"Here is a line drawing of the earth, represented by concentric spheres." He traced the outline of the different spheres with the shadow of his pencil. "This outer sphere is, of course, the surface of the earth. From the center of the sphere out to the surface—the radius, in other words—is 3960 miles. This solid ball at the center is the earth's mantle, estimated to have a radius of eight hundred miles." He paused, scanning his audience for attentiveness. Both Adrian and Marie seemed mesmerized simply by the presentation medium. Suresh, having studied geological science extensively, scrutinized the diagram intently.

"You might add that the mantle is made mostly of iron, which is the primary source of the earth's magnetic field," Suresh added with pompous academic certitude. "Until recent findings, the source of the magnetic field was purely conjecture."

François felt relieved that Suresh had pointed out this rhetorical detail. It indicated that his attention had shifted from the deleterious ramifications of his forecast to the primary focus: the inestimable amount of power they stood to gain. "Excellent point. You have been staying abreast of recent geophysical research," François remarked, avoiding placation. "Now we know oil is not as deep as the earth's mantle, which—as Suresh has pointed out—is a seething ball of molten metal. And we know we're not swimming in oil, nor are there seas filled with oil, so it is not stored on the surface of the earth either. Its reservoirs must be within the vicinity of the surface, for as we go deeper, we find ourselves closer to the mantle, a hostile environment for oil deposits." He paused once more, scanning his audience inquisitively, inviting questions with his poignant penetrating eyes and focusing eyebrows.

"So, you're saying, oil lies in pockets close to the earth's crust?" Marie blurted as if awakening from having been engrossed in the screen projection.

He smirked as if the most profound insight emerges from the most naïve, unstrained and innocent. "Marie, that blue-blooded schooling of yours rears its head conspicuously," he retorted with sarcasm. "You are absolutely correct. As a starting point, we have to make certain assumptions—reasonable, educated assumptions, mind you. Let's assume a thin continuous concentric spherical shell of crude oil, one hundred feet thick, lies five hundred feet below the surface of all land masses." He shot an acknowledging glance at Marie, then he pointed to the layer below the surface of the earth on the cutaway of his projection. "The volume of this fractional mass in cubic feet would be 1.65 with seventeen zeros behind it—a very large number—165 quadrillion cubic feet. A barrel of crude oil is approximately 5.6 cubic feet." He switched to another display showing his calculations. "Dividing the assumed available volume of oil by five point six, we get 29 quadrillion barrels of oil." He stopped, allowing his friends time to absorb the almost unfathomable quantities he had just recited. He smiled briefly, thinking to himself that he had picked his friends well as they were all intent upon his presentation. The issue of toxic contamination from waste seemed to disappear as quickly as it had emerged.

"I, for one, do not believe that much oil is under the earth's surface," he resumed. "I—"

"Nor do I," Suresh interrupted. "While working on my doctorate in chemistry at Oxford, I read various treatises hypothesizing the origins of crude oil. Considerable august and erudite sources believe it evolved from millions of years of heat and pressure on organic matter, mostly plankton. The volume you calculated would not seem to jibe with these theories."

"Absolutely. I agree," François retorted. "Certain august and geologically erudite sources suggest that no more than two hundred fifty thousand square miles of exposed land contains crude oil readily available for pumping. Recent geologic surveys report approximately four and one half million square miles of land above water. Hence, after doing the recalculations, the number of available barrels of oil is reduced to 146 trillion. That's it. That's the planet's total supply of oil. Now as I've put forth, I've extrapolated two billion motor cars operating by the year 2020. We must make further assumptions regarding the amount of fuel consumed per unit per day. I've only worked with the four-stroke engine you see in the other room, but cars will become bigger, stronger, faster. We know there's a limit to the fuel supply, but the capitalist incentive will not take dwindling supplies into account and will behave as if the supply is infinite. In so doing, automobiles will be designed and built without accommodating fuel efficiency. Let's assume each automobile, having to traverse large distances daily, will consume an average of ten gallons of gasoline per day. Suresh, do you remember the number of gallons of gasoline retrievable from a barrel of crude oil?"

"Indeed, as I remember, it was eighteen, but refinery techniques could improve," Suresh replied.

His friend's immediate recall of such obscure information impressed him so, a wave of euphoria raised his spirits even more. "Eighteen is the number I used as well. Given these broad assumptions, with only automobiles using gasoline, the supply of gasoline contained within the earth is 361 years," François stated, remembering to not sound as if he were delivering an academic lecture. "Now, here's the rub. I have a very strong intuition that automobiles will not be the only—if not even the major—utilizers of oil-related products."

"I place your intuition above another man's facts," Adrian inserted. "But, what, exactly, would you propose consumes crude oil in the future?"

François rejoiced at the question his friend had put forth, almost as if he they had rehearsed the interaction. He had lived in this research for several years, pondering each possibility to its logical extreme, and then exhausting every conclusion coming from the precipitating answers—obsessing, waking in the middle of the night with new inquiries, revelations and perspectives on every emerging discovery and technology. "Carbon compounds pervade our future— not only for energy but also for materials and medicine," François replied as if he had capsulated his life's obsession over the past three years in this single statement. "Steam power will become obsolete. Ships, trains, automobiles—all will rely upon energy derived from petroleum. Electrical generating facilities will utilize petroleum to power turbines. Air travel will become common place, most assuredly powered by carbon sources as well. And you've heard of plastics? These materials will multiply like insects, infesting everything we build and consume."

He surged with reverent pride. He had become the minister fostered and nurtured into him since his childhood—his message finally penetrating his congregation—his sermon: automobiles and oil.

"Based on my rather broad strokes of mathematics, if we cut the time, I calculated by one-third; the earth contains a 120-year supply of crude oil from now. In other words, by 2025 the world will have run out of petroleum. By that time, the basis—the standard—for global economies will be petroleum-based energy and materials. However, replacement resources will not be readily forthcoming. The reason? Corporations and governments, bloated by the riches derived from these relatively short-lived technologies, will not have planned transition technologies and energy sources. Bandage efforts will emerge, but a deluge of desperation in energy shortage will sweep the globe." He saw Marie poised to blurt her question before anyone else had a chance to speak.

"Knowing you," Marie suddenly inserted, "you've worked out a solution to that contingency as well."

He felt ambivalence, realizing he had a plan, but he had not fully acquiesced to its consequences. "I have—yes. It's not a pleasant one. But I'll ask you—an expert in relieving yourself of unpleasant and spent relationships." He smirked at his desired effect, noticing her acknowledging wince. "What do you do—personally—to end an affair?" He tried to mitigate his directness by softening his voice, but she evinced an air of discomfort—not from the question itself, but from François' intimate knowledge, aware that her last lover committed suicide after her sudden loss of interest. She subdued her guilt, having been consoled frequently that his actions were not of her responsibility.

"I'm sure you ask the question in earnest, so I'll respond in kind," she remarked on the edge of defensiveness. "I end it. Period. No transition. No cooling off time. No promise of friendship in the future. I've found this method best for all parties involved, even though at that particular moment it appears and feels cruel and unsympathetic."

He was pleased she was candid, forthright in speaking her mind. "Indeed. And that is exactly what I propose. The world will experience a love affair with oil and its ancillary economies and products. At the time the global crude oil supplies are dwindling to within ten percent—we end it. We end it all."

Chapter 5

Jordan Éclair

Southern California, 2026

"I am the Prince of Doom," Jordan Éclair whispered in the young woman's ear, sliding off to her side and stretching on the king sized bed. He quickly repositioned himself, propping himself sideways to view her straight on. A man of many women, she was the most beautiful woman he had ever encountered. Her skin, smooth and blemish-free; her muscle tone, taut and complete; her proportions, sculpted and mathematical. Her metallic blue eyes, chiseled chin and cheekbones transmitted a goddess-like quality with her light brown hair framing her rare face. He watched her mull over his comment, sporting a coy grin.

"You're the Prince of Bullshit," Rebecca retorted. "I'll say that for you! But you're such a good lover," she cooed.

He had long relinquished the hope that friends and lovers would know him for who and what he is—the last in a lineage of self-appointed kings, a royalty affecting the world more than any in ancient, medieval, or modern times. His anguish was deep, buried far enough now to be undetectable. He rolled on his back, waiting for her to take the lead in their love-making session. She nestled her head on his shoulder and softly rubbed the hair on his chest. "I'm telling you the truth? How could I prove it to you?" He noticed she seemed almost impatient with his comment, preferring to relax intimately with him rather than wrangle over his claim to dubious notoriety.

"It makes no difference," she replied with feigned apathy. "You are who you are. I don't understand why you insist upon these wild stories. And if they were true, I'd say, be who you are—not who you think you were born to be. You are your own man. The tales you've told me: your grandfather, a man who put the seeds of nuclear fission into the brain of Einstein; your father, mastermind of the Iranian revolution, among other things, and your mother—a good one—the creator of the AIDS virus. If I didn't love you, I'd leave you for being so delusional."

The familiar emptiness started tugging at him. "It's all true," he said, pulling her on top of him. "I could prove it to you, but –" he added, cutting his comment short, by laughing. Yet, he felt guilty, knowing his cavalier behavior took risks with Rebecca's life. If she had any verifiable evidence whatsoever of his true identity, she would have to die.

"You may be weird and crazy, but there's not an evil bone in your body," she insisted, now becoming more active with their sex play. She started rocking and undulating over him. "With such an odious family lineage, then what's on your agenda? What is your evil mark in the world? Other than to addict me to you, and make me long for more?"

He resented being thought of as evil. "My evil mark? More like my fate. Want me to tell you? I'll tell you," he declared, flipping her around, so she was under him again. He propped himself over her with extended arms. "I'm here to complete what my father started. And his father, and his father. I'm not sure how far back it goes. My guess? Much further than my grandfather. I've helped fuel Iran with enriched nuclear material. I've provided them with scientists and technology to build medium range missiles to deliver nuclear armaments. They will attack Israel, decimating the entire Israeli state—illogical, since they'll kill the Arabs there as well, rendering it so radioactive, the cradle of western civilization will glow—which I think is a metaphor come true." He paused, laughing nervously. "But that is their intent. And the dirty trick is—they will also decimate the major cities of the Middle East as well as annihilate all the oil reserves and refineries."

Rebecca stopped moving, her mouth agape in awe. "Even if what you say is a lie—and it is—what a god-awful tale. This fantasy of

61

yours—you'd kill millions of people and put the world's economy in a tale-spin."

He noticed that for once she evinced a glimmer of emotional recognition to his story. Ambivalent, he wanted to refrain from continuing, but he yearned for her to know him for who he really was, and not for the fantasy she believed. "Yes, I know. That's the point," he replied. "I know my family and predecessors all too well—with my mother and her cronies raising me—no—training me."

"And your father? Where was he all this time? Was he out digging for the uranium to make it all happen," she snapped back in her crisp Queen's English accent.

Recognizing her sarcasm, he ignored it. "My father? I never met my father. I told you that before. Someone murdered him."

"Killed for his wretched life, no doubt?" she retorted, still wedged below the weight of his body.

"Killed because it was part of the plan," he replied with a flair of flippancy. "Now let me concentrate on what we're doing. We have to finish. I have an appointment."

After leaving Rebecca in the bedroom, he turned on the water to heat up to heat up the shower. He wanted to stay in her apartment with her. She loved him for what she saw and heard, and not what she knew about him. He reflected. If she knew his true identity—the one of which he tried in vain to convince her—she would recoil in terror and disgust. Something about revealing himself freed him from guilt, but it exposed him to the insecurity of her eventually tiring of what she considered his "fantasy game," and she would leave him.

"Rebecca," he called. "Please, come join me. I didn't mean to be an asshole. I apologize." He waited a few moments, and she entered the bathroom just as he stepped into the shower. He rubbed a hole in the steamy clear shower door and peered through to see her standing naked in front of him.

"You really want me to come in there with you? You going to tell me more of your silly stories?" she inquired with an acrid tone.

"Absolutely not. No more stories—ever," he responded, raising his hand in pledge.

She opened the shower door; he immediately pulled her next to him. "Really, I apologize for all that bullshit I tell you. Maybe I don't think I deserve someone as beautiful and intelligent and kind as you, so maybe I'm just trying to drive you away."

"Wow. That's too much psychobabble for me. But there's better ways of driving a girl away. You tell your stories with such detail and consistency. I wonder, if, maybe, you're writing a book or living in some fantasy world you dreamed up as a child, and now you're still immersed in it. I don't know. I know I love you, but your tales of conspiring evil concern me."

Tortured in silent ambivalence, he could not keep her, and he could not leave her. He played a game with himself, realizing that if he really thought she would actually believe him, he would not have told her. "As I said, it's history. No more stories," he responded. He stroked her back down the grove of her spine, the slippery soap suds creating a silky path along the furrow of her back. He turned her around gently and soaped her from neck to foot. "I wish I could ask you to accompany me, but I've got work-related business." She rotated to face him, asking with body language to finish by soaping down her front side. "I've got to drive all the way to El Segundo. We're testing a new guidance system, and, well, I can't really tell you much more—you know, it's a defense project. But I'll come back here to Newport Beach later tonight, if you like."

Rebecca took his chin in her hand, rotating his head to stare into his eyes. "Remember, you said you'd go to my department's party with me? You know—at the psychobiology chair's house at Dana Point? He's been bugging me, looking forward to meeting you." Jordan

63

winced as if he knew what that was all about. "No, not because he's gay. He wants to talk to you about your work with nonintrusive electrode technology."

Guilt coursed through him as he had deceived her by not divulging yet another tale—one closer to her own reality; one she would not believe as well. Her department chairman, Dr. Chamberlain, was very much on his own agenda as well. "Oh, yes. I forgot. Damn, how absent-minded I am." Rebecca cast a stern but disappointed glance, and then put her arms around his neck as he had finished soaping her. "Even if I had planned something else, I'd cancel it and come to your gathering, Rebecca." He kissed her, separated himself, rinsed, and left her in the shower.

Dispassionately, he dried himself and got dressed. He knew that any emotional interplay with Rebecca would cause another delay, though he longed to pull her from the shower and take her back to bed. He had to be at his destination on time. Others depended upon his reliability and punctuality, and he had maintained an impeccable record. He was the king of the world and the mechanic of its fate. He built the tools, yet he was, himself, a gear of a process, set into motion more than a century earlier. His function was unquestionable, irreversible and indelible. Until now, he had never sensed a permeability. His function had remained his reality.

Always focused and singular in purpose, he had never considered an alternate direction. Such fancy carried a taint of self-destruction—even suicidal ideation. Contemplating abandoning his purpose was akin to standing at a high cliff's edge, considering jumping off to his demise. The thought was so out of bounds, he shuttered at the notion. *I'm deluding myself, thinking I can be like others, live like others, die like others. I cannot escape my life, except by death, and that time rapidly approaches. Perhaps it's fear I'm avoiding—not my life, work and association. Perhaps I'm afraid of dying. And why fear*

death? Pain? No! Afterlife? No! I fear death because I have not lived
my life. It was not the one I would have chosen to live. Yet, my mark on
the world will be the most traumatic and least notorious.

He dressed quickly while Rebecca was still in the shower. She had just emerged when he approached her from behind, put his arms around her, and kissed her neck. Convincing himself he had no choice but to leave, he disregarded the emotional tug to drawing him back to her.

"I'll be back later this evening. We'll attend Chamberlain's party," he promised, posing a thoughtful stance. "You'll witness some of my tales come to life tonight," he added, winking, then turned to depart without further explanation. He could sense her exasperated curiosity behind him.

Five minutes from Rebecca's apartment, he raced his 2020 electric Audi down Jamboree toward the San Diego Freeway, having forgotten the speed limit along the stretch. His laser detector howled a strident warning, shocking him to decelerate from eighty to fifty within two seconds, just in time as he rounded the crest toward the freeway. He glimpsed the scowl on the face of the CHP cop poised between two parked cars, having been on the verge of taking off after him.

An empty, dull, disconnected remorse lingered—a feeling that he had lost something that he had become used to, and now he would never see it again. Yet, that was not the case with Rebecca. He would return there that night, to be with her, to go to her research department's party. The speeding ticket he almost could have received jostled him. *That was close. I'm glad I wasn't playing any music. I've got to pay more attention. Rebecca distracts me, but I like it. What is this emotion? Me or her? Or is it an interaction between us? I've never felt connected, never felt like someone should know me, never felt as if I wanted to be around someone and I never really gave a damn. Certainly, Mother would not approve as I'm sure she has already had her background thoroughly investigated. I have to make certain no harm comes to her.*

He checked on the status of the cop in his mirror and then accelerated onto the full circle on-ramp. The exhilaration took his mind off his dilemma. He decided not to listen to music, but focus on the upcoming meeting with his mother, Zora Green, and other scientists who worked for their corporation. He had wanted Simon—his right hand man—to attend, but Simon had more urgent business elsewhere. *I'll have to get my gun from my desk, but I wanted to use one of Simon's Berettas.*

Helming the most advanced media company of the twenty-first century did not reveal nor exacerbate Jordan's forty-four years. Driving, he reflected on the early years—the joys and triumphs of their developments—marvels in holography, 3-D presentation, and sensory immersion. He had forged his company's fortune through brillance and innovation. He had injected the company's technology into major medical, business, and entertainment media over the past fourteen years, especially penetrating films and gaming. He chuckled to himself, recalling how his non-intrusive holographic maser electrode, the centerpiece of the company's technology, had been publicly released through a stroke of innovation and desperation. They had always meant to shroud the technology to be used for future projects, but circumstances forced them into an accelerated product introduction, unveiling a product that entrenched itself into every media device marketed. He had conceived a strategy to advance the technology, moving it not only into consumer electronics but also spearheading it into biomedical research, a move he realized would divert public attention from his and his cohorts' true intentions.

The commute along the 405 stretch from Irvine to El Segundo seemed instantaneous as he mulled over his life, his company, his fate, his mother and Rebecca. His meeting with Zora Green and other corporate research scientists marked a critical occasion, requiring his presence. Otherwise, he would have opted to not attend. He loosely tolerated his mother's involvement in the workings of their organization—the organization for which BrainLink was the impenetrable face; the organization for which his predecessors had lived and died; the organization about which he harbored spurious second thoughts. The cult consumed his life. He sometimes preferred it were she, and not he, whose role was to spearhead their purpose to its finale.

Almost missing his off-ramp, he turned sharply, crossing four lanes to exit at Rosecrans. After a cursory scan of the traffic, he barreled west to arrive at their five-story building in the midst of other aerospace and defense contract corporations. He pulled into his parking space, eager for the outcomes of the forthcoming test trial, but ambivalent about the means, and the scene he would encounter once he entered their covert research lab.

After navigating through five layers of security, he arrived at a third level basement laboratory. Zora Green greeted him at the door, flashing eyes displaying both officiousness and motherly pride. Jordan dismissed any motherly inclinations she had ever displayed toward him, concluding genuine matronly attributes cannot reside in the same woman who had invented HIV and AIDS and who preferred using human subjects over test animals during risky research procedures in order to achieve optimal methodological validity.

"We're ready, if you are," Zora commented monotonically as he brushed through the last electronic security gate.

He allowed his eyes to rest on Zora's face only momentarily. Then he looked beyond her, searching for indications of what lies ahead. He did not trust her and, although he, himself, was an integral part of the movement, her involvement and contributions had been equal to any Éclair. *And, of course, carrying me full term was worthwhile as well.* "Good. And the subject?" he inquired with equal impartiality. He noticed Zora's demeanor brighten with his question.

"A perfect subject. One who will not be missed, yet this one is not the vagrant homeless diseased-brained variety we're used to. This one is void of the brain damage associated with alcohol, drugs, mental illness, and improper living," she replied. "One of our female operatives procured her. She appears to be from a middle-class background, a loner, some college, unemployed, no family or friends to speak of. She had the interesting idiosyncrasy of impulsively traveling, leaving her usual domicile for one to six months. Our operative discovered her in Hermosa Beach, where she was leasing a flat."

Jordan glared at Zora. A gust of anger burst forth unexpectedly, forcing him to refrain from striking her. He labored at containing guilt. Knowing that they had to test a human, he managed his own negative internal backlash. He had always used contrived justification killing their research subjects, rationalizing that at least a homeless person would serve a function to science and a less drain on society. "Mother. You did not abide by our agreement. This individual is not an indigent," he responded tersely.

She immediately glared back. "I thought you would be pleased. The subject eliminates many extraneous variables that could confound the results should they turn out disagreeably." She hesitated, her expression segueing from stern to harsh. "And please, do not call me 'Mother.'"

He always felt mildly refreshed after having triggered an emotional reaction from her, no matter that it was negative. "The subject is set up and ready?" he asked with an impatient reconciliatory tone.

"At your disposal," she responded and then tugged on his elbow as he headed toward the closed lab doors. "Perhaps you could explain to me sometime—and I deserve an explanation since we all serve the same calling—what is the purpose of your contrived conscience? I've noticed this development of late, particularly in the past three years since you've been associated with the university," Zora asked in hybridized benevolent austerity. "We've killed billions, yet you display trepidation over one—one from whom we will gain scientific insight and information."

If he could simply make her disappear, he would. All the programming in his life could not remove the burgeoning despair etching at his insides. He was raised with his purpose, with his clan's purpose. He knew all too well his calling. However, something had percolated within him, a foreign element over which he had no control, and the lack of control worried him as he was sure it worried his mother as well. They could not afford an uncontrollable—an unpredictable—free radical altering his temperament. All the cogs and gears had to be oiled, lubed, and synchronized harmoniously.

He wanted to return to normalcy; he wanted to reset, going back to his self a mere five years ago. *Is it Rebecca? Am I allowing the fantasy of middle-class romance to sway my conviction? Zora is correct. This subject's life's purpose has never been greater than now, the subject of our experiment, the culmination of every thinker, leader and philosopher's dream—to control the thoughts of another—to completely alter another human's memories and personality—to make his whim, my whim—to do my bidding without question or reservation.* He stopped in mid-step, facing her directly. "You're right. I could not agree with you more. Nevertheless, I would like to speak with her, given she is such a prime specimen. Any objections?"

She squeezed his elbow affirmatively, then released.

"None. No objections. In fact, it's a good idea," she replied, uncharacteristically sycophantic.

He strode toward a door-less, window-less wall. A tiny blue light on the ceiling flickered, and the wall split, opening to an anteroom. They tore open cellophane bags containing white clean room apparel, donning the garments which covered them, leaving only the face exposed to air. Each put on a diving mask-looking accoutrement with an air filter over the nose. They walked into a second anteroom where high-powered fans showered them for three seconds. Then some double doors snapped open, revealing a spacious, sparkling, well-lit expanse stretching over one hundred feet in all directions. The walls were lined with enclosures and racks filled with electronics—twinkling lights, digits, counters, monitors. Additional flat screen monitors were mounted on bench-like work stations sprawling intermittently throughout the lab. All seemed organized around the object at the center of the room: A person sat contained in a large, dental-looking chair. The area, ten feet around the center away from the chair, was clear. Directly above, the ceiling arced into a dome, forty feet in diameter, its center adding ten feet to the already twelve-foot high ceiling. Along the surface of the semi-spherical opening, various lengths and thicknesses of densely packed clear and opaque plastic rods protruded through the ceiling, all directed toward the sedate occupant seated in the spaceage lounger.

A cylindrical platform three feet high and eight feet in diameter protruded from the floor at the perimeter of the circle, away from the focal point of all the screens, lights, buttons and indicators— the figure in the chair. A long table with keyboards, smaller monitors, and other controls were positioned in front of the platform. A hologram of a brain shimmered directly over the platform. The holographic, three-dimensional image—four times larger than an actual human brain, rotated in jerky gyrations, shifting colors, and periodically displaying deeper brain layers, graphically peeling away sections of neural tissue, exposing sub-cortical activity in real time. Sparkles like fireworks scattered and crackled across its surface then dived toward

70

the center, illuminating internal brain structures, boomeranging back to the cortex in a symphony of light and color.

Jordan and Zora approached the console facing the holographic brain. Two of their associates silently awaited them, moving aside, giving the new arrivals access to the controls. Jordan paused to study the huge shimmering brain twisting and turning in space. He typed into a keyboard, causing a smaller hologram to appear directly in front of him. Then he stretched a pair of wire mesh gloves over his cleanroom—or bunnysuit, as they preferred to call their garb—and grabbed the virtual smaller brain with his right hand. As he oriented the smaller holographic image, the larger image moved in synchrony. With his left hand he took a probe from the console and directed it toward the brain's center. The outer regions faded, displaying midbrain structures.

"The subject appears completely content, Dr. Egress," he said, turning toward one of the onlookers. His neuroscientist colleague stood at the ready to respond.

"She is in a dream state as if she believed she belongs here. She is aware of her life; she has memories, but being here is part of her will and volition—incorporated into the induced dream state. She's dreaming but not anticipating awakening from the dream. She's cognizant, aware, can tell you what she did when she was ten, but, as far as her will—this room is where she belongs, the culmination of her life. Believe me, she harbors no ill will nor does she experience distress," Dr. Egress explained, her arms folded tighly across his torso. The bunny suit mask concealed her face, but Jordan sensed an ambivalent tension uncharacteristic to this respected and trusted scientist.

Knowing Egress lacked basic social skills and could bend easily under pressure if she, indeed, felt uneasy about her performance, he decided to question her. "Dr. Egress, which of our operatives

71

brought this subject here to our facility? It wasn't Simon, was it?" He immediately sensed his colleague's unease. But he sensed a shared curiosity as well.

"No, Simon did not provide her. Actually, the person who brought her in was someone I had not seen before. She was a female operative—dark hair. Zora met with her briefly, and she left before I had a chance to query her, as I always get some background information on all our research subjects," Dr. Egress responded as if on a witness stand. "But not this subject."

Jordan was compelled to ask a question, differentiating this subject from all the rest. "The alterations are temporary, based on feeds overriding her cerebral and limbic interactions. Is that not correct?" Egress looked confused, glancing at the other scientist in a sophomoric plea for assistance..

"Yes, Dr. Éclair. Is that condition not what we had determined for this test?" the second scientist, Dr. Ranvier replied with a defensive edge.

"Oh, yes. No problem," Jordan responded assuredly. "I simply wanted to talk to the subject beforehand; I wanted to verify that she had not been drugged. All these altered consciousness parameters are programmed through the maser holographic neural matrix as standard protocol. I would assume it's safe to say, the experiment has been successful so far. As I recall, our last subject suffered irreparable brain damage at this stage. So, if we can alter her brain templates permanently without cellular or functional damage, then we've arrived. Am I not correct?" He poked Dr. Ranvier on the shoulder then glanced across the room at Zora, who seemed to be containing a mounting impatience.

Jordan checked a few more controls on the console, typing a command on the keyboard that cast a green glow over the center area, a safety marker indicating it was safe for him to enter the test zone.

"Let's not forget you could get cooked and explode like an egg in a microwave oven if the settings were unsynchronized," he remarked cryptically. He glanced at Zora and the two scientists who stood stiffly waiting for him to give them the OK to conduct the experiment. Then he walked to the woman reclining relaxed and unfettered. Approaching her from behind, he moved cautiously to her side so as not to startle her.

He sensed within an uneasiness—a free-floating anxiety. It disturbed him. *I am Jordan Éclair, descendent from the dynasty Éclair. One woman. What's this gnawing at me? Have I absorbed too much middle-class value and morality? Morality does not exist. It is a corral for middle-class behavior. I believe the same hogwash we have circulated to keep the people in check. Yet, I feel a concern for this woman's safety. If I could, I'd let her go. Perhaps continue to work with chimps—even killing a homeless man seems foreboding to me now. I've got to conquer this resistance.* "Comfortable?" he asked smiling. She turned toward him, nodding her head slowly in agreement. Her smile was genuine, unexaggerated, serene. She had deep blue eyes inset within an oval, crème-colored face. Even without makeup, her lips were pink; her nose, lightly sprinkled with freckles. "I don't know you, but you are familiar," she asked lackadaisically. "I've seen you before, met you before. Were we in the same grade school? Are you from Grand Island, Nebraska?"

His smile transformed from contrived to genuine. He caressed her cheek with the back of his fingers. He was awestruck by her familiarity. *I've seen her somewhere before!* "No, but I feel the same about you. We've met somewhere before. Tell you what. Sit tight, and you'll be leaving soon. OK?" he commented with the genuineness of a seasoned nurse. Without waiting for a response, he returned to the control console. After tapping some keys, a 3-D display showing interconnected geometric forms materialized.

Appalled at what he observed from the 3-D generated graphic, he turned to Zora, again glaring at her. His immediate thought, though not acted upon, was to snatch the female subject from the chair and replace her with his mother. "A Vegas hooker? You've programmed her new identity to be a prostitute? You're acting out your prurient curiosities with your research subject. If you're so curious about it, you could have easily assumed that identity and done that yourself twenty years ago. I'm going to change her substrate programming—now, before the test." Zora's unaffected posture and resilience to his insults provoked him more.

"We thought this was the most reasonable venture," Zora commented without shame. "Should the experiment be successful, external agencies would not investigate rigorously once she turns up, even if someone were to discover she's someone else—another case of multiple personality disorder."

Perplexed, he did not understand why Zora offered such flimsy rationale. He suspected ulterior motives, realizing he could not pry the truth from her during an impromptu confrontation. "MPD is extremely rare," he snapped as if he did not need to remind her of inane psychological trivia. "She might attract even more attention. We have so many government people at our disposal, why worry about something like that? Besides, everyone knows how to fornicate. How's that teaching her something unique?" He paused, waiting for a reaction he did not receive. "Since one object of the experiment is to instill a talent to demonstrate the system's capability, let's choose something more complex," he continued. "How about being a violin virtuoso? Or, a helicopter pilot? I know we've got both skill substrates in memory files currently." He banged on the keyboard, probed and poked in the 3-D holographic display until the images changed, and he paused to ponder them. His eyes darted furtively at the others who were in huddled in focused conference. He quickly added more keystrokes. He felt his guilt-infested resistance overtaken by enthusiasm, overturned by the scientific adventure facing him. "OK. Got it." He swiveled to Dr. Ranvier, Zora and Dr. Egress, who had moved to give him ample room to work. "Rene, when we first developed this violin substrate, we had a violin around here to verify the skill set had been implanted. Would you fetch it, please?" Dr. Ranvier immediately turned toward the opposite far end of the lab, commencing a jog. "Let's get this over with," Jordan remarked with an assertion, pleasing Zora.

Jordan operated the same hemispherical control that illuminated the center area green, reverting the center hue to red. He hesitated as Dr. Ranvier returned with a violin tucked under his arm. He glanced over both shoulders as if verifying his right of way. "Initiating sequence," he said, again operating the hemispherical control by rotating his virtual object sideways. The large brain hologram came alive, rotating, changing hues, alternating patterns in specific brain regions. A powerful, low frequency hum inundated the area, vibrating surfaces and tingling their feet through the floor.

"High voltage modules have activated. Reference maser fields are established. Primary maser source is online," Dr. Egress announced with the flair of a NASA launch director. "Neutralization of diencephalonic and sub-cortical areas commencing now."

The three dimensional brain spun upside-down then displayed only the outer cerebral cortex alternating with layers just beneath it. The areas showing the brain stem and cerebellum were no longer displayed. The cerebral surface expanded, showing in detail the composite substratum. These layers alternated colors and patterns, ranging from green to bright red, with patterns ranging from tightly clustered dots to cross-hatch. Suddenly, miniscule speckles of light exploded across the surface of the cerebral image like tens of thousands of tiny flashbulbs. The underlying midbrain undulated in synchrony to this eruption of light and color.

Jordan caught himself fixated as all were mesmerized by the spectacle emblazoned before them. Even though they had conducted this test hundreds of times with living and non-living substrates, he knew this experiment was critical—this time their subject was a human who they hoped would live—and prosper—through the ordeal. If she lived, and if all the aspects of the experiment were satisfied, their next phase could be expedited within weeks. He worried about his mother's tactics as they were all too familiar to him. This subject had to survive. *I'll take her to Thad's hospital. She should be safe there.*

He had lapsed into rumination; his colleagues drifted into the background of his awareness. Twenty minutes had passed before he became refocused on his immediate environment. He had decided to transport their subject to his psychiatrist friend, who ran a hospital in Laguna Beach. He anticipated his decision would not bode well with his mother, Dr. Ranvier or Dr. Egress since they had planned on conducting the post-experiment research. Still, he had conceived of the entire research design, as well as all of the neurological and neuropsychological tests. It was his research, his experiment and his destiny. He would record the post-neuro-programming procedures if they were that interested in the outcomes. Besides, the success of the experiment—the bottom line—reduced to only one factor: They implement the next phase of their ultimate project.

The tug on his arm coaxed him from the remainder of his ruminative retreat. Initially irritated, expecting a comment from Zora, he was relieved to hear from Dr. Egress instead. "Dr. Éclair. The procedure is in its final phase. All life signs are stable. EEG readings are at expected levels. You seem to have been pre-occupied. I wanted to make you aware," Dr. Egress' metallic-nasal voice whispered apologetically. *Does he think I'm going to reach out and kill him if he irritates me too much?* He mused at the possibility, realizing that if he were a pure hedonist, with less impulse control, he would easily do just that and with little chance of recourse or retribution. His own power disturbed him. *Rebecca doesn't know me. I AM above reproach.*

Chapter 6

The Power of Mind

Jordan fixated on the instruments measuring functional brain activity, aware that the woman's vital signs could still be strong although her higher cerebral functions destroyed. Constantly observant of the holographic maser matrix cycle, he waited. The system would not display verifiable results for several seconds. He yearned for this subject to live. She represented the success of their program for the next three years—the climax and culmination of their grand historical drama. His breathing was shallow as the 3-D brain monitoring image stabilized, slowing its gyrations and pulsating, indicating cessation of the process.

"Her vitals are strong!" Dr. Egress announced uncharacteristically excited.

He's killed so many subjects, her not dying means success? Jordan scorned silently, befuddled at his colleague's remark. His mother noticed his frustration. "Brain function, doctor. We can't use a living vegetable," Zora scolded, reflecting her son's silent condemnation.

The flat screen monitors flashed: *Program Complete – Systematic monitoring initiated.* The 3-D brain returned to a pattern he recognized as routine. The glow in the staging area around their subject segued from reds and oranges to green. Jordan's gaze jetted across the control monitors, checking for discrepancies. *Perhaps Zora was right, not using a subject prone to disabilities and brain malady. She performed a function of which she is unaware—a favor to me and humanity.* Eager to confront his experiment, he tore off the clean room helmet, dropping it on the floor as Zora and Dr. Ranvier half-heartedly restrained him. "It's good, or it isn't. Either way, we're way past particle contamination now," he growled high-pitched, pulling away from them. "And I don't want the first human face that she sees after

78

her modification to be masked behind a space suit. Lois and David, please ready the functional MRI. I want to run through a complete motor, sensory and cognitive battery. And we need to do this within the next three hours." He could sense his mother's suspicion without looking, and without her saying anything. *I still have to deal with her.* He strode toward the young woman lying motionless in the high tech chair, dominating the center of the room.

He startled, gazing at a face full of warmth and comfort as if he had just encountered a long lost twin. She smiled broadly, and he returned the gesture even more thrilled. Emotion welled from within, and he restrained a sob. Self-conscious, he glanced at the others who busied themselves with the functional MRI equipment in an alcove on the far side of the lab. He spied Zora watching him furtively, masking her interest by keeping busy with shutting down the systems and downloading data from the experiment. He looked up, verifying the camera had been turned off.

He insisted this subject be treated with genuine regard, and not as a lab rat. "Hello," he greeted her, continuing an open-face smile. "You are in a hospital. You are well, but we found you. You had an accident. Do you know your name?" he inquired, not expecting a response. She appeared confused but not alarmed.

"My name? No—no. I don't seem to know my name. That's odd," she said. He glanced up at one of the maser matrix projection rods, verifying it continued to generate the anxiolytic effect necessary to prevent her from panic.

He feared she could break or fracture at any second, that somehow the success of their experiment was only momentary, and that she would regress given the slightest provocation. "Your name is Hyperia. At least, that is what you were muttering when we found you; let's assume for the time being that's your name. We were able to bring you back to consciousness here after you lapsed into a coma. My name is Dr. Éclair, but please call me Jordan. Are you comfortable?"

"Yes," she smiled peacefully. "I feel—so serene and mellow. I'm in a hospital?"

Eager to remove her from the lab, he welled with paternal protection against an impending toxic element: Zora and the other scientists. "A hospital of sorts. I'm going to take you to another hospital soon, but first we have to perform a few tests to make sure you did not suffer any brain damage—from whatever ordeal you encountered before we retrieved you."

Hyperia nodded serenely, turned, facing forward, and closed her eyes. Jordan was concerned—once they removed her from the anxiolytic beam, her anxiety level might soar, possibly leading to a severe panic attack. He wanted nothing to interfere with her safety and well-being. He jogged to a nearby white cabinet and extracted a hypodermic kit, bottle and sterilization supplies. Upon returning to her side, he caught Dr. Ranvier's attention and motioned that she should join him. "I'm going to administer three milligrams of Lorazapam. As soon as I start the injection, I'd like you to shut off the tranquility-inducing maser hologram matrix."

Ranvier nodded affirmatively and walked swiftly to the control console from which they all had observed the experiment. Jordan swabbed her arm with alcohol while Hyperia studied him calmly. "This won't hurt," he said, changing his demeanor from serious to pleasant. He looked over to Ranvier and nodded. As he injected the tranquilizer, a low frequency undulation halted. Just as it stopped, Hyperia's eyes widened and her pupils constricted, but the drug took effect almost immediately, and she dropped her head back, smiling languidly.

Ranvier returned to Jordan and Hyperia. "I don't think the benzodiazapene will affect the results of the magnetic resonance imaging," she remarked, second-guessing Jordan's immediate concern.

Jordan glanced over to her, briefly provoked by her comment over the test results. *Our first, live, successful subject—a complete substrate eradication without damage to structure and function, and she's worried about imaging accuracy.* "Let's disengage the chair from the floor and wheel her over to the MRI," Jordan responded, without addressing Ranvier's apprehension.

After two hours they had scanned and observed most of her higher and mid-brain functions. Jordan recorded: "Her primary, secondary, sensori-motor and association cortex responded perfectly to stimulus interrogation. Her low limbic and thalamic pathways demonstrated unimpeded functionality. The only deficits the team detected were absolutely appropriate—memory fields made blank by the eradication of memories of her life. The music program had been implanted, evidenced by the activation of sensori-motor response pathways when we applied auditory and visual fields with musical stimuli." He observed closely as other response sets matched program protocols. They could not program a new life for her. She would have to learn that on her own, and Jordan would transport her to the man to do just that.

"Please ready her for transport," he said, gesturing to Drs. Ranvier and Egress. He turned toward Zora, who was busy completing transcribing the notes from the MRI tests. "I'm taking her to Throckmorton's hospital." He subdued his surprise as Zora looked up at him unfazed.

"I assumed that. It was a given. You thought I'd object?" she responded monotonically but with a twist of confrontation.

He wondered if anyone, even in history, experienced such a mother, but he knew he was the only one. She is the woman who almost single-handedly concocted one of the most deadly and insidious viruses over all human evolution, who gestated him in her womb from a Petri germinated egg, giving full-term birth. Other than her service of giving full and natural birth, she had offered no maternal compassion, even denying him the benefit of referring to her as mother. Nannies, servants and household service personnel had offered higher models of human warmth and easily substituted for her as maternal surrogates. He hated and loved her. If she were to die this instant, he would feel only inconvenience, handing off dealing with her body to Simon. Yet, he would feel deep loss, knowing one of the few people who really knew him had disappeared from his life. Her genius and perceptivity incised his intent and planning before he had a chance to unravel it himself. Was she smarter than he? He thought not, but she operated without the burden of empathy, emotion and sentimentality which bound him in ways he was unwilling to surrender. Indeed, he realized his weakness of empathy and compassion escalating, and this realization pressed him, not to stop and argue with her or quibble over her second guessing, but to press through to the pragmatic, collect Hyperia, and depart for Laguna Beach, so he could later rejoin Rebecca. With all this mental clamor converging simultaneously, he smiled at her warmly. "Thank you, Mother," he replied. The flash of her eyes almost blinded him, mindful that he had referred to her as "Mother" but aware that her reaction could be contrived as well. *She's allowing this transfer without the confrontation I expected. Did she want me to take Hyperia?*

Zora helped Drs. Ranvier and Egress dress Hyperia for the trip with Jordan. They escorted her to his Audi, buckled her in, tucked her in another blanket to assure her comfort, and closed the door. They nervously waited for Jordan to come out as he urgently attended to belated chores he had postponed during the final testing phases with Hyperia.

After downloading and transferring the logs of the test, including the notes Zora had herself logged, he emerged in the car dock harried but determined. As he approached the group standing about the car, he focused on Hyperia who remained serene and calm. He glanced at the wheelchair, thinking it was an authentic touch. He worried that the tranquilizer injection he had given her might wear off. Knowing psychoactive medications as he did, he realized the rebound effect of this drug would thrust her further into panic—more so than having given her nothing. He recalled reading the diaries of his deceased grandfather, who would make constant notes and memoranda to himself—to create this, or make that, or invent a device—based upon a need at any given instant. Jordan wished he had known him, but he died decades before Jordan was born. Right now he needed an improvised device: a portable tranquilizing field to replace the sorely inadequate drugs upon which he depen ded to maintain the stability of his precious cargo. He carried another syringe with two milligrams of Lorazapam which would have to do until their destination an hour away.

He drove west on Rosecrans toward the freeway with a troubling but unidentified worry gnawing at him. *What was Zora up to? Perhaps she's worried that I will run asunder.* He glanced over at Hyperia, who was staring at him. Her gaze penetrated him with deep, round brown eyes and beautiful rosebud lips.

Fearing the effect of the drug was wearing off, he considered returning or pulling over to administer his extra syringe. "Who am I? Really? I feel as if I should know. I feel as if I should be afraid, worried, scared. But I'm not. What's my full name? You told me Hyperia, but I don't know my family name. I don't even remember my parents. Where am I? Where was I born? How old am I?" she inquired in a voice not pleading or desperate but stoic and sane.

"Your full name is Hyperia—" he paused momentarily. "Your name is Hyperia Reson. We are close to Los Angeles International

Airport—they tell me you were found roaming about on the beach—
and now we are driving to a place about an hour away, Laguna Beach,
in Orange County. I'm taking you to a special hospital where they can,
hopefully, restore your memory. Otherwise, I cannot answer your
questions, mostly, because I do not know the answers. I only know
your name because that is what you were babbling when we found
you." He saw her bow her head in confusion. He worried that her
anxiety would escalate; though, since she had nobody identifiable to
miss, she might better cope with her amnesic state.

"I feel as if I were just born, yet I am very old as well. But you
and your group of doctors are the only parents I know. How old am I?
I'm not just born. I can speak just fine, so where did I learn to speak?
And I understand what we're doing. I even know how to drive. I had to
be somebody, but it's a complete blank," Hyperia said, more fascinated
than dumbfounded with her lack of recall.

He had accelerated onto the freeway, then crossed over to the
carpool lane and engaged the cruise control to maintain seventy miles
per hour. *All the wars, oil, disease, famine, genocides and draughts. It
wasn't religion, race, cultural malfeasance or economic imbalance. It
was us. And I feel this woman is the key to end it all.* He refrained from
pushing the gas pedal, accelerating to one hundred twenty and
hastening the progress to Jerome Throckmorton's hospital. "Tabla
rasa," he commented, turning to her briefly, smiling. "Blank slate. I
think you're quite lucky; I envy you. So many unhappy people choose
suicide to end misery. But, what is misery other than bad feelings
triggered by memory? What if they could simply have their minds
erased and start anew?"

"But whoever I am, I don't think I chose to have my mind
erased. Besides, how could that be? Yet, here I am. I could have been
anybody," she replied, dreamily. He reached over and touched her

exposed hand protruding from under her wrap. She gripped his fingers gently. "But it seems like I have known you."

"You've been through quite an ordeal. We really don't know what happened to you to cause the catastrophic loss of memory you've experienced. But the hospital I'm taking you to—they'll find out. Dr. Jerome Throckmorton is a leader in neurology and brain function. I suggest you rest. Try not to think about it. You're alive. That's the most important thing. You're alive, and from what we could tell, very healthy. Sleep, Hyperia. Put your head back and try to sleep." He could sense her gazing at him drearily. He took his eyes off the road, patted her on her hand once more and nodded affirmatively. "You'll be alright."

Sleepy and tired himself, he refrained from disengaging the cruise control, squelching his impatience to accelerate around the traffic. The exhilaration and speed would wake him, but, given his precious cargo, the compromise of risking an accident, or being asked difficult questions by some CHP cop, he restrained himself. He repressed his guilt about the risk of ending a random person's life as well, justifying that the experiment did not render her dead or brain dead. Still, she had a life prior to their interference, and he pondered glumly. *I wonder who she is. She's beautiful, bright, and seems to have possessed a faculty of reason and insight. Zora doesn't make mistakes. And definitely not mistakes bringing negative attention to our organization's activities. She hasn't become complacent with our power and control over politicians and officials. I can only trust she would not have plucked someone out of a life of family or notoriety. Who was she then?*

In a ruminative trance, he noticed their off ramp was in one half mile, and he darted across the double yellow lines of the diamond lane for the exit, causing other drivers to swerve, honk and gesture. He relied on his driving skill, diplomatic plates, and luck to protect him, but he realized the laws of physics superseded all three, and he would have to be more careful and less reckless.

As he sped westward on the hilly road, heading toward Laguna Beach, he pressed a button on his steering wheel. A female voice with a German accent said, "Number please." He recited a number rapidly, and a receptionist answered: "Clarity Center."

"Please inform Dr. Throckmorton that Dr. Éclair is ten minutes away," he responded crisply, then pushed a button to hang up after the receptionist confirmed the message. He grimaced as if he had forgotten something, and then pushed his steering wheel button once more, reciting another set of numbers. "Guten Abend," the voice answered.

"Verbinden Sie mich mit Herrn Kirchmayr, bitte. Ich bin Doktor Éclair," he responded, greeting a German receptionist in her native tongue. Within seconds, a friendly, but formal, male voice came on the line. "Hans. Thank you for being there," Jordan said. "Please transfer two million dollars from an account with the code name Sigma Three Omega to Recipient Four Zero Alpha Five. The destination account has been sent via an encrypted message."

"Very good, sir. And how far are you from the mean?" the telephone voice asked, to which Jordan responded, "A Z-score of positive four point five." Then he hung up, appreciating the seamless manner in which the banker requested his secret pass phrase.

He stopped at a gated driveway and glanced upward into the camera. The gate opened, and he drove through. He parked in front of a shaded villa overlooking a cliff and the ocean below. Four hospital personnel scurried outside, one with a wheelchair, one with a gurney, and two others with equipment, meds and expressions connoting concern for the patient. He motioned for them to wait.

He studied her serene face, her lips slightly parted. He quickly—embarrassingly—repressed the attraction he felt for her. He wanted to awake her gently, so as not to alarm her with the renewed activity and strangers. "Hyperia. Time to wake up. We're at the hospital," he whispered into her ear calmly, tenderly squeezing her thigh. Her eyes opened as she remained expressionless.

"I was dreaming. I was in front of a room full of people. They were listening to me tell them something. They took notes and seemed intent upon my words," she remarked without pause.

His feelings were stuck, lodged between abandonment and nurturing. With the energy and bustle around the car now, he wanted to release her to the system. He almost yielded to an internal, uninvited entreaty to nurture, nudging him to remain at the hospital a few more moments, just to observe her immediate well-being. "We're at the hospital. We'll discover who you were—" he commented, catching his misuse of tense, stammering briefly, "—are," he restated with conviction. Looking over his shoulder, he acknowledged Jerome Throckmorton who had just come outside to join his crew and was leaning next to him over the car window. "Here is Dr. Throckmorton. He's going to take good care of you, Hyperia. Please go with these people now. They're going to open your door and take you inside. Don't be afraid. I'll return and check on you soon." She nodded, and the nurses and technicians escorted Hyperia into the building. As soon as she was out of earshot, he motioned for Throckmorton to come closer to the window.

"I just transferred two million to your account. Follow the program I provided—vigilantly, rigorously, without deviation." He paused, drawing back to consider Throckmorton sternly with long eye contact. "Demonstrate the alternate program to Zora or to one of her representatives if they come here asking," he remarked. "Then call me immediately. In fact, call me as soon as they arrive if you have an opportunity. An unannounced appearance would be inappropriate, but I would not put it past Zora given her trepidations about the logistics for our project." Throckmorton, a medium build, middle-aged man with graying brown hair and thick wire-rimmed glasses, stared at him with sharp blue eyes as if he were insulted that Jordan even felt obliged to deliver the instructions.

"Your wish is my command, Mein Kommandant!" he replied wryly. He hesitated, smiling. "We designed the program together. How else would I do it? How long have we known one another?"

"It's in my genes," Jordan responded apologetically. "But that's correct. We have known one another very long. So, you should know—I don't trust my own mother."

Chapter 7

The Brain Cartographer

Rebecca, naked and sopping wet, yanked the door opened, staggering Jordan as he prepared to enter her apartment. His key remained in the lock as the knob repelled from his grip. Outside, she latched on to him while he stood at the door threshold. She put her arms around him, kissed him with fervor, and shimmied up his body , legs clamped on his torso as if she were scaling up a tree for coconuts.

He worried she would feel the lump under his belt at the small of his back—the gun he concealed there. "You're a naked little sloth," he said surprised but exuberant. "Why the passionate greeting? And, ya' know, someone could have easily been here with me. Then what would you have done?" He saw she was truly jubilant at his arrival.

"I guess I'd have to service you both," she replied dreamily. She jumped off him, grabbed his hand, and pulled him inside. "I'm happy to see you—and you're back on time. Usually, when you go to the office, you get delayed. And—I've been thinking about you all day." She hesitated, an impish expression overcoming her face. "Think we have time for a quickie?"

Rebecca's long, lithe body, wet and shiny beckoned him. He couldn't resist her as she flirted with him with her green, saucer eyes and long, dark hair draped over her breasts. He concealed his frustration as he had been obliged to favor the dutifully rational over matters of his emotions. He winced disdainfully. He had just departed Hyperia, having wanted to remain longer. For the second time in an hour he must delay a satisfaction, denying a beckoning that was even more compelling. He grappled with his attachment for Rebecca—did he love her, or did he simply love having her? Being around her? Looking at her? Smelling her? Hearing her rapturous voice? Was she an object of pure hedonism or was she what he believed he felt—a deep belonging, an attraction involving both mind and body?

He heard himself before he spoke, and he did not like the parental-sounding quality to his comment. "If we get side-lined now, we'll be late. You know that," he replied, expressing whimsical impatience. *Good. I don't want to sound officious, or pissed, even.*

"Fashionably late. And sexually satiated," she responded, slowing to ponder the issue. "But you're right," she relented. "It's just that, since you've gotta change clothes, I just figured, you're almost out of them anyway; I might as well take advantage of the situation. And now, since you're all wet from me, you've got to get out of them even that much faster. But, your right. We can't keep Dr. Stan waiting."

I should be excited about being with her. She is beautiful. I envy the men who can put off their appointments and obligations for intimacy with their loved ones. I owe my schedule to history and progeny. What have they given me? Few will know what I've done. Few will know what generations of my family has done. For good reason, I suppose. But then again, who would truly believe our identities or the results of our actions? We are not super-human, yet we have made decisions—interceded into the events of the world—having a million times more leverage than world leaders or megalomaniacal despots. "Tomorrow. Let's spend the day together. How about if we drive down to San Diego and stay at that hotel you like so much?" he offered with compensatory affect. He watched her mood transition from playful to serious.

"I'd like that," she sighed. "But I wish you could let go sometimes."

Offering her a pressed-lip smile, he walked toward the closet as he unbuttoned his shirt. A thin, dark film covered him. He recognized this despondency—the same abysmal glum that vexed him sporadically as an adolescent. He had concluded as a boy—no matter what he had at his disposal—toys, money, vacations, people courting his friendship—something deeper disturbed him. He knew he would

90

never be happy until he found himself, salving that obscure irritant that had vexed him for a lifetime. *Some commit suicide to escape the constant poking, the chronic nuisance masked as pain.* But he knew it was not pain. He could hover, but he could not soar. The irritation was the blisters from the shackles on his ankles, the shackles holding him down. "I have something to confess. I was not being completely candid with you," he offered suddenly, impulsively. "I want to meet your advisor, Dr. Chamberlain, as much as he wants to meet me. You may not have realized this, but this trip, this meeting, was as much my finagling as your planning." He paused, assessing her reaction, noting the cocked head of a curious puppy. "And—what I've had to deal with at work—it's overwhelming. I don't think I'd ever admit to myself, let alone to anyone else, that I'm overwhelmed and exhausted. I—I love you, Rebecca. And I love you because I can say what I'm saying now." While she was distracted, he had slipped his Beretta into his rear pocket. He disrobed down to his underwear, laying his folded pants— gun-side down—on the bed. He threw his other clothes in a laundry basket in a corner. "So, if I'm not the free spirit you'd like me to be, give me some time. Things will change; I will change, I promise you."

His comment had the desired effect as she approached him and caressed his face. He recognized she was cooling emotionally, and he had to keep her enthused and vitalized about him and their relationship. He could not afford dwelling over any guilt about meeting her and arranging being in her proximity several times simply to evolve a relationship—the reason to get close to Chamberlain on a social level.

They readied for Chamberlain's party, exchanging forced, atypical chit-chat during the brief process. Jordan despised what they were preparing to accommodate: gatherings intended for similar social classes to appraise one another, reinforcing their mutual quests for status and wealth. Onlookers recognized him as a successful industrialist, entrepreneur and scientist—thus emitting appropriate sycophantic diatribe—but they were completely unaware of his real motives, intentions and power. Only until now did Rebecca comprehend his alternate agenda for accompanying her, and he worried that her silence reflected her continued contemplation of his disclosure.

Driving away from her apartment building, Jordan continued to feel depleted. Blocks away, they stopped at a local coffee shop where he indulged in a quad espresso, revitalizing himself to socialize with Rebecca's academic cadre. He could have arranged a business meeting with Chamberlain, but that would have set the wrong tone. He anticipated—depending upon the ambiance of the event—his approach could be either amicable or harsh.

He wanted to gain Chamberlain's enthusiasm, trust and intimate knowledge of functional brain substrates—processing, memory and all mental factors defining human being. Jordan and his company could erase memory—perhaps even the vestiges of personality—but they could not reprogram. They could not transform someone into someone else; more ideally, make that person do what he or she would otherwise never do. Chamberlain's research had laid bare these secrets, but he had neither the technology nor the ethical bravado to take the next steps. Although Jordan believed Chamberlain had considered what he wanted to propose, the man was under too many moral constraints and social dictates to even propose such a venture to Jordan. Jordan's team had no such restraints, and indeed, Jordan's clandestine organization's sworn duty and purpose now focused on Chamberlain's capabilities, to be materialized by their efforts and technology. He would do whatever it took to recruit Stan Chamberlain to their fulfill their interests.

The route to Chamberlain's house presented a challenge to Jordan's patience as well. He would have preferred helicoptering there. The Pacific Coast Highway was the most direct path, but it was wrought with tourists, beach goers, traffic signals, and zealous cops intent upon enforcing speed limits. *Eighteen miles as the crow flies and the damn trip takes over an hour. A worm with miniscule importance does not have to make himself so inaccessible. Simon and I have routinely flown my helicopter from Orange County Airport to San Clemente in under ten minutes.*

Dr. Stanley Chamberlain's house overlooked the Pacific Ocean from a high rocky cliff-side perch at Point Dume. A reclusive, wealthy citrus fruit magnate owned the land, before the oversight era of the Coastal Commission, and had carved the granite shelf of the cliff in order to accommodate a three-hundred-foot staircase riveted into the rock wall. Upon purchasing the lot, Chamberlain exercised a loophole grandfather clause, allowing him to reconstruct the staircase and add an elevator, allegedly for the handicapped. This leverage of opportunism over environmental conscientiousness made Jordan believe he could harvest Chamberlain as a partner. Jordan knew that Chamberlain, for all his ethical posturing about the individuality and the uniqueness of the human spirit, wanted to reprogram a person into another person. His technology, coupled with Jordan's holographic maser, offered psychologists what the scalpel had offered to surgeons.

Once through the gated entrance, he passed his keys to the valet, and he and Rebecca entered the double doors, invited by an alluring entourage of colleagues, friends, neighbors and sundry courtiers. Jordan gloated inwardly as he noticed Rebecca was perceptually impervious to the social dynamics of this party. Though delighted that Rebecca was not a member of this enclave, he would have preferred that she had more insight regarding the lair into which they had ventured. *The grand professor, Nobel Prize winner, philanthropist and entrepreneur is a hedonist. I should have known. Now I know my business tack with him.* He furtively checked his inside coat pocket, where he had stashed his pistol. Glancing about, amused at what he had just spotted, he nudged her to notice the topless woman playing pool in an adjacent room, evidently losing to a savvy hustler.

"This is going to be an interesting party," he whispered into her ear and then looked up, smiling as a mid-fifties, very well preserved and youthful woman approached them. He felt impressed by her openness and exuberance.

"Rebecca! I'm so glad you could make it here tonight. I'm Margaret, Stan's wife. You may not remember me—we met probably over a year ago. I seldom get to the university, but I met you at a faculty party there." She cordially held Rebecca's hand, caressing her arm as if stroking it with dry rub marinade.

Rebecca honed on the woman's face, focused as if nothing else were in the room. "I do remember you. How could I forget such a stunning woman!" she responded with convincing gusto.

Margaret dwelled briefly, deciding whether the comment was sincere or not, then switched eye contact from Rebecca, demurely segueing to Jordan. "And you must be Jordan Éclair—famous gaming magnate, the man responsible for revolutionizing media!"

"Present—guilty as charged," Jordan responded, lightly snapping his heels together and grinning modestly. "Though, to be accurate, I didn't revolutionize media, only its presentation. Its content is still up to the writers and developers." Margaret flowed to him catlike, still pressing Rebecca's arm, but shimmying up to him seductively. He braced himself for some personal question he presumed she would pose.

"How do you stay out of the public eye? Stan had his business manager check every possible resource, trying to invest in your company, or one of its holdings. Nothing. He's upstairs now, stuck with the chancellor, but he wants to talk with you. He'd kick me under the table if he heard me tell you—he's been waiting for weeks. He even plays games with your company's—what's the term—cerebral cap."

He winced silently at her contrived lapse of memory, a tactic used to demean or demote in importance. *Of course she knows the name of the device. She probably knows the serial number. If he's been playing with it, he's probably connected himself and her to one of the erotic games. She knows damn well what it's called.* "Did he tell you our company controls the minds of the nation's youth with the device he had so cavalierly donned?" He smirked, observing her stealthy surprise to his remark. "Or had he moved beyond the popular tripe the boorish conservative pundits were spewing, despite positive endorsements by the FCC and FDA?" She unconsciously retreated a step, though not losing eye contact.

She should be a politician's wife—or a politician herself—not the wife of a hedonistic scientist with delusions of grandeur, he mused. *I'll bet she can change the subject on a dime without appearing abrupt.*

"Let me take you upstairs. I'm sure he won't mind the interruption, and the chancellor would like to meet you as well. But be careful. I'm sure the old fool will try to recruit you into lecturing some class, or being a guest speaker. God forbid—you, a faculty member!" she warned, talking down to faculty member status. She turned to Rebecca. "My dear, I'll return immediately," she chuckled apologetically and gently pinching Rebecca's forearm. "As much as I disdain the myth of 'men-folk conversations,' I think these two deserve a bit of privacy." She rotated around, spying a brunette woman about Rebecca's age, and beckoned her over. "Joyce, my dear, please meet Rebecca Ramsey. And here is Dr. Jordan Éclair. I'm escorting Dr. Éclair up to Stan's library. I'm sure you two women have a lot in common."

She reminds me of Hyperica. His gaze dwelled on her a split second too long; she had noticed. *I hope she doesn't think I'm interested. She'll corner me later when Rebecca is distracted elsewhere.* He nodded politely and then looked away with purposeful curtness. "Shall we?" he commented to Margaret and then kissed Rebecca on her neck. "I won't be long, babe."

Jordan paced after his hostess through two interconnected, lushly carpeted, and exquisitely decorated hallways, pondering if anyone else traipsing through this house wondered how a university professor—granted, a Nobel Prize winner—could adorn himself in such opulence. *Perhaps it's family money*, he thought. *Had I been my mother, I would have had Chamberlain thoroughly checked out, and I'd already have the answers to my questions about his background. Perhaps my mother is right in chastising me for preferring the experiential route.* So consumed in his thoughts, he ran into Margaret when she stopped in front of some heavy double doors. Embarrassed, he backed off silently, gesturing to the artwork as if he had been too absorbed to watch where he was going. She smiled empathetically but seemed to take pleasure in the split second of body contact with him.

"He's in there with the chancellor," she whispered. "Let's not make a big deal of it." She knocked lightly but assertively and nudged the door open, sticking her head inside, not obsequiously.

"Stan, you know, you have guests, and though I understand you relish in Fitz's company, I have someone here you've been wanting to meet." She swung the door fully opened, revealing Jordan standing in the door well next to her.

"Fitz," Stan Chamberlain said, speaking to his friend, Dr. Fitzgerald Jung, chancellor of the university. "Here is the young man we've been waiting for. Waiting? No—I won't keep secrets— discussing! Margaret, thank you so much for bringing Jordan up. I'm old and absent-minded and self-absorbed, and I forgot to ask you specifically to bring up Jordan as soon as he arrives. But you've seen through my flaws, and here he is." He jumped up, bowing and mewling, motioning Jordan inside. Jordan took a few steps toward his host and then checked to his rear to notice Margaret had stayed behind, furtively closing the door after him. The chancellor stood, moving to greet Jordan as well.

Jordan did not like prejudice, especially coming from himself, but there was nothing he could do about it: Jordan was a fatist—a racist if excess body blubber had a color. Chamberlain's form went beyond portly, and his mere outline discouraged him from truly respecting the renowned professor. *Makes sense and fits my assessment of him as a hedonist.*

Jordan saw both men approach him in shadow, cast by the fully involved fireplace framing them from behind. He knew why he preferred experience; why he liked going into situations garnering information without preconceived notions or advanced intelligence. He was keenly adept at garnering clues and gleaning insight richer than what extraneous sources could provide. Still, he was relieved he had taken Simon's advice and allowed his assistant to scour all of Chamberlain's international financial holdings, especially the ones the IRS was unaware of. Jordan settled into confidence, now assured of the targeted rapport with his host. *Chamberlain set this up. The chancellor will excuse himself, offering to talk with me later. In the meantime, Chamberlain will lay his pitch. He wants something, which is why we're meeting in this setting instead of in an office.*

After cordial greetings and introductions all around, Fitzgerald Jung remained standing as Stanley Chamberlain motioned Jordan to take a seat—the same chair Jordan had observed the chancellor had occupied when Margaret had first prodded open the door. The chancellor seemed pressured as if delivering difficult lines from a script. "Gentlemen, I've left my wife to her own devices for much longer than I am allowed. No doubt she'll greet me with pursed lips, furrowed brow, and narrow eyes." He laughed and shook his head with feigned disgust. "It's a game! I know as well as she; she enjoys my absence, but I must return to her side nevertheless."

Jordan plopped himself down casually, readying himself for the next volley from Chamberlain. Recognizing they both had something the other wanted, he repressed a certain smugness—he knew what he wanted was subterfuge, whereas what Chamberlain wanted was an entrance to true psychological technology. *I'm the amicable old lady in the candy-laced gingerbread house, beckoning Hansel and Gretel in for a little snack. The witch is hungry; the children are hungry.* He amused himself with this little whimsy, realizing he was the witch in this scenario, as the chancellor made his way through the door, and both men exchanged partings. He waved quickly as the chancellor bid him an awkward farewell.

He remained sitting nonchalantly, committed to letting Chamberlain lead the conversation, wondering just how he would do it. He felt perfectly at ease in this interplay, knowing that whatever Chamberlain said or wanted, Jordan would get his way. Chamberlain returned to sit squarely across from Jordan, stone-faced and silent, contemplating his face and sporting an expression between a poker and chess player.

"I'm not sure where to begin," Chamberlain finally opened. "You want to navigate the mind; I have the maps. The problem is you and your company pose some ethical problems into which I must tread carefully, or not at all." Chamberlain's comment jolted Jordan briefly as he instinctively suspected Chamberlain knew something of his true intentions. Chamberlain had paused to view Jordan's reaction and then continued.

"The ethical dilemma is two-pronged. First, a working technology—as I conceive you would develop—has the potential to spawn hundreds of industries out of which billions, even trillions, would flow. Vast wealth has its own pitfalls. Secondly, I must deal with the public's outcry—that the mind is a sacred domain, private and out of reach from all but God." He paused again to take in Jordan's reaction to the word, God. Jordan remained stone-faced. "And there is a third issue, a personal one. I'll mention it later—as embarrassingly—I must include it as a contingency for our future partnership."

Chamberlain's comment enraged Jordan, and lava surged to the crust. Jordan clutched his hands, fingers interlaced, as he braced himself between restraint and onslaught. He had killed before, and the arrogant, hedonistic, self-important insect-of-an-intellectual before him had raised his ire. He calmed himself, realizing diplomacy and tact had to be observed. He had dealt with magnates, royalty, high heads of state and members of his own clan, all wealthy and powerful beyond the comprehension of this academic politician. *This plodding pedantic who obsessively drove his graduate students from one boring set of research to the next, trudging along a path of discovery, publishing twenty articles for every nuance of novelty unearthed until a body of work finally emerged which appeared to have wholeness and substance.* He maintained a Cheshire cat grin as he pushed out of the chair.

"Contingency for our future partnership is as follows." Jordan got up, walked to the double doors and locked them. As he returned toward Chamberlain, he detected his host feared him—such an uncharacteristic move was worthy of apprehension. *A wise decision*, he thought, still grinning. He strode toward Chamberlain without flinch or expression change. Standing over him, he pushed Chamberlain's forehead back forcefully, so his head pinned against the chair, then reached into his inside jacket pocket and placed the Beretta gun barrel under the Nobel Prize winner's jaw. "I'm not going to play games with you. I'm going to have what I want, one way or another. You've got more problems than some phony, trumped-up ethical concerns, fretted by religious fanatics, publicity lime-lighters and limousine liberals." Chamberlain emitted torrents of sweat, his breathing fast as if having just finished a long jog. "You're going to work for me—with us—and you're going to commit yourself to it. If you do, you'll be a very wealthy man. I've deposited five million dollars in that secret Zurich account you believe the IRS doesn't know about. I want you to call Zurich to verify the funds are there before we leave this room. As of now, you're five million dollars richer, but your next decisions will be crucial to your well-being, as well as your family's. As we meet certain milestones, I'll deposit more. By the end of the project, I will have deposited fifty million dollars into your account, tax free, to do with as you please. But you will work with me and do my bidding, or you will die; your wife, Margaret will die; your daughter, son-in-law, and both your grandchildren, three-year-old Todd and five-year-old Amber, will die—painfully and brutally. I'll see to it the children are flayed alive in front of you before I kill you. Do you understand me?"

As if he had awakened from a nightmare, only to discover he was not asleep after all, he nodded his head within the range Jordan allowed his head to move, his skull still pressed against the chair back, his eyes white with narrow black dots in the center.

"Say it! 'Yes, Dr. Éclair. From here on I am your partner. I'll work for you, do your bidding without questioning, and I understand I'll be rewarded very handsomely,'" Jordan demanded. Jordan's hand was slipping off Chamberlains sweaty forehead, and he released him to speak. "Say it, I said!" He moved the gun barrel from his neck to his forehead.

"Yes—yes, Dr. Éclair. I'm your partner. I'll do as you request. And you'll reward me handsomely," Chamberlain repeated, trembling, but his countenance stabilizing with the mention of the money.

"We'll endow a few million to the university to quell their curiosity and make it appear as if the research you're doing is for them. But make no mistake—this is not a research project. This is a design and manufacturing project, and you are the project leader. I'm going to release you. If you disavow your oath to me, now, or ever, I told you what would happen. I'm going to release you, then hand you a phone with your bank information already entered. You can verify it online. Then I want you to call Zurich and verify the amount personally. Then I'll explain what you're going to be doing for the next two years." Jordan quivered at the exhilaration he experienced, pressing Chamberlain's head back, gun pressed against his throat and head. He considered the man an arrogant, undeserving windbag—the worst kind of academic, a cockroach with a Ph.D. and Nobel Prize—but an insect nevertheless. He believed that many academics are not very talented, certainly not brilliant, but many are persistent and diligent and hard working and refrain from airs and pretensions. Chamberlain was a politician who gave science, research and academia a bad name. He released his head, squeegeed the sweat from his hand onto the armrest upholstery; he slid the phone from his jacket pocket into Chamberlain's quivering hand.

"Stop shaking and whining. You're still alive, and five million dollars richer than five minutes ago," Jordan hissed with disgust.

"I—I—I thought you had gone mad," Chamberlain whispered. He looked at the smartphone display; his expression lightening almost immediately as he viewed his Swiss bank account balance.

Jordan feared Chamberlain might make a run for the door or provoke him to detain him physically, which he did not want to do. He already knew he would not have to shoot him, knowing that the five million dollars would not only calm his nerves but also assuage any ethical qualms he would voice about mind-access technology. However, had he died of a heart attack or stroke during the altercation, he would have had no another recourse.

"No. I'm far from mad. How could I possibly be mad, you idiot! Now call your bank in Zurich. I want to start working immediately." He watched in silent amusement as Chamberlain skulked to his desk.

Soaked in sweat and limp from the immediate trauma, he looked up the number to his Swiss bank. Jordan's impatience climbed as he waited for Chamberlain to ask to speak to someone in English in his broken German. The process was fascinating, he thought, how a large sum of money could overcome a man's physical and psychological trauma so quickly and completely. Here was a man he barely knew, a stranger to him only minutes ago, a self-important chest puffer, who now subordinated himself completely. Chamberlain replaced the phone receiver and smiled at Jordan. "Looks like you're my employer," he said calmly. "What do you want me to do?"

"I want you to recover your previous disposition and act normally. When the chancellor asks you what we discussed, tell him my corporation has given your department an endowment for five million dollars." He hesitated as he saw Chamberlain's dismay. "Another five million—not yours. You can remain the principal researcher in name, but I want you to grant Rebecca all privileges of co-principal investigator." Jordan waited for Chamberlain to balk slightly and then recover to concurrence, clearly still thinking about his own glory.

"Her dissertation is complete," Jordan continued. "I've studied it; it's brilliant, and you know it. Grant her doctorate. She is to lead the project. You will spend more than half your time at our research facility in El Segundo—and another location soon to be disclosed. Needless to say, we're merging your neural cartography with our maser electrode technology. We'll discuss technology and project specifics soon." Jordan viewed Chamberlain's change of affect with mixed aversion, seeing that he had transitioned from cowering to mewling.

"You mentioned fifty million dollars," Chamberlain whimpered in Uriah Heep fashion. "Will there be a contract based on goals, vesting in stock, how will that work? Naturally, if we can negotiate a tax free incentive, I would—"

Jordan truly hated Chamberlain, a feeling that he realized as he caressed the Beretta in his pocket. Pondering his indignation momentarily, he goaded himself to the positive. *The science he claims in his name has been the laborious and painstaking work of others over the past twenty years. He is not a scientist; he is an administrator, a pompous bureaucrat of supersized proportions. He keeps the keys to the kingdom. I have to work with him.* "We'll work out the paperwork tomorrow, as well as the details for the project. I said fifty million dollars, and that is what I meant. I'm going downstairs now. I suggest you join us shortly—normally." He pulled the Beretta out, so Chamberlain got a glimpse of it, then returned it to inside his jacket. The same flash of peril waxed over his expression, like when Jordan held the instrument to his throat earlier.

Downstairs Jordan approached Rebecca and Joyce, the woman with whom Margaret had connected Rebecca prior to his departure for upstairs. Margaret, Chancellor Jung, and a group of Orange County dignitaries stood close by. He grinned evilly as the Orange County aristocrats eyed him self-consciously as he approached, then he continued, past them. Though removed from his grandfather's mulatto stature by two generations, he still sported a complexion suggesting he was not purebred Caucasian extraction. He recognized all too well that these simpletons held a deep and inexplicable belief in superiority based upon their religious, political and racial roots. Yet their dilemma, a source of perplexing distress for them, was that he was not a member of their politics, religion, nor race. Paradoxically, by their very own standards of success and hierarchy, he occupied a loftier status than they. He decided to wiggle the dagger deeper, making certain they would find no assurance their ideals were secure or well-founded. Rebecca noticed her companion, Joyce, was distracted, and looked in the direction of her interest. She caught Jordan descending the stairs and immediately looked at the adjacent group, seeing them smiling in wincing agony.

"Have you made a new friend?" she asked him as he approached her. Without a word, he pulled her close to him by her narrow waist and kissed her firmly on her lips for three seconds.

"I missed you," he responded playfully. "Friend? No. But I do have a new business partner. And you have a new job," he added. He glanced at Joyce, who annoyed him, as she sported a smile so wide and obsequiously exaggerated it could have severed her head from ear to ear. Having to put an extra effort in ignoring her irritated him that much more. Knowing him extremely well, Rebecca turned him in another direction, hoping to distract him, only in time to have Dr. Jung, the chancellor, intercede.

"I'm sorry for having left as abruptly as I did. I had already promised my wife I would not talk-shop before we left the house this evening. So when I ended up in Stan's study—well, needless to say, she was already irate."

Jordan liked the chancellor more than he liked Chamberlain. He perceived Jung portraying an amicable, humble persona which seemed genuine. Amassing research funding for the university was his agenda, not feathering an abysmal megalomania. "I understand completely, though I can't really empathize. I've not been married." He put his arm around Rebecca's waist, pulling her closer to him. "But I believe your university will be happy with the arrangements Dr. Chamberlain and I have worked out." He hesitated with an impish smile. "Indeed, Stanley was beside himself." He could see that the chancellor was maneuvering to introduce him to the nobility around which he had detoured to avoid. The others in the adjacent group had positioned themselves for introductions.

"I'd like to introduce you to a few of the university's benefactors, as well as some of our community's leaders and spokespeople," Dr. Jung said, gently leading Jordan under the elbow.

Jordan grabbed the chancellor by his other elbow, gently halting his progress. He glanced at the small circle waiting to greet him, and he smiled as if he'd join them shortly. He recognized Congressman Doorman, and he remembered the congressman had threatened to filibuster legislation aimed at providing expanded healthy lunch programs to public schools nationwide—Coca-Cola, Lays, and McDonald's had been among his major campaign contributors. Rebecca had mentioned that he had been a frequent guest for various pundits on Fox News. He had read when Doorman's father had held a congressional seat for Orange County during the Fifties and Sixties. He had filibustered against Civil Rights legislation in 1966 during the Johnson administration. Some of the other noteworthy guests included Chas Foxworthy, owner of the Orange County Country Club. They had vigilantly sought to exclude blacks, Jews, and other ethnic minorities from joining until an order from the State Supreme Court five years ago mandated that they open their doors, or risk severe civil liability.

Jordan could neither face these people with a congenial air, nor could he contaminate himself with hypocrisy. He was neither liberal nor conservative, but he felt toward this group the way they felt toward the most miserable and down-trodden of minorities. He reveled in a fantasy about this elite, entitled crowd. He would Shanghai the lot of them and ship them off to Sudan or Somalia, where they could be put to use, forced to traipse across fields, hunting for land mines. He surpressed an evil grin. He cautioned himself, mixing his distaste for those of their ilk and the aims of his covert organization, for he was powerful enough to have any and all of them murdered without fanfare at any given time. "Chancellor, as much as I'd like to meet your excellent congregate of social nobility here, I'm afraid we have a pressing appointment, and we have to leave immediately."

With a quick and officious handshake, he left the chancellor standing. He nodded farewell to the circle of guests. He turned and kissed Margaret on the cheek from behind. "We have to leave in a hurry. An emergency just came up," he said apologetically. "But we'll see one another soon. Your husband and I will be doing a considerable about of work together." Rebecca looked at him in mild awe, but offered no resistance.

Outside, he spoke to the valet briefly, and then turned back to Rebecca as they awaited the arrival of the car. Regretting having to remove her from a situation she seemed to enjoy, he was assured telling her the outcome of his meeting would assuage any resentment she had toted away with her. "I hope you don't think I interfered with your affairs and your life, but here's the situation. I crafted a deal with Chamberlain. There are two aspects to the work—corporate and academic research. He has to work with the company. Since he's not going to be around here as much, the project needs a project leader—you. And your well-deserved and overdue doctorate is included with the deal," he whispered while kissing her neck. "You can thank me when we get home."

Chapter 8

World War One

"These Black Hand fanatics are not to be taken lightly, François," Gershon whispered, leaning over the table, assuring that nobody in the Sarajevo Café heard him. "You cannot go with me—no—absolutely not!" He paused, peering at his friend sternly, hopeful that François took his unswerving stance seriously. "I've spent months negotiating this meeting, making payoffs, setting up schedules, playing roles!" He enunciated his comment in a conclusive hiss. "Three and a half million pounds, and you want to risk it—our plans, our lives—on a whim, a fancy?"

François' cheek cooled from the rush of Gershon's breath, extruded by exacting and pointed words. He felt excluded from the excitement, but he understood that Gershon's words were true. He fantasized about adventure, but these emotion-laden images existed only in his imagination—his plans, his schemes, his projects, all executed by others. He ventured one more excuse. "But if I dress as one of them and bear arms for the assassination, and know names and locations, certainly they would believe that I am part of the organization." Gershon slumped back in his chair, dejected by having to continually deny his friend and partner.

"I am Russian; you are not. God forbid—they don't even know I'm a Jew. And need I remind you—you're half Nubian!" Gershon stared at François intensely. "You have planned this venture so well. Only you could have devised such a perfectly precise scheme, like clockwork in its intricate juxtaposition of parts. All the gears, cogs, wheels, springs—in perfect harmony." Gershon leaned over the table once more, easing toward François' ear. "The world at war. Is that not what we have planned?" He hesitated, without moving. "And oil! François! Do you realize how the resulting war will alter the global economies?" He stopped again, realizing what he had asked. "Certainly you do—you designed it! Petroleum energy for autos, ships, trains. And very soon—as you've predicted years ago—airplanes. This war will consume more oil than—"

François' flight of fantasy dissipated to reality, and he settled back into his role of grand designer. Discouraged, but not dejected, he understood generals who insisted on accompanying their men onto the field of battle. "To speak of ourselves as wealthy is truly an understatement," François interrupted. "Very well, I give in. You are absolutely right, but I had to try. If they shot us, believing we were Potiorek's spies, all our hard work and planning would have been in vain. And frankly, they'd be justified in shooting us for being so careless, underestimating them as idiots. They're fanatics and low-lives, but not stupid," François admitted.

Gershon's expression eased. "My old friend, at times I'm not sure when, and if, you'll relent. I remember on that blizzard-like night in Bern, the eve of 1904, ten years ago. You stated we could own the world. How many men in history wanted to own the world, said they would own the world, and even had a plan? But you? You had a plan and the means, and it didn't require dictatorships, megalomania, or marching bands in your behalf. You said it could be done with oil, science, money, and stealth." He paused, touching François' sleeve. "It's June 26, 1914. That meeting was over ten years ago. Today, our various organizations and corporations own ninety percent of the oil deposits and reserves in the world, as well as patents for the major technological advances."

François caught himself gloating, a transgression against humility about which he was genuinely vigilant. He could not allow himself the simple egotistic pleasures other men with simpler successes afforded themselves. "The nations of Europe—of the world—could not have aligned themselves more advantageously. And the band of Bosnian hooligans you're meeting could not have played into our hands

108

better. The world can never know that we paid Potiorek one million pounds to invite the Archduke here—for an inane opening of a hospital."

Gershon wiggled nervously at François' comment and shifted his eyes about. "Just saying that in a public place is dangerous," Gershon murmured. "Changing names, wearing disguises, trusting nefarious types with large sums of money, clandestine meetings, all to finalize a conspiracy by any definition. I must say, Potiorek held up his end of the agreement. Ferdinand and his wife are due here in two days."

François felt empty. This grand scheme culminating in a world at war was nothing other than a simple puzzle to François—a domino effect to which he had provided the initiating finger. He foresaw a termination point far into the future which he knew he would never experience. He feared his ilk's death affliction approaching, and he longed for another fifty years of life. "When they assassinate Franz Ferdinand, knowing the Austrians as I do, they will countermand by issuing a demarche to Serbia. The Serbs cannot—will not—abide, and the international alliances will set off a chain reaction. All of Europe will be at war."

"And the man who caused it—" Gershon smirked coyly as he flashed a glance at François, "—the man who caused it will be caught. Some poor, deluded wretch will be tortured, his life squeezed out of him in a Serbian dungeon."

François flinched inwardly, Kafka-ishly fantasizing that the man who would be caught would be himself. "Yes, but hopefully they do not kill him too hastily. We don't want suspicion cast in Potiorek's direction. Indeed, Potiorek should be the one doing the catching and interrogating." He nonchalantly kicked at a leather bag beneath Gershon's stool. "The chemist—he provided you with the weakened cyanide capsules?"

"Everything's in the bag," Gershon responded. "Capsules, maps, ammunition. And speaking of the bag—I'd better be underway." He pulled out his pocket watch, checking the time. "These Black Hand fanatics—they're just smart enough to ask the wrong questions should anything arouse their suspicions—which is why you cannot accompany me. I'm to meet them in perfectly miscreant surroundings, on the banks of the Miljacka in an abandoned warehouse near the Bosnian National Library. I expect anywhere from three to ten of them—all with aspirations of martyrdom—to achieve the dubious distinction of killing the Archduke—and Sophie, if they're lucky."

A surge of fulfillment inundated him. He would be the unknown agent of history's most spectacular events. As if he were astride a giant snake, winding and slinking its way through time, he controlled the reins of an otherwise uncontrollable beast, guiding it to the vicinity of its prey, but never able to direct its actions with precise accuracy and volition. "I'm glad there are many of them and not simply one overzealous martyr. The probability of success increases, like sperm struggling toward an ovum." He noticed Gershon suppressing a guffaw.

"The verbal pictures you paint create indelible images. Now when I meet these men, I shall visualize them as semen, sprayed into the chamber of history to conceive a war of all nations, solidifying global oil consumption," Gershon recited with sacrosanct conviction.

"Be off, my old friend," François said hastily, not wanting to dwell more on desired outcomes. "Make beautiful music. We'll meet at my house in Zurich. At that time, we'll have to decide if we want to ride this out in Switzerland or retreat to the United States."

Despondency and loneliness overcame his near grandiosity from moments ago. He watched as Gershon disappeared among the old market pedestrians and vendors. Startled at his sudden change of mood, a feeling spawned from no clear cause, no apparent thought or deed, he

110

searched inside himself for reason. *I love living, and I see the end. I must arrange my own death. I will not die an old man, surrounded by grandchildren and doting admirers. My protégé back in Austria—he'll tend to this war, and I must make certain he survives.*

***

Gershon's arms fatigued from the burden carrying his satchel of assassin's supplies. He switched the weight between hands every five minutes. He had realized the load was too heavy at the Café with François, but he wisely did not mention the burdensome bag. François would have loaded that fact into his arsenal of reasons to accompany him. He furrowed his brow in annoyance, thinking that as brilliant as his friend was, he disregarded basic contingencies as if they were details to be discarded. He mulled over the recent conversation: *Of course, he could not be with him when he met these men from the Black Hand. He had not been part of the association before—what would they think if he arrived with a well-dressed mulatto, claiming to be part of the Bosnian resistance?*

When Gershon arrived at his destination, he could smell the rotted timber, human sewage, garbage and river waste that had accumulated around the unkempt area. A Bosnian ghetto—the stench underscored why these men wanted to kill Archduke Franz Ferdinand.

Gershon had strolled through the area twice before, making certain he knew exactly where to meet his accomplices. Most of their meetings had been in one of the leaders' apartments. The wealthier of the members, Balkan military officers and teachers—the founders of the organization—owned homes on the outskirts of the city. Gershon's holding companies had financed much of the Black Hand's activities and weapons. His last donation he had advanced personally to Danilo Ilić, with whom he was to meet today along with some young zealous followers of the clan.

Breathing slowly through his mouth, he did not want to inundate his nostrils with the vile air, though in the course of his journey, he became used to the stench. So it was, he concluded, people acclimate to their environs. *Yet, some awareness of the pestering presence—the chronic injury—must persist at an out-of-awareness level, though one must become numb to what would otherwise be torture. How could slaves survive, or tortured inmates, or impoverished families, or a mother who cannot feed her children as she watches them slowly die—how could any of the downtrodden human existences live on with such external pressures to bear unless the human condition was to adapt as a defense to the onslaught of nature? What wall does this pain construct? Or, perhaps it builds weapons? Defense or offense against the burdens and toils we must bear? People who experience strife over their entire lives, who know nothing but hardship and misery—how do they persist? This stench is their life.*

The door behind him creaked open, and a roguish, scruffy, black-bearded, potted face protruded from the shadows. A crackly, guttural voice beckoned to him in proletarian Russian. "Guspadin Dostoyevsky. Please, come in. Quickly."

He yanked his bag upward from the ground, attempting to make it appear a lighter burden than it was. Distracted from his rumination about how people cope with lifelong hardship, he flashed on how he currently coped with pangs of fear. Instead of basking in the wealth his family had provided for him in St. Petersburg, he gallivanted about the world, implementing the projects of François and of his group of clandestine comrades. He deflected the pang of fear he felt as he entered the dank, dingy, shoulder-width brick stairwell leading to an underground sewer labyrinth.

Yellow, filament-glowing, incandescent bulbs dangled from hastily strung wires along the top of the semi-circular passage. Surprised his guide did not light their way by torchlight—the smell of kerosene accosting his nostrils—he wondered about the source of the electricity. He knew the wiring in the city was scant, and only the wealthy and well-established businesses were able to afford this luxury. Thus, the owners of the source did not know about the diversion of their power, or the people who operated this clandestine meeting hall were better connected than they let on. Nevertheless, they were not stupid, nor did he assess them as careless; so apparently they were indifferent to his awareness of this casual opulence.

Knowing he could never retrace his steps if danger beset him, he resolved intrepidly that he would emerge victorious after having passed on the materials in his bag, including the assassins' supplies, a map of the Archduke's proposed route two days from now and his schedule. Finally after walking back and forth, up and down, through narrow, dank brick passageways, they stood before the threshold of the cleanest door he had seen along his path. His guide knocked furtively and in distinct code. Gershon chuckled silently, amused that secrecy and security would still be a concern this far into the bowels of Hell. *If ambushers had made it this far in, they certainly would not be so gauche as to knock with cryptic signal.* A caricature of his guide opened the door—looking cautiously as if the Austro-Hungarian secret police had stalked them in their footsteps—he ushered Gershon and his guide inside.

As if a bubble of royalty had broken off from the main palace and had floated unobtrusively through the rabble and decay of the city, it lighted here. Gershon was immediately irritated but withheld the expression. *If they wanted him dead anyway, why have we paid so much for them to do it? It's to insulate Potiorek, no doubt, but his influence here is obvious.*

"You're right on time, my Russian friend!" Danilo Ilić yelled robustly. He slammed an empty glass from the vodka he had just downed on the rustic wooden table. "My boys! Gather round. Here is our benefactor."

Gershon's plight escalated, observing that Danilo was drunk. Predicting sober behavior was precarious enough, but actions loosened by alcohol were stripped of the rationale he used to judge men and assess character. He disdained drunkenness. It was a lie, a flimsy bravado facilitated through deadened senses and obscured reasoning—a trick propagated by the waste products of bacteria in vats of grain and fruit. And now he had to deal with it on the brink of his group gaining superlative power: Europe thrown into turmoil. He sighed in silent disgust.

Worried more about the success of the plan rather than his own safety, Gershon considered all the roles he could play. He had learned—growing up in Russia and dealing with drunks—playing the kindred spirit gains more than a tee totaling critic, but the role jeopardized his anonymity. He did not like the business relationship polluted with false camaraderie. *I cannot allow this drunk to disrupt the plans. But if not now, what about later? They know me as Fyodor Dostoyevsky. This fool will be apprehended, but only after the job is successful and complete.* "My dear friend, Danilo!" He dropped his bag, rushed to Danilo and hugged him. "You've saved some vodka for me?"

Danilo burped loudly and spun in a guffaw. "The finest!" He looked at the assemblage gathered around the table and against the walls. He picked the youngest and most amenable to commands. "Marko! A clean glass for our friend," he demanded boisterously.

Gershon tossed the vodka down his throat, dropped his glass to the table, then kicked at his bag with the side of his shoe and gestured to the men around the room. "If I knew we were having a party, I would have hired the Dervishes!" Gershon commented with frivolity.

"Ha! A party. These men, they want to throw a party. With these men, we cannot miss. And that is what we are here for, is it not?" Danilo shouted, now suddenly more sober than he appeared when Gershon first entered. "They are serious men, all of them. They won't even drink vodka with me! That's a damned good sign, though maybe not such a good omen!" Gershon surmised that Danilo's drunken state had been a test, not only for him, but to test his men for stability and focus.

The warm glow spread in his gut, the vodka diffusing but not yet affecting his brain. Though now more at ease with his situation, he felt pressed to get on with the transaction. "I've got everything here— in this bag. Money, guns, and—" He hesitated. "—the tablets, in case you are caught."

Danilo turned a grave eye to him, not suggesting resistance, but rather a restrained plea for help. Danilo moved closer to Gershon. "I want you to hand out the tablets. I would feel like the marksman at a man's execution," he whispered. "Call me weak-hearted, perhaps even a coward in these matters. I've known many of these boys for most of each's life. Their families." He angled his head toward one of the young men. "Gavrilo, there. I just spoke with his widowed mother this morning. I cannot be the one handing him a poison pill."

Danilo's request pleased Gershon, and he graciously accepted the task bequeathed him. He could be certain the suicide tablets his chemist had concocted—secretly weakened so as to not to cause death to the imbibers—would be distributed properly, and not replaced. And he had a macabre, if not grandiose, interest in looking in the face of a man who would be the final instrument to instigate what Gershon and François planned as nothing less than cataclysmic. "Very well, my friend. If you wish. However, if I do this—and I have like reservations—I would ask you to introduce each man to me. I want to shake his hand, for he is a hero, and if I give poison to a hero, at least I

115

can look him in the eye, hear his name pronounced, and shake his hand."

Danilo's demeanor softened close to tears. He touched Gershon on the shoulder, nodded, and gestured that he should follow him. Gershon yanked his bag to the table, several glasses crashing to the floor. He carefully unbuttoned it while still displaying the haste that this somber moment demanded. Holding a hand-sized silver tin, he slid next to Danilo's side. The men seemed to understand what was occurring, and they lined up against the wall, ready to receive their sacraments. Lagging behind Danilo, he assessed the lineup of potential assassins—hard, hungry, gaunt faces with a touch of compassion. He pictured that one of these men could rip your heart out with a fork, make a broth from it, then spoonful by spoonful, nurturingly feed the broth to a sick child.

"Lazar Djukić," Danilo said, starting with the first young man—dark, serious, intent—the young man bowed his head. "Gavrilo Princip," Danilo continued, announcing the second man, the one to whom he had referred earlier. "Here is Muhamed Mehmedbašić," he said, moving to the third. Facing each man, Gershon handed him the round, gray tablet, shook his hand, looked him squarely in the eyes, and emoted a gesture of pride and spirit. He handed out sixteen of the twenty capsules from his tin. At the end of the line, he handed the remaining capsules to Danilo.

"I'll leave the bag. It's all there," Gershon commented furtively, but maintaining his somber demeanor. Gershon saw Danilo did not want to count the money in the presence of the men, either because the transaction cheapened or diminished their mission, or because Danilo wanted it for himself. Gershon did not know, and he did not care. From all that he had observed, the men who might usher in the end of the world had been rightly served. He departed believing these men were, indeed, the correct choices for the job to be done, and he had every confidence that success would be the outcome.

Chapter 9

Dolchstoßlegende

Marie Rothschild glowered at Gershon, squaring off in a hostile stance across her office. Perplexed by her own ambivalence, the conflict between business and personal obligations had besieged her. On one hand, she had to deal with the labor union's demands at her family's weapons factory. On the other hand, her cohort's crafted subterfuge to which she had given tacit—if not explicit—consent, vexed her. The workers' strike had achieved full momentum at the crest of the war, at a critical time when munitions and weapons were urgently required at the fronts. Fifteen years ago when she had abandoned herself to François' fervor, she had not realized the repercussions of the alliance and the personal and business discord it would cause once implemented.

"This is nasty business, Gershon," she enunciated deliberately as she looked out over one of her weapons factory floors from the window of her office in Frankfurt. "You, François and Adrian—you engineered this strike. You channeled and concealed funds; you make it appear the German government reneged on contract payments. Then you incited the workers to strike." She sensed Gershon's icy stare behind her, melting as he erupted into one of his inspiring crescendos.

"Marie! It's not enough that you comply; you must be avid; you must embrace this strategy with pure gusto," he broadcast with evangelical declaration. "This operation requires not only cooperation, but it also requires relentless fervor—impassioned commitment. We are shaping a global future. A new world. Our world," he paused, "—and you are subverted by a sense of loyalty to the workers? Or, a sense of German nationalism?" He stopped again, not really expecting a response but timing his entreaty. He knew she responded more keenly to rationale when it was mixed with drama. He was aware that Marie

118

Rothschild had remained intrepid about their group's ideal—or at least its romance—since 1904. However, he had noticed her waver since they had implemented what François, Gershon and Adrian had cavalierly labeled their "world at war plan." She felt increasingly uneasy. "You cannot maintain a milligram of caprice, Marie. This is not like dithering over the selection of a gown to wear to the opera." A pulse of fury heated her, but she remained silent, continuing to stare out at her factory floor.

A forlorn mist consumed her as she had procrastinated implementing a promise made years before. Since then, she had continued to affirm her decision. She despised questioning her decisions. Yet, making a decision meant losing options, and she hated losing options. She considered lost options, lost freedoms. "I've been coming to this same office since I was a little girl. My father would bring me to work with him. He treated me as an apprentice, even when I was eight years old. He expected to me carry on—to run the companies as he did. You mentioned nationalism and loyalty. Gershon, I thought you knew me better. You misinterpret me. I don't feel compassion for the workers, nor do I feel any sort of German patriotism—it's a government from which I profit. But I learned my father's lessons well. Shutting down the munitions plants through your conspiratorial scheme in order to dampen the German war impetus— well, that just plain bad business," she finalized in an exhaustive huff. She turned to look at Gershon as she leaned against the railing in front of her window. She knew him well, perceiving his tenuous balance between compliance and opposition.

"I understand the values with which you were raised. I must confess; I was raised with similar values—work ethic, candor, morality, competitiveness. I know few who were not raised with those values. You are not unique in this respect. I don't presume to be philosophical about what I consider middle-class standards. Now is hardly the time for an ethics debate, so let's keep it pointed. It's good business if you keep the long-term effect in sight," Gershon shot back. "It's good business if you realize that within ten years your manufacturing facilities will triple; that within twenty years, your operations will reside worldwide.; that your corporate umbrella will cover not only weapons, but also construction machinery, automobiles, farm equipment, ships, airplanes. Virtually everything built now, plus all to be built in a new world—governed by the power of petroleum. Marie, the monotony of this company has made you short-sighted. Do not lose sight of our goals."

She repressed the impulse to scream at Gershon, to get the hell out of her plant, and never come back. Fifteen years ago she was a young girl, swayed by idealisms she had not fully thought out. Today, she was not so easily swayed by her old friend's fervor-spiced logic; her family business had priority over lofty goals and world-conquering aspirations. The technological utopia she had imagined was not as important now. Manufacturing quotas, production schedules, and shipment deadlines—she had been numbed by the banalities of her station in life. And she pined at the realization. She knew what business had done to her, and she didn't like it, yet she recoiled from leaving it. She battled with herself to let go, to recapture the freedom to aspire, to inhale the vigor of life, and the exuberance of change. Like the suffering Freudian neurotic paraplegic hysteric whose mind tells her she cannot walk, but her rationale knows otherwise. She forced the kernel of herself—what she had concealed with so many layers—out of atrophy.

"Gershon," she exhaled before leaping. "Please explain again. What is the timetable for this labor strike? What happens next and in what order? My family will not understand, and I will need to fend off someone taking control of the factory from me. The German government may force me to employ soldiers as workers, and that would lead to bloody strife. Tell me, my friend. What have you geniuses planned for Germany?" She saw Gershon's face ease as he detected her resistance melting away.

"Germany cannot be allowed to win this war. Our plan—François' plan—is to induce an armistice for at least twenty years—an unofficial armistice. A consolidation of resentments, if you will, allowing a nationalistic indignation to better fester and spread. One that has all the appearance of a peace, but is merely a twenty-year cessation of overt hostilities. We are deploying agendas to weaken Germany at the fronts. Depriving the armies of needed munitions by initiating labor strikes is simply one ploy. Calling an end to the war will devastate the troops who are, in fact, winning on many fronts. The soldiers will consider themselves betrayed—stabbed in the back. To deepen this wound, we have crafted proposals in the peace treaty requiring Germany to pay war reparations for an absurd amount of money and time into the future, out to 2020. These terms will agitate the populace even more. Given the right catalysts and another twenty years for us to engineer more electrical and petroleum technology, the war will resume. Its next incarnation will evolve quickly with even more devastation, more carnage and a massive invocation of technology that will usher in a connected globe. The nationalisms and tiny cultural infestations of Europe will dissolve."

Having a disposition tempered by experience and life, Gershon's soliloquy disturbed her. It caused her to reflect. She had never considered herself a humanitarian—not even one who cared whether the masses suffered or thrived. However, he had delivered his vision with such exuberance, such momentum, such zeal. She had always known Gershon to be very level-headed, not prone to flights of passion or philosophical fanaticism. She felt danger, even threatened, though he had not issued an assaultive gesture, nor had he implied retribution had he not obtained her full cooperation. *Now is not the time*

121

to sprout angelic wings for the fight against human suffering, Marie. What Gershon offers—what we have planned for years—puts business first, governments second. This voice of conscience whispering within me is the remnant of a little girl, afraid of the dark, clutching her dolls, and whimpering for mommy. We play a game, a game to win. And whether the stakes are honor, fortune, pride, or sacrificing the lives of millions, it is still a game.

She felt her resolve congeal. "Gershon, my apologies for my adverse departure from our goals. Please, my reservation was short-lived and inconvenient. I'm the same Marie you have known. I'm intrigued about this treaty to bring about the war's end. What's next?" she asked, dispelling her skeptical countenance. The expression of determined tension dissolved from Gershon's face. His relief meant her relief.

"The plan is simple, elegant, and allows the German people to be themselves, without the necessity of imposing propaganda and smear campaigns. Given their own devices, they will be the narrow-minded, conformist society we expect. They will blame their plight on Jews, Gypsies, Communists, intellectuals, and other fifth columnists. François has been grooming a man, a man he claims is better than Satan's own seed. This man will ride the wave of this national indignation. He'll materialize and organize the resentment and fury into a Germany unsustainable within the world. He'll create positions of hatred about which the German people will rally. Once the nations of the world discover that this new Germany is inconsolable, they will rush in to crush it."

His description of the inspired venomous leader of the new Germany captivated her. She wanted to know more about him but refrained from asking. "You say these things as if they have already happened. The war has yet to end," she remarked blithely.

"The war will end within weeks. François is in Versailles as we speak. He is preparing for the hammer to fall," Gershon replied, noting that she had still not capitulated to verify her ultimate intentions.

The turmoil from which she had sensed an undercurrent of threat had subsided. Whether the threat was real or imagined was inconsequential. "And I should continue to provide tacit consent to this strike?" She contained her dissonance as a labor strike disgusted her profoundly.

"Not only tacit consent, Marie," Gershon responded pointedly. "You must fuel the resentments with subterfuge from above, where they least expect it. Who would ever suggest you have conspired to motivate labor disputes within your own factories? It's absurd!"

"And my family's business concerns? Half of our revenues come from weapons production. It sounds to me as if the end of this war is the end of munitions manufacturing in Germany," she replied, turning abruptly from Gershon to survey the manufacturing floor, confirming that it was still there. He noted her worried expression.

"True. For perhaps fifteen years German weapons manufacturing will be non-existent; it will be banned. However, you have facilities in South Africa, Argentina and Indo-China. Double your manufacturing and stockpile the weapons." He reached into his long leather satchel and extracted several rolled-up blueprints, maps and documents. "Don't worry about money, Marie. Your operations will be well funded. But see here." He unrolled the papers like a fine silk merchant might unfurl a bolt of his finest material.

She marveled at how she could actually fear her oldest friend. He had changed—driven, singular, obsessed, even fanatic. She hoped he had not noticed her panic when he reached into the satchel, as she feared what he might extract. "Of course, you have more than some words for me—you come with a plan," she commented drolly.

"This factory here," he emphasized, twirling his hand in a circle over his head. "Forget it. Once the labor strike is over, the war will be over. And when the war is over, this factory will no longer be able to build weapons and munitions." Referring to his map, he pointed to blue stars in the vicinities of Buenos Aires, Johannesburg and Sumatra. "But you can manufacture munitions here, in the factories we have already constructed and supplied for you." He turned to Marie with a blank expression, intended to not bias or taint her own reaction.

Still grappling with ambivalence, she was miffed that they had not conferred with her regarding her own business affairs, but she readily comprehended how this proposed operation would expand her family's holdings, securing their financial future well into the next few decades. "I must say, you and François seem to have wrapped up the future into a tight little bundle, ready to deliver to the world. And they won't even realize the gift they receive," she commented while doting over the map Gershon had unfurled. He unrolled a blueprint across the map. "But what's this? You would not have brought it out if you had not expected me to see it." She smirked as she saw his eyes sparkle.

"Ah, my dear perceptive one. This is what you will produce here instead of guns and bullets," Gershon replied coyly.

Marie already felt revived and invigorated by Gershon's redirection, though; as she scrutinized the plans, she was puzzled by what she saw. "These schematics and chemical symbols over here," she pointed. "This looks like an expansion of our explosives or gas facility." Noticing organic chemical formulas next to the floor plan schematic, she scanned the equations looking for familiar notations. "But this chemistry is unfamiliar. These aren't explosives, and they aren't gas."

"So true," Gershon responded with matter-of-fact poise. "The post war inspectors will look into every nook and cranny of this facility—especially into this facility since they will no doubt be aware

124

that you are manufacturing munitions on foreign soil, and they cannot do anything about it. They'll harass you here. They'll use extra scrutiny. But they'll find only pharmaceutical boons, optimizing German reparations." Marie cocked her head, perplexed. "These formulas are not chemicals for warfare—at least not today's war." He stopped briefly to assess how his comment affected Marie, finding her steadfastly attentive. "These chemicals are for the German people. They are pharmaceuticals, but they do not fight off viruses, or bacteria, or fungi, nor parasites. They fight off lethargy, depression and ill-will. These are a new class of drugs similar to cocaine, but without the narcotic overtones of bliss and semi-consciousness. They are medicinal in quality in that they treat the mind. This particular formulation is called amphetamine. The name is a contraction of alpha-methylphenethylamine. It is a stimulant, much more effective than coffee or chocolate and considerably longer-lasting, easier to ingest and cleaner than cocaine."

"So you want me to convert my gas warfare factory into a pharmaceutical factory? What an interesting concept," she responded, musing over the notion outwardly, but harboring renewed resistance at the outlandish notion. Gershon sensed the subtle reticence and promptly assuaged her inner rebuke with information.

"Marie, listen to me. This drug is insidious. It dupes the user into believing he feels more energetic, and moreover, better about himself and life in general. It creates a marvelous euphoria, luring the user into a whirlwind of activity. It quells the appetite and represses the need for sleep. Given repeated and constant dosage, these positive effects are short-lived. The user develops a tolerance to the drug very rapidly—it is highly addictive. After a while, even with higher and higher dosages, a different mood tone overtakes the user. Instead of feeling all is well with the world, the user feels paranoid, hypervigilant, resentful, even psychotic."

Amazed by what Gershon had explained to her, her brain buzzed, overwhelmed by the sheer genius and manipulative eloquence of the plan. Though he had not explicitly described the implications, the outcomes were clear to her. *A downtrodden and demoralized German population, disgraced by reparations, massively ingesting a chemical to help them become more upbeat, while, instead making them feel even more resentful and indignant, manifesting paranoid notions of unjust culpability and indignation. Not able to immediately turn to violence and war, they would subjugate and repress these bitter feelings until the dam would eventually burst.* "We'll feed this drug to the German people? It's brilliant," she whispered in an elongated snarl.

"François found it as he researched drugs developed to treat opium addiction—the point being that the treatment would supposedly have the opposite effect," Gershon explained, nodding with appreciation at Marie's insight. "This drug had been developed in Berlin in 1887, but it was widely ignored. Indeed, it continues to be ignored. But we will resurrect it as a boon to the productivity of the German people."

She had transformed within her brief encounter with Gershon, migrating quickly to her old self—her younger self. Aware of how quickly her mettle—the very foundation upon which she entrusted her ideals—had altered, she silently wondered what had happened to her. For an instant she drifted into her temperament of fifteen years ago. She had lost sight of the higher purpose, having been persuaded by her family to entrench herself in the family business. She had to become practical, staunch in sober thinking, and become as unidealistic as business demands. The benign decisions of business administration had muddled her passion—the prospect of changing the world through radical and uncompromising methods. "Gershon, thank you for reviving my memory." She took his hand with both of hers and squeezed it, holding it in close comradeship. "Where is François right now?"

"He's crafting the next Great War," Gershon replied with matter-of-fact serendipity.

Chapter 10

The Treaty of Versailles

"You must reject this treaty unconditionally, my dear Herr von Brockdorff-Rantzau. You must distance yourself from it as far as possible," François insisted brashly of the German foreign minister. He leaned toward him intrusively from the velvet armchair, almost toppling off. They had met secretly, urged by a highly influential government official's insistence to the minister, two days after his arrival in Paris. François understood he was a stranger to the foreign minister, noting that the bureaucrat did not trust him. François perceived the misgivings were due largely to his influence among high government circles who obligated the pompous minister to give him audience, compelling him to hear François. He compensated his ego by treating the meeting as nothing other than a formality.

François brimmed with energy and intensity. He had taken some of the experimental drug for which Marie Rothschild's factory would soon be converted to manufacture. And though Gershon had warned him against experimenting with the drug on himself, he had become to enjoy its effects. Already electrified with energy and perception, his feeling of insight and all-encompassing influence soared.

"You already know the stipulations of the treaty, Herr Éclair?" the German diplomat asked with entreaty and skepticism. "How could you? It is a most carefully guarded secret, assembled by the French, British, and United States governments. How could you know? You are not even a political or appointed official."

François' tact was swift and direct. Answering the minister's questions was commensurate to negotiating with him—and he had decided negotiation or discussion would be not only unproductive, but also intolerable. "I want you to contact your secretary in Berlin after our meeting. He will inform you—frantically—that the whereabouts of

128

your wife, son and daughter is unknown. That they were kidnapped, and that an unknown emissary informed him to tell you that you could discover their location and insure their well-being, from here in Paris— and that you will have been informed of the conditions for that information. Then have the hotel send a telegram." He pushed a folded piece of paper across the table. "Verify the amount deposited in this bank account in Zurich." He paused while the minister studied the paper. "Comply, and you and your family will be wealthy for generations to come. Fail to comply, and your progeny ends here." He saw the minister's already ruddy face turn crimson as he pushed back his chair to leave.

François' rage surged, as he had no patience for arrogance superseding rationality. "Don't get up, you fool!" François reached over and yanked von Brockdorff-Rantzau by the sleeve. The minister recoiled but complied. "You will be revered by the German people, rejecting this treaty. This treaty is a national dirge for Germany. It calls for Germany to accept absolute responsibility and blame—total guilt. You—your countrymen, for generations—must pay reparations for the next century. It forces you to give up vast quantities of land; you must disband your armies, and you will not be able to manufacture munitions. I know this," François paused to form his next words with articulation, "because I wrote it. Well, I designed its content with intent, and our emissaries positioned it to be received well by Allied officials. Georges Clemenceau, Woodrow Wilson and David Lloyd George have been advised it is within their best interests to endorse these measures." François paused to ponder his next words, uneasy that he had already disclosed too much. "I never seize goals that are not already highly desirable by the persons over whom I try to exert influence. These conditions are desired mostly by the French. You, yourself, will be officially privy to these conditions in their entirety on May 7, in two days." He stopped to fix the foreign minister in a vice-grip stare, making certain he had his complete attention. "Reject them unanimously and return to Germany. Do not attempt to negotiate for better terms. Fly off in the face of an outrage, just as you had prepared to do moments ago with me. Your victors will have their way with newly elected officials from a Republic of Germany." François noted the German official already seemed less agitated, his abrupt departure more obligatory histrionics than genuine outrage.

"And what of the new, elected president?" the minister asked with reserved incredulity, now sounding conciliatory rather than pompous. "Will he not accept, or at least renegotiate the terms, and ask why I did not remain to do the same?"

"He will resign rather than accept the terms of this admittedly heinous and obnoxious agreement. My man will eventually move into to seat of power, and sign the treaty." His words swayed the German foreign minister's emotions to and fro, and he watched him freeze in aghast.

"Scheidemann will resign? After such a brief term as the first elected chancellor of Germany?" the minister responded, appalled.

François liked the minister, assessing him as rational, clear-minded and unfettered by personal issues. However, he was an aristocratic intellectual—an Aryan—too entrenched and unevolved to comprehend an abstract and unfatalistic circumstance, not to be trusted with more than what he feared to lose. "Indeed, the current government administration will be replaced by select officials. The new republic, das deutsche Reich, will spearhead a new German democracy," François replied cautiously. "But mind you, please abide by my instructions. Do not tamper with the process I have described, or the circumstances about which I warned you will be implemented. Furthermore, I suggest that you not discuss the contents of our discussion, though I doubt many would believe you. You risk damaging your credibility should you divulge the details. Simply walk away with indignity, and you'll maintain dignity; balk, and calamity will interrupt your life."

The minister departed, shaking François' hand obligingly, but François noted the minister was decidedly stunned and disoriented. Lodged between shock and mortification, von Brockdorff-Rantzau's values and beliefs had been torn asunder. He knew what the diplomat was thinking: "How could a half-breed non-German—a heathen by the minister's standards—threaten his life, his family and collude to manipulate Germany to conform to his own nefarious and fantastic scheme? It's more absurd than Grimm's tales come true." Yet, the foreign minister had heard of this man's power. The foreign minister verified to the exact Pfennig the next day that the money François had assured him to be deposited in the Zurich bank account was there.

As François had predicted, on May 7 the Allied Powers had crafted conditions requiring Germany to admit to full blame for the war and pay astounding reparations. The minister composed a diplomatically indignant posture, withdrew from the negotiations, and promptly returned to Berlin, much to the praise of the mortified and dishonored German people.

Chapter 11

Credit Where Credit Is Due

1927—New York, New York

François viewed Americans' predilection for racism as a virtue rather than as a vice; it pleased him immensely. Racism was superstition—they embraced it so mindlessly, effortlessly as if it had been genetically interwoven into their carnal fabric. Each time he traveled to America, visiting even an urban cosmopolitan enclave like New York, he encountered racism—unsubtle, gauche, barbaric. And he marveled at the singular brand of racism—mostly targeted toward American negroes; though, he observed that any people of color or diverse ethnicity were negatively marginalized as well.

His encounter with the lobby personnel at the Waldorf-Astoria underscored Americans' intrinsic racism. Interestingly, he noted, the prejudice manifested itself differently among the Caucasian social castes. The lobby clerk, displaying far more haughty airs than his social rank warranted, presented such a testy posture as to deny François even had a reservation. Being a French mulatto rather than an American negro would usually make a difference, but the clerk— either swayed by his own disinclinations toward persons of color, or maintaining a position which he believed would impress the hotel dignitaries— sustained his intransigence. Ever vigilant, François' assistant had already subtly departed to make a phone call, so when a zombie-faced manager approached the desk, curtly dismissing the clerk with a shove and a huff while extending sycophantic, groveling apologies. François recognized that William Astor had called from overseas on his behalf at the behest of his discerning secretary.

After settling in his room, he stared down on Fifth Avenue, reminding himself that if he were to meet Adrian Morgan on Fifth and 79th Street, he needed at least an hour to make the four-mile walk. When in New York, he insisted on walking unless time or weather absolutely did not permit. An airplane flew overhead, and he wondered how people would adjust to the rapid shift in time zones once transatlantic flight provided day-long trips between Paris and New York. He had already acclimated to the nine-hour time difference during the ten-day voyage, but one day would be quite a jolt to the system, he thought. *It will come. It's 1927—give it twenty years.*

He wished Adrian were not ensconced in his aristocratic social enclaves. All social trappings were cultural accoutrements, not vested in reality. He knew Adrian was well aware of this postulate. They had discussed so much philosophy and sociology over the years, and he knew Adrian was not such an adept liar or actor to have fictionalized his position as they conversed. Yet, they could not meet at the Waldorf-Astoria since Adrian's social circle included the Vanderbilts, and the Astor-Vanderbilt cult feud rivaled the ancient family resentments he had heard documented in the backwoods of Kentucky between the McCoys and the Hatfields.

François' temperament segued from his scientific vigilance, observing the New York environs, to relaxing with his long-time associate. "I don't care for New York," François commented to Adrian Morgan, upon first seeing him, arriving at the corner of Fifth and 79th. "In fact, I don't really care for America or Americans." He had worked himself into this resentment lather while walking. But before he had put a check on his candor, he remembered his colleague, Adrian Morgan, son of a great American financial icon, was an American. He flashed a guilty glance at him, but Adrian seemed more in agreement than being put off. "But it is for those very characteristics that I find distasteful that our plan for the expansion of credit should be as successful as I anticipate," François continued unabashed. Adrian appeared charged, eager, more youthful than his forty-two years would otherwise disclose.

François fretted. Four years senior to his friend, he had outlived his predecessors. He knew his genetic lineage differed from

133

the rest, granting him more time. Still, he worried that he could not forecast his end, and if he had at least ten years remaining, he could see his grand scheme come to fruition, as well as produce the progeny needed for the succession. Knowing that Gershon could take over in the interim put him at ease—but his obsession with his longevity consistently interrupted his flow.

They were close to the Metropolitan Museum of Art, on the east side of Central Park. Since their appointment was on the west side, in the Excelsior Hotel, they had decided to walk through the park. En route, they sat on a park bench at François' urging. Adrian's sheer ebullience fostered engagement.

"François, your war in Europe was pure genius. You have set the stage for a world consumed with consumption," Adrian remarked, seeming flabbergasted at his colleague-of-twenty-five year's prowess. He stopped to allow François to react to his witticism, but François, having delayed sitting, finally sat, appearing more taciturn than amused. "Americans are hedonists, but they are also full of religion and fear. It is for that reason that they remain self-servingly subservient and will remain even more so as we implement this expanded credit system—the reason you are here," Adrian continued.

François had resisted leaving Munich to come to New York. Two years after the Great War's finale, 1921 Europe still festered in the devastation of the war and was slow to recover. The negative impact of his plan engendering resentment into the German populace had made the recovery even more anemic, slowing motivation and growth. But Americans were euphoric, manic about creating a better America, resolute now about staying home and out of the rest of the world's problems. To him, America represented the same fertile soil for consumerism that the garden of Europe sowed over centuries of nationalistic and cultural feuds, resulting in the war ending two years ago. As Europe continued to stagnate, François aimed to cultivate an

134

American consumer embroiled in work and debt. "I wanted to stop here and listen to you before we meet with your business associates," François offered, pondering his words. "I believe you've mapped the perfect strategy for expanding the use of petroleum and other petrochemical products here. But I want for us to talk. I haven't seen you since your financial interventions in Germany over two years ago." Adrian seemed supercharged, and François wondered if he had been using the same amphetamines with which they had inundated the localities and workplaces of Germany. He wanted him to slow down.

"You've just completed that long voyage and hardly had a chance to settle into your hotel room," Adrian remarked, acknowledging the pace at which they were moving, "but business matters move at a different clip here," Adrian added.

The warm spring air, the buzz of people, the drone of the city distracted François from his inner thoughts, the place where he had conceived and materialized more fiscal and human reality than the Wall Street tycoons he was preparing to meet could ever fantasize. During the twelve- day Atlantic journey, he had tried to put his mind at ease, trying to contemplate the next fifteen years in Germany—with and without his existence. His protégé had progressed—public speaking and heavy-handed influence in a burgeoning political party suited him well. He had become more autonomous and independent, signaling an escape velocity where momentum would propel the loaded projectile on its trajectory.

Annoyance begat annoyance. Though François had garnered the capital required to implement Adrian's credit funding plan, he was uneasy. Was it simply an issue of control? He had not been fully involved in the plan's development, though he was key in the inception. *No, that's not it. It's the others—the banking, stock market, automotive, steel, real estate and petroleum men. They don't know what we're doing. They have no stock or investment in the outcomes other than*

becoming wealthier. They cast their level of success, the essence of
their lives in their fortune. An enumerated soul is a measured soul,
valued no more than the local economy and defined only by empirical
instrumentation. They are purely business, and Adrian has been defiled
by his niche in the same manner Marie had become jaded by her
family's businesses. His plan is sound, but the plan without the ultimate
resolve is merely a blueprint, spawning an aimless device.

François put two fingers over Adrian's mouth, dampening his
companion's monologue about capital gains, stock leverage, and the
wealth François' funding efforts will generate. "Oil, Adrian. Oil. We
are fashioning a globe dominated by the energy created by burning
petrochemical compounds." Adrian stopped talking abruptly, shocked
by François' physical intrusion. "Remember what I showed you
December 31, 1903 in Bern? The Great War was merely a prelude to
the encore. Do not lose sight." He twisted toward Adrian, grabbing him
by his shoulders, holding him at arm's length, assertive, pressing his
position as a father would do to an autonomous older son.
"Dominated," he enunciated the word. "All classes, nations, races,
ages. All will depend on oil. It will be the life-spring for living. And
when a global population of seven billion is consumed in oil
dependence, the origin of their existence and motivation—oil—will
have been camouflaged and sublimated. The common man must not see
his world created by oil and definitely should not detect that it was
spawned by us. We remain more secret than secret. We do not exist.
You're talking as if we'll have a symbol on the New York Stock
Exchange. These men we go to meet—they are not partners, investors,
or stock holders. They are pawns—victims. They do our bidding, and
they make a lot of money. But the underlying goal remains out of their
sight and reach. Is that understood?" He relaxed his grip from Adrian's
shoulders, noticing that his friend's muscles had suddenly gone limp.
He knew Adrian's tactics well—he utilized the survival tactics as

animals in the wild: defer to the alpha male, the wolf pack's leader, the head of the herd. And he knew Adrian was a pragmatist—he would rather advance than waste time fretting or complaining.

"I understand completely, François. Am I not the individual who helped Marie diversify her manufacturing and production abroad? Am I not the one setting up hierarchies of holding companies, masking our real estate holdings? Not all assets can be deposited in Swiss bank accounts, you know—our Texas and California oilfields, holdings around Los Angeles and central California, Venezuelan properties! But you mentioned ticker tapes. The automobile manufacturing cannot be hidden forever. Eventually, these holdings will fall under the scrutiny of the United States government. This country will not be a fiscal free-for-all forever. You, above all people, must realize that. Especially after we vastly expand credit. The euphoria will be short-lived, then they will realize they cannot repay."

Frustrated, François had witnessed the pull of real world forces on his close friends and allies. Marie's family business and fortune diverted her from focusing on affairs of their cultish organization. Adrian's standing with Wall Street and his father's connections had weaned him from his earlier idealism. Yet, he thought, did they not see the world forming according to their plan and design? Did they not foresee that by adhering to the global schematic, their power would extend beyond local, state, or national wealth? "Adrian. We have discussed these matters. Please, you are deeper than quarterly earnings reports and profit ratio projections. I'm here with one billion dollars to give to your bankers, but they must distribute the money as they are directed, not as their financial advisors and stock holders direct," he asserted, pausing. "As I direct—so these men we meet today—each must understand that if the funds are misappropriated into any investments or holdings other than toward opening credit lines for the common man, his life, as he knows it, will end. His personal, financial, professional, social—all aspects—will unravel. On the other hand, if our guidelines are implemented accurately, each will be wealthier than all of the stock portfolios could ever deliver." He hesitated, smiling at Adrian. "But you know these things. Why should I repeat them to you?" As he wound down his lecture, he noticed Adrian's face turn tense. He saw an emotion wash over Adrian; one he had never seen in his friend before—guilt.

"François, since we talked, an issue has arisen. Once this billion dollars is dispersed, there will be a wave of financial euphoria. I'd be so bold to venture, the surge will cause an uptick in not only the economy but also in the culture in general. So, here's what we did not discuss. This money will affect the American culture and, inevitably, American history. You, of all people, must have thought this out. Think about it. Once a culture of credit is underway, we'll see an escalation in amounts floated for payment, occurring at all levels of society from consumer goods to home mortgages, to cars, and upward even to stock and commodity purchases. Now, what if a point in time is reached when the payments are suddenly called in? What happens then?"

Embarrassed, François had committed the characterological sin for which transgression, in his view, was unacceptable: He had underestimated a colleague; he had underestimated Adrian. His lack of candor had omitted the latter aspects of his entire plan. But, he quickly rationalized with good reason. Adrian stood to lose more than half of his fortune in the financial calamity François had hoped to forge. The economies of the nations of the world would lose inertia, toppling over like tops losing their spin. He needed this calamity between his wars. Great economic strife would fuel his next war, bringing all nations into a heated conflict and superheating the resulting economies thereafter. "The economies of the world will implode, like deflated dirigibles plummeting from the sky," he replied in a monotone. "Adrian, I should have given you the core reasoning here." He spoke slowly, even with self-consciousness as he looked at Adrian's face wane from ecstatic to apprehensive.

"François, we've known one another a lifetime. I know you; I'm aware you frequently have secondary, tertiary agendas. Frankly, in my heart of hearts, I thought this process was too smooth, too simple. Something else must be at play, but I didn't want to press the issue. My own unwavering naiveté brought it to the forefront."

Having been too self-absorbed in the plan, François regretted not being more involved in the process. He had left most of the footwork and logistics to Gershon, but he had insisted upon implementing the American Project, as they had named it. "Adrian, we're seeding greed. It's that simple. Your investors will most likely get wiped out by this venture. Our one billion dollars in seed capital will balloon into twenty billion dollars and quickly deflate." He hesitated, pondering whether to divulge more of the plan. "We installed triggers within Swiss banks to call in loans, worldwide, once a threshold debt-to-asset ratio is reached. Currencies will collapse, the gold standard will be re-established, banks will be mobbed, the stock market will crash, and massive worldwide unemployment will ensue. We anticipate this crisis to continue well into the next decade. The next Great War will be the world's savior and downfall. Tens of millions will perish. Like the gash of a blade excising gangrenous flesh, the societies of the world will accept without wincing, numbed by chronic grief for two decades." Adrian was listening attentively but had already formulated his response.

"Men with vision; men with dreams and foresight will attend this meeting, all looking to you, the great, elusive François Éclair, mysterious, omnipotent millionaire—some say billionaire. A man with power beyond identity, even beyond comprehension. I've even heard the term 'anti-Christ' tossed about." Adrian noticed François had twitched nervously, a tick he evinced whenever he was presented with this much avoided public persona. "The world at large does not know you; certainly, the common man is completely unaware of your existence. But, these men at the meeting today—they know you. Some of them have profited by your shared innovations: Thomas Edison, Henry Ford's son, Edsel, Thomas Watson, Charles Coffin, Alfred Sloan. Other executives from Chase, including me of course, will be in attendance, all eager to expand this alluring middle class credit market you've been hawking," Adrian exhorted with vehemence, his tone now phasing to resentment.

He suddenly felt a disheartened, pang of despair jolting him. What had happened to the euphoria for the future, that glow of advancement beckoning him toward every question with curiosity and astonishment? At the turn of the century he was ignited from within, burning with prospects of a posterity unlike any known to previous millennia. What had happened to that glow? He quickly retraced the times, the epochs in his life since he felt so uplifted and optimistic. He searched his past, like a troubleshooter repairing an engine, looking for causes of misbehavior, a source where the operation went awry. As he dug deeper, the culprit emerged. Oil had happened, he concluded. And without oil, these advancements would wither as textbook notations and university laboratory engineering projects. What would power Edison's incandescent bulbs, or burn in Benz's or Ford's automobiles, or fuel the advancement of aviation, or energize the thousands of other devices he was sure would spawn from this new world of technology? Yet, he was still prone to forget—his nostalgia goading him into a comfort zone which he had abandoned and disinherited years ago. He sank, but re-emerged swiftly, as was his coping strategy. Yet, he could not shake the ultimate euphoria. *This scheme is part of the ultimate agenda; I am merely enacting my role. I've lived longer than the others. Perhaps my longevity was planned as well.*

These men with whom he entrusted the steps of the logistics of his schemes—they did not truly understand the scope of oil. Yet, the vision was so acutely simple and clear; it blinded him as would staring into a stark sunrise. Technology demands mobility; both demand power. The source was undeniable and singular. Hydroelectric, wind, geothermal—these sources might as well not exist, given the technologies and populations to come. Millennia of agrarian civilizations have seen to that. The economies would never move forward with these passive energy resources. Then, he had asked himself. *Perhaps they should not move forward. What is the source of the premise for progress? If civilization is an outgrowth of human evolution, and, if civilization is not a dead-end branch, then what should drive civilization but progress? The question should perhaps be: What is progress? In simple, observable terms—larger populations? Longer life spans? More leisure time? Less manual labor? More material goods per citizen? Social equalities? Elimination of natural inconveniences? And, if not these changes, then what? Stagnation? With new tools and methods at our disposal, we choose to not implement them? To sit idly as a populace and wait for a sign from God? I think not. We can turn night to day; turn winter to summer; soon transform a month's journey to a day; witness events from afar within seconds; bring vast stores of information to our fingertips; perhaps, visit the stars. These wars, these adversities, a necessity, a mere blip in what is otherwise a glorious evolution.*

"Adrian, I never promised you hedonism. In fact, I've been forthright in my own demonstrations of parsimony. I'm the richest, the most powerful man on earth—certainly the most influential. Tell me. Who knows me? Look at any of these people in the park. You think I bear a hint of recognition with that woman there? Or, that couple sitting on the bench across from us? When we walk down Wall Street, who there recognizes me? What if we go inside the Exchange and mosey up to the Chairman's office? Think he'll leap out of his chair, hand obsequiously extended, ready to offer me a brandy and some insider tips?" He stopped to size up Adrian's reaction who sat intent and steadfast, listening.

"Adrian, we aren't building careers for ourselves. You and your family are wealthy beyond the imagination of every common man—and most uncommon ones. You took on these endeavors, knowing self-sacrifice was the reward. We will never reap any humanly acknowledged glory, fame, or acclaim from what we have done, or will do. Indeed, our efforts must remain as subverted and clandestine as ever, else, what we've done would be undone, and whatever is not undone would earn our names the most hellish notoriety and make whatever posterity we leave behind, the targets for retribution for generations to come. Who would reward massive wars, propagation of poverty and hunger, genocides, economic devastation, the general promotion of human despair? And, if your answer to them is—I did it for your own good; after careful consideration of all the possible choices available, what I did yielded the optimum response in the long run—you could never prove it, never demonstrate it, never even present a convincing argument that could not be rebuked by any yokel with half your intelligence, though you know it to be true. So, you're not only evil, you are mad as well. Stay with me, stay with the plan. We must initiate this next stage. It fertilizes the soil for the next decade, and it provides the implements and tools for the devastation and harvest to follow." He felt unnerved, noticing Adrian had bowed his head, weeping lightly.

"My father died eight years ago, in Rome. He trusted the family fortune with me—and my brother and sisters. He looked to me to carry the wealth beyond mere ledger sheets. When I was a boy, he told me he believed the next century would unlock new and amazing opportunities. So, here I stand at the brink of the opportunity well,

142

looking down that dark tube and what am I about to do? Piss in it. He would never understand. But I understand. I remember your presentation back in 1904 all too well—the graphs and diagrams, the depiction of the pockets of oil around the earth, and your rather erudite and eloquent prediction of the use of petroleum over the next century, occurring partly because you caused it. We caused it." Adrian paused, looking up and squeezing François' knee. "How could I say no to the man who caused the Great War? I'm with you. I could only become richer by abandoning your cause. Only invest in more stocks, more companies, buy more land, build more railroads. My current wealth, or twice my wealth, will not allow me to live a year longer than I would anyway. I certainly cannot buy any more time; I cannot purchase immortality. I do not have enough wealth to elevate each man, woman and child on this planet from ignorance, famine and poverty. You've—we've—got the best show on Broadway. Let's see it through."

Chapter 12

The North Sea, 1939

The ocean spray invigorated him. François welcomed this Atlantic journey. He had declined the time-saving flight to America in order to reflect on his group's accomplishments over the past four decades. At a recent meeting, he recalled one of his members accrediting him with the "foresight to unravel the future," but François had corrected him, pointing out that unraveling infers previous entanglement. They had wound the fibers, avoiding kinks. The spool had spun unhindered.

He had just spent a week in Istanbul with his Japanese counterpart, Yoshi Suma. Istanbul was as far east as François cared to travel. He recognized his flaws, and one was his eurocentrism. He realized Asian influences played equal, if not greater roles in the human social evolution—he preferred to manage that factor more remotely. Still, he needed to ponder the dynamics Yoshi and his Asian group had masterminded, and he needed to contemplate his next meeting with Albert Einstein—an unannounced visit from a spurious acquaintance in the acclaimed professor's past.

François trusted Yoshi Suma, and for that acknowledged state, he knew he was not a racist. Yet, a certain insidious skepticism of Asian trustworthiness haunted him, and he battled to root it out. He remained vigilant about his decisions. Though not a Freudian, he realized some thoughts were anchored deeply, embedded within the bedrock forged from sensate passion rather than rational cognition. For this reason, he examined his decisions—not using rumination or obsession—but rather from a scientist's perspective: *Is my thinking purely logical? To what set of factors and evidence to I owe this conclusion?*

He was void of guilt. He was not a sociopath; he resided on Olympus. The worldwide economic collapse he and Adrian had devised worked so well because they had mastered human nature. Of all the pitfalls available for coercion, greed provided the easiest access. He and his brood gained access to influential circles, then unleashed an onslaught of irresistible monetary lures. Greed and seduction were the greatest snares of all. Had he been entrapped? He thought not—merely superseded what would have been random access. He stood on the bow of the Atlantic ship, amidst the wave of misery he had engineered. Yet, he rationalized, he did not cause it; he simply laid it at the doorsteps of those who had the power to implement it—or not.

He wanted to talk with someone, if only to organize this own thoughts. He decided to write a letter to himself, then throw it in the ocean. With paper and pen always at the ready, he wrote with Gattling Gun speed, recounting the steps they had taken to accomplish their current position.

The Depression was essential to the global plan, not just in America and Europe, but in all Asia as well. Yoshi colluded to strengthen the Japanese military and weaken the parliamentary system. He provided behind the scenes actions to dissolve the multiparty system into the single party, still answerable to the Emperor. Being the Emperor's concubine certainly improved the permeability of the Japanese upper echelon. Yet, I've always perceived his influence as unidirectional. The culture was simpler to influence because of the centuries of military rulership. Still, his Cherry Blossom Society was pure genius—his brain progeny, and no one else's. He brought into being the military machine which is now Japan. Germany and Japan, each convinced it should be ruler of the world. They are allies now, but will be stopped before they ever have the opportunity for their inevitable opposition against one another—which leads me to my current trip to New Jersey.

Albert's a pacifist. I'll have to play up his utter distaste for the Nazis. I'm sure he's already considered the possibility of them

145

enriching uranium, but my sources tell me that they're too bigoted and concrete to develop an atom bomb—given the source of the science. Ridiculous, since their top scientists tell them they could win the war with such destructive force.

The Nazis will lose once the United States enters the war. The amphetamines will make that deranged, megalomaniacal proletarian even more paranoid and unable to listen to his generals or to make rational decisions. The issue is not really the Germans. The issue is who has the weapon first—the Americans or the Russians. Once this war is over, the real war will commence. He ripped the paper from the pad, crumpled it and threw it into the dark water.

François' ship was three days from docking. He stared at the icy North Sea churning below the bow, wondering how many thousands of feet the ocean floor lay below him. He contemplated if he jumped in now, when would his body reach the bottom, or would the physical and biological forces prevail over gravity to avert his corpse from ever settling. He guessed the temperature of the water—the mist condensing on his face was not a convincing probe. A salve encompassed him as he immersed himself in the serenity of the trip to the floor of the North Sea.

I cannot die yet. I must wait. I've lived longer than I believed I would, given my affliction—my destiny. I've outlived my predecessors by more than a decade. But I'm tired, so tired. Even with the forces we've enacted, I'd gladly bequeath the efforts and fruits to my son. My son, Kristoph, two years old now. He will continue the lineage. If he is to learn any lessons soon, it will be to live with the masses—breathe and love and suffer, and even wallow—but always fully recognize the separation and be prepared to relinquish the tether at any time. I know that Gershon will see him through and raise him with his daughter, Zora.

146

He hugged the railing, caressing it to give way, yet depending upon its supportive endurance. He longed for the fervor and zeal of his twenties when every observation spawned an innovation. As he looked forward to a meeting with his old acquaintance, Albert Einstein, recollections of that evening in Bern on the last night of 1903 converged to lighten and darken his temperament. Despising nostalgia, he was suddenly victimized by it.

He pushed away from the railing, aware of the distress he was imposing upon himself. He did not want to see the end. But he looked forward to meeting with Einstein. He grimaced as he returned to his cabin, knowing he always had an agenda—the Agenda. He would prefer to spend hours, talking with his old acquaintance, discussing philosophy, physics, and even politics. He was most interested in the mass-particle duality dilemma, realizing the problem was Einstein's most egregious barrier. Resolving the separation between statistical physics and relativity had resisted solution even by the great professor Einstein himself. *We each have a crescendo, then we ride the wave until it diminishes. Then we perish with the entropy brought on by the rush.*

Chapter 13

Princeton, 1939

"Your group lacked celebrity status," François confided to Professor Leó Szilárd as they strolled the Princeton campus. He realized immediately he had chosen the wrong word; Szilárd seemed both incensed and confused.

"Celebrity! I do not understand the meaning of this word. What does celebrity or celebration have to do with a viable missive to the leader of the United States government, warning him of imminent threat from the Nazis. As much as these animals may condemn the science of Einstein and other Jewish scientists who have fled the country, that drug-crazed madman will stop at nothing to develop an atomic bomb. With such a weapon he would most certainly win the war—first Europe, and eventually, the United States. America WILL get drawn into this war!"

François felt Szilárd was more than a scientist—an academic with a knack for investigative empiricism. He saw Szilárd as a visionary as well—perhaps more so than Einstein. Yet, he knew Einstein, the apolitical pacifist, had to be convinced to endorse a plea to develop a weapon of extreme devastation. *A weapon of mass destruction*, he thought bemused. One that would no doubt embody his name for whatever amount of mayhem it would cause. He stopped in the middle of the campus path to face his companion. He needed Szilárd's full attention. "Roosevelt did not heed your warning—not because of incredulity or rebuff—but because of politics. He weighs his choices based upon public opinion and leverage. His decisions must have clout—substance. You know this word, clout?" He continued without waiting for a response. "Clout is force—a walloping force. Americans are impressed with fame, and they have a short attention span. And—the American public perceives fame as a greater force than academic notoriety. You, my dear Professor, have astounding

148

credibility in the field of physics, but the public does not know you. Dr. Einstein has both public notoriety and scientific credibility. Roosevelt will take notice if he sees Albert Einstein's name penned at the bottom of a letter. Your previous letter had been signed by leading figures of science, including yourself, but Roosevelt could not justify major national financial and defense decisions based upon the exhortation of a few Hungarian scientists." François could tell Szilárd was not accustomed to direct personal discourse, but the noted scientist remained focused and amicable.

"Albert is my friend and colleague, Mr. Éclair. But I fear he may decline our invitation to lend his name and—celebrity—to our entreaty," Szilárd replied, assuming a solemn demeanor.

A gust of mid summer breeze caressed François' face. He realized he tired of the game of manipulation in which he had been immersed for over three decades. Time slowed. He focused on his immediate environment, sensing only the air, hearing the birds, smelling the aromas of the Princeton campus at that time of year. He had often wanted to move to the United States—especially to Southern California—a locale where the temperature was more temperate. He tired of seasons—both climatic, political and sociological. The instigator of calamity yearned for consistency. The pan continental war he and his cult had groomed was coming to fruition. He had already achieved one of his goals: Oil was the centerpiece of energy. His second undertaking was close at hand: the development of nuclear weapons. One to start; the other to end.

François recovered from his brief tangential reverie, realizing Szilárd's concern was genuine. Convincing others to embrace his emotional and cognitive perspective had tired him as well—he knew Einstein would comply. "Professor Szilárd, let me assure you, your old friend and colleague would have approached you sooner or later, had you not approached him today. Dr. Einstein is aware of German advances in nuclear science—advances toward completing an atom bomb. He knows the German propaganda machine has targeted him publically as a scapegoat, and they have put a virtual price on his head. His life and his science are at stake here. He cannot risk the Germans winning the war and jeopardizing his security here in America." He saw Szilárd's countenance turn grim, not knowing whether the despondency was due to a remote possibility of Nazi incursion on American soil, or from fear of confronting his friend, Einstein, with such threats. To defuse Szilárd's spiral, François beckoned him to continue the walk toward Einstein's office. "Come, we should continue. He's expecting us at three."

François remained silent as the two men walked along the arboreal canopied pathway, seemingly on autopilot, each knowing the way since both Szilárd and François had visited Einstein on the Princeton campus on different occasions.

Upon reaching the building entrance, François stopped suddenly, tugging lightly on Szilárd's elbow. "Professor, you've already written the letter once. May I propose that you take the initiative and write it again, offering to Einstein the courtesy to modify it as he sees fit once the letter is complete. This method allows him to remain relatively hands-free of the process and allows you the control of expediency. He merely needs to think and sign. And as I've explained, he's already done his thinking. You'll probably have your missive sent within a month," François offered, expressing an enthusiasm aimed at ameliorating Szilárd's angst.

"I believe you are correct, Monsieur Éclair," Szilárd responded, unknowingly mimicking François' upbeat affect. "My indecisiveness was an artifact of previous scientific collaboration, which I confused with our current political necessity. I agree with you. Professor Einstein has already reached the same conclusion. He will sign such a letter."

Chapter 14

Tryst in Vienna - 1979

Zora Green enjoyed Vienna in the winter. The air was cold
and damp, the sky was seldom without overcast, and a general gloom
dominated the populace, especially during January and February. She
had squared herself in perfect posture in a firm velvet armchair facing
Philharmonikerstrasse, her back toward the walk-in-size fireplace in
Hotel Sacher. She sniffed the scent of freshly baked pastries and
espresso, wafting throughout the opulent guest sitting room adjacent to
the main lobby. She focused on certain passers-by, reflecting on each
one's individuality: face, body shape and size, gait, clothes, shoes,
companions, if any, and if not, the reason why. Each had an aura,
though she denied she sensed what one would describe as extrasensory, magical, or supernatural. She picked up information from the
whole, and she had yet to operationalize what the information entailed.
But she contemplated each. *What was it like for that person's mother to
bear him? How much love or brutality was bestowed upon him during
his childhood? What kinds of friends did he have? Where did he go to
school, if at all? What is his sex life like? Does he have a single lover,
or any lover at all? Who would cry if he were to die suddenly? What
would he look like in a casket? How much does he think about his own
death? If she could intercede on his life at this very instant and give
him anything he wanted, what would it be? Mundane self desires, like
wealth, power, happiness, sex? Or mundane philanthropic wishes, like
world peace, the end of all hunger, global national coexistence?*

Her designer disease had yet to be unleashed on the general
populace. Her laboratory subjects remained—unbeknownst to them—
quarantined and isolated in remote African villages in Sudan and
Kenya. She disliked it there as much as she liked Vienna, and for the
same reasons. Heat, sun, and clear skies deadened her. *Why live in such*

152

conditions, she asked herself. *It saps the motivation from you, gives you no reason to move about, think, imagine and create. They should die. They make perfect lab rats.*

That inner verbalization stunned her, and she stopped herself. *I'm not a racist. I have no disdain for those people. I could conduct my research here in the inner sanctum of Vienna, maintaining the same emotional detachment. Black Africans or white Europeans—what's the difference? They all procreate the same. The genetics are identical. Each could be transplanted at birth to the other's habitat; other than features related to epidermis, there is no difference. Edgar Rice Burroughs had the correct tack.*

She nodded curtly at the waiter, watching him precisely position her Sachertorte and espresso on her table; his gesture hybridized between dance movement and military drill. Skilled and practiced, she recognized him as a true professional. Service at upscale establishments like Hotel Sacher was mandatory for her; she would not dine anywhere that exposed her to the vulgarities or gauche nuances of proletarians.

***

Kristoph stood furtively across the street from Hotel Sacher. He had spied Zora through the large plate glass window, but she had not seen him. The Vienna cold needled him, entrenching his despondency even further than last week in Paris. He disliked Vienna— the constant gloom, the Dostoevskian starkness where a bleak reality was covered by a veneer of style and class. He detested the stark winter in Vienna. Its cold conducts itself inside one's viscera by a humidity that stubbornly would not condense. The cold fascilitates a feeling of lifelessness. It nurtures the frozen nodules of dog excrement plopped along the sidewalks, and the eighty-year-old automaton-like widows around whom the dogs orbited. The women looked at him with blank,

153

yet piercing, stares, all covert minions of Death himself; all primed to seize him and drag him to Hell.

The reality of Austria was different than the quaint nuance most Americans attached—from *Heidi* to *The Sound of Music* to friendly yodelers helping mountaineers in the Alps—the friendliness was a facade, masking the coalesced seclusion of isolated in-bred villagers over the centuries, creating a shadowed, cultural grave out of which neither reason nor global modernization could extirpate the soon-to-be zombies who remained there. He winced when he heard the Viennese dialect spoke around him, despising what he believed to be a denigration of the German language, promoting the fantasy that the multitudes of warped dialects were somehow endearing or indicative of cultural preservation. Austrian German did to high German what American English did to British English, and the crass, vulgar Viennese dialect did to Austrian German what the Brooklyn dialect did to American English. The guttural aural machinations around him blended into a raspy, grating whine. Even the subway station announcements were proclaimed by a renowned actor with the archetypal Viennese dialect. Still, he took the subway since the cab drivers sounded worse.

Staring at the hotel lobby window, he knew she had spent the night there, and he knew what was forthcoming. Ambivalence disquieted him. He loved her, and he hated her. He felt sexually aroused, imagining her nude body—not only the flesh, form and texture, but also the scalpel-like, incisive, unfettered mind connected to it as well—a body and mind like no other body and mind. He wanted it; he had known her his entire life; they had never been romantically involved. The detachment had seemed almost planned, as if their guardians had overseen their relationship, and actively—though covertly—had engaged in severing whatever intimate alliances spawned, though he could recall nothing negative—nor positive—ever mentioned about Zora Green or her ilk.

Vienna engendered his internal fog, the gloom he carried around, that blossomed from within. He wanted his opaque emotional outlook to dissipate, but Vienna mustered more doom for him to consider. He feared going inside, yet he lusted it. *She already knows the intent and the outcome. No romance for us. No dates, pining at night over your romantic interest, obsessed about what the other is thinking and doing; no anticipation about our next meeting, deciding we could no longer bear the intervals, and choosing to live together. No family, friends and common ties. No vacations and holidays. No anniversaries or shared experiences, reminisced fondly. No arguments or grievances, later to be resolved with affection. I could invoke one of my local agents and have her shot dead as she sits there within the half hour. That would be the most intimate act I could perform with her. And what a bold move that would be, ending a cacophony of history, appearing as a cadence—wars, governments, nations, economies, revolutions—all orchestrated, initiated by my predecessors.*

A chill reverberated through him—not the thermoregulatory jolt meant to activate the flow of blood, but a chill reminiscent of a fever or the reminder of a harrowing event whose recalled image still elicits imaginative trauma. These sentiments cast a pall over him, as he reluctantly skulked from his burrow, in the shadows across the street, and directed himself toward the entrance of Hotel Sacher.

***

"What irony! Two hundred Schilling for a tiny piece of chocolate cake and a small cup of coffee carries a vulgarity greater than the vulgarity from which consistently try to escape. There's no escaping the tawdry condition you despise as life—which makes you an object of gross humor," Kristoph commented, standing out of sight at the back of Zora's high-backed chair. He knew, rather than be offended, she would take derisive glee in his observation for whatever

155

negative rationale levied toward her; she defeated it with her own brand of self-esteem.

"Kristoph, you need not have shivered across the street in the cold. And that group of off-duty laborers standing in your vicinity must have added to your shivering agony," Zora replied, delicately sipping her espresso and replacing the cup precisely into the saucer.

Off-guard, the manner with which she spoke riled him—such presumption toward the most powerful man on earth—and the fact that she had seen him there after all. Her attitude reduced to the perspective of a mother two steps ahead of her otherwise precocious child. He decided to ignore it. "When we were children, I could sneak up behind you and startle you. Please don't say you were always aware I was there. You didn't feign the shock and tears of having the wits rattled out of you. As I remember, once you urinated in your underwear when that garden snake I had planted under your pillow slithered out," he commented, casually sitting while motioning to the waiter for attendance. He saw the corners of her lips compress. He had evened the score.

"I understand your message and motives during the video conference last week, and if I know you and myself correctly, we have both arrived at identical conclusions. I've booked a suite in which I have already spent a night. It's quite comfortable," she blurted, changing the subject promptly.

He did not feel disposed going there yet. She plunged into the cold water; he eased in, one limb at a time. "The Shah has vacated Iran. Khomeini, our exiled Ayatollah, has landed, ready to lead the nation into an Islamic theological state. All is well," he said, turning as she nodded toward the waiter approaching.

Even the Viennese wait staff galled him, officious without warrant. Serving a cup of coffee here, in Paris, or Los Angeles, or Lubbock, Texas, does not change the essence of the process. Adding flair, pomp and circumstance to the method is merely entertainment value, at best—a play intended for those with the disposition and acquired taste, lacking in new information or advancement of skills. Even the waitresses in Linz and Wels emit a certain sanctimonious aura as if to say, "I'll do your bidding reluctantly since you are here, but, if you were a decent, socially-abiding individual, you'd be at home, eating at your own dining table." He ordered a cognac, offering neither nod nor emotional inflection. The waiter repeated his request with military precision, turned and marched off in a stride between a waltz and a drill step. He glanced at Zora during the brief interaction, noticing her concealed amusement at his general irritation.

"You and I—we've known one another since we were children, and we've never had sex," she said, ignoring his comment about Iran and the waiter. "We've never had an intimate moment. You know me well enough to know I'm certainly not into love affairs. And certainly a relationship between you and me would have caused great alarm among our curious occult organization as a whole. But now, this situation, here. This is something to look forward to. Like readying for a nice massage after a stressful day," Zora whispered, head cocked slightly, grinning faintly.

Wedged between arousal and performance anxiety, he wanted to sit awhile and delay *the massage*. Under any other circumstance, he could easily control his trepidation with his mind and using simple breathing techniques. He had never been given to panic attacks or stage fright. *I'm a man who has toppled governments, ordered murders, committed murders myself, pushed the button for detonations to disrupt the lives of millions. The Iranian revolution itself sets the stage for—* He stopped his thought in mid-sentence as the waiter had fortuitously returned with his cognac. "A massage? I like it! Here's to our massage. May it relieve stress and muscle fatigue." He raised his glass and sipped away half of the snifter's contents. "Tell me about HIV," he said abruptly, sipping from his glass and leaning forward as if readying for the rendering of an exciting tale. "And AIDS. That is what you're calling your virus? I've got to admit," he paused, muffling laughter, "what a cryptic acronym—as if it were, possibly, a universal antibiotic, aiding that which ails you." She offered a rare genuine smile, as she knew he knew she had chosen the name intentionally.

"Auto Immune Deficiency Syndrome," she remarked, whispering the syllables slowly, almost sensually.

He always felt deficient when in her presence. Even now as she named the designer virus she had engineered from molecular infancy to its current clinical trials in the field; human life had no bearing or impact on her goals. Try as he did, he could not help but dwell on the potential for human suffering. Still, he could not expose his frailty; he had to emote resolve, without hesitation or remorse. "I understand using Third World nations as grounds for clinical trials. But, why Africa? You have no racial biases. The data suggests a slightly higher optimization of our model if you were to unleash your new virus in the Arabic Middle East—especially in Iraq," he countered, already aware of the answer before he posed the question.

"You realize the reason, though I would have preferred the Middle East as well. But the very reason I would have preferred Arabic lands is the reason they present a poor fertile ground for a sexually transmitted disease. Their entrenchment in their religious beliefs, and the fear these beliefs have cultivated, make them poor candidates for the rapid incubation of a virus—its contagious characteristic relies on frequent and varied sexual contacts. Homosexual copulation is a capital offense in the Middle Eastern lands, as is adultery. Iraq, Iran, Saudi Arabia, Jordan, Syria, Lebanon, even Egypt—on the African continent—make poor laboratories," she replied in a perfunctory manner, as he had been privy to this reasoning before the decision had been made. "It's January, 1979. In one year we'll hear of a case of an unknown disease developing in the United States. The disease will probably make its way to America via the Caribbean Islands from Ivory Coast or Nigeria." She paused, looking at him expectedly as if she were unsure what he wanted. "Are you ready to go to the room?"

Kristoph had never had sex with someone he knew well—always pick-ups, one-night-stands and prostitutes. He preferred prostitutes. The engagement had meaning and purpose: You pay her; she performs in a manner which is sexually fulfilling and complies with your requests without trepidation or emotional bartering. The transaction was honest, genuine. He abhored religion—all religions—and especially the sanctions and stigmas placed against prostitution. *If it doesn't make sense, look to religion as the source of the confound.* "You and I—we've known one another all our lives—your father, my father. Frankly, having sex with you is akin to having sex with a sibling or close relative. What I'm saying is—you know what I'm saying—humor me awhile. Let's talk. Tell me about what you remember of your father, Gershon. At least you had some physical contact with him before he died." Her shoulders relaxed; she blinked less. She seemed to soften, abandoning the officious air distinctive to her persona.

"I only remember glimpses, fleeting images," Zora recalled with restrained melancholia. "Oddly, I remember him moving my mother and me from Jordan to London in 1946, the year he died. I was five years old. That's the year you and I met. That move to London—it seemed almost too purposeful—they decided to put us together like that. Then again, he moved for other reasons as well. The first and foremost, I know, was because he was already privy to the formation of Israel, and he did not want to be in an Arab land when that happened. He wanted to position himself to move to the newly-formed nation whenever it was stable enough to insure my safety. He left a journal for me to read—the shape of things to come and where we come from. But you've read the same journal, so there's nothing new."

159

He dismissed the mentioning of the journal he had read many times with biblical intensity. The thought distracted him from his current motive: Kristoph hoped to elicit a fuzzy response from her— something about her father that had touched her emotionally, some endearing memory, an image sealed by emotional connotation. A realization dawned on him—he simply was not biding time before he went up to the suite with her. He wanted to get what he had never gotten from her—what no one who knew her had ever received: a tear. He wanted a virgin response. It would not come from confrontation. It would emanate from the place she held in seclusion. Barring herself made her more vulnerable, he surmised.

"Your father died shortly after my father died. Mine died in 1941 when I was two years old, so I really do not remember him—very fleeting glimpses, which may or may not be actual memories. They could be resemblances from what I've pieced together of him, seeming like memories. But I was an only child. You had an older brother—he died with your father? It was an airplane explosion?" He saw her hardened expression turn harder as was her way to combat grievous emotions.

"Yes, my older brother. He was not supposed to be on that flight—only my father. But Kristoph, this is somewhat of an inane conversation. You know the reason for my father's death as well as I do," she replied with implore.

"I know the reason for François' death. And the exact circumstances. But let's put it on the table, shall we?" She nodded casually, though her countenance suggested she would prefer to avoid the ordeal. "Each pinnacle male member of our tribe must die an untimely death. We begin evolved and enlightened, but each of our cells is a timer, readying itself to erupt. Eventually, each and every one of us must be put down, as a lame pedigree horse, else the agony is too much to bear. It's a euthanasia of kings. There is no going back, no

160

backing out, no regression to the starting point. We implement grand plans, execute designs affecting the lives of millions, billions. François outlived the ones before him by two decades, for reasons I'm unsure. Perhaps his atypical racial strains. But then, we both know that."

"The price to be paid—we remain unknown and die at an early age—at an unknown time, unknown place, by an unknown agent. I know it all too well, obviously. I now face the same fate, one for which I assumed voluntarily, but not necessarily, volitionally. I was groomed for the job, in the same way a eunuch is groomed. He volunteers, but, given the choice at a very early age, if he had possessed the mature faculties to make a decision, he would never have chosen that particular career path; nor would I. I realize that now, and I think—ponder, ruminate—what would my life have been like without it? Yes, I know, I have been the prime mover of events over the globe. But, as blasphemous as this may sound—what of it? What would my life have been, had I not been groomed, goaded and molded into what I am and do today? I feel somewhat akin to a recent movie titled *Logan's Run*. The populace was young, beautiful and vivacious, but the price each individual had to pay: Each had to die at the age of thirty. They never knew old age." He saw Zora repressing amusement, probably mulling of the idea as having merit.

"Are you saying you regret your life? Certainly, you're not dead. You could have many years ahead of you—still," she inquired, her tone emoting more than earlier. "What's the difference between you and someone who randomly dies an untimely death from the whim of probability?"

"What's the difference? The whim. The whim is the difference. My death is not determined by probability—it's determined by plan. And I have accomplished a major goal—replacing the US controlled Iranian administration with a fundamentalist theocrat and set the stage for a major showdown between the state of Israel—which our fathers were responsible for creating—and the middle of the Arab world. And the hapless United States, the naive and unwitting interlocutor." He paused, inhaling deeply after not taking a breath during his monologue. "It's time," he added, giving up on extracting the tear from Zora.

"It's time? For you to die?" she asked, confused.

"No. It's time for us to retire to the suite," he replied, throwing back the remainder of his cognac.

He allowed her to lead as they traversed the hotel lobby floor. Though this staff had been trained through education and experience to be composed and detached, he noticed an energy, an attention directed toward them. He was always diligent—avoiding attention, remaining as innocuous and benign as possible in every situation and environment. *They knew her? This was a favorite haunt of hers, a frequent retreat for trysts with various lovers?* The concierge, the hotel manager behind the counter, both clearly evinced more attention than the situation would normally have called for.

The liquor had helped. He felt more at ease, even though his favorite prostitutes provided some petting and foreplay before entering the bedroom. Zora remained staunch, business-like and directed. She opened the door and entered the room without contrivance or gesture, removing her coat and hanging it in the closet. "Unzip my dress, please," she asked, turning her back to him. "I realize you're not really sexually excited. I understand. I'm certainly not a seductress, and we're basically siblings as you mentioned. So, I'm thinking, perhaps you can fantasize. I know you, and I know you appreciate nude women. Though I'm not passionate, my body is beautiful. So, I'm going to get nude, then I want you to direct me to sit, stand, kneel, pose any way you like until you become excited. Will that please you?"

He thought it odd that he had not thought of her being naked yet, given that sex was on the agenda. The last time he saw her nearly

unclothed was when they were teenagers on a sailboat on the
Mediterranean, and she was lying on the deck sunning without a top—
not a provocative act in her geographical and social sphere. She was
fifteen at the time. He was seventeen, and, as he watched her, his mind
drifted to the beauty of her form—and to lust. Suddenly aware of
lascivious fantasies, he quickly vanquished the image and never
pondered it again, escorting the thoughts into a mental cage of banished
images. But just then, the pent-up feeling burst from the cage unbound;
he experienced the same jolt of adrenaline exciting him so many years
ago. "I'd love to see you nude," he replied, his breathing shallower.
"But I'd like to undress you as part of the—" he paused, "—foreplay?"
Uncharacteristically, she grinned a coy grin, signaling her amenability
to his suggestion.

"Do you want me to sit, stand, kneel? I'll do it," she replied
with a docile, almost submissive attitude which excited him even more.

"Sit, there, on the edge of the sofa," he said, pointing to the
location.

She complied, taking a seat. "Leave my shoes on as well?" she
asked.

He had leaped from ground level, zero lust, to a heightened
sexual appetite he had not undergone since a memorable meeting a year
ago with Rita, his favorite prostitute in Paris, who was well-versed in
all manners of role play and sensorial techniques. Concomitant with his
erotic feelings, he had lost his shyness. "Are you wearing panty hose or
stockings?" he posed. Her expression approached shock—not that he
asked the question, but an expression emoting pique.

"I do not wear panty hose," she replied curtly. "These are
stockings, held by garters. Old fashioned, but I prefer the look and feel.
But you should approach and discover yourself."

Flush, almost feverish, he slid the cocktail table in front of her
away with his foot. He kneeled before her in a bowing position—an

163

outsider would have construed the pose as worship. Removing each fine leather, high-healed shoe, one at a time, he held each over his nose and mouth, oxygen mask style, inhaling and exhaling as he would with a bottle of fine wine. He slid his hands up along each side of her right calf, beside her knee, and slithered under her dress along each side of her thigh until he felt the rim of the garter belt and the upper edge of her stocking. Then he wiggled his fingers further along, probing the presence of underwear. Satisfied—though disappointed—by the existence of the garment, he slid the stocking off her leg, allowing it to fall gracefully to the floor. Then he performed the same ritual with the left leg.

"Stand, please, and turn around," he commanded her in a firm but gentle tone. She complied. He unhooked the top snap of her sequined, metallic blue, satin Versace dress, unzipping it completely to the small of her back. Repelling it on both sides from her neck, the top melted from her firm, feminine shoulders. He nudged the lower part over her hips, where she lifted her feet, one at a time, to free herself of the accoutrement. She stood with her back toward him, adorned only by her black panties, the smallest contoured garment he had ever seen.

For memories long forgotten, his mind jolted to the visage of her fifteen-year-old tan frame glistening on the deck of the sailboat in the Mediterranean sun. Her body remained untainted from aging after twenty-three years. With outstretched arms, he skated along the groove of her spine with the fingertips from both hands, one starting at the small of her back and the other the top of her neck, converging in the center and then diverging at opposite ends. She remained submissive, silent and motionless. His familiarity with her as a lifelong friend and companion had waned, replaced by an object of feminine beauty, even an aesthetic, artistic object.

He had remained mindful of not looking at her face, but now he desired her body, from top to bottom, front to back. Now far

164

exceeding the arousal of frolicking with his favorite prostitute, he spun her around to face him. He gasped at her dark beauty. Though she had ebony hair, it carried a blonde appeal, a quality he did not understand but felt immediately. He pinched at the silk strands around her pelvis and pulled them over her thighs, around her knees and down to her ankles. She obligingly lifted her feet, allowing him to disentangle her from the frail garment.

Maintaining control overwhelmed him. A demon entered him, driving him to consume her, ravage her without regarding limits or standards. His thoughts were muddled as he fumbled with lines of reason or rationale. He let go.

***

Unaware of how they had gotten to the bed, he felt exhausted and spent. More than drained of energy, he had become woozy. The ceiling spun as if he had too much alcohol to drink. He dragged his hands over his body, verifying he was naked. He heard noise in the bathroom, so he knew his recollections were not completely a dream. He opened his mouth and voiced, "Zora," but the words did not come out. He had lost track of time. He tried to turn his head to see the clock, but his head would not turn.

A presence was next to him. It was Zora, but he could not see her. She bent over him and kissed his forehead.

"Kristoph, I do love you," she said, "but we have a much greater responsibility to what we've already done and will do."

The pang of realization was not painful. She was to be the one. The end did not feel as foreboding and ominous as he had imagined, probably because of the drug she had administered to him, or perhaps because he was prepared if not hopeful. Life had lost its meaning—the meaning he lived was for the purposes for which he was raised and the meaning he desired he could never own. Being stranded in the middle—in a chasm between objectives and unfulfilled fantasies—had taken its toll. He felt the mattress depress next to him.

"You should know, I was at the height of ovulation. I have other methods to guarantee pregnancy, and a male child. But given that my methods fail, I brought a small canister of liquid nitrogen with me, some glucose solution and some vials, so I was able to freeze enough of your semen for future use. Indeed, I might use it again even if I am pregnant—I like you that much." She kissed him on his lips. "Good-bye, Kristoph."

A Turkish room maid found him the next day. He was the third dead man she had discovered in a room, naked on a bed, in the five years she had worked as a guest worker at the hotel. Without drama or excitement, she returned with the hotel manager. He called the house physician and chief of security, a formality in case the death was a homicide and not the usual heart attack, drug overdose, or cerebral hemorrhage. The doctor examined the body, assessing a heart attack and indicating that no drugs or foul play was evident.

They could not identify the body. After searching the room thoroughly, they could not find any documents or identification to call the next of kin. They notified the city morgue and Kristoph's body was taken away—to be entered as a John Doe—weeks later—to be transferred to a medical school.

Chapter 15

Genes and Witchcraft

What is this conflict I feel? It's tormenting me. My mother, Rebecca, my genetic history, the myth of my foretold early demise? Zora could not have gotten close enough to me, long enough, to alter my memory with the maser electrodes. She's always hidden something from me and told me she has been nothing but forthright. Yet, I know differently.

"In coming call, Dr. Éclair," his car AI interrupted his ruminations. "It's Dr. Throckmorton of Clarity Center. Do you want to take the call or shall I take a message?"

Alarmed, he feared Throckmorton's call could only be bad news; otherwise, he would tend to Hyperia's recovery until Jordan would have called him. "I'll take the call," he responded with despondent resignation.

"Jordan?" Throckmorton murmured.

Now he was even more troubled by Throckmorton's tremulous voice. "Hello, Jerry. What can I do for you? You sound troubled. How's Hyperia?" he queried with an upbeat tone.

"Hyperia. She's the reason I'm calling. No worries. She's fine. She's in good health. In fact, better health than you could possibly imagine. I can't tell you more. You need to get here as soon as possible. Where are you?"

He knew Jerome Throckmorton would not over-dramatize— always the objective observer, making medical decisions through measurement rather than with supercilious intuition. "I'm close to my office in Manhattan Beach right now. I had an important conference to attend, but this sounds more important." He paused, sighing. "You can't simply tell me what's going on?" He sensed Throckmorton had changed since he last saw him three days earlier.

167

"Jordy, you know me. If I could tell you, I would. Just get here as soon as you can. Say, two hours?" His friend sounded transformed—sincere as if recently inspired by some nirvanic insight.

"I'm on my way, Jerry. I won't even drop by the office," Jordan replied, now feeling relieved Hyperia was healthy but concerned by Throckmorton's plea for alacrity.

Thoughts of Hyperia had haunted him these last three days. When he had seen her in the lab for the first time—even before he had laid eyes on her—her presence, her existence, her very being seemed to emanate a force he could not explain. He had never experienced such an influence; the feeling vexed him. He did not like the inexplicable, the idiosyncratic, the effect without an observable cause.

When he had transported her to the Clarity Center, she was more than a passenger. *What is this feeling? What is this attraction I feel for her? It isn't sexual—god, no. But I've known her a lifetime, and I've never set eyes on her before. Where did she come from? Perhaps I've associated her with someone from my past, someone who looked like her, or she triggers a memory which is otherwise long subdued and weakened. Perhaps a girl I knew in my childhood?*

He turned abruptly off Pacific Coast Highway onto Rosecrans to get to the freeway. The meeting he had to postpone was an exclusive contract with MultiDimensional Gaming Corporation. They were incorporating certain facets of his company's Brain-Link technology into their online games over the next five years. Recalling the contractual potential of billions of dollars over the next five years and the board's strong reaction if he were to mishandle this marked opportunity, he decided he could not cancel it. He would send Zora Green in his stead.

"Call Zora Green's office at Brain-Link," he commanded his car AI.

Suddenly uncomfortable with a festering irascible temperament, he tried to mellow his tone once the car AI connected him with Zora's office. "Dr. Éclair. Zora has not been in the office for three days," Zora's assistant said. "She hasn't called in. I thought, perhaps, that you would know her whereabouts. We are a bit concerned about her." He disconnected his line without comment.

Aghast, he was appalled no one had seen her since he last left her. Not so much worried about her well-being, he was suspiciously concerned about her machinations for the past three days. "Find Zora Green!" he erupted, commanding the onboard AI. Tempted to exit the freeway and return to El Segundo, the urgency to get to the Clarity Center in Laguna Beach prompted him onward. He was baffled. *She's not available? What the fuck! She knows how disturbing this behavior would be perceived—especially by me.*

Chamberlain's technology preoccupied him over the past three days. As he drove south—intent upon meeting Jerome Throckmorton, his curiosity was ablaze after the beseeching phone call—the exigency to find Zora began to overwhelm him. He reasoned her presence was required, if not simply to take his place at the meeting with the video game company. He was needled, confined to his car, grappling with the circumstances of Zora's disappearance and coincidence of Hyperia's appearance.

Designating technology to do the footwork, he trusted the artificial intelligence equipped in his automobile to find Zora. Jordan had designed the communications system in his car, fashioning it to autonomously reach anybody, anywhere, anytime. Its logic algorithms traversed several hierarchies, first pinpointing the target's location using GPS. Then it cascaded through a multitude of triangulating methods: calling the primary contact numbers; searching to verify if other known correspondents were in the vicinity; calling friends, neighbors and business associates. Simultaneously, the system encircled locations around the person of interest and called all numbers simultaneously, talking to respondents with a human-sounding voice, using such advanced electronic cognition that the person at the other end of the line could not detect they were talking to a machine. Jordan had designed what he coined "Holmes mode." If it could not locate the sought-after party after calls to the primary numbers, it incorporated both overt and covert tracking operations: calls to ancillary locations, searching financial and credit computers for ATM and credit card use, phone record scans for recent utilizations, email logins and use of security access pass codes.

"Zora Green located, Dr. Éclair," the crisp midwestern accented female voice declared ten minutes later.

He had been bogged down in a mire of suspicion and angst. Now, he wavered between relief and regret. He felt relieved that he had found Zora. Not being able to find her would have signaled an onslaught of even more catastrophic worry. Yet, he regretted finding her as well. The need to discover her whereabouts suggested to him that she wanted him to find her—a game with rules with which he was unfamiliar up to now. *What is the relationship between Zora and Hyperia?*

Jordan sped toward Laguna Beach, now even more compelled to see Hyperia—this strange, angelic presence. Momentarily, he had a burst of panic, fearful Zora would harm her. He quickly dispelled the notion to not making sense. *If she simply had procured her from one of our operatives, as she said, why would disposing of this woman be so important? And, if for some reason, she wanted her dead, why not just kill her? Why did she bring her back to the lab? Simply to experiment on erasing her memory, with the possibility of rendering her brain dead? She's hiding something from me, and I've been too preoccupied with enabling our Middle East project to investigate.* "Do not attempt to contact her. Where is she?" he queried the onboard artifical intelligence, a system he had designed, built and tested five years ago.

"Target is in the Santa Monica mountains in a shallow valley accessible via Mulholland Drive. The data is scant. Seventy-eight percent probability the facility is a biological lab, based on shipments, phone records, and employment records linked to the location. They operate cryogenic equipment. In addition to other apparatus and supplies, the data infers research or maintenance of biological systems. Based on receiving records from shipments to their address, it would appear to be a cellular development or fertilization facility."

The ambivilence vexed him: should he turn around, drive into the Santa Monica mountains and confront his mother, or continue toward the Clarity Center. He was forty minutes from Hyperia, over an hour from his mother. He could drive to Santa Monica airport and fly his helicopter to the location his AI had pinpointed, but he resigned that notion. He thought, *what would be the point? I'll see Zora later, and she is no immediate threat to Hyperia-- my primary concern right now.*

He depressed the accelerator absent-mindedly, motivated by an ever increasing conviction to get to Laguna Beach. "Call Dr. Throckmorton," he barked. "Use his private number, not the Clarity Center number." The AI connected him within seconds.

"Jordan," Throckmorton's voice bellowed through the car, as the computer had adjusted the internal volume loudly based on ambient noise. "How close are you? The gates should be open for you if you're outside now."

An uneasiness gnawed at him. He had traced his angst to two sources: Zora and Hyperia. He was accustomed to Zora's untoward behavior, but he was sensitive about Hyperia. His sensitivity made him vulnerable to Zora, and he needed to protect the source of his vulnerability. "I told you to call me if there were any changes, or if anyone tried to get to her. Has there been any suspicious phone call, visitor, someone trying to get in?" Jordan sensed the lull on the other end was an extension of his last conversation fifteen minutes earlier.

"No, no one has tried to get to her. I'm sorry I seem evasive, but her condition is something you have to experience. I cannot explain it," Throckmorton replied with conviction. "Where are you now?"

Without usurping power from him, his mother could still exercise considerable influence with little apparent effort, and he was thankful his qualms were not verified. "I'm on 405, about twenty minutes away," he responded hurriedly then pressed the hang-up button on his steering wheel.

"Monitor Zora Green's location," he ordered while still driving. "Download all changes in activity. Access any and all satellites, servers, remote cameras, repeater stations—track all activity. No need to respond."

As Throckmorton had promised, the gates to the Clarity Center were opened, waiting for him. As soon as he drove over the threshold, he noticed the gates closed behind him. He spotted Jerome Throckmorton, who started a slow jog toward him as he drove toward the entrance. He seemed inordinately animated, almost consumed as he approached Jordan's open car window, not waiting for him to disembark, intent upon talking first.

"Remember that time we once got into a heated discussion about Carl Jung? You essentially dismissed his theories, especially his notions of collective unconsciousness," Throckmorton remarked excitedly as Jordan tried to exit his car.

Throckmorton's question irritated him as it seemed tangential to why he was there in the first place. "Jerry, you've never called me about anyone I've brought to you before. I never hear from you unless I ask. And now, you call me a couple days after I deliver a patient to you—with highly sensitive credentials? Jerry, tell me what's going on." He paused, assessing him, seeing an expression of exhilaration tempered by calm—a nirvana. "Let me see her—now!" Jordan demanded without waiting for a reply.

Throckmorton responded with a youthful grin. "My friend, I don't know what you've been doing or who she is, but—" He stopped for lack of words. "Is this the result of one of your experiments? If so, you'll get ten Nobel prizes," he continued as he led the way through the automatic double doors and into the hospital lobby.

Four armed security guards stood ominously around the lobby, impressing Jordan with their skeptical scrutiny even of him. He spotted another two formidable psych techs standing watch at the end of the long building wing they traversed. Previously miffed by Throckmorton's evasiveness, his angst was eased by the appearance of the tight security. "Her room—at the end of the hall?" Jordan asked impatiently. Throckmorton nodded passively, his mouth immobilized into an upward crescent. He stopped in front of the door, blocking the way. He grasped Jordan's forearms, squeezing them briefly, muttering. "It's for you. I wish I could see what you will see."

Jordan smiled nervously, unsettled by the doctor's rambling. "OK, Jerry. It's for me. What's gotten into you? Let me through," he remarked with pensive reserve.

Sunshine inundated him as he opened the door to the windowless room. Throckmorton had unwittingly prepared him for a shock. A warmth saturated him, emanating from an unknown source. Reminded of brain research subjects with stimulated occipital lobes, they saw bright light when light did not exist. So was his experience—the radiance stunned him only briefly. He glanced around hastily, realizing his perception could not be of true light, but the sensation of light—but how? Throckmorton had a Brain-Link maser electrode array within the Center but in another part of the building. The apparatus was bulky and cumbersome, and it had not been outfitted with updated remote technology. Its presence and influence would be obvious; he would have realized he was being affected by his own invention. *Something's playing tricks with my mind. Was Jerry able to develop the remote Brain-Link? What I've spent millions of dollars developing, threatening and conniving with Chamberlain—was it all for naught? Is this his big surprise, the bait to the surprise birthday party, the meaning to all the subterfuge? I don't need to squint because the light is not real. My brain's projection is not creating radiation that will harm my eyes.*

Masterful at containing his reactions, he jumped at a voice whose source he quickly concluded came from within as well. His greatest fear was madness, losing his ability to perceive, think, and act accurately. [Hyperia] *No, the light is not real, my brother. Open your eyes and join me. Come to me as we have been parted for millennia. Come to me and let me touch you. Yes, it is I—Hyperia—your sister. I speak to you, not through vibrations of air but through vibrations of space. An ancient and pure science—lost over tens of centuries—only now being rediscovered through your efforts. Walk through the light.*

His heart rate pummeled his chest, then suddenly calmed as if controlled by an external source. The blood draining from his head, returned. His panic—the fear of losing his mind—dissipated. He trusted the voice but, at the same time, knew it could not be real. The equipment, the technology to access his neural sensory activation centers was not local—nothing close enough to present this level of sensory intrusion. In his lab back in El Segundo—yes—but not here. *I'll go with it. I feel it means me no harm.*

[Hyperia] *I'm not 'it' Brother. I am Hyperia, your blood sister, recast into flesh, and made alive by our mother. Come to the center of the sun. I await you.*

Light washed over him, immersing him, coating him, enveloping him. He looked at his hand, and it had vanished in the luminance. Ahead, an outline, a silhouette of radiance, formed.

174

[Hyperia] We were called prophets, angels, seraphims and cherubims. Hyperia's face appeared before him sparkling, glowing, beaming with the joy and energy of ages. *We come from the same seed. The boys and girls were separated as we each had different purposes, different goals, different training. Our type was protected through the millennia from invaders, power-mongers, and intruders. Sit.*

He viewed her now in full form, standing at the side of her bed—bright, shiny, dazzling—yet his distrust persisted, maintaining that this visage was a manipulation of neuronal channeling, the same way his Brain-Link device worked. "I do not think I am mad; therefore, my sensory functions are being manipulated. It fascinates me. I'll sit. Let's discuss what I experience." The lighted figure motioned to the edge of the bed to sit. She sat next to him.

[Hyperia] Our kind evolved from the ancient Canaan City of Ugarit, over six millennia ago. We were a special class, bred to forecast, teach and record. Our parents and benefactors were the first masters of genetics. As young children we were protected, separated from the society and culture at large. The high priests—ones like us— cultivated our talents. These priests were not connected with the Baal worshipers at the time but rather pursued a separate goal: identifying reality. They questioned the world around them, just as scientists today. They had learned that by gathering information through observation and experiment, they could draw conclusions about the origins of past events which led to the prediction of future events. The boys were particularly adept at garnering information from the environment, combing through inter-relationships and coincidentals to forecast future events. They were not fortune tellers; they were analyst precursors. The girls had similar, but still remarkably different, skills. The memory of the culture merged into the fabric of their brains. They contained true collective unconsciousness—cultural memory. Over the centuries, these talents were genetically honed and bred so that these

175

girls owned the memories of all the past—each generation put its
mnemonic mark in the memory engrams of the girls. You and I—
brother—we are the progeny of this ancient cult of Canaan.

Jordan had abandoned his resistance to this hallucinatory specter. Entranced by her personal account, he yearned to know more. "How are you here? Why now? Your appearance—it could explain so much. My ancestors. My father. My grandfather. Where they came from. My purpose. All my life I've wondered, but suppressed, for fear of making myself miserable and unable to fulfill my obligations; yet, I asked in the darkness, 'How can a child be born with obligations?' I made no agreements, signed no contracts, entered into no covenants. And then, there's the affliction—the promise of the untimely demise— the sacrifice—that we all share."

She placed her finger over his lips. *[Hyperia] You need not talk. We are together. I will touch your head and take you on a journey of answers. You will see the past through the eyes of our ancestors. Are you ready?*

Still bound to worldly concerns, his first thought was to ask how long it would take, quickly rebuffing himself at the inanity of the question. He discarded such trivia as her hand approached his head and neck. Afraid to ask, always avoiding the thought, he knew his own time was drawing near. He parted his lips, stopped, then decided to confront the fear from which he had always shrunk. *I've never asked, always hoping the looming future would vanish. But, perhaps, I can discover: Why must I die before I am ready?*

Chapter 16

Visiting Canaan

Ugarit-1192 BC

His feeling of a free fall was lessened only by a loose association to his body as if connected by a long tether. He remembered dreams of falling, but always remaining aware he was dreaming. His experiences in jumping from airplanes were cradled by his hand on a ripcord. This time the comfort of awakening eluded him. He unconsciously grasped for a ripcord as he plummeted through a silent narrow undulating funnel, oscillating luminescent gold, ambers, browns and yellows. Sparkles and bright flashes demarked the nebulous rim which seemed close but out of reach. He wondered about gravity— since a vacuum or alternate pressure or grappling force was not apparent; the only force propelling him downward had to be gravity, which meant a massive object was at the bottom of his decent. *I started this plunge without stepping off a precipice or ledge. I'm not accelerating as a gravitational force would require. And there's no wind from velocity. Clearly, then, I cannot be in a true physical environment. This sensation is an experience of mind.* He glanced at his torso, legs, and feet, observing form without detail. He held his hands before him, displaying like characteristics—no texture, color or size— simply form.

Instantly stopping, dust, bright sunlight and an unfamiliar stench assaulted his senses. He grappled with the opposing forces of reality discernment versus focusing on the current experience. *I'm me, but I'm not me. I am as if observing another from within, yet I feel what he feels, smell what he smells. And I'm frightened. The noises. The muffled sounds of screaming; horses, moans of anguish and pain.* Befuddled, he heard words—not in English—but he understood the message.

"Lotan, my brother, they will break the walls down and find us," the soft female voice echoed to his side. He recognized his sister's voice. He realized she was not a sister of family but of close association.

"We wait here for Yassib, Hurriya, my sister. He has arranged a passage away for us out of Ugarit," he replied with hesitation as if mouthing the words through an automaton. "And when Yassib arrives, I must impart information: a shadow of the future which will insure our survival and revenge."

The boy and girl heard the stone wheel door crunching the surface beneath it. Initially alarmed, both Lotan and Hurriya knew only their teacher, Yassib, could have unsecured the passage normally. "Lotan. Hurriya. Are you here, huddling in the dark? We must depart!" Yassib whispered with stark pitch into the candle-lit darkness.

"Light the lantern by the passage, Yassib. Come to us, here in the Room of Life. We hide under a ceremonial birthing platform in the far corner. I must tell you what has come to me before we leave," the young boy, Lotan, replied with urgency.

Yassib, the children's teacher, keeper and master of the eugenics cult, lit the lantern and desperately peered through the pasty yellow light, over the infinity of stone conception and birthing tables. He could barely discern his prize eugenic products, Lotan and Hurriya, standing timidly in a dark corner of the stone-crafted tabernacle. He scurried to them, fearing harm might befall them even in this isolated, yet besieged, environment.

Lotan immediately clasped his wrist and yanked him into a huddle with himself and his sister. "Write these words after we depart. Make them part of the scriptures to live forward forever, for these words will come to pass. We shall create their future. The weapon we shall wield will be the ebony muck oozing from the depths of the earth. I have smelled, tasted and handled this death elixir, this black unholy

178

mixture. I have mixed it, dashed it among the rocks, water, wind and sand. Its blackness blends with naught. And, when I subject the ooze to fire, it takes on a life of its own, ablaze as if a spirit was waiting to burst forth. This odious amalgam is the substance of life gone past, many eons before us. Its essence still contains that life, and, once lit by flame, the life, which took refuge under the earth, springs forward as heat and flame. Use it to destroy them as they destroy us. For just as the black repugnance takes fire, the life from which it is made will burn with a destructive glow. Make them dedicated to this wicked substance. Make them worship it as they worship their invisible god. Make them covet and adore it, for it shall light their torches, drive their chariots and energize the hearths of their homes. And the more they invite its creeping death into their families, homes, cities and cultures, the more it will entrap and consume them. This loathsome substance resides deep under our feet, in the earth, where all the living things, both plant and crawling creatures have retreated. The spirits of the long since dead are the stuff of this vile pitch. Write this, Lotan. Write this, and more. Make these words part of a living scripture, always our goal, but never their knowledge, for their doom and devastation will be our priority. First, destroy them morally, usurping the fabric of their characters, as individuals, families and cultures. Then ultimately ignite it beneath their feet, consuming them in an inferno all together." Yassib paused, winded from his trance-induced soliloquy.

He stared at the boy, who glared at him with the intensity and brilliance of Baal. He stroked the boy's head, and his sister rubbed his shoulder. "I shall do your bidding, Yassib, as I know you see what others cannot." Yassib stood, unfurling himself slowly from Lotan's clutch, gently attempting to coach them upward and toward the exit route he had prepared.

"You did well hiding in the tabernacle—Lotan and Hurriya— my children. We must get you out of Ugarit. The others are already on the boat, waiting for your arrival. The invaders kill every living creature in sight—man, woman, child, beast. You and your kind will be our last hope, our chance—to procreate and avenge, to nurture and preserve our truth throughout the ages."

Yassib reasoned their timing was critical, but haste without means would be futile. Escape was imperative, but, without arriving at the safe haven for shelter, all would be lost anyway—and the destination was far away. "And the fabric, on the vertical poles of the floating vessels? Did you attempt that before the marauders' arrival? Did you construct the vessels? We had the time." Yassib altered his hastened expression, looking at him as one would gaze upon Baal himself.

"Yes, the priests and laborers recreated your designs flawlessly—they put your fruitful imaginings to the test. You envisioned magic! You craft flies in the water as a bird soars in the air. You have saved your own life and the lives of your brothers and sisters, for your craft offers the only method to escape and outrun these Sea People and the Invisible-God invaders from the South. Please, children, we must go. The labyrinth leads under the walls of Ugarit, where the transporting party awaits you. You, Hurriya, Babib, the other high priests—you will flee in your own craft." Yassib noticed Hurriya's consternation.

"Yassib? Your words suggest you do not accompany us!" Hurriya commented, her panic unconcealed.

"My duty lies here, to protect the temple and guard the image of Baal with my life so that his image is not desecrated by these savages, these believers in this invisible god—this god who neither loves nor procreates with his people. Come now."

"Why do they attack us, just to kill and burn? They do not steal, rape, nor plunder. Is their object to exterminate us?" Lotan asked, an uncomprehending naïve curiosity prevailing his tone.

"So it seems is the will and word of the questionable authority whose will they abide, their god they call Yahweh. You are powerful and wise beyond your years or mine, Lotan. And your sisters will assure that your meaning and memory live throughout the ages." Yassib squatted to eye level, squeezing the boy's shoulders. "Exterminate them as they exterminate us, but one thousand fold over," Yassib pleaded with command—his rage apparent by his raised voice which he suppressed mid-sentence.

Lotan's eyes welled with tears, knowing he was bidding his beloved teacher farewell forever. "I shall exterminate them, Yassib. I will preserve your memory here in their ashes," he paused, allowing Yassib to caress his hair.

"You must perpetuate your seed to perfection in your new land and keep our scriptures sacred. Listen to your sister, for she has the memory of past ages as well as the log of the present." Yassib paused, his expression signaling Lotan that Yassib would impart the most significant teaching ever. "Here is the way: The dead from ages past will arise from the deep and flow from the depths. Sparked by the fire of the sun, it will lay waste to the surface of their countries. The inferno will blaze across their farms, forests and cities, destroying them as they destroyed us. This I promise you."

Lotan and Hurriya realized the necessity for haste, but they did not want to leave their home, the place to which they felt bound. The yearning to remain was at odds with the inherent drive to survive; they could easily decide to die with their brethren. But their duty buttressed survival, and they reluctantly filed behind Yassib. They heard crushing and thumping at the stone door.

"Come children, the secret passage awaits in the corner, through a corner stone of which you were not even aware. Once they break through the door, they may not find the passage, but we cannot take a chance. Let us not tarry," Yassib cried beseechingly.

Lotan had caressed every stone, corner and crevice in the great fertility chamber. It was to him his beginning, his life, and he had always imagined his end. Yet, the truth they had discovered, the improvements they had made through birthing new babies, destroying those which did not have the desired traits and nurturing those who evinced the desired stock, had given him hope for an ever-lasting life—virtual immortality—but they had yet to discover the cure to the affliction vexing his kind—his special breed. He would die as all of his unusually bred caste did at forty-five years. To spare him the agony and excruciating suffering of his atypical death where each cell of his body imploded over a single week, they put him to a ceremonial merciful death.

He felt comforted as Yassib gathered him and his sister together in the corner, standing together on a single stone tablet. Slowly—as if the force of their combined weight sent a signal—the slab slowly descended into an already torch-lit cavern below the fertility chamber's floor. They stepped off the platform, and it rose slowly, returning to its original position in the floor above. Lotan observed, although Yassib stressed alacrity, that he had paused cautiously to uneasily observe the tablet ascend to the floor level above.

"It has never been tested," Yassib remarked, noticing Lotan's and Hurriya's inquisitive expressions. "If it had not returned to its original position, my angst would increase tenfold. Those invaders will break into the chamber shortly. Please children, follow me, and watch your steps."

Through alternating blackness and flickering murkiness, Lotan kept his mentor's back in clear view—always aware of his sister's footsteps behind him. The bleakness of the dreary cavern hall had already taken its toll on his mood. He wanted to cry, but he reasoned that as close to extinction that they were, crying was the least of the productive options; it would only tend to slow them down and harry Yassib.

After tenacious perseverance from tracking Yassib, he smelled sea air. The dank stiffness of the catacomb was replaced by a freshness with which he had experienced only four times in his life—whenever they had travelled to the seashore for the ceremonial disposal of the fetuses and newborn corpses. During those journeys he ruminated that he could have been one of the failed children. And though the success of the process was unarguable, how did they ascertain success from failure? He wondered. What was the benchmark? The measurement? He had only become privy to the sacred test ritual shortly before their city became embattled by these Israelites and Sea People.

Jordan occasionally phased into his own consciousness. Deciding not to struggle, he perceived an anesthetized state, where the line between himself and Lotan was as blurred as the line between existence and nonexistence. He experienced Lotan through Lotan, not through an external omniscient peephole—not even as a clandestine rider or benevolent parasite, viewing from the inside. The perspective was far more personal. If he were dreaming, he could not awake, nor did he want to; the intrusion of self perturbed him. He submitted fully to his first person perspective, and his host, Lotan.

Lotan's thoughts mingled with Jordan's, presenting as a soothing lullaby. *[Lotan] My thirteen years seem like thirteen centuries, and both are equivalent solitary flaps of bird wings in the eyes of God. My sister, she foretold of this catastrophe. She must write a book. She and her kind must write a book of many chapters and many verses. And it will be passed on and translated, told and retold throughout the ages. This book of scripture will spawn worshipers and prophets. But the words must never convey the truth. Light. I see sunlight ahead, and the screams of torment and violence have ceased. The sea smell entices me, and the sound of sloshing water is near.*

183

He stopped abruptly behind Yassib, noticing his teacher had become drenched in water splashing through a cave opening three-man lengths above them. Yassib moved the ladder over the hole as more water splashed in. "The tide is high, children. The sea water moves in and out. Lotan, you will quickly uncover the forces behind this ritual of earth and water," Yassib remarked, irritated that the water had caught him as soon as he had positioned himself with the ladder.

"If I may, brother and Yassib," Hurriya commented with assertive stillness, "Our ancestors were aware of this periodicity one thousand years ago. It is caused by the Moon. It is a force. They attributed it to the Moon god, Lotramas, who has been lost and unnoticed for centuries. But the wise understood the attraction the Moon has for the Earth, and the Earth for the Moon. They had no way of measuring—of testing. And since only a blasphemous act can presume to measure or test a god, any such action would have been punished by the sacrifice of the perpetrator." Yassib's expression appeared more resolute with her words.

"And so shall the book you and your sisters will write continue to denigrate and defame those who would measure to seek the truth. For we must remain in shadow from now on, and the outsiders must fear seeking knowledge through methods of observation and measurement. Your book must seek to perpetrate ignorance in the guise of righteousness, piety and faith," Lotan replied, assured that his sister had read his most recent thoughts.

He had crawled through the cave to the outside where rock, water and sand met. As he watched Yassib pull Hurriya through the opening, he became painfully aware of his teacher's expression. When he recognized that one of Yassib's journeymen had come to accompany him and his sister to the boat, he pleaded. "Please. Please, Yassib. Come with us to the sea vessel, then take your leave. You return to your death to sacrifice yourself as the savages sacrifice animals and the children of their conquered." Yassib deferred Lotan's request.

From the boat, Lotan watched Yassib disappear into the hole; his head last to sink below the threshold of the Earth, propelling him into a fantasy of death and envisioning the last sunset he would ever see. He knew he would see many more sunsets but never again his beloved teacher, Yassib. He, his sister and their kind would go about to forge the future of this insidious lot of human infestation to insure that the centuries ahead convoluted into a noxious and calamitous finale. He watched the shoreline fade away. He heard the water lap against the vessel as the wind caught hold of his wing design, tugging the craft ahead. He wept.

***

The boat pilot had mastered Lotan's water wing, steering the stern to the left. The change of angle and a gust of wind yanked the boat forward with ferocity. As he glided effortlessly through the waves, Lotan's thoughts segued to the advantage of wind over oarsmen.

The sudden jolt separated Jordan from the visage, gliding through the water. No longer part of Lotan, he floated motionless in a tight vortex of glitter—surrounding and engulfing him—moving him without a sense of motion. His identity as Jordan returned, but he remembered the experience with Lotan. The dream was real; he had not really awakened. His sense of loss for Yassib persisted—Lotan's memories and emotions were Jordan's own now. With the return of his own identity, his sense of loss for his host identity—Lotan—spurned grieving.

He recognized this foray into consciousness past was manipulated by Hyperia. He trusted her at his helm, but he questioned whether she understood the emotional torment arising from the suddenly plucking him from Lotan's plot. They were like intimate characters experienced lovingly in a story, but now the story has ended.

185

I do not hear her words; she speaks to me through experience. The play I witnessed. It was not a past life, nothing as gauche as reincarnation. She transmits her memories to me as engulfing sensory experiences— true immersion—but the story itself, the characters, the setting, they are memories, shadows from the past. I was not Lotan in past life; he was my ancestor. She is a carrier of cultural memory, an organic scribe, storing the events of our people in her own genes.

Jordan remained stunned, almost in a trance. He recounted his experience, trying to recall the meaning of his journey. *Time has no meaning. Lotan made this simple observation millennia ago. I wonder where he is—where was he buried? When did he die? How did his progeny continue? Where did he go? I did not stay long enough to find out. I understand now; I am part of a lineage of bred humans started in ancient Canaan. My kind—we all sprung from a well of genes as if we are a separate species. And Hyperia, she is guiding me, showing me my history, my ancestors. The maelstrom around me, it appears to be slowing, the bottom widening as if I'm falling through a hole, but no sense of falling. The light—brighter than the sun—I'm falling through—*

High atop an exposed island peak, an older Lotan's robes fluttered in the strong breeze, his beard flexing with the intensity. He squinted through the magnifying tube; this was the first clear day in months that he could reveal the far-off landmass to his sons and daughters. Anxious to get a view, they all clamored about to see the rest of the world. He had repeated the tale of adventure and exile—how he and Hurriya escaped invaders conquering their land, invaders who had posed for years as the good neighbors to the south. He told of the Sea People assailing them from the west. He recalled Yassib, always with tenderness. He told of their lost peoples of Canaan, who had landed on this island east of the large continent bordering on their home's sea. He repeated the story of their people, entering this massive expanse of water—fearless of the monsters foretold to devour them, should they venture through the narrow passageway to the extreme west. Twenty ships had been outfitted with his invention, the fabric wing that makes boats fly through the water. And they had sailed through the strait without leviathan molestation, just as Yassib had assured them.

He recited their thirty-year history on this island, their population doubling in the interim. They had constructed a city rivaling Ugarit in beauty and design. The inhabitants experienced comforts unimaginable to the people from whom they were separated a mere three decades earlier. Lotan and his kind had fashioned systems with water running through tubes, and boiling water in closed containers so that the escaping steam provided movement and work—propelling boats through the water, turning mills to grind grain, even pumping water through the tubes. But they could not depart from their massive island, nor could they have outsiders aware of their existence. They were completely self-sufficient. And to insure against invasion, they had designed formidable exploding weapons and devices that could accurately deliver the projectiles to their targets. Unfortunate explorers and ships forced off course were aggressively obliterated. Of the very few who were able to return to their home ports, the agitated sailors told of fire-breathing monsters, dragons and death's own brigade inhabiting the island group to the east of the large southern landmass. Lotan expected these stories would persist throughout centuries, protecting and isolating them. He realized they would eventually have to reassimilate into the world culture, but the correct time would avail itself to one of his wiser descendants in later centuries if not millennia.

Jordan sensed he had not lost his own identity completely during this glimpse into the past—the split impression of being part of the more aged Lotan yet observing him from outside as well. He had learned what Lotan knew, and from that union, a feeling of foreboding and anguish encompassed him—dissociated him from Lotan's identity

187

and highlighting his own. The earlier feeling of emptiness and forlorn departed as he was reunited with the elder Lotan. He strained to fill in the thirty-year gap, concluding the younger Lotan and his party must have journeyed west along the entire length of the Mediterranean Sea to emerge at the Straits of Gibraltar. He wondered how they navigated, reasoning that Lotan may have discovered celestial navigation; it appeared he had already invented a telescope, harnessed the power of steam and had devised a system of running water.

"My children, our essence of purpose is survival and improvement," the elder Lotan announced. "Each generation hones the sword of our blood sharper, exacting its toll not in meager and mundane hostile exchange on the battlefield—we survive. The conqueror's game is a fool's game. We conquer the conquerors through persisting, through surviving. We avenge our people by waiting, abating exploration and curiosity until the day comes when we reassimilate ourselves among them. And, when we wage battle, they will not be aware of our presence. Like the affliction eating your body from the inside, the conquerors will hit and stab at themselves, attempting to remove a malady about which they have no location nor remedy." A boy bearing Lotan's resemblance stood to ask a question.

"Sir, those who we are against, our enemies—none of us will ever see them. Nor will our children or our children's children. The years about which you speak run into the hundreds, perhaps the thousands. What if our enemy has long since vanished? And, what if we lose sight of our aim?"

Jordan marveled at the insight and wisdom of this boy. He wondered what part of his own self had been inserted into this vision. He continued to observe through the split blend of insider and outsider. He could feel what Lotan felt, and he sensed a pride well inside Lotan that this boy, his son, could be wise and insightful enough to conceive such a question. And he was saddened by the possibility of the boy's query coming to fruition. "The ravagers of our civilization may disperse; they will live among their subsequent conquerors and their conquerors' conquerors. But the books and scriptures of their religion will carry prophesies—prophesies we shall have implanted—which will draw them back to their homeland—our homeland. And when they are all together, under a single, united nation—we will strike them and all those who have been complicit." He approached the boy, kneeled, and looked him in the eye. "You—" he paused, rotating to include the other children, "We," he added, standing up and stretching his palms upward, "will never waste your lives here as I believe is the question you actually asking. You will all have tasks in the outer world. You will not sit on this island, idle, waiting as millennia pass you by. Our people, our progeny, will take an active role in the formation the usurper's fate. The unfurling of their future and fortune will not be accidental and random. We shall set the course or their future, surreptitiously directing their cultures, gouging trenches and erecting dams to guide the flow of what will appear to their societies as fate designing their outcomes."

He noticed another child, the daughter of his sister, stand to be recognized. He amazed at her strength—a strong child, her gift of memory extended not only into their past, but seemed to overlap the future. Her eyes glowed an iridescent blue, different from the light brown and amber common to the others. "Delia, please speak," Lotan remarked calmly.

"My uncle, Lotan. Bringing me up here, the air, the sea, the visage—it has spawned a vision I would like to share." She stood erect, cocking her head back and clasping her fists to her sides; she shuttered briefly, then turned to the west and pointed. "I see in the far future---the people of the large land east of us, devastated. They are Nubians to be traded by peoples who are yet to find themselves. The slavers are the northern people from the lands currently inhabited by barbarians and

189

savages. They will take up the banner of scriptures we will implant—of the spiritual emissaries we will send to dissuade them—and colonize another land far to our west, across the great sea. They will discover through exploration that this world is not flat, but that we live on a great globe. The globe's essence is a force from within, which holds all things to it. We must participate in this great migration to the west. Power will accumulate there. And the our enemies will disperse to the northern and western lands. We must move with them. We must assimilate when the movement begins—when the slaves from the land to our east are herded and transported. Their plight is our cue. Moving with them allows us invisible passage into their culture." The girl unfurled her hand, slumped her head and shoulders, then collapsed. The other children seemed concerned, but not overly anxious, and circled to her aid. Lotan moved in her direction, and the children made room for him. He hoisted her into his arms, and they commenced a trek down a narrow switch-back trail.

Instantly, the picture of Lotan and the children receded into a pinpoint as he sensed himself being sucked away. Flashes around him—as if surrounded by hundreds of brilliant stroboscopes discharging asynchronously—disoriented him. An instantaneous hint, a nudge from within, directed his attention to each flash's center. Rather than view the light as blinding and distracting, he gleaned information from each after image—each a glimpse of history as he knew it, as he had studied it in school, as if a video log had been recorded thousands of years ago. Now he was privy to it at triple time. Thousands of scenes surged by him, displaying the events of three millennia.

He imagined himself as a high velocity bullet, only shot through time, absorbing the visages of each layer as he penetrated them, the images immobilized him like a fire hose pressing him against a wall. His emotions could not keep up with his eyes, draining him and leaving him numb. He could liken this experience only to the fast-action, high-risk sports he enjoyed: bobsledding, aerobatic flying in two-seat jet airplanes, and parachuting. Yet, even these real activities did not generate his current rapid pace of scenery, disconnecting his recognition from his emotional breath.

In rapid succession he witnessed snapshots of carnage and destruction—all geographically and culturally diverse—ranging from battlefields to ancient cities, he supposed, were now in ruin. Some scenes he recognized; some he did not. At first he noticed only what appeared to be the Near Eastern races; however, as the display raced on, he discerned Asians, Nubians, Caucasians in a mix of paraphernalia—all engaged in the common denominator of strife and war.

Like a child on a carousel ride, he wanted to leap off to the safety of his mother during the lulls within the onslaught of images. Panting, but his lungs full of air, he felt desperation. He introspected, attempting to calm a surging panic with reality—the images were in his mind; his mind and body were in a room. But, holding on to even this crutch of sanity was fleeting.

He noticed plateaus of peace, advancement, stability—only to be followed by further surges of savagery and fields of blood. He imagined himself in a time machine, hurling through the past toward the present, glimpsing at events without garnering detail but still being able to extract shapes, forms, meanings. He gasped at a sudden nirvana—everything he witnessed seemed to be through the eyes of a perceiver at the scene—not himself, but of an ancient agent who had observed, possibly participated in the action. What he saw was not an omniscient camera flying through time for his amusement and benefit, but a distant relative viewing the action as it actually happened.

He could discern the relative time period by the sailing vessels, the weapons, and the armor, but only as after-images. The millennia to which he had been subjected left him lonely, in need of some human contact. He wished he could hear voices, track languages, see writing, but one image merged into the next; his brain could merely categorize loose and approximate placements in history.

Occasionally the frame speed hovered around a geographical area and period. Jordan had lost awareness of himself—his own bodily state. His heart beat wildly, his pulse tapped out a hard-driving rock tune, and his eyes felt like he had not blinked all day. The presenter of the slide show seemed to operate the speed here with volition. Without impugnment, he studied each slide carefully. Occasionally he could focus on a single life, and each seemed to whisk by within five minutes—slow compared to the last fifteen hundred years sliding by within what felt like ten minutes.

The pace of the images suddenly hastened, blending into a blur too indecipherable to glean any information from a single scene. He felt relieved, able to reflect on his experience but still trapped within this vortex of cascading images of historical significance. *These pictures I'm seeing, it all seems like a dream. No, more like a psychedelic adventure. My Brain-Link technology could not implant images this rapidly, causing the brain to acquire and perceive implanted images so quickly. The visual data cannot come from an external source—the technology does not exist. Yet, I do perceive what I perceive; so, either the technology does exist, and I am not aware of it, or the images come from me, trapped within. That Hyperia could produce such an effect—from touch.*

He saw himself bifurcated, pondering the purpose of this dreamscape presentation; simultaneously appalled at its scope and magnificence, breathless at the detail. He had concluded could only be generated by own neurons—his own brain—locked deeply inside memories otherwise inaccessible. *I see this cascade of images as if they had happened, like a world history book, its pages flipping rapidly. Yet, I'm looking at his array of events from a participant's perspective.*

The world's civilizations and cultures did not evolve as vacuums,
especially within the past millennia. Cultures have interacted with one
another around the globe—effecting, changing, stimulating,
destroying—so it would not make sense, given my host is Hyperia, that
I would be privy to merely the Western view. This viewpoint that I
witness—if it is not a cultural or political viewpoint—it must be my
viewpoint. I see the world as my ancestors saw it, as they were involved
with it. So, the sequence of frames, the locations of time and place—
that's where my ancestors had trod.

He cleared his mind of cluttering ruminations, hoping to more
carefully focus on the cavalcade of images flowing in a stream of
pictorial unconsciousness. He fought back skepticism—the tendency to
dismiss the experience as a mind control ploy devised by Hyperia for
some manipulative reason. He chastised himself quickly, concluding
the level of detail and point of view could not have been contrived. Nor
was he drugged or manipulated by a more advanced Brain-Link device
since he himself had designed the most advanced Brain-Link device in
existence. Still, his ruminations continued. *Calm! Calm! Stop and*
observe! He commanded his inner voice to cease and desist its chatter
and clamor.

He focused on a single spot in the barrage of image flashes
inundating him. He quickly sank in. He tried to identify scenes as they
occurred, some faster than others. He seemed like a desparate
commuter, running late for a train, scrambling for it after it departs, and
finally grasping a handrail of the last car. Once the passenger is in tow,
the train accelerates, yanking him along with it.

As the frames of time raced by, he thought each scene was
separated by a century. In glimpses he recognized Babylonia, Assyria,
Chinese civilizations, Rome, Greece. The succession of pictures
slowed, and he peeked into a scene similar to the one of the elder Lotan
teaching his children and followers on the island mountain top. The

people surrounding the man appeared distraught but abiding as they listened intently. Their garb was not unlike ancient Greek attire, but something broke the congruency of the scene. They spoke, but their lips did not move. Emerald, ruby and amethyst-looking gems adorned necklaces and bracelets. In the background he noticed flying devices, like airplanes but smaller.

A motorized vehicle rolled close to the main speaker, and the driver emerged referring to the speaker as Darius. Again, Jordan felt drawn into this visage, more as a participant than an observer. Darius paused as if expecting the new arrival to convey vital information.

"Darius, our geo-physicists have confirmed your hypothesis. A major tectonic shift will occur within the next seventy-two hours. We must evacuate as the island will be engulfed by the sea."

Darius seemed down-trodden by the news but assumed an upbeat air. "This seismic event is untimely but fortuitous as well," he remarked solemnly. "Our civilization could not remain here much longer without intrusion from the outside world. They have not yet embarked upon experimental science, but thinkers in some of their cultures now delve into logic and observation. The time has come for us to disembark and blend into their cultures." He stopped and scanned the area, searching for something. "Hyperia, my sister. Please come join me here."

Neither dream, nightmare, nor nirvana could describe Jordan's astonishment. He wanted to awaken, to reassess with reason or rationale what he had witnessed, for out of the small throng of people emerged Hyperia, the woman guiding his dream-tour through the past—the woman who claimed to be his sister. She joined Darius at the center of the group.

"We will be united through Hyperia. We will continue to communicate and unite, either through her dream-thoughts, or through a medium to be developed in the future. She will bring us together, serving as a conduit for our combined thoughts and goals. Much of what we must do is laid out, and we all know our purpose."

"Hyad will depart for Greece and relay how our land was destroyed. We cannot leave remnants of truth about our existence." He paused, searching the small group. "Josif, you must leave for our former homeland, now controlled by the Romans. As planned, you will plant the seeds of dissent into the sacred scriptures of our conquerors. Plant the untimely messiah into their midst. Demitrius, ready our people to abandon this island. Remind them that this island was merely an eight-hundred-year interlude—that we survive millennia by changing and adapting. Each knows his purpose; each must ready himself to immerse into the outside cultures as we have practiced and rehearsed."

Once more the momentum of time swept him up. He departed Darius and Hyperia and assumed a new perspective. He soared high over the island mountains, the wind roaring, his long hair snapping his face like tiny whips. Hyperia sat at his side as he rode atop a flying machine similar to the ultralights he knew in his century but propelled by a power plant with which he was unfamiliar. Part Jordan, part Darius, he turned to examine Hyperia's face. *This woman— could this be an illusion, a mental implant meant to tie something familiar with the unknown? Does she look identical because Hyperia wishes me to make the connection between her and this specter from the past? And the woman with whom I ride, she seems so real. Could she know that her relative from twenty-five hundred years in the future accompanies her, watching her through this genetic portal connecting distant times?*

The blast of the air was interrupted by a more strident sound from below. He looked down to witness a massive wave approaching the island. The atmosphere rocked with shocks from the ground and water below. He twisted to glance behind him, observing the sky speckled with airborne devices like the one he and Hyperia flew. "The earth swallowed our island home, and we all escaped timely and unscathed," Hyperia remarked as if reading his mind.

He felt obliged to respond but unsure whether to identify himself or not. "I'm Darius, but I'm Jordan—from your future," he replied, unknowing whether his words would even be heard. Her eyes flashed as if she had understood his words, though he had the odd perception his mouth really did not move.

"I speak to many personages from the future. From which future are you, my brother?" she replied, smiling as if he had made a routine comment.

Stunned, he had not completely sloughed off the sensation of dreaming as he phased in and out of the personas of these visages. Completely merged with Darius, he seemed to be communicating through his host's body, sailing through the air over what he had concluded was the Atlantic Ocean close to the coast of Africa. "I am Jordan Éclair from the year 2023," he replied stammering, remembering that the method of defining years had not been developed yet. *English does not exist yet.* He thought. "I mean—about two thousand five hundred years from now," he paused, waiting for a sign of recognition as she continued to exude an aura of near omnipotence. "I'm guessing this is approximately five hundred BC," he continued with resignation, knowing that "BC" would be an anachronism. She grinned coyly and looked away.

"We are familiar with the calendar metrics and our relative position on a timeline," she responded with dryer affect than her expression bore. "My sister—your sister—hosts your journey here. No doubt my appearance is identical to her own as it should be." She assessed his countenance, allowing him to adjust. "It is how we know the future. We speak through our blood—or as we have learned, through the genes. We have honed the art of speaking to our progeny when they seek us. They tell us of what is to come, and we make adjustments to our present."

"You are Jordan, the last to expedite the Final Rite. You are the last in a caste of males in our lineage to push the frontier of the future and resecure our place on the earth. You see—you comprehend—what you do, what your father did—what your grandfather did—and all before them—we are all one in motive and purpose. You will execute the final deed---igniting the dead beneath their feet, consuming them in body as they are now consumed in spirit. They carry a vile seed—selfish, blind, corrupt. This planet is unable to support them; they are unable to support this planet. A variation of man doomed by its own self-destructive tirade. Go back now, Jordan. Go back and complete our mission."

The wind's roar and cathartic silence pervaded him after BC-Hyperia had made her pronouncement. The realization of his essence, the reason for his family's success, the explanation for his uncanny insight and mobilization of technology—all elucidated by a managed dream into the ancient past. *I'm on a hypnotic voyage, tethered to my mysterious sister sitting on a bed in a mental hospital in Laguna Beach, California, and suddenly the truth of my being is revealed as if I were on a psychic archeological dig, unearthing relics of myself as I scramble through the ruins of a long-dead civilization. I see myself through a distant mirror, held to my face by the shadowy power of a genetic collective unconscious, channeled by my sister to meet her ancient counterpart. It flies in the face of what I know, but it is not impossible.* A calm permeated him.

Ever the opportunist, he clamored for more knowledge. Desperate to discover more while under this uncanny trance, he grasped her hand as it rested on the handrail of their flying device, hoping to anchor himself before being swept away to his own time. "If my journey is to end, I must know—my grandfather and father. How did they die?" He saw in her face an elated compliance as she squeezed his hand in assurance he would not leave without his questions addressed.

"You are returning now. Your journey must follow the only timeline that exists for you. The line is a delicate textile, and within the fabric is woven the history of your blood's essence. Toward the end, you will witness events to answer your questions." She squeezed his hand gently, then let him go. The wind's force diminished, the roar became fainter, and the sea of sky chariots behind them vanished into the blue as he faded away into the now familiar soundless vortex of gold flashes and swirls.

Chapter 17

Escher's Timeline

Incapacitated by dizziness, an inexplicable vertigo had overwhelmed him. The connection with his external sensations and the attributions associated with stimulated memories and feelings reinforced his self-ownership—nothing had invaded his psyche, eluding him to believe what he was not. Yet, he remained within this swirling time vortex. He pondered the physics—if not simply the mere utility—of the visual effects of motion, light and color if only his mind were inundated by the sensory medium.

I am not actually traveling through time. My body resides in Laguna Beach. So, why the pretense? Why the contrivance of a journey through time? Why can't I simply awaken from this trance—if that's what I'm experiencing—and go about my business? I was just told I would witness my father and grandfather. And, if this is truly time travel as I sit physically in one spot, I do not understand the maintenance of the illusion of linearity as if the fabric of time requires time. I seem to have velocity without the sense of speed. The flashes, crevices, curvature and undulations of the surface of the fabric through which I appear to fall—these are no doubt meant to represent nodes of time in my past. Her implication was that each timeline is unique. Then I experience more than a simple trance, for, if this were a trance, I could simply emerge from this altered state into a normal conscious state, remembering what I had experienced during this perceived journey. A dream? No. It's too real; yet, reality? No, the laws of physics were violated—or at least the laws of physics which I am aware of—and I'm not aware of an alternate law of physics. He rattled his body, shook his head violently and blinked his eyes rapidly, but he did interrupt his current state—he continued whisking through the nebulous funnel.

Boredom set in, the same congealing boredom arising from looking out an airliner's window, watching the patchwork of terrestrial geometries appear and reappear, never actually resolving to a finale until you're finally descending toward your destination.

He resolved not to second-guess his guide, yet he doubted the veracity of his apparent time travel—if it's a dream, then he should simply awaken. And furthermore, why should time be required to travel through time? This quandary needled him—he experienced either dream or reality—neither of which met the expectations of his logic. He thought his floating through space was illusory as well since it lacked the concomitant vestibular sensations. His vision was intact; his acuity detected small incremental changes and shifts in the surface of the vesicle through which his journey was contained.

He remembered beseeching Hyperia of Canaan to allow him to witness his most recent ancestors' lives. For his entire life he had silently longed to learn of the history of his grandfather, François Éclair. He had never seen a photograph, nor read a letter, nor seen any account of him in a family album or keepsake. He had an even greater lust to learn of his father, though he had seen photos of him, read his writings, and observed his signature on many drawings and designs. He was keenly aware his father and grandfather were responsible for the events of today, as were most of his family before him. And now he knew the reason—they bore an ancient covenant, or curse.

But, if I am the last in this long line of generations spanning centuries, then what is to become of my seed? My offspring? I've postponed thinking of the inevitable, but am I to die an untimely death like the rest of my male predecessors? What becomes of my male offspring? We are an advanced brood, perhaps more advanced evolutionarily than the population at large. How does our DNA define us from the others? If I am the last, then would my male offspring live on with a normal but prosperous life from our fortune? What would

become of my female offspring, vexed and burdened by the barrage of
unconscious memories from a bloodline disconnected from its ancient
purpose? Did our forbearers not plan for the end, that we accomplish
their goal, or did they wash their hands to the ultimate outcome,
knowing that their ancient vendetta against the world and humanity at
large would have been consummated in their absence? When I return, I
will carry on with even greater passion, but die? No.

The sparks around him and illumination slowed as he perceived his body elongating, melding and blending with a single bright bead, a window through this wall of time. For the first time he experienced some physical unpleasantness—stomach queasiness, a mild sea sickness as he was extruded through the wall of time and into a point of view to which he was unfamiliar. He saw the world through another's eyes, identical to his experience with Lotan.

Relieved that the tedious ordeal had taken some variation, he was suddenly elated at the prospect that he had landed during his grandfather's time. His sensory awareness activated slowly—seemingly awakening from a primordial sleep. He had not realized his senses had been so deactivated during the dream journey he had now become to accept as real. Even tactility had morphed to imperceptible, underscored by the rush of cold air around him. The colorless foggy blur had not rendered detail, and white noise dominated the background. Exhaust fumes and fresh bread filled his nostrils as he sensed himself upright and walking. Sounds undulated with more contrast, and form assumed more contour. Briefly panicked by his lack of control, he wondered how he guided himself not being able to see. The distinct sounds of autos and traffic exacerbated his concern. With equal haste he calmed himself, knowing he perceived this environment through the senses of another—whom he assumed was his grandfather, François Éclair.

Joyous at the onset of greater clarity, he discerned the voices of passersby speaking German. The cold air he had felt earlier rightfully placed him outside on a winter day, walking briskly along a busy sidewalk in an apparently bustling early twentieth century European city. He empathized with the plight of a quadriplegic as he himself struggled with his lack of autonomous mobility—he wanted to browse a passing newsstand, but his host continued by it. He was as integrated with this personage of the more recent past as he had been with Lotan, who lived three millennia before his time.

Through whose eyes do I peer? I feel as if I identify with this person, not like the ancient ghosts to whose lives I was privy. Perhaps because I have returned to modern times that I am more at ease. He passed a storefront window, but his personage did not look at his own image as he himself would have done. Jordan now felt more than mere sensory perception; his carrier's emotional state touched him. He was gravely sad yet determined to arrive at a destination in a timely manner. He became more integrated with the man's emotional and intellectual being—he was François Éclair.

Through his host's eyes, Jordan recognized Marienplatz; he was in Munich. François slowed as he approached the Frauenkirche Cathedral. He paused before the grand wooden double doors and tipped his head straight back to look up the front of the structure. He removed his right-hand glove and caressed the door's ring handles, then passed his fingers over the wood texture. He opened the door; the musty air blew him back. He hesitated, having thoughts of fleeing with the escaping gust. Jordan's ambivalence had diminished into François' forlorn.

Shouldering the heavy door open, he protected the leather satchel he had gripped in his left hand since he and Jordan merged. Unaware of his eavesdropper, François stepped through the dank, cold,

202

dimly lit cathedral, pausing occasionally as if the environs held some special significance.

Adjacent to the altar sanctuary and a confession vestibule, he prodded open an ornate iron-work door blocking the way to a steep narrow spiral stairwell descending to depths unknown. He repelled occasional surges to retreat using an emblazoned badge of duty—a tenacity toward obligation so rigorous that, if the duty were shirked, the resulting guilt would avenge the dereliction one-hundred fold.

What is the face of death? I remember as a child, thinking about my final end. I wondered when that person—who would render the final blow to my mortality—was born. At any given second of my life, I asked, "Where is he? Does he wield a weapon, drive a vehicle, or dispense a violent assault?" Finally, I discover the identity of the grim rogue avoiding my probes, unbeknownst to him, readying to close the door to my mortality.

The narrow brick-lined passageway reminded him of historical accounts of ghostly clandestine labyrinths spanning the depths of cathedrals, hiding secrets of forbidden rituals using jars containing the aborted and unaborted remains of broken covenants. *A fitting place to end.* He followed the dim lights through the corridor, finally reaching a chamber expanding into more shadows and colorlessness. An indistinct form of a man appeared from behind a pillar.

"Even as late as last century, the Bavarian royalty colluded with the church to use this chamber for torture and execution. Before that, it was an embalming chamber which doubled as an excellent location for nuns to have abortions," the figure remarked tenderly before allowing himself to be recognized.

Mixed elation and despair confounded François' reaction. "I thought he would send a trusted member of his SS. I realized you had infiltrated into the highest level, but still—" François remarked, surprised and resigned. Gershon moved closer, sliding slowly between the marble slabs spaced between him and François.

"It's the only secret, the only thing I have ever kept from you. Ironic, if not macabre, I wanted this meeting to be a surprise. I could not bear not seeing you for one last time. And I did not trust his Aryan Neanderthals to do what had to be done, let alone do it correctly and with passion," Gershon responded, his voice trembling with hesitation.

François felt relieved, as if informed of a painful surgical procedure that warranted anesthesia after all. "I can't tell you how many times I considered turning back. But, I couldn't—I can't. My bloodline, this wretched infliction damning me to the status of a shooting star." He hesitated, reflecting on the paucity of his lifespan. "Which reminds me—business before pleasure." He patted the satchel, spotted with sweat from his clutch. Gershon motioned to one of the slabs, then illuminated it with a flashlight. François opened the satchel, unfolded the drawings and blueprints and spread them out.

"He'll be filled with empty self-confidence and grandiosity after he sees these inventions. I've pumped him up with expectation, and these designs will not disappoint. He'll put his top scientists on the project. I've already lined up someone to lead the project, a Wernher von Braun. You know him, don't you?"

"I know of him. He's done some interesting designs with toy rockets. His designs take rocket design into space and beyond. These designs will eventually be the delivery medium for munitions, perhaps the fission bomb I told you about," François commented with jaded enthusiasm. "The Germans will dump research and manpower into the development, only for the Americans and Russians to take it from them." Peering through François' eyes, Jordan focused on Gershon, gloating over the designs.

"We are closing on our goal, my old friend. We have others undercover negotiating with the British about Palestine. When the last

204

bomb explodes on Berlin, Britain and the United States will ameliorate their guilt—having allowed this madness you cultivated to mutate as it did—with the gift of Palestine." Casting a solemn glance downward, he paused. "Then the stage is set. Our progeny will continue the task." François detected tears.

Disconnected from reality, the mind of Jordan and reality of François occupied the same space, the latter not aware of the other's presence. And he was disconnected from affect, caused by the disparity between discussion of the future and knowing what must occur within moments. "My son, Kristoph? And your daughter, Zora?" François inquired, refraining from the outburst of tears lurking below.

"Kristoph and Zora are both in Jerusalem, safe from harm," Gershon calmly answered. "Once the Palestinian transfer is accomplished—Exodus! As we agreed, they remain in the new capital, Tel Aviv, until the Arab unrest ignites. Whether to raise them together or apart remains to be seen." François sensed a distressed pause as Gershon weighed whether to mention an issue seemingly beleaguering him. "Your sister, she will raise Kristoph and Zora. She appeared suddenly three months ago, confused about why she had even come to Suresh in Bombay. He took her to Jerusalem."

As shock can invigorate an injured man, so had Gershon's unexpected announcement about his long-separated sister jolted him, distracting him from immediate matters. "My sister? You've seen her? Where is she? Where has she been?"

"I hid her existence from you, my friend. And my motivation was not to be secretive or clandestine. No, my reason was to avoid prolonging your pain. To avoid giving you false hope." Before François rebuked, Gershon put his hand on his friend's shoulder, squeezing it to allow him to continue to speak. "She is a seer of considerable skill and insight. Your line's power is strong. She has full access to the past— but what is more astounding, she's had glimpses into the future, not as

205

detailed images---but she seems to be able to glean ideas, concepts, even some basic forms." He squeezed again, signaling he had not yet finished. "She said—she said the process of disintegration had already started with you—and that you concealed great pain. She said you had discovered a way to chemically retard its progress. And she foretold that a reversal, a cure, will be discovered—in the future—not our lifetime. There is hope—but only for your son or grandson."

The words from which he had refrained suddenly crumbled as if constructed from a rapidly oxidizable material. He had suspected a link with his sister, but he could not verify it and dare not search for her, risking forfeiture of her power to view through their line's ages; the power corrupted if brother and sister were to come in contact. He bowed his head in dejection then slowly looked up. Gershon stood two feet before him, with one hand still holding his shoulder. François had postponed the pain of degeneration—the genetic affliction the males of his ancient line suffered—but it had gained momentum and ate through the chemical barrier he had concocted. He had redirected all of his cognitive and emotional resources, aiming to withstand an indescribable agony permeating his entire being. Comforted by his old friend's touch, he felt Gershon's hands gripping his shoulders, pulling him closer. Gershon's face drew toward his. He felt his friend's mouth on his, his lips engulfing his as an old lover might bid farewell to his betrothed before departing on a long unwanted journey. He sensed Gershon's cupped hand hovering around his neck, his hand opening to bare the needle projecting from his ring, and a pinch before the world went dark.

The vortex yanked Jordan from brief darkness, returning him to a scintillating luminance causing him to squint. The previous episode had left him sad and disquieted. Yet, another undefined burden lurked, marginal, casting a weighty but unforboding melancholy. *A personally involved tale without denouement, I feel alone. More than alone, I feel lonely. We connect to no one. From Lotan to François to me—other human souls are absent; the do not pervade our being the way other humans go about their lives. Parents, siblings, friends, co-workers, even enemies—pull and push, leaving traces, even foundations upon which new beginnings are born. We do not participate in such human sharing as if each life has a schematic, a script, that we each follow and execute without question or resistance. We who wield such power are merely programmed automatons, written by algorithms and scribed in genes by ancient eugenicists.*

Cold air on his face, the sensation was more biting—a frozen dankness. Dropped quickly from the time swirl, his senses were suspended within a conundrum, not discerning the outer physical reality from the inner vision. Immediate motivations charged with discriminating the obscure segue between inner and outer, shadow and light, color and white. He tilted, caught by the wall where he found himself standing, inside yet another host from his ancestral past.

He opened his eyes, his sight met snowy gravel and the vision of his own feet. Teutonic voices again surrounded him, but the dialect seemed different—he recognized Viennese immediately. He looked across the street at an oft-visited hotel—Hotel Sacher. He had been there only four weeks ago, but the scenery and environment seemed off as if an anonymous neighborhood decorator had swooped in, making retrograde alterations. He panicked. *The division between reality and fantasy—between this dream journey induced by Hyperia and my true senses—is no longer pronounced, no longer obvious. I see the world through my father! My father! If only I could view you from the outside, see you as others see you, and not as you see yourself. I want to tell you, to let you know: We can change. You are not a robot, an unwilling and unsatisfied monarch wishing to experience life as you choose, and not as your subjects demand it. I feel you now.*

Kristoph stood furtively across the street from Hotel Sacher. He had spied on Zora through the large plate glass window, but she had not seen him. A hunger possessed him—a hunger with which he felt shame and abandon. If he were to surrender to it, he would finally be unhindered from his tethers, released to roam—to live, to die. Raised together as siblings, he knew she was not his blood sister. He wanted her. He had wanted her all his life, but especially since he had spied her swimming naked in her father's pool when they were fourteen. Thirty years later, and he still pleasured himself with the memory. If he were to have her, today had to be the day. The pain had started, and he knew the end was nigh. The aversion he felt from the neighboring, conversing construction workers pressed him away from his hiding place and across the avenue. As he walked, he rationalized, even if she saw him dawdling across the street, the message would have been sent: She has never seen him indecisive, so his intent must be uniquely directed toward her.

Jordan, the quintessential voyeur, marveled at the visage of the woman of his host's focus. The surge of awe triggered sensations in his own body, reminding him he existed elsewhere. *Zora! What a beautiful woman! A paragon among Venuses, how can flesh have such impact? My mother, before I was born. I have abandoned all skepticism, believing I experience what I sense. Yet, how am I to contain myself if I occupy the body of my co-progenitor? Witnessing myself conceived— participating in my own conception—I'm not prepared.*

Kristoph's heart fluttered—a teenager reluctantly phoning the girl he had only heretofore fancied from afar, already having hung up four times, trying once more, mustering the courage to go through with the interaction. "Two hundred Schilling for a tiny piece of chocolate cake and a small cup of coffee carries a vulgarity greater than the vulgarity from which you seek to escape by engaging in the purchase and consumption. There's no escaping the tawdry condition you despise as life—which, ironically, makes you an object of gross humor," Kristoph commented, standing out of sight at the back of Zora's high-backed chair. She seemed different—receptive, kind, even passionate. Her eyes were hungry, yet sad.

"Kristoph, you need not have shivered across the street in the cold. And that group of off-duty laborers standing in your vicinity must have added to your misery," Zora replied, sipping her espresso and replacing the cup precisely into the saucer.

Jordan, the eavesdropper—the Pauli Principle violator—phased in and out of complete integration with Kristoph. He realized he relinquished his self-consciousness through abandon, thus losing awareness that he was a hitchhiker. The preceding surrender to François' experience was novel. Complete assimilation came effortlessly, and it provided a safe haven from the overwhelming feeling of dissociation. But a stark reality evolved from this situation—one confronting—and confounding—the boundary of reality: He would witness his own conception; he would not only witness it, he would engage in the full sensorial encounter. A humorous thought reminded him that he had not lost touch with his own exclusive autonomy: *What Oedipal conundrums will arise from what I am about to behold?*

Within this infinitesimal moment, he was reminded that an instant or a millennium is composed of the same fiber, and that substance is void of measurement domain: weight, dimension, wavelength, not even quantum consistency. A barrage of conflicting emotions battered him suddenly. Sexually aroused, he did not know whether he felt his father's arousal or his own. It felt like his own, but differentiating between self and other was tenuous. Indeed, if it were his own, then he lusted for his mother. And as he pondered this apostasy of values, the concomitant shame was countermanded with a typhoon of lascivious passion. *Is this passion my father or me? I want this woman more than any woman I've ever desired. I can feel him; he is unaware of me. Does he interpret my passion as his own, is his mine, or have we melded to create a resonant passion? He hides his lust for her with repartee and references to their childhood. He's the most powerful man on earth. Simply tell her he wants her—he wants her now. What childish game playing is this?* He noticed Zora stiffen, apparently aware of the burdensome triviality barring an otherwise lustful episode.

"I understand your message and motives during the video conference last week, and, if I know you and myself correctly, we have both arrived at identical conclusions. I've booked a suite in which I have already spent a night. It's quite comfortable," she blurted, changing the subject promptly.

His father's reluctance and procrastination irritated him. Like a viewer of pornography, he wanted the actors to cut the obligatory small talk and get to the core theme of the film. Yet, this impatience was one more reminder that this altered state—this journey through his own genetic ancestral memory—maintained all the trappings of reality.

He heard his father's bitterness, distraught about his scheduled death, his lifelong execution sentence. Yet, his words indicated a misunderstanding of his demise. He stated he believed he would be put to death on humanistic or moral grounds—that he had become too powerful and that the only solution to the ending of such a reign was indelible termination.

Confused, Jordan silenced his thoughts, endeavoring to glean what he could from the conversation between his Zora and Kristoph. He observed her listening, even challenging his father's perception of his situation, but she did not offer an alternative viewpoint—and certainly no elucidation. Jordan knew his mother, having spent a lifetime with her, negotiating with her, watching her social interactions, and how she dealt with subordinates and her inimitable goal-directed execution of tasks. He knew her as iron-clad, pathologically lacking empathy. Yet, here she was, conversing with Kristoph with more amity than he knew her capable of. She could not have changed so thoroughly within these subsequent four decades during which he knew her as "mother". He concentrated on Zora, attempting to exclude thoughts and conversation not related to her.

He heard her voice as if she whispered, yet she had maintained her conversation with Kristoph. She spoke but not in the intercourse with Kristoph. *If he knew his demise were a genetic malady and not due to his status, he would not concede his life. So many times I've wanted to tell him I love him. I've spent countless hours in laboratories attempting to isolate and reverse the effects of his Canaanite gene—the God who shines so brightly, only to be extinguished by his own luminance. It's so ironic—I discovered HIV in my quest to cure it—I created the disease his ancestors strove for—the affliction striking weakness, sickness, and death toward those who procreate.*

Silently aghast, he perceived the faltering whisper surreal—a note served up by the wind in the trees, a dissonant melody composed by ambiance—its common denominator was Zora's voice. She had spoken to him, unaware. He heard her like he had heard his father—blood's essence speaking to him through time.

His heart pounded as he stepped into the hotel elevator. Zora's perfume enlivened him. Abandoning his inhibitions, he stroke her hairline at the back of her neck. The taste of her mouth, the sensation of her undulating tongue, catapulted him to rapture, unable to disengage as they reached their floor, the sliding door opening automatically.

Unlike Zora to tote such a large handbag, Kristoph stepped into the hallway, watching her nonchalantly gather her purse while an elderly couple tarried disapprovingly in front of the elevator door. He cringed at the impending interaction, hoping it would not ruin the moment. He knew she did not appreciate strangers casting judgmental aspersions in her direction, especially if the source were elderly or those apparently cast into a rigid belief system. Though poised to pounce on the detractors, she blocked their entry instead, stared at them in mutual silence, then stepped aside just far enough to force them to skirt by her.

"The room is at the end of the hall, to the left," she said cheerily, approaching him with improved affect. Then she mumbled, "They should keep the bourgeois out of here."

Engulfed by the passion in the elevator, Jordan was disaffected by the interruption. Kristoph's ambiguity disquieted him as well, having already abandoned himself to the situation; his father's diffidence had an edge of neurosis.

Once in the room, she directed him to unzip her dress, so he could see her nude. Though she claimed she was not passionate, she evinced otherwise in the elevator. He was disappointed she did not resume her previous state of sensuousness. Instead, she seemed to take a more direct tack.

Kristoph—and Jordan—braced themselves as Zora rotated with the teasing heat of a glowing ember, her form's perfection revealed from all angles in her turn. Zora's nude figure catapulted Kristoph into a frenzy; Jordan had ceased to entertain her as his mother. His awareness became diasporic, residing in many states; he lost perspective. Aware he was participating in his own conception, he was unable to focus on any sensation without segueing to another, like a slippery tomato seed evading a fingertip. He quickly disavowed the notion he was participating—he was merely along for the ride. His view resonated through aspects, phasing from Kristoph, to Zora, to himself, to an omniscient perspective, floating in the room with the participants unaware of his presence. He concluded these varying references emanate from Kristoph. Unexpectedly, what had been kaleidoscope of sensation and image seemed hazy and dull. He realized his host had lost consciousness—the time spent with Zora was a fleeting instant, though perhaps hours had elapsed.

When François died, Jordan had experienced being yanked away from the scene, as the living genetic material through which he had observed the world had been terminated. Stuck in this sensory murk, he was confused about Kristoph's vitality. He felt sad, even bereaved, knowing his father could be dead—would be dead very shortly. But he experienced a story already enacted—he already knew the plot and climax and the ending was no surprise. *My father cannot be dead, or else I would have found myself in the time whirlwind shifting me from one ancestor to another.*

He heard Zora's voice—soft, tender—not the woman he knew as his mother.

"My dearest Kristoph. I've loved you since I was born; I was created to love you. You were raised to do what you do; I was raised to do what I was taught to do from early on—to save you. My father, Gershon, loved your father. He loved him so much, he charged his only daughter with the task of discovering a cure for your genetic affliction—without robbing you of the powers embellishing you." *She's crying. I hear her crying.* "I failed. I was close, but I failed," she murmured, heaving silently. "I know you are already feeling the pain. I was the natural choice to carry out your release." She paused as he felt her fingers caress his nape. "From our time together today—I have enough of your sperm to impregnate myself if I am not already pregnant from our sexual intercourse. I will not fail our son. I will name the boy child for where your ancestors began—where free will ceased and destiny began—Jordan. I will cure him!"

He winced at the pinch on his carotid artery.

"Good-bye, Kristoph," she murmured.

213

Chapter 18

Business as Usual

His first sensation was warmth—it inundated his arm as if treated by a hot pack and gentle massage. The flashing vortex, which he had assumed sensorially symbolized time passage, had vanished. *Perhaps I'm in another location. Perhaps I can see the future as well.*

Fighting back turmoil, his perception was disheveled as if awakening from a sedative-induced long sleep. Other than his arm radiating, he felt only the pressure from being seated. He was unsure whether his eyes were open, and given the experiences from his tour through his ancestral past, he was uncertain about where he was, or even if he was awake. He did not like being unaware of his body parts or doubting the veracity of his sensory perception. He squeezed his eyes tightly—the pressure on his eyelids verified they were closed. Then he opened them slowly, his sight met by the unsaturated colors of a dimly lit room. Variation of pressure on his arm—Hyperia's grip pressed and released. Woozy, he recognized Hyperia's room in the Clarity Center.

"Welcome back, my dear Jordan," she whispered melodically.

Uneasy about this new set of circumstances, his coping responses had not equipped him to manage the barrage of stupefaction, wonder and epiphany he had just encountered. He hovered between action and inaction, unable to react, yet feeling his legs, jaw and arms poised to spring. He did not care for dreaming, as he had no control over the outcome—not of the dream itself but over the emotional sapor remaining from experiencing the dream. Bemused by what he had seen, he was sure he had not been dreaming. The reality of Hyperia's voice confirmed his conclusion, yet impaled him with the knowledge that she was his sister; she had just emerged from an altered state of awareness. As more of the surrounding ambiance reminded him of his current life in 2023, he accepted having made a safe landing from his genealogical expedition. "I am back. You are my sister," he remarked with dreamy affect. He looked over to her and reversed the grip, holding her hand in his. "I need a few moments to digest what I just experienced. You were responsible for that ride, just now?" He inquired more gently than his usual demeanor.

"I facilitated the journey, but I did not experience the outcome. Yet, the world you saw, the people—their lives—no matter how far back—they were real, or at least as real as they were at the time they lived," she answered with matched tranquility.

Dazed, he needed to establish a frame of reference—a footing based on what he thought he had experienced. "And you are aware of where I went? Of what I saw—in general?" he added.

"Yes. You went to your—to our—beginning. We were the chroniclers and soothsayers of Canaan," she explained. "By some breach of mutation, a very small fraction of the priestly court became highly specialized. We were protected and our abilities were cultivated eugenically. The boys were highly sensitized to social and natural trends; the girls were gifted with an ability to use bloodline as a medium of awareness. We have been protected and nurtured for millennia. But—"

His emotions—always restrained—surged within him; the mother he wanted; the siblings about which he fantasized as a child— they were real. He pulled her to him, hugging her as if finding a long-lost child. Yet, a black spot—an indefinable, unidentifiable barrier— kept him from full appreciation of the moment.

Am I a puppet, like the men before me—so powerful, yet succumbed to their destinies like dominoes in a chain? A champion of sensory experience, am I to disavow that which I witnessed? My mother euthanized my father. Zora never told me of my sister, yet she lured me to her, allowing me to depart the premises with Hyperia—and allowing me to believe I had saved Hyperia from Zora's own mind-destroying

215

experiments. I suspected she let me depart with her too easily—without a major row. This, too, could be merely a ploy. How am I to believe that which I experience? At what point does paranoia end, and gullibility begin? What is the reliable middle ground? I'm no fool, yet she has manipulated me—played me like a common hustler. Nevertheless, she has led me to a joyous epiphany, giving me insight into my ancestors, my father and grandfather, my sister, and a heretofore unseen side of herself. The journey has been real—not an illusion.

With racking ambivalence, he struggled to trust the wakefulness to which he had surrendered in his altered state. "I named you Hyperia during the drive here, to this hospital—I suppose the name conjured the image of rising above it all. What is your real name?" Jordan asked, still feeling extended compassion for this woman—his sister. He watched her ponder his question.

"My name—is Hyperia, as you named me. My own memories are slow to return and my name—of no important consequence—escapes me. I seem to be void of a sense of self. And my awareness of self is only through contact with you," she replied softly, genuinely, deliberately.

Poised between confusion and impatience, he realized he could advance his interrogation only without pressure. "I'll be honest with you. I don't trust this situation. I feel as if I've been propelled into a plot written by Zora. And since you are an integral part of the story line, as much as I want to, I don't know whether to trust you or not. The mind trip I just experienced certainly was impressive—too profound to not be real, I must say." He paused to assess her reaction. She touched his hand as he talked. "Where have you been all my life? Why hasn't Zora told me I have a sister?" She clasped her hand around his wrist.

"I haven't been all your life," she responded straight-faced.

Her response slapped him awake. Awash with resolve, he envisaged the entire schematic—Zora, Hyperia, his father, the Cult and himself. "Hyperia, I'm going to leave now, but I'll return for you soon—within the next couple days. I'll call you—" She flashed a puzzled look. He extracted his phone and showed it to her. "I'll use this device, and you can hear me from a distance as if I'm in the room with you. Dr. Throckmorton—the man who has been caring for you— will remain at your service. You evidently made quite an impression, as he's the one who summoned me here—with some urgency, I might add. He will continue to care for you. Whatever you need, you let him know. When I call you, he'll bring my voice to you." She smiled, nodding her head in understanding. Part of her memory is intact; part is not. *She doesn't know what a phone is, but she knows me. It's not amnesia, so how can her memory be selective?*

Jordan passed Throckmorton as he breezed through the door, resolute and purposeful. Throckmorton picked up his pace, shadowing him through the hallway to the hospital exit. "You were right to summon me," Jordan stated in the tempo of his retreat. " I'll return soon. Make sure she has any comfort she desires—except do not let her leave the premises." He stopped in the lobby to address Throckmorton more directly. "I told her I'd call. Evidently, she remembers only certain things—a phone not among them—so when I call, you'll have to take her the phone, and maybe, show her how to use it." Throckmorton seemed to ignore him, possessed by a more pressing agenda.

"Jordon, there's something you should know. As part of a thorough screening and assessment procedure, we ran a gene study." He paused, holding Jordan from moving away from him. "Her cells are perfect—unworn and new—like a newborn."

"I'm not surprised," Jordan countered without rebuff. "Your assessment fits my suspicion. I've got to go. Call you soon!"

217

As he sped away from the Clarity Center, his onboard AI spoke just as he prepared to make a request. "Dr. Éclair. You have a meeting with Dr. Chamberlain at the UCI Medical School in one hour. You are currently forty-five minutes away. Shall I call to cancel, postpone or map the most efficient route for you?"

These recent revelations had distracted him so, he had forgotten about issues for which he had prepared for years. Stymied from his recent objective, he resigned to meet his business obligation. "No calls. I'll keep the meeting. Please route me. It's 4 PM," he said, glancing at the clock. "Let's stick to these mountain roads to avoid traffic. In the meantime—find Zora—but do not contact her. That facility we discovered in the Santa Monica Mountains—I want a closer view. Use whatever non-public satellite imagery you can acquire."

He drove south on Jamboree, making haste toward UCI's NeuroNetworks Center, where Chamberlain's office and laboratory were located. Normally, he relished the quiet commute to meetings, according him time to ponder contingencies and thinking over the upcoming event. He did not try to second-guess or control the future but rather consider the chess game before him, anticipating the possible moves. He grinned inwardly, knowing this melding of Chamberlain's research with his own technology marked what he had described once to Rebecca as an "unholy union." He reminisced about how far he had advanced with the science of neural access, bringing him to his upcoming meeting.

Requiring focus and a clear mind, he freed his thoughts of Hyperia and Zora, instead recounting a history of his company. Brain-Link Corporation had ushered in a variety of the most innovative control systems and peripherals, now used in computing, medical, and behavioral sciences. Twelve years ago, the Department of Defense had given his company exclusive contracts, designing and building piloting systems for fighter aircraft and drones. Hands-on guidance and on-board piloted aircraft had become obsolete—systems were controlled exclusively by the pilot's mind while he sat in sensorially-controlled, stationary cockpit in an undisclosed ground location. The jet responded instantly to the most subtle nuance of mind control without the encumbrance of hand-eye coordination or muscle activity—manned, yet unmanned.

Working diligently, he never gloated over his accomplishments. He had advanced the theories and research catapulting his company to the financial glory it had attained. And though systems and machine control, maintained strictly by mind, was still a foreign—if not foreboding—concept to many; he had undercut a growing tide of religious and ethical resistance by developing a consumer gaming market, much to the disgruntlement of the defense department who wanted him to harbor his proprietary patents and products strictly for defense and warfare.

He relished the total immersion his Brain-Link apparatus gave him—more than he enjoyed any other activity. The use of his consumer entertainment and gaming peripherals avalanched internationally, boasting over seven hundred million users playing his massive multiplayer role playing game worldwide, with some one hundred million players online at any given time. He played anonymously when he played the game as well as masterfully as he had invented the hardware. Playing was the ultimate escape, assuming a role completely out of reality and life. He assumed the role of a female refugee from Atlantis with limited powers of time travel. Wearing the Brain-Link apparatus connected to an Internet-linked computer running his software, he was that character, completely absorbed in all five senses, immersed in the digital environment. The technology motto: One's reality is what one's brain makes it to be. He believed this adage to be true, with or without including the technology.

He had written several academic, peer-reviewed treatises on the subject of nonintrusive neuronal intervention of sensory-motor experiences, which he referred to as technologically simulated hallucinations. But he had maintained that organic memory—brain engrams—could not be treated as standard read/write binary digits. Social technology ethicists abhorred the possibility of brain programming—and reprogramming—and Jordan's articles attempted to assuage their angst, endorsing that the feared neural reprogramming was not achievable. Without guilt, he had proselytized this position, knowing fully well that he deceptively advanced a faulty viewpoint. He rejoiced in the fact that the military had tried and failed on countless occasions. He gave them just enough so that they would fund his company and his efforts.

Daydreaming and reminiscing en route to Chamberlain's lab, he had lost track of time. He mused that perhaps the genealogical time expedition he had experienced with Hyperia today had primed him for these dissociative experiences. When he arrived at the research facility, one of Chamberlain's lab technicians was waiting to escort him. As he approached the door, he prepared himself for Chamberlain's distinctive palaver.

"Dr. Éclair, I—" Chamberlain announced as he sprung from his chair with sycophantic enthusiasm. Jordan cut him off, gracefully, but with assuredness.

"Please, call me Jordan. We're going to be working together pretty closely in the near future, and the 'doctor this, doctor that' accolade takes its toll. We both have PhDs," he commented curtly. "Please, sit down. We have much to discuss. You've verified your bank account?"

"Jordan—indeed I have. Quite satisfactory," Chamberlain replied with the satiation of a man finishing a Thanksgiving feast.

Nevertheless, he sat back, noticeably anticipatory, if not nervous, about this encounter.

To Jordan, Chamberlain represented corruption in academia, and the entire "publish-or-perish" mentality within the respected institutions of higher learning. Yet, he was not sure whether he did not like the man's character, or whether it was simply the man's role within his ungainly position he found distasteful. Whatever bothered him about Chamberlain, he knew he did not trust him. He pulled his phone from his coat inner pocket and voiced, "Scan area." After three seconds, the screen glowed red. A white arrow pointed toward Chamberlain.

"You've a live recording device on you. Give it to me—now," Jordan demanded firmly. He noted Chamberlain exhale in dejection, knowing he would not put up any resistance. Without comment, Chamberlain handed him a small digital recorder from his shirt pocket.

Jordan realized this man had to cower emotionally and intellectually in order to trust him. "Recording what we're going to discuss would not be good for you or me—but worse for you," Jordan remarked intently. "We're going to work together, amiably— amicably—but you should fear me. Don't try anything like that again. The consequences will be most severe. Do I make myself clear?" Chamberlain, red-faced from being caught, nodded nervously and swallowed.

"Our technology has mastered memory access. I learned long ago in my own research that thought is, simply put, compilations of processed hierarchical memories. One does not think thoughts that are not already stored in memory. Oh, yes, one would ask, 'Well, what about imagination and creativity?' To which I would respond, these processes are novel, but only novel because of the permutations and combinations of the existing thoughts from which they are derived. Change memory—change thought; change thought—change feeling;

221

change feeling—change action. We can detect thought; we can implant new information; we cannot supplant memory. Hence, we cannot—through our technology—coerce an individual to engage in an action against his will." He assessed Chamberlain, who had dropped his obsequious demeanor and listened attentively, but readied himself to insert a comment.

"Your Brain-Link games, the entertainment systems, your other consumer markets—I suppose even your military applications—require the user to don the head gear?" Chamberlain queried in a reserved manner—prepared to hear an opposing response.

Jordan recognized he was dealing with a keen and shrewd man, understanding his new business partner suspected other than what he had asked. "I think you already know the answer to that—which is yes and no. Yes—the consumer market and the defense department applications must wear head devices well within proximity of the brain, but without any electrode contact. No—our cutting-edge technology does not require proximity. In fact, we could infiltrate someone's brain from a room-mounted controller, from a remote station, even from a satellite." He paused, waiting for Chamberlain to respond, but he remained in a thoughtful daze. "But, you suspected that all along, didn't you?"

"I did, yes. Why else would you need me? You have everything except that which my research with the primate brain can provide. But armed with what I have, given the right organization, you could control the world," Chamberlain replied with near-religious ferocity.

"I don't want to control the world—only certain individuals in the world. And them, not very long at all," Jordan responded.

"Please, elucidate me," Chamberlain responded with sincerity. "Jordan. You and I—I think we understand one another. I've had it with this game, fending off one ego-maniac after another, bulldozing cohorts and adversaries alike with my own home-grown megalomania. I'm good at it. Perhaps I should have been a politician, but I over-educated myself. What—" he stopped emphatically, then continued. "What exactly are you doing? Can you be precise. I'm with you. For the money, and the opportunity to reinvent myself just this once—I'm with you. You've trusted me thus far. Trust me further if you can."

Chamberlain's shift from reluctant consultant to familiar consort caught Jordan off guard. The change was so radical and sudden, he was tempted to trust him. Given the situation, he pondered, he had nothing to lose. What would Chamberlain have to gain by deceiving me. Even if he were to go to the top guys in Homeland Security, NSA, the FBI, or the CIA, it would not matter. I know many of them, and he would incriminate and discredit himself. Still, discretion won over candor. "I'll disclose more as we proceed with the project. What I can tell you right now—you've already deduced the obvious—I need not only remote brain access capability, but also I need to be able to erase and rewrite. And these links will be mediated from various sites, including satellites, cell relay station towers, and direct application—I'll explain later."

"May I ask—where?" Chamberlain inquired, unfazed by Jordan's response.

Jordan had never fully learned to fully quell his temper, though he moderated it by subduing the rage responses which arose occasionally within him. Chamberlain unknowingly stimulated such impulses—like the other night at his home. Pressing Jordan after he had already established the rules challenged his authority—his reasoning. *What's he trying to communicate? He's smarter than me? He has more facts at his disposal? He's an arrogant bug. If it hadn't been for smarter people than him, working under his presumed tutelage, he would have been just another fat bureaucrat.* "I must access the memories of two hundred thirty-four individuals around the world. I

223

must change each memory—each person's intents—without his knowledge or awareness. And each person must operate in a clandestine manner. Those with whom the person works must not be aware of any change. If anybody becomes aware, the person must kill the other party instantly. That's all I'm willing to disclose right now. Do not ask me more. I'll tell you more when I decide it's time." He noticed Chamberlain shuddered, then recovered as if he had just sucked on a lemon.

"I'm ready when you are," Chamberlain said with an upbeat flair. "May I ask, what is the timeframe? The completion date?"

"Two years from today—tops. We may push the deadline." Jordan responded, brusque enough to signal he was willing to answer that, but no more questions regarding purpose. Chamberlain's demeanor phased to officious, and he stood.

"Then, we have no time to waste. Shall we begin? I've prepared a demonstration for you—if you would kindly accompany me to the lab," Chamberlain offered, rising from his over-stuffed office armchair.

Jordan followed Chamberlain, watching his bulbous frame lumber through the corridor. The incongruity of Chamberlain's body against the clean, crisp, defined lines of the interior architecture abraded his sense of athletics. He disliked every morsel of him—his movements, shape, voice, expressions, even his smell. He hastened his pace to be at his side, avoiding the rear view.

After walking through labyrinthine hallways, Jordan and Chamberlain paused in a wide hallway, peering through a continuous set of windows running the length of the adjoining room. Jordan deduced they had paused close to their destination. His own company's research and development facilities had similar labs—pristine, brightly lit, white, breathlessly clean at a single glance. Knowing these were Chamberlain's animal research labs, these levels of cleanliness were excessive. Jordan's facilities required high levels of particle filtrations, where researchers developed microcircuits. Even a one micron particle could deter the accurate functioning of the molecule-size circuit pathways. Chamberlain, he thought, should be using real-world test scenarios for applications which must be readily externalized, and the effects of contamination did not pose unpredictable confounds.

"The look on your face tells me you're worried about controlled situations. Don't jump to conclusions until you have the facts, Jordan," Chamberlain remarked, eyeing him sternly.

Prone to worry on hair-trigger stimulation, he knew Chamberlain was right. He was embarrassed he had appeared so obvious in his concern at all. "You're right. You read me well. Please, proceed. Don't let my preconceived notions get in the way of my enlightenment," Jordan responded apologetically. Chamberlain's attention shifted toward the goings-on inside, on the other side of the window.

"Your initial impression of this facility was correct. It is absolutely clean; absolutely controlled. This lab is dedicated to testing the efficacy of memory re-write in primates—the entire spectrum of memory. Starting from down there," he gestured toward the far left end of the elongated room, "we test object recognition, place and spatial memory, sequential memory. We also assess various levels of explicit and implicit memory storage, recall, and memory consolidation."

Impressed by the diligence and industriousness of the staff, Jordan surmised Chamberlain's researchers must enjoy their work. "There appears to be a wide mixture of talents, specialties, and skills in there," Jordan remarked, hoping to hear an elaboration. Chamberlain posed a smug grin.

"Indeed. We employ biopsychologists, neurologists, neuroengineers, and neurophysicists—even integrated circuit designers—and our newest specialty, carbon-based organic circuitry.

225

Our university is one of few in the world boasting a doctoral degree in neurophysics and neuroelectronics." He paused, slapping Jordan gently on the shoulder. "I think your company recruits from us every year."

Ignoring the camaraderie Chamberlain had tried to instill, he had become impatient to view some results. "You had mentioned demonstrations," Jordan commented, trying to not sound pushy. Chamberlain's demeanor shifted to austere.

"Let's go into this ante room to suit up," Chamberlain replied, directing Jordan to the locked double doors behind them. "It's a dressing room leading to the airlock for the main lab."

After donning the clean room bunny suits and entering the lab, Chamberlain ushered Jordan into an opened ante room, which he had noticed outside, but about which he had not inquired. The equipment had perked his curiosity since he saw some of his company's own devices partly concealed across the room.

"Chimpanzees are quite clever, Dr. Éclair. They respond well to all of our memory protocols. Some of the other primates are suited for specific research, like object recognition or place memory tests. But with chimps, we can teach sequential tasks, and even some elementary language skills. Indeed, we've isolated the neuron locations for both the storage and processing of verbal as well as sign language. We've modified some of your gaming hardware, so the chimp is immersed in certain environments, given select challenges and scenarios. A few of our subjects—this one for example—comes to us straight from Africa. Since we did not want to derange him—or otherwise taint the generalizability of our research findings—we brought over his entire community." Chamberlain glanced at Jordan for a reaction, as he knew Jordan would know this procedure as highly irregular and illegal, but it satisfied both the quantitative and qualitative purity of the research.

"Using your modified hardware—and software—we immerse this fellow in his natural habitat through a unique integration of multiple sets of scanning masers—one set simply vigilantly maintains a neural reference point. The reference point is not physiological, but centers on alternating shifts of the cerebral processing centers. We have overcome what has befuddled others. The brain shifts processing centers. It is not a physical, geometric center about which the brain functions—it is, in fact, a processing center, which shifts and meanders based upon the organism's level of activity, parallel processing capability and directiveness. Humans, we have found, have highly changeable and malleable centers. Chimps run a close second."

Jordan was gratified hearing Chamberlain's descriptions. He was well aware of the processes Chamberlain had described, but, since his company had the focus of the military, public, and press, he could not openly conduct experiments using chimpanzees, let alone humans. Their secretive research had rendered volumes of findings, but these results did not lend themselves to profit-oriented endeavors. "Your talents are truly a gift to behold," Jordan remarked with obvious cryptic obsequiousness. "You're impressing me—it appears I've selected the right business partner." Chamberlain had been distracted, directing two assistants to complete the demonstration setup.

"As I was saying, we immerse this fellow in his jungle habitat. We view an animation of what he sees here." Chamberlain pointed to a monitor. "We hear what he hears; his other sensory experiences we monitor here." Chamberlain waved at a console marked off in sections: Olfactory, Gustatory, Somatosensory, Vestibular. Jordan noticed each section contained unique displays, labeling appropriate factors for each sensory domain. "His motor processes are rendered paralyzed as if he were in a dream state. Essentially, he is dreaming, yet he is quite awake and conscious. He runs, but his legs remain quiescent; he lunges, but his body is still. Whatever he has learned in his environment from natural development, we can un-teach it, if you will, and implant new learning—new memories—with absolutely no detriment to any neural structures or function." Again distracted, his assistant signaled that they were ready. "I should add, the detriment could come from the behaviors associated with the altered paradigms. For example, we could alter his taste for certain foods. Left unchecked, he would starve to death. We could even alter his taste for females, replacing his sex drive for same-sex partners. Given that scenario, his place in his society would change radically, also affecting his survivability." Chamberlain returned to the control console, displaying the sensory readouts. He seemed particularly proud of the monitor designated for monitoring what the chimpanzee saw.

Jordan suppressed his curiosity about this panel. A master of focusing his mental energies, he had become slowly overburdened attending to Chamberlain's pomp didactic with background ruminations of Hyperia, Zora, and the genealogical history he had not yet fully digested. "You mentioned this display of visual experience was an animation. Please explain," Jordan asked with thoughtful enthusiasm. Already agitated, Chamberlain ignited with childish gusto.

"This display, Jordan, is the meeting between sensory experience and computer animation. You see, we cannot fully distinguish the true colors the chimp experiences; perception of shapes, angles, and relative sizes are, as you are aware, largely molded by cultural experience. The computer fills in the blanks, so to speak. It interprets colors, shape, perspective for us. Furthermore, it allows us multiple perspectives—omniscient viewpoints, one might say. We can zoom out and observe the subject as if he were observing himself."

This same feature was slated to be released in the next expansion of his massively multiplayer role playing game hardware and software, but since Chamberlain was unaware of his company's internal developments, he hoped he would not assume he had stolen it from him. While Chamberlain appeared enamored by his own research hardware, Jordan noticed the assistants preparing the chimpanzee demonstration seemed concerned. "Your people appear to be ready to get the show on the road," Jordan remarked, pulling Chamberlain by the sleeve of his bunny suit. Chamberlain startled as if he had forgotten the reason they were there. He nodded, signaling to proceed.

Jordan observed as two more assistants emerged from another room, leading a chimpanzee, each holding its hand as they walked in tandem toward a small round room constructed of what appeared to be clear plexiglas. *If it's straight from the wild, it seems very tame and docile. He's domesticated it with his equipment, no doubt.* The chimp hugged each technician with affection, then walked into the chamber-like room voluntarily, and they shut the door.

Familiar sounds aroused him—coils charging the maser generators for the neuron electrodes. The displays came alive—he saw a cartoon version of himself in the visual monitor. He looked back to the chamber, and the chimp was starring directly at him.

"I have to admit, Dr. Éclair, this fellow is used to this process. He was the outcast of the group, attacked frequently by the more aggressive males. Basically, we removed the 'wild' from him, though all the parameters making up what we consider 'wild,' we've stored, and we could replace. Nevertheless, the staff have taken a liking to him, so we haven't returned him to his original state. Needless to say, we can't keep him with his chimp community any longer."

Jordan suppressed more disquiet. Chamberlain's experiments with Jordan's hardware had led Chamberlain to results and demonstrations identical to his own. Yet, Jordan did not intend for these discoveries to be released upon the consuming public—or even upon the governments—for many years. He was concerned that this research was under the auspices of university research from private and public grants. With instantaneous insight, he perceived what Chamberlain had developed: The cure to mental illness—and exactly the tools required to complete his life's task—that which was furthered

229

by his father, and his father's father, and by all the predecessors to whose lives he had just been made privy. *These men did not work toward cures, or betterment, or enrichment of the human condition. What they engendered, what they plundered from men and soil, was stagnation. God did not create man—my predecessors created man. And they did it in an image necessary to accomplish that for which I am the end pin, the piece that makes the stack complete. But what I saw today—was it genetic revenge, or a culminated wisdom which over the centuries has become the stalwart vision of the future? I'll complete my life's goals, my family's goals, my chromosomal essence—but for what purpose do I then die?*

"Within the room is a stash of bananas under a panel. The subject retrieves bananas from this location with the ease you or I might brush teeth. To retrieve the bananas, he simply presses the series of buttons you see spaced along the walls. He has to press them in an ordered sequence, and the duration from one button to the next is timed specifically, so he cannot be too late or too early. The procedure takes five minutes—it's more complicated than operating a combination lock, for sure. Nevertheless, he learned this procedure very early—and I might say, very quickly. The assistant will talk to him, reminding him to go get his lunch from the repository." Chamberlain gestured to the assistant to proceed.

Jordan mused, as the technician referred to the chimp as "Winchell," telling him that it's lunch time. Winchell seemed to start the process without prompting, which pleased Jordan since he wanted to see some autonomy. Chamberlain, whose habit was to pull on Jordan's elbow to get his attention, tugged once more.

"Your gaming equipment centers brain location by maintaining a physical location—a marker on the user's headgear. As I mentioned, we center by constantly updating brain processes. We monitor these processes remotely through the unique brainwave patterns of the subject. We've discovered harmonics in brainwave patterns more unique than fingerprints—as unique as DNA. Remote distance remains a challenge, but I'm sure, based upon your needs, you'll figure it out in due time." Chamberlain paused for his assumed sly remark to have an effect. "The chimpanzee—named Winchell by a few of the staff—is unencumbered by any monitoring apparatus, as you have noticed. Here, on these monitors, you see how his brain activity shifts as he proceeds from place to place. He must count, wait, and remember the position of each button in the room. Both sequential and place neural centers are taxed in these analytical and memory processes. Now, we will completely alter the sequence and timing of the buttons, so he will fail at the task. He'll try again and fail. Then we will erase his memory, write the new procedure—to which he has never been exposed—and then observe him successfully executing the new programming."

Inwardly appalled at Chamberlain's success, he shuttered at all the human subjects whose memories Zora had destroyed trying to achieve these same results—which brought him back to Hyperia. *All staged for my benefit.* Chamberlain—sensitive to Jordan's expressions and temperament—noticed that his attention had drifted.

"Dr. Éclair, is something wrong?" Chamberlain asked with the hypervigilance of an eighth grade boy on his first date.

Impressed as he was, he vowed to himself not to display it. "Nothing. Everything is right so far. I'm curious how you're going to carry this off, transferring this technology to me, while rusing the university and your grantors simultaneously. You need to handle that. I don't want your business entanglements to get in my way." He hesitated, smiled, then tugged even harder on Chamberlain's elbow. "Please complete this portion of your demonstration; I believe everything you explained. You seemed to have a grand finale planned, at least from how I read you. Please, get on with it." Chamberlain cut a sly grin, as if caught in a mischievous act and twirled his finger around in the air for the assistants to speed it up.

Jordan returned his gaze toward the chamber, observing the research team conduct the experiment precisely as Chamberlain had described. Winchell's new memory of the procedure was implanted painlessly and effortlessly within less than a second—receiving his the new instructions in mid-stride—and carried out the newly implanted program. In five minutes, he was munching on the feast of bananas and other appealing fruits hidden under the spring-loaded floor door, hatching it with the transferred deciphering code as well as if he had studied it for a month. Jordan could not fully suppress his awe, and he knew Chamberlain saw it.

"Dr. Éclair. All this equipment is of your design. We've made modifications here and there, but the basic process is yours. As I'm sure you're aware, the devil is in the details, and that's what we're good at—details. There is another modification you're not aware of. It's not an electronic or mechanical alteration; it's a physiological one. We've surgically modified Winchell, our research chimp. And not his brain." Chamberlain remained coy, seducing and whetting Jordan's curiosity.

Jordan disliked Chamberlain, and when he made his pronouncements during the demonstration, he reminded Jordan of a ring leader of a three-ring circus. He remained constantly irked in Chamberlain's presence, his irritation ebbing up and down depending upon whether his willingly coerced business partner was talking. "Chamberlain, you're a smart man. You should realize—I would not have transferred millions to you—I would not have talked to you—had I not already been assured that what you are now so superciliously expounding, were not already a reality." Unbattered by Jordan's remark, Chamberlain grinning even more placation.

"This you're not expecting," he retorted self-confidently while gesturing another signal to his research team. "Indeed, you may not even need this feature for you whatever it is you're doing, but we've taken your work to the logical extreme."

The equipment resonated a marked vibration, denoting to Jordan the implementation of a longer and more radical procedure. The clamor in the walls behind him confirmed what he had suspected—the power supplies for the maser electrode matrices were housed behind thick concrete slabs. He moved as close as he could to the chamber, having noticed that Winchell had lost all interest in his culinary heist; he had come to a complete stand still. Jordan peered at the chimpanzee's face, fighting the illusion that the animal's eyes segued from blank to sagacious. Chamberlain remained silent, but fixed on Jordan's reactions.

"Pick a number between one and ten, please, Dr. Éclair," Chamberlain asked him upon receiving a head nod from his main assistant while balancing a stack of books.

Engrossed in figuring out what had occurred with the chimp, he recognized the process had not gone as sourly as Zora's experiments with people. "Four," he replied absent-mindedly.

The lab assistant—acknowledging Chamberlain's four upheld fingers—counted from the bottom of the stack to the fourth book, extracted it from the pile, and said, "Moby Dick," then she went inside the chamber and handed the book to Winchell the chimp. Chamberlain's attention remained transfixed to Jordan; Jordan was acutely transfixed on Winchell. He watched him fumble with the book in an ape-like fashion, inwardly disappointed by his initial conclusion. *What was I suspecting? For the chimp to turn to page one and start reciting verses? Yet, if he's developed what I think he's developed, no wonder he wants the collaboration with me. If he hands this technology over to the government, he'd lose it. Still, he's blinded by the catalyst the partnership with me could provide—I'm a terrorist, plain and simple. My clan has wreaked the terror of ages. We've engraved the*

trenches through which history has flowed, all tributaries toward this
river—my river. But if I am the final piece of this elaborate scheme of
historical determinism, what happens next? Nothing. How well
conceived—planned without me. I die off; no one is here to replace me;
the Cult is dead; we've accomplished the retribution we set out to
incur. And as I look at the world, the conflicts, the extravagances of
corporate economies, the deliberate aversion to alternate energy
source, I realize, we've created a world that must be destroyed. We
masterminded not only checkmate for destruction, but also the
rationale for apology. Fine, but I refuse to die with the Cult.
Chamberlain has the answers—he simply is unaware of the questions.

"Dr. Éclair, sir, if I may intrude upon your thoughts,"
Chamberlain commented with less presumptuousness than usual. "My
father was a salesman. He had a saying for exemplary sales talent. He
said an outstanding salesperson could 'convince the buyer that
monkeys can talk.'"

During the period he had been distracted by Chamberlain's
comment, a foreign voice enthralled him—captivated him. He watched
as Winchell read *Moby Dick*. He read with purpose, conviction,
meaning, as he not only comprehended the words, but also that they
told of prophesy as well. The voice—not male, not female, not
computer synthesis—a voice distinct among sounds, perhaps like a
raspy violin in the hands of a virtuoso player.

"Now small fowls flew screaming over the yet yawning gulf; a
sullen white surf beat against its steep sides; then all collapsed, and the
great shroud of the sea rolled on as if it rolled five thousand years ago."
Winchell read flawlessly, with the grace and finesse of an orator.
Jordan starred at the chimpanzee, and the chimp starred back as if he
knew him—as if he recognized his inner workings, his plans, his
desires.

234

Not the beginning—rather, the end of Moby Dick. Surely, I am not Ahab.

Chapter 19

Epiphany and Evolution

Jordan's thoughts were ablaze; he teetered between nirvana and confusion. Chamberlain's demonstration of a chimpanzee reading *Moby Dick* bombarded him with flights of fantasy. Driven by the imminence of his project's fruition, the proximity of the apex of success, he pressed himself to leave or be consumed by the marvels of the research. Still bombarding him was the question: *Could the chimp comprehend what it read?* Nevertheless, the demonstration had gone far beyond Jordan's expectations. Within the magnitude of Chamberlain's efforts, Jordan's requirements were met and exceeded. He understood, with an inner gloat, that he himself was Chamberlain's only route—his only course of action—if Chamberlain were to profit from his genius and scientific exploits beyond colluding with the government in toppling other nations, and polluting rivals' economies.

He grappled with his priorities—he had pried himself from Chamberlain after the display of simian literacy. A profusion of emotional and intellectual revelations hammered him for attention. Yet, Hyperia persistently bubbled to the surface, as if she had singled him out. She had shown him the truth through the most bizarre medium.

Seldom at a loss for an answer—seldom appearing to stumble indecisively—he found himself uncomfortably at odds with what to do next. His mother, Zora, was proving to be even more of an enigma than he had heretofore experienced. *Since I was a boy, I never trusted her. How bizarre is that? A twelve-year-old boy, feeling he's got to guard himself, to watch his back to protect himself from harm from his mother? And why not? I saw what she had been capable of from an early age. She had no regard for human life and seemed to take a certain glee in human suffering. The level to which she could engage in genocide astounded me. She could push a button, or create a disease, but she could not look a man in the eye while she twisted a blade into his gullet. Too cowardly, or simply a misguided softy?* He smirked. *She takes pride in her discovery and proliferation of the HIV virus. It was the perfect gift to humanity. No one takes credit; the source was untraceable; she sits back for decades, gloating in her achievement. What a woman. And today I discover she is, in fact, a purveyor of my longevity—according to an out-of-body experience into which I was cast by this strange woman—this woman who, for all intents and purposes, is my sister. I should have a DNA check performed immediately—but I believe her. She comes first. I return to her; take her out of the hospital. But where, though? Who could I trust other than Throck? Where could I place her, so I can be assured of her comfort and safety, away from Zora? Why not trust Throck implicitly? Because, if I could buy him, then Zora could buy him. I must leave her with someone Zora cannot influence. I can only think of one—Rebecca.*

Consumed in rumination, he had absent-mindedly driven so far south on 405, he had to exit an off-ramp and drive back north. The uneasiness of indecision had waned, as he had an epiphany: He realized Rebecca and Hyperia belonged together. With resolve, he ordered his car AI to find Rebecca and get her on the line. Not accustomed to the high of ecstasy, he mistrusted his newfound elation, as he had believed both depression and glee were extremes of an emotional spectrum signaling either misguided thinking or an unconscious effort to escape reality. Alter your behavior, and the thoughts and emotions will follow, he repeated to himself. He reduced the pressure on the accelerator, slowing from ninety to seventy, then sighed in relief that he had not been stopped during his lack of vigilance. He winced suddenly, reacting to an internal body sensation bordering between a cramp and a tickle. *Extremes exacerbate the process—it's starting.*

"Dr. Éclair. Rebecca Eisner is waiting on the line," the soft voice of his AI interrupted his decline toward panic.

Feeling relieved to talk to her, did not hesitate to confirm his wishes. "Put her on, please," he commanded. "Rebecca. Please, before you say anything. Listen. I've always known this, but never felt it. I've never said it to anyone. I'm sure my father never said it; his father never said it. I know this because I know my family history very well—something that I want to explain to you in great detail. But here's what I want to say: I love you." He paused, waiting for her to respond. The moment of silence seemed elongated. His onset of dejection quickly detoured at the sound of her voice.

"Jordan, I more than love you. What I feel for you—you have no idea. And I know, you have some dark secret—something that you've held from me; something that has kept us apart. It's an invisible barrier, indefinable. But I always knew you'd eventually let me in, or at least share some of that pain with you. Yes—I know it's pain. I feel with you; I sense with you. I don't know what it is, but sometimes I know where you are, what you're doing, what you're feeling—it's like a waking dream."

Having so many events and feelings focus at an apex simultaneously pushed him upward, toward the elation he had averted earlier. He exited the El Toro Road off-ramp and stopped, uneasy about mixing his feelings with driving. *I've been trained—bred—not to feel, not to fall in love, not to be prone to these kinds of frivolous wanderings of mind. And yet, here I am, like a schoolboy having received a Valentine's card from the prettiest girl in his class. No. It's more than that. I share something deeper, more profound with Rebecca. It is that connection that I feel. I've felt it since I met her.* "Rebecca, when I told you I was the Prince of Doom, I meant it. There's so much I must explain. But, I need to remain focused. I have a sister. I just found out. She's at a certain hospital; I'll explain the circumstances later. I want to pick her up and take her to your apartment. Could she stay with you? Her name is Hyperia. She's quite unique, even gifted, as you'll probably discover." The silence did not disquiet him this time, as he realized she was shocked, assimilating all he had told her.

"Of course she can stay with me. When will you bring her?" Rebecca responded with a why-would-you-presume-otherwise tone.

His AI distracted him, reminding him that this mother was attempting to contact him, and that she was still in the Santa Monica Mountains location. "One second, Rebecca," he said as softly as he could muster, then put her on hold. "I can't talk to her now, but please let her know I want to see her today. Do not inform her that we are tracking her location. Tell her I will return the call in two hours." In the interim, he looked outside, noticing a throng of school children—he surmised, kindergarteners—in the crosswalk in front of him, all escorted by three teachers. The vision triggered another mild bout of the painful sensation taunting his body moments ago. He returned to Rebecca. "I'm on my way to the hospital now, to pick her up. I'm about thirty to forty minutes from there. Another hour to your place. Say in two hours?"

"OK. That works. I dropped by the South Coast Plaza on my way home anyway. By the way, I heard your visit with Chamberlain was a big hit," she replied with enthusiasm.

He laughed, thinking that "big hit" was an understatement. "I'll see you in two hours, then," he replied curtly and hung up. He immediately had the afterthought that he should have told her he loved her once more. But then, how many times must he say it in order for it to be true. He had said it once. Must he repeat it in order to reconfirm it, or bolster its veracity? *I'm human, yet I feel like I'm learning to be human. No, it's not humanity I'm learning. It's this culture. It's alluring, yet toxic.*

He pressed the button on his steering wheel to summon his car AI. He was determined to move Hyperia with Rebecca, then have the son-to-mother conversation he had never had. "Please call Dr. Throckmorton. Tell him I'm returning to pick up Hyperia. I'll be there in forty-five minutes or less," he barked brusquely. His self-awareness intruded on his focus, as he had decidedly become disoriented, forgetting where he had exited the freeway. He glanced at this navigation map, emitted a self-deprecating sigh, put his car into gear, and sped across the main avenue to access the northbound on-ramp.

"Dr. Throckmorton is on the line. He wants to talk to you," the simulated voice said, interrupting his silent vigil northbound.

Irritated, he was finished for the time being. He wanted to drive and reflect without the intrusion of someone else's thoughts and wishes. "Throck. I'm on five, in San Juan Capistrano. I'll be there soon. Please have Hyperia ready," he repeated with a brusqueness and impatience that had remained with him all day.

"Yes, I understand. But I have so many questions," Throckmorton interjected before Jordan could disconnect. "My experience with her—well—it's yielded far more than your typical patient-doctor relationship." He stopped, seemingly panting.

Jordan sensed desperation, a completely alien trait from his learned and highly respected colleague. *Is everyone going bat shit, or is it just me? Throck is one of the most composed men I know.* "Throck. I'll talk to you briefly when I get there. Meet me outside, but make certain Hyperia is ready to accompany me. OK?" He hung up the line before Throckmorton could respond, as he did not want to become another casualty of lost composure.

The winding canyon roads leading to The Clarity Center offered him some respite. He had asked his AI to put all calls on hold until he arrived. The uninterrupted journey facilitated a consolidation of the day's experiences. Between Hyperia's genetic time travel, Chamberlain's talking, a literate chimpanzee, Zora's more-than-usual clandestine activities, and his decision to include Rebecca into his

240

fold—he complimented himself—he had not only coped well, but also had made strides forward.

The Clarity Center's grounds gates were open—a violation of security standards—but he was far from fretting the issue now. Dr. Throckmorton was waiting for him at the entrance; he did not see Hyperia with him. He noticed the transcendental daze on Throckmorton's face had diminished, replaced by the angst of a junkie uncertain of the whereabouts of his next fix.

"Jordan. Who is she? What is she? OK, I realize I'm digressing from our usual very discreet relationship, but please—indulge me—I feel as if all my education and training as a psychiatrist has been made obsolete," Throckmorton entreated, intercepting Jordan at his car door.

Though Jordan had known Throckmorton for over ten years, he had always maintained a very topical relationship with him. The psychiatrist had helped Jordan with some human subjects problems a few years back in the midst of the development of the Brain-Link technology for consumers, and for those services Throckmorton continued to receive a hefty royalty. Jordan did not want to alienate his trusted associate, nor did he want to rectify their existing relationship. He empathized how the contact with Hyperia had affected his friend's perceptions. Indeed, Jordan was curious about just how Hyperia affected the doctor since she was neither related to him, nor was she directly related to anybody in his family or organization. He had assumed the effect generalized across specific genetic similarities, but, if she could delve into the consciousness of non-relatives with equal vivaciousness, her power of mind would be astounding. *I am my father's son. I am the servant of his cult*, he mused. *I'm thinking about how her power could be analyzed and mapped to technology. Such an ability to delve into and alter via remote brain link could even up the*

241

ante on Chamberlain's chimpanzee. He inwardly chastised himself, realizing his thoughts diverged from what he had already concluded.

The drive had helped, removing an irritable, impatient edge which had been gestating throughout the day. He saw that this man who was a stalwart of cognitive neurology and psychiatry had his world severely perturbed; he could not cope. "Throck, I'll explain what I can. If not today, sometime very soon. Hyperia is—well—very special, as I'm sure you realize. She's my sister. She has some very unusual gifts with which even I am just becoming aware. And because this is newly-found knowledge, my insight is limited as well. Because I'm going to learn far more very shortly, I need to take her with me. I'm on a very tight schedule. But I promise, you'll get a full debriefing," Jordan pronounced with greater empathy than when he answered the call. He felt heat on his face. Both he and Throckmorton looked toward the double entrance doors. Hyperia sat in a wheelchair, smiling, staring at the two men. Throckmorton gestured that the attendant should wheel her outside.

"Dear David," Hyperia said, looking at Throckmorton. "My brother's actions will explain everything very soon." Throckmorton looked even more puzzled, then glanced toward Jordan for an explanation.

Though his sister's comment merely alluded to the future, he felt off guard. She violated ground over which he was not prepared to tread—not with "civilians." "She is gifted with the rare ability to combine imagination and fantasy with factual relevance. Certainly not a mental disorder, nor is it magic. Is what she says true more than what random chance would predict? I don't know—I doubt it," he interjected with didactic authority, attempting to deflect further questions. Throckmorton did not seem convinced, assuming an offended posture.

"Jordan. I'm not one to explain a UFO sighting as swamp gas or missile testing. I know what I saw—what I experienced. She effected an altered state of awareness without obvious hypnosis, trance-inducing equipment, or psychopharmacology. But you appear evasive, even secretive," He paused, looking bewildered. "Fine. There's secrets you want to keep. I won't pursue the issue further. Perhaps at a future date, you could indulge me?"

"As I said, Throck. I'll explain everything soon. But for now, thank you for your services. You've been a great help to me personally, to my family, and to my company. More compensation is in order—I'll see to it shortly," Jordan remarked. He noticed Hyperia had left the wheelchair and crept up to Throckmorton, escaping both of their attention. She gently touched his fingertips. He immediately lapsed into the same blissful state Jordan had observed in him earlier.

"You see, my friend. She did it again," Throckmorton commented, smiling. "I'll see you when I see you." He turned to Hyperia, wanting to hug her, but he refrained. He nodded to the attendant for them to go inside.

Feeling uneasy Throckmorton had pressed him to answer questions he did not feel disposed to answer; his sister approached him to calm his temperament. He startled, stepping back before she could touch him. "Hyperia. I must ask you to not attempt to alter my mood or thoughts in any way. Please, will you abide by this simple request?" he stated sternly while holding the car door open for her. She seemed puzzled and enlightened simultaneously, a condition he found discomforting.

"Whatever I say or do will alter your thoughts and mood, brother. The environment—every second you experience, every sensation that impacts your being—changes how you think and feel. I am merely a condensing conduit," she replied.

Annoyed by her seemingly oppositional response, he motioned to her to fasten her seatbelt. "You know what I mean," he responded bluntly. "I'm sorry. I don't mean to be curt with you. I've had too many surprises dealt me today—mostly by you, dear sister. Indeed, you are one of them," he glanced at her compassionately, reaching over to squeeze her hand. "I'm taking you to a friend's. You will stay with her. I like her very much. You'll like her as well. Her name is Rebecca."

They drove in silence for fifty minutes, finally stopping in Rebecca's apartment building's parking structure. He slid out of his door, aiming to open the door for Hyperia, but she had already disengaged herself and sprung out with similar alacrity. "I like Rebecca," she offered without prompting as if the conversation were continuing from an hour earlier.

He took stock in the sincerity of his earlier discourse, rationalizing that he had not deluded Throckmorton, as his only option was to put him off. Hyperia possessed a talent which, before today, Jordan had always mocked as chicanery when touted by other soothsayers and psychics. His thoughts returned to Zora. *Why didn't she just tell me?* He froze in his steps. The same tickling pain rushed through his body as if unnerved by a thousand prickling nerve endings. Hyperia stepped quickly next to him, fingering the base of his spine. The sensation subsided. *It's starting. I've acted as if I had forever, but it's starting. And I feel as if my life had just begun. She made it go away—or would it have vanished just as quickly had she done nothing?*

Uncomfortably wavering between gratitude and embarrassment, he cranked his head as if to relieve a muscle spasm in his neck. "I don't see her car. I called her to prepare her for our arrival, but we may be early. I have a key, in any case. Let's in go, shall we?" he said, gesturing the direction. He was consoled by the ease with which Hyperia agreed without overt gesture or expression; she radiated amicability and composure.

He stopped as if recalling an overlooked item on a checklist. His personal assistant—a man he trusted above all others—needed to be here. Knowing Simon's predilection for punctuality, he would be at Chamberlain's now, expediting a move which Chamberlain was sure to consider premature and rude, given Jordan had purposefully not given him a definite timetable—and he certainly did not inform him the move would be immediate if the results were compelling. He texted Simon to please come to Rebecca's as soon as practical.

As Jordan and Hyperia walked through a side gate leading from the parking area to the main building grounds, Rebecca sped up the driveway, dashing into a parking space. Hyperia had turned in her direction, just as she had come into view. Jordan looked to see what had caught her attention. His comfort level escalated. Between the two women, he never wanted to leave, though, Rebecca was not yet even in their presence.

How is this possible? I feel protected as if I were a child shielded from harm by a caring, protective parent. Yet, I have nothing to fear. Hyperia exercises powers of the mind not yet discovered—not yet even considered. She seemed to transport Rebecca's affect and love here—to us, to our location—before she arrived here just now. Her essence is here, but not her body. I feel surrounded by her loving disposition before I turned to see her. And my affliction—I don't feel angst or worry as if she spreads an ephemeral opiate. I must confront Zora, see what's she's doing, inspect that facility, if it exists. Perhaps the AI was wrong. But Hyperia came from Zora, and Zora lead me to her—to take her away. Why? He broke his trance as Rebecca emerged from her car, approaching them with more glee than he had ever observed from her.

"Jordan! I felt empty while away from you," she said, her words jostled by the vibration of her jog. She held him closely, then parted to face him, her joy tainted with glum. "I don't know how I know, but I know—you're sick, very sick. And somehow, I seem to know your mother can help you. She awaits you." She paused, looking down. "And I know very bad things are going to happen, and very good things as well." She hesitated, looking to Hyperia. "And I know she is central to it all—and that, somehow, she told me—but we've never met." Rebecca released Jordan, side-stepping to Hyperia to face her. "I've seen your face, felt your presence—I don't know where. I feel as if I've known you all my life, yet I fear you. I fear looking into your eyes, gazing at you."

Now even more convinced of Hyperia's charismatic lure, he witnessed Rebecca affected just as Throckmorton. He thrust upon himself an edict to resist the same alluring persuasion—for as much as he wanted to abandon his will and surrender to the serenity Hyperia's ambiance seemed to promise—she could be a product of Zora Green—venom with the allure of milk and honey. He watched as Hyperia caressed Rebecca's cheeks, then gently tilted Rebecca's face upward with pressure on her chin. "I am not to be feared, sweet Rebecca. What fears me is that which clings to you, unwanted," Hyperia remarked as if whispering a lullaby.

Watching the interaction transpire with the distance of a scientist, he suspected mind intervention. *Maybe someone is using our equipment, or applying Chamberlain's technology to mine, beating me to the gun. The only one capable of doing that would be Zora, and she wouldn't undercut my efforts with some tangential project counter to our efforts. Then technologically, it would be impossible to intercede in Rebecca's mind without going through me. Hyperia is truly gifted with a power, but up to now, I thought it was short-ranged, capable of affecting only those within her field of encounter. And the only way she could have known of Rebecca would have been through me. She must have become privy to my memories and feelings during the mind trip she subjected me to. Still, she has something not controlled by technology—it comes from her, and her alone. I can't waver now. I've made up my mind—she is not a threat. I can leave her with Rebecca.*

246

Impatient to discover Zora's whereabouts, and to unravel the puzzle connecting Zora and Hyperia, he interrupted the transfixion between the two women. "Rebecca. Hyperia. I must take my leave. As you both have mentioned Zora Green, I must go fetch her, as she has been far more clandestine and duplicitous than I ever have known her." He winced suddenly, as another wave of pain cycled through his body, leaving no tissue untouched. Rebecca reacted, looking alarmed. He was too distracted to notice Hyperia stopping her advance toward him. Hyperia placed her left open palm over his sternum, and her right open palm pressed against the back of his neck.

"Stay still, brother. Stay perfectly still," Hyperia commanded softly. Then she emitted a sound, alternating between a whistle and a shriek—a discordant sound which seemed to emanate from her chest, throat, mouth, and lips simultaneously. She pushed him forward into a standing fetal position as his body went limp, yet remained sturdy enough to stand. He twitched and jerked mildly, then as he calmed, she released him. She turned to Rebecca, now staring at Rebecca aghast while fearful for Jordan's well-being.

"You'll do fine for the time being. Rebecca and I will remain here. We have much to discuss. Once you find Zora, she will explain all, as she has set this sequence of events into motion—a sequence of events parallel, yet superlative, to your own agenda. Together, all things will come to pass, as predicted, my brother. Go now."

Jordan succumbed to his sister's compelling proposal. Facing Rebecca and Hyperia, he understood Hyperia had induced a healing power—one that he remembered observing while visiting the descendents of the secretive Cult of Canaan, as they had assembled on an island vanquished by an ocean. He hugged Rebecca. Then, feeling awkward, he hugged Hyperia. The warmth of her cheek against his penetrated his face.

"The power is yours, brother. The culmination of all things is soon to come. You bring forth a new era, but you must survive to do it. Trust our mother." Hyperia's comment haunted him as she took Rebecca's elbow and coaxed her through the gate to take their leave.

Chapter 20

The Shadow

Jordan liked Simon Laslow—the man did not mince words. To Jordan, this was a trait engendering trust. Jordan's right-hand man, assistant, implementer, cleaner, and all-around administrative guru, Laslow seemed to be multi-tentacled. Ambidextrous and coordinated both figuratively and literally, he was Jordan's expediter, taking care of all that needed to get done.

Simon arrived at professor Chamberlain's laboratory shortly after Jordan's departure. His job was to make certain the technology transferred efficiently and quickly. He had spoken with his boss briefly before his arrival at the Irvine Research Facility. Laslow had wanted to meet with Jordan briefly before dealing with Chamberlain, only to see Jordan speed off just as he arrived. Frustrated that Jordan seemed distracted and unable to wait, all he had was the text message Jordan had dashed off a few minutes earlier: He had seen all he needed to see, the money was in place; start the process. *Yet, was Chamberlain truly ready to do what he would be told to do?* Simon pondered. He knew that Jordan would not have informed Chamberlain of the imminent transfer, so Laslow's appearance with demands, schedules, and moving trucks would present a trauma designed for a guidance counselor to handle—not him. Jordan tend to leave the "shit work" for him—which Simon belived was OK. That was his job—but he didn't have to leave it "extra smelly," he thought.

Jordan had morphed into a dilemma to him—a paradox of entities that cannot occupy the same body at the same time. Laslow recalled fond memories when the company recruited him. Jordan found him through a clandestine network, interlinking the CIA, NSA, Interpol, and various international military intelligence agencies. Jordan had told him at the outset of their first interview that he needed a scientist, an engineer, a psychologist, and a guiltless killer, all rolled into one. Jordan realized he had met his future boss—and his ideal career. He silently reminisced, recalling when Jordan had described him whimsically as the perfect golfing partner—apolitical and amoral—a person who could accept that the impossible is real, and the probable is an illusion.

To Simon Laslow, Jordan Éclair was the most brilliant, versatile, tactical leader he had ever known. He saw his boss as razor sharp, crisp, exacting, unemotional, yet able to feign the most subtle of feelings in order to manipulate or control. And the man had never been in the military. *The military probably would have dulled his senses*, he mused. Yet over the years, he believed that Jordan—though never losing his brilliance—seemed to have become softer, more prone to human weakness, swayed more by opinion than by hard fact. *Perhaps it's age; perhaps he has so much to do, he's taken on too much. But then again, that's a weakness. He was always the one to know his shortcomings. After all, that's why he hired me.*

Laslow parked his gray Carrera in front of the primary research compound, blocking the parking lot driveway. For the next three hours, he did not want anyone coming or going. And should someone insist upon leaving, that person would lose his job. He needed the area cordoned off legally, and he had arranged for the police department to lend a hand on the scene, bestowing an official appearance to a surreptitious maneuver. He exited his car, then signaled the trucks parked a few blocks away to move in. A police cruiser rolled next to him just as the trucks were lining up, blocking the street.

"Captain said to give you whatever support you need," the officer remarked blandly, his arm resting outside the window.

Laslow did not like the police—not because he feared them, but because he thought the people who are attracted to the career do it for the wrong reasons. He believed an ideal police force should induce and employ highly intelligent, well-educated members, adept in legal and moral philosophy. Given these criteria, most infractions could be resolved through means other than a judicial system extolling merely a veneer of democracy. *Let the military handle the gangs, cartels, and perpetrators of true antisocial violence*, he thought. "Good afternoon, sergeant. Our operation will be moving equipment from these facilities over the next three to four hours. We need to operate free of traffic and onlookers. Also, anyone trying to gain entrance, even if they prove they work here, should be forbade passage." He paused, ascertaining the officer's demeanor, making certain his level of obsequiousness was sufficient. He reached into his pocket, extracting ten one-hundred dollar bills. "My contribution to the police fund of your choice," he commented, handing the officer the money. The sergeant's mood instantly became amicable.

"We'll take care of it. We'll post a car at all street entrances. We'll have a traffic detail handle the detours," the man said cheerily, slowly rolling away. Laslow scowled inwardly as the officer drove off. *Piece of shit.*

Turning toward the building complex, he recalled his recent conversation with an attorney in the California UC Regent's budget and accounting office, assuring him the transfer of equipment and intellectual properties would go smoothly, given Jordan's generous research endowment. *That may be smooth, but these people will be confused and pissed.*

As he had programmed his phone to remain silent unless Jordan tried to reach him, it suddenly blurted the familiar signal. "Sir," he answered assiduously, yet respectfully surprised. He expected for Jordan to launch into whatever was on his mind, skipping the usual polite salutation.

"You've no doubt noticed I've been distracted as of late," Jordan blurted, seeming to not know where to start. "Simon," he paused, venturing into an avenue other than business, "these last few

251

days have been challenging—more than simply business as usual. I truly wish I had some answers to the mysteries I've—" he stopped as if to choke up. "I'm in a rather tenuous position." Simon preferred to listen rather than talk—a trait Jordan appreciated—so Laslow remained silent, waiting for Jordan to continue. "Remember when I told you— long ago, when we first met—accept the impossible as real? Well, now I must heed my own advice. I'll relate the details later, but the high point is—I discovered I have a sister. I have a sister, and she has some rather bizarre—talents, for lack of a better word."

Simon listened faithfully, with focus but without reaction. He remained silent. He had experienced Jordan during crises in the past, and he was confident Jordan would say everything that needed to be said.

"As far as Chamberlain goes—don't hurt him," Jordan continued with renewed vigor. "For god sake, don't kill him—or any of his staff. If he seems resistant or defiant, maybe a strong, assertive discussion will work." Jordan paused with introspection. "I probably went overboard, putting a gun to his head the other night. I wanted to cut through any resistance. We don't have the time. As you probably guessed, he's not expecting you. Just transfer everything in that building—equipment, files, people—even animals." A lull ensued as Jordan was met with silence when he expected a response. "We've prepared enough space to receive everything from the Irvine lab. Dr. Ranvier will direct activities from there. Let's meet later. I'll call you," he said, ending abruptly, and he hung up.

While stuffing his phone in its holder, he noticed a paunchy, middle-aged man, approaching him from afar, lumbering laboriously. *There's a man in dire need of a StairMaster, and a vitamin and water diet. I hope this isn't Chamberlain. How could a mind like his allow himself to slip into such slovenly lethargy? It's disgusting.* He had focused on the large center figure so intently, he had not noticed the two female assistants accompanying him.

"What's going on here," the man he assumed to be Chamberlain queried abruptly, slowing his approach as he discerned Laslow's demeanor from afar. "One of my people told me his way was blocked. That he was not being allowed to pass," he continued with mellower tone.

Laslow felt the pressure in his forehead rise—it indicated an impending emotional reaction from which he tried to distance himself. Jordan had already advised him of guidelines for behavior, but he preferred someone else actually conduct the social interaction and diplomacy. Laslow did not lack in self-insight. He keenly knew his own limitations, and he would just as soon put a bullet in this man's head, than have him exhaust breath from his whiney speech, and blow it in his direction. "Dr. Chamberlain?" Laslow uttered inquisitively, offering an alternative option to what his impulses craved. Chamberlain nodded affirmatively, then catching Laslow's expression, halted the momentum of his objections. "Dr. Chamberlain. I'm Simon Laslow, Jordan's personal assistant," he said, introducing himself and extending his hand. Chamberlain returned the handshake, remaining humbled by a sense of Laslow's unpredictability.

"Dr. Chamberlain. I understand you and Dr. Éclair have an agreement. All arrangements have been made to move you and your staff to an alternate facility closeby—well, in Southern California. Before you object, let me inform you, all arrangements, both legal and financial have been finalized. I need for you to go back inside and let your staff know what's going on. Tell them the truth since they're probably unaware of the deal you and Jordan's company worked out: Your technology, research, patents, everything, has been sold to Brain-Link Corporation. For now your staff can accompany you. If anyone decides they do not want to make the transfer, we understand. By the way, please be sure to tell them that all will receive a moving bonus worth fifty percent of his or her current salary. But for now—for security—we require that everyone stay put until we make an accurate assessment of who's here, doing what." He knew Chamberlain was in his power, consumed by his dark, penetrating stare. "Dr. Chamberlain. It's imperative we expedite the transfer of your technology, staff and equipment immediately. I understand Dr. Éclair made no mention of this transfer. His lack of candor was not meant to be deceptive, but rather for security purposes." *This man is made of mush. If he's what it takes to become powerful in academics, no wonder the students graduating today are more interested in iPhones and Facebook, and not in the politics of who's fucking them faster.*

"I—I—I just didn't expect to move so fast. Jordan just left here. He told me to expect change quickly and to prepare my staff, but I assumed I'd have days, even months. I'm not offering resistance— merely surprise," Chamberlain replied submissively.

"We're on a schedule, doctor." Laslow gestured toward the trucks lining the street, and the police cruiser passing by, the policeman offering a perfunctory nod. "As you can see, we are prepared for transport. And as I've explained, the state and university officials are well aware of the exchange. We've got to get you and your staff back to work—for us. So, without any other further delay, perhaps we can get going?" He watched as Chamberlain glanced at his colleague nervously, wanting to save face without upsetting Laslow. Laslow's face shallowed as his impatience mounted.

"I'll go inside and prepare at once. Once I inform the staff of Jordan's generosity, I'm sure my people will lend their full cooperation," Chamberlain remarked. "How much time do I have before your people come in?"

"Ten minutes. I'll give you ten minutes. Then we've got to get going," Laslow replied, asserting the imminence of the situation.

He watched as Chamberlain and his entourage reentered the building. At times he craved certain benefits of his old job with the Israeli Secret Service, as few questions were asked whenever he had engaged in errant acts of impulse. He did not like Chamberlain—not when he had heard of him; not when Jordan had described him, certainly not after this personal encounter. Laslow's stare followed Chamberlain's bulky frame. He fantasized about vaporizing it—the same way he imagined being able to fire a missile at slow cars in his way, jeering at his target as its occupants dispersed into insignificant particles of metal and flesh as he drove through.

The text message signal from Jordan broke his trance—fantasies upon which he knew he would never act; he allowed himself the freedom to take whatever action he desired in his mind.
"Please go directly to Rebecca's as soon as practicable. Stay with them until I return. Me— helicopter to SM Mountains."

Laslow felt a shudder, realizing what the message conveyed. He loved life and avoided pain whenever he could. He would not want to experience what he knew Jordan would have to undergo. And he knew he himself would have to confer with Zora very soon as well. He agreed with Zora's reasoning: Knowledge alters the future. *It's that time. It's hit him. He's sick. Zora needs to administer the solution as soon as possible. It's coming together.*

Chapter 21

Anima

Alone, quiet, except for the rumble of the engine, he enjoyed an unaccustomed serenity inside the cockpit of his helicopter. No longer was he Jordan Éclair, captain of electronic media, whiz of the gaming industry, genius of neuro-mech-integration. The Pacific Coast Highway receded below him, ambling northward, coastal dwellings clinging precariously to sandy foundations, intermingled by tell-tale bare cliffs where once stilt pincers lost their grip to the rampage of the ocean, and the assault of periodic rainy seasons. Looking up occasionally to dodge southerly air traffic bound for Santa Monica Airport, he wished he could remain aloft. He intuited his trip was not his choice, but rather designed—if not determined—by Zora Green. *I don't believe in circumstance. Too much appears to be converging for all this to be random chance. She's waiting for me. The mere fact she's made her presence known to me, without telling me where she is, or what she's doing, is a ploy, a game, a manipulation to draw me in. And of course I'll comply. Does she mean to kill me, like she killed my father? Will she know I've already seen it all through Hyperia? She doesn't have to explain—it was necessary. It was euthanasia, I know. The affliction had overtaken him, and like those before him, he had to die by the hand of a friend to avoid a death too brutal—too excruciating—to even consider. She knows me. I would gladly accept the option—the truth—presented to me as fact and reality. Why the game—the foxhunt? Perhaps because she does not know me well enough, thinking that she must lure me with mystery and intrigue. True, we have not discussed the affliction, as it applies to me. How blocked and restricted our relationship—that we never discussed the most vital aspect of my life. But it applies to all our male family. And sooner or later, I must deal with the reality of an early demise. I have not left progeny, and perhaps that issue remains. Has she procured a female for me to inseminate? I had an inkling of a notion that was Hyperia's purpose, until I discovered she's my sister. Zora could have just informed me.*

He jolted to awareness like the sleeping driver awakening suddenly as he veers off the road to the admonishing crunching of the shoulder under tire. The AI interrupted his pondering with a message: "Dr. Éclair. You indicated you preferred VFR instructions. Deer Creek Road in five miles. Then follow it north through the canyon for three miles. At that point, we must diverge from the road, as the site is inaccessible except by all-terrain vehicle or helicopter. Zora Green's position will be four minutes from the point of divergence. It is underground—undetectable from the air, or to hikers. She has radar and infrared area surveillance—she'll know when we arrive. I've been monitoring analog and digital transmissions from the area. All seems quiet, though the spurious static could be encrypted carrier waves."

Beset with a sense of the inevitable, he was bedeviled by a sense of looming doom—the kind of forlorn he had imagined men on death row must feel whenever the long awaited actual ritual walk to death arrives, when they emerge from their cell one last time, when each footstep occurs within a finite series, counting, aware each draws closer to the last. *The duration of life—short, miniscule, sub-atomic— from a universal perspective—is endless and expansive until a point, a threshold when somehow the inevitable is within eyeshot. The infinite collapses to the very finite. I must behave as if I'm returning—as if I'm going home, to wake up tomorrow and show up at the office.* "A fog bank is lurking over the Channel Islands. Is it likely to move on shore soon? I've got to be sure to get out of here before nightfall," Jordan asked his AI assistant. Not really concerned about the fog bank, he simply wanted to hear the artificial intelligence he had designed respond one more time—another footstep. Oddly, its voice was similar to Hyperia's, even though he had constructed it and given the system its voice characteristics months before he had ever known her.

"There's a ninety-five percent probability the bank will remain offshore. An easterly flow is developing, causing the marine layer to dissipate," the AI responded, sounding like a chirpy TV morning weather reporter.

After following Deer Creek Road at an altitude lower than safety would advise, he became concerned his intrusion might cause the few dwellers of the area to become suspicious, especially since they were very sensitive to fire danger and think his helicopter was on other-than-routine fire patrol.

"Correct your heading ten degrees east for wind velocity. One-half mile on your new heading. The signal is getting stronger. One-thousand feet. Slow to ten knots. Now hover. You are directly over Zora Green's facility, based on all information I could gather." He thought the AI even sounded more human than he had designed it, as he detected a defensive tone, as to say: "It's not my fault if it's not there." But he was sure it was there, as he was certain Zora wanted him to come to her.

He fought off the despondency badgering him for the past few months. He realized now it had been a reaction to repressing full recognition of the affliction—his imminent demise. Even as he disembarked from the helicopter, each action was one recorded with nostalgia: last landing, last shut down, last flight. He stopped short of saying farewell to his car AI.

Standing in the middle of a clearing, he turned his face into a predusk warm breeze whisking through the canyon, and he basked in the solitude. From his vantage point, he did not detect any line-of-sight house, avoiding the various ranches and secluded homes nestled within the crevasses and nooks of the mountains. *Where is Zora?*

"I'm below you, son," Zora's voice announced, ringing clear in his mind, but not in his ears. "You see the large boulder on the north side of the clearing? Go to that boulder."

Less surprised at her method of communication was how she addressed him—son. *A bit of affection and motherly endearment before saying adieu*, he mused. He had spotted the boulder earlier, and he walked to it as directed. It was shielded by trees at different angles, making it impossible for anyone to view it unless they were standing at the clearing with him. And even with the helicopter in plain view, it was not at all uncommon for hikers to fly into the area then trudge further into the wilderness.

He had already suspected that the boulder was artificial, even hollow. The entrance would have to accommodate a protrusion from the ground, and not simply a rabbit hole into which one might drop. Even this fleeting scenario brought with it wistful memory of one of his favorite childhood stories, *Alice in Wonderland*. An undetectable seam in the boulder widened to reveal a hollow interior. "Go inside, please," Zora's voice commanded. He was impressed and bemused by her utilization of the "voice-in-the-head" technology, which the company had abandoned for consumer marketing five years ago. Its chief developer believed VITH to be the next step in communications, as it stimulated auditory neurons directly rather than being stimulated by the ear's cochlear nerves, which are activated by air waves—ambient sound. Now it was used somewhat sparingly among the deaf; it required extensive neural maser electrodes—more elaborate that the gaming equipment for which the company was now famous. As he stepped into the hollow boulder, he scoured the area once more, searching for the maser electrode array she used to transmit the voice signal. Since a sizable portion of Chamberlain's technology was to be used in long range transmission of holographic maser signals, he rejected the notion she had procured the technology before they could have gotten Chamberlain's lab operational inside their LA facility. *They're in the process of moving him now—she's not that fast.*

The sunlight diminished to a slit as the rock enclosed him; the platform upon which he stood descended. He had been completely unaware of this facility until now. *Zora's deception seems obvious. Like a rat in a maze, I've followed the food pellets leading me here.* Humbled, he had always been led to believe that he was the most powerful man on earth, as was his father and his grandfather. And though he was, perhaps, the most powerful man on Earth, it stood to reason Zora Green was the most powerful woman. The platform stopped inside a dimly lit chamber, perhaps an anteroom or airlock to the main facility, he surmised.

A wall panel slid open suddenly, and Zora appeared, stepping through it with grace and eloquence he had never observed in her. Dumbfounded, he was stunned by her countenance, never having paused to appreciate Zora's beauty. Though a woman of sixty-eight years, she had maintained the youthfulness of a woman in her late thirties. The tautness of her skin defied surgical procedures; her muscle tone, obtained by others only with devoted hours on training equipment; her thick black hair, gracefully striped with white, had never seen a coloring product, and every strand remained steadfast to her scalp. The cold officiousness to which he associated her had vanished. *How can it be? Within hours she has transformed herself? Perhaps a technology she's been hiding from me—a personality transplant, perhaps. She's managed quite well concealing this facility, so her secretiveness and ability to maintain deception remained intact.*

Though awestruck, he regrouped seamlessly to not appear caught offguard. "Mother. Needless to say, all this is quite a surprise." Instead of the cold innuendo he expected, she remained silent, approaching him. Coming closer than she had ever been to him— probably since his birth—she stood inches before him, looking up into

260

his face, endearingly, lovingly as if beholding a long lost child after many years of separation. She pressed his face between her hands, holding his cheeks like delicate porcelain. Then she hugged him, remaining silent.

His angst soared—he did not trust her so close to him, especially with her hands behind his back. He had the indelible image of seeing her with his father only hours ago during Hyperia's guided tour of his ancestral past. Witnessing his father's death through his father's eyes underscored the need to keep Zora in clear view. And even then, like the magician performing seemingly impossible tricks, one watches him with unveering scrutiny, only to be deceived once again by the master's sleight of hand. Yet, her proximity was not entirely overwhelming—as the experience touched a chord, perhaps a set-aside childhood memory; a forgotten longing for the maternal associations his friends had, but he had none—so he did not bolt away, or reject her affection. As she held him, he remembered seeing movies of mother and child reunions. They had always touched him, and he reserved admitting to others that he had secretly cried during these sentimental scenes.

What is this I'm feeling? I'm Jordan Éclair. Now I'm standing emotionally beholden to a woman who is mother to me by birth only. She could have cloned me, and I would have had more affection. What is this welling up inside me? It's like a dam holding two rivers apart— joy and despair—and it's bursting. He started to heave, and she squeezed him tighter. Still trying to hold back the onslaught of emotions surging within, he looked around self-consciously, wondering who else might be watching. No one else was there; they appeared to be alone. He let himself go. Sobbing and heaving, he returned her embrace, sobbing vehemently on her shoulder. She embraced him even tighter, comforting and consoling him.

261

"Jordan, my son. I know. I know you hurt. I'm so sorry you feel the pain you feel, and I want to take the pain away. Jordan. I thought—I thought I had to take your life like I had to take your father's. But son, I don't. I don't have to. I've found a solution. I have so much to explain. So much to explain that I couldn't tell you before. But now, now I have the answer, and it fits. It fits so well. Jordan. You don't have to die. You don't have to suffer any longer. We are at the end of our long journey, and you are here with me—your mother," Zora whispered, never releasing Jordan, always speaking into his ear.

A wind had just blown through him, sweeping the rubbish and debris away. The burst of emotion was novel, invigorating. Still, he thoroughly recognized that Zora used human beings as research subjects; she was the inventor of HIV; she engineered draughts, political upheavals and genocides in Third World nations, and secretly financed Arab terrorist organizations—all to achieve an economic end involving the centralization of oil production and distribution. He cut his silent reverie short, noticing she inspected him introspectively.

"I know what you're thinking—that you cannot trust me. And given everything you know about me—about us—and everything you've seen, you're wise to heed your thoughts. Of all the males from the beginning, you have been the most protected, the most cuddled. You may realize that—you're every bit as brilliant as your grandfather. One could say your grandfather almost single-handedly engineered World Wars One and Two. He literally crafted the world's petroleum economy. Your father was directly responsible for most of the status of the Middle East as we know it today, while my father was behind the scenes, dealing with the British, Americans, and then with the newly-created United Nations." She touched his shoulder, rubbing it maternally. "You know why, my son? You know what we are? Who we are?"

He had acclimated to his mother's altered mien, deciding that even if it were a deception, it made no difference. He had resigned to the fate—the affliction killing the males in his bloodline. "I've known it before. I grew up knowing who I am, who we are, and what our intent is. I could never truly socialize or mingle with others, knowing what I was meant to do—what I was born to do. That any child I played with, there may be some reason why I would have to push her into traffic, or feed her poison in her lemonade. And I've carried out my birthright faithfully." A surge of affection, of love, welled within him for Zora as she observed him with a matronly wisdom.

"You saw it, induced by your sister. You saw your beginning?" she queried with an exuberant curiosity.

Her question confirmed his suspicion—Zora had planted Hyperia, but at this point he did not care. "Yes, I thought I saw, through a dream state. But I'm still not sure I really experienced—that I really saw—what I saw. It seemed real. But you knew enough to ask, so you may have orchestrated the whole thing—not that I believe you did. But you did know that she would have the effect on me that she did. You let me leave with her, thinking I was saving her from another one of your brain cleansing experiments, like the others you've done—to no avail."

"All that was for a reason, Jordan. All that was for you. What did you notice about her? What specifically, other than the effect she had on you—and others?"

Baffled by a disinclination toward anger with her, he wished she would be more forthright. *Tell me. What is it about her you want me to know.* "Notice? That was it. There really was nothing to notice. She didn't seem to have a personality, history, any memories," he replied, drawing a blank about Hyperia's distinguishing characteristics. He noticed Zora's face alight with acknowledgement.

"Yes, Jordan. That's correct. She did not. Come, follow," Zora said, offering a slight tug on his elbow.

263

The sliding doors snapped shut behind him as he followed Zora through a seemingly endless curved hallway, the wall material enhancing the effect with shiny iridescent blue porcelain. The passageway was a work of art of overwhelming color and brilliance. He had not fully acclimated to Zora's garments—they were not her usual attire. A flowing, silk-like material adorned her, clinging to her shoulders as if glued, flowing, yet clinging, around the form of her slender, youthful body. The material sparkled, not of glitter or gems, but as if each weave contained some shimmering essence. He remembered he had seen this material before: The island to which the children of Canaan had escaped, then centuries later escaped from, to avoid the ocean engulfing it. He witnessed his ancestors through his ancestors' eyes—three thousand years ago. They fled their island paradise to reemerge on mainland, integrating themselves surreptitiously with the people and cultures. He wondered—*Their goal was clear then. Why didn't they just conquer? They knew something unspoken at the time, but unapparent to me.*

She led him into a stadium-sized room, the size of ten basketball courts. The floor was shiny marble, smooth, yet not slippery. Arrays of pictographs defined directions to sections of the room containing different equipment and furnishings. The wall material continued from the hallway—the fired, glassy bricks, crimson, cyan, and dark blue. The center of the room had elongated, pedestal-like stands. He had seen these before as well. They were in the secret chamber deep inside Ugarit, where Lotan and his sister hid during the Israelite invasion of their city.

Flabbergasted from the spectacle he had encountered, he needed clarification. "Stop, please," he commanded, moving to take control of his perceptions. "Zora—mother—what is this? How could you possibly have all this—" he exclaimed, gesturing around himself, "—and me not know about it? Did you develop this facility aside from the corporation? I know where all the corporation's holdings are, and I'm fully aware of our hidden LA facility. But where did this come from? The capital? The time? The expertise? It there a company within a company I'm not aware of?"

"Yes, you know where most of it is. But you're not aware of the artifacts. Over the centuries, some of us had to maintain the progenitor standards, shielding the perpetuators—you—from the burden of sustaining our essence: the historical holdings, the archives, the history of cultures, the original scriptures, the blueprint of mankind. This lab—this temple—is a monument to what we—you—are. Where you came from. What you mean. The purpose. The history. The spirit. The Gods." He inwardly winced at a near manic intensity to which her affect had segued. "This lab has existed since my father, Gershon Akerling, and your father, François Éclair, migrated to Southern California during the Thirties—I forgot the exact year. At that time, they saw an area ripe for the development of automobile transportation and the construction of highways. They had this sanctuary built, knowing this area would be key to the Cult's operations, aside from the visible business ventures. They moved many of their ancestral archives here, in light of their machinations in Europe, and what those ventures would instigate over the next two decades. We have maintained archives here you have yet to see—documents and artifacts which will widen your eyes. And here, in this facility, I mixed the archives with our technology to work in parallel with your work—and to discover a solution—a cure—for the affliction gripping you now, as we speak."

Jordan crumbled to his knees; the tingling permeated through and around his body like pins penetrating every cell, deeper and deeper. Zora rushed to his side, extracting a black, metallic vial from her pocket; she pressed it against his carotid artery.

"It's a temporary fix, but we must initiate the procedure. We need your sister here. Simon's bringing her as we speak. Rebecca will go assist Chamberlain," she said with finality.

He felt almost instant relief from the agony aflame throughout as if his body had been thrust into boiling acid, then removed quickly without incurring any damage. Hearing Zora tell him that Simon was on his way, in light of the fact that he had told him to stay with Hyperia and Rebecca, alarmed him, even during his physiological reprieve. "Hyperia. I named her Hyperia, since she did tell me her name. I told Simon to stay with them after I left. Why do you need her here?" The pain having subsided, he sat up, with Zora supporting his arm.

"The serum should hold you for a few hours. Dizzy?" Without waiting for a response—or answering his question—she tugged on his elbow. "Come with me. I'll show you while we wait."

Disoriented from his near collapse, the winding corridors were surreal. He had experienced them before, with Hyperia, while traveling to Ugarit. The temple passageways were adorned with similar designs and pictograms. The composition of the walls and floors, though having the texture of fired clay or porcelain, had qualities of plastic and stone combined. The colors were strident, working to subliminally awaken and stimulate him. *An entire world has existed without my awareness. Where did all this come from? I believe her—that she did not want me involved for fear that it would distract me from my primary purpose—invent and devise, shaping technologies and economies for our ends. But where do I fit in here? That's the answer. Normally, I would not fit in here. Normally, I would die, none the wiser. That means there is an echelon of which I am unaware. Like what I saw in Hyperia's trance—priests, cultists, scribes, maintaining an existence that appeared to vanish eons ago, only to be preserved here. They did not show this to my father, nor was François aware. I must know more.*

"Mother—forgive me if words stick in my craw—it takes some getting used to." He hesitated, allowing her to absorb the impromptu apology. She stopped at the intersection of two corridors, turning to face him. "Mother. You're showing me all this. I've gotten over feeling as if I've been deceived or kept in the dark. I comprehend the purpose—especially after Hyperia—my sister—guided me through my ancestral past." He paused again, fighting for words, his face contorted with regret and confusion. "There's so much I want to ask. So much I don't understand. But my primary question now—is—why show me all this now?" She seemed ablaze with purpose, motivated to keep moving.

"Because you will survive. And because you mark the end, and a new beginning." She touched his check lovingly as if to convey motherly patience. "Follow. All questions will be answered."

He noticed as they paced through the hallway that he had not seen any doors leading to other rooms, concluding that these rooms must be enormous as well. Finally, they arrived at a set of clear sliding doors. Curious about the material, he touched it, feeling a warmth that would emanate from neither glass, plastic, nor crystal. Zora grinned, observing his fascination.

Chapter 22

Animus

The two-door halves parted, allowing them entrance to a room every bit the size of a football field. He stood in amazement, not only from shock at the size, but also from the familiarity. It was an oversized version of the temple room in which Lotan and his sister hid within Ugarit. Zora watched him intently.

"You've seen this room before, haven't you?" she asked as if already knowing the answer.

"A smaller version of it. Yes. I watched Lotan and Hurriya escape from a chamber like this one with their teacher—"

"Their teacher, Yassib," Zora interrupted, saying the name for him.

He nodded agreeably, acclimated to her familiarity with all he had seen and experienced. As he scanned his perimeter, he turned around to his right, examining the wall behind him, which extended for at least three hundred feet. Glass, fluid-filled cylinders, compact and regularly spaced, receded isometrically away from him. On edge with curiosity, he looked at Zora, who motioned he should move closer to take a look.

Approaching tubes that looked like lava lamps, he had already primed himself for what he would encounter. Somewhere in his cognitive formations, out of his awareness—that place where solutions are discovered and puzzles are solved without the active participation of the person seeking enlightenment—he knew. He sensed what his mother was doing, and what the experiments at the company were all about.

The first tube he approached emitted an eerie yellow glow. Peering inside, a mass of skin-coated flesh resembling a partly assembled human, only malformed and contorted, floating and jostled by the moving fluid and bubbles. Undisturbed by this image, he moved to the next cylinder where a faceless toddler bobbed back and forth in a darker yellow froth. He continued down the row, examining tube after tube of lifeless flesh—humans at various stages of development, though, he surmised, not from in vitro gestation. Caught by surprise, he spun quickly, as his fascination with the myriad of bottled corpses along the wall distracted him from noticing the columns of identical cylinders extending in another direction behind him.

He flushed with pride, as he mulled over Zora's brilliance. Always fascinated by cloning, especially neural systems, he had never had the time or opportunity to pursue this domain. And since he always had to operate the company in the public eye, the extent of the research he would have preferred would never have been deemed acceptable, let alone ethical. "Zora, I'm very, very impressed. Now I understand completely," he commented, his eyes full of awe. "I only wish I could have participated. But now I understand. Those experiments of yours—those weren't homeless whose memories you were—" he stopped as Zora interceded.

"They were not homeless at all. Their origin was here. And I wasn't trying to erase memory—I was attempting to implant it, mplanting not simply memories, but an entire schema of human existence—all that the brain acquires from existing, from gestation through birth, and onward through post partum development," she explained with exuberance. "But you've got one thing wrong. These are not clones."

An inertial glue seized his body and mind, suddenly consuming him with a paralyzing realization. The out-of-awareness solution percolated to his consciousness. "Hyperia?" he queried with a fleeting gasp. Without a wince or eye blink from Zora, he knew the answer.

"I haven't been cloning, though I have learned—after many trials and errors—how to gestate to adulthood. Gestating to infancy—

well, we can do that. But gestating the fully developed adult—that's the achievement we've recently accomplished. These are not clones. They are recombinant DNA integrations from cellular samples maintained over thousands of years. All your ancestors are here. And each ancestor, in turn, has contributed his or her DNA to the pool. This process—the in vitro gestation of humans to embryonic stages—has been viable for millennia. It's one of the secrets devised by the escaping Canaanites—the ones you witnessed leaving Ugarit."

The deeper realization came, not as nirvana, but as the waking cognizance that the nightmare was real. "I'm—I'm not born of woman—of you—am I?" he asked, choking out the words.

"No. Nor was your father, nor your father's father. You all came from labs—from priests' chambers—similar to this one. It's similar to the room in the temple you saw, where Lotan hid during his last day in Ugarit. He had escaped with the secret of life and with an indelible goal—to destroy those who slaughtered his people, trespassed his home, and dispossessed him of his culture and heritage." Accustomed to Zora expressing little emotion, let alone fervor, her escalating affect confused him. "They destroyed all he was—all because of disillusioned beliefs and mythologies about their Gods. The invaders and outsiders of Canaan—the so-called settlers—and those who followed them. And all the nations that supported them, and hid them, and had acculturated them—all who were complicit—will soon experience the same fate."

The revelation of his pedigree effected him contrary to the emotions he believed he should feel—instead, they normalized him. He could live a normal human existence because, indeed, he was not really human. "Zora—mother—I'm certainly grateful for your diligence at finding a cure, or at least a partial remedy for this apparent genetic affliction, but—" he stammered as she cut him off once more.

"Why you? Why now? Because you—your genes—are at the pinnacle, the apex of the progression, the lineage. Any further engineering with your DNA will lead to regression, somewhat like the inbreeding engendered in the European monarchies. You are the highest born yet, with the optimal of the characteristics bred for over four thousand years. It's you. And how fortuitous, since soon we can mark the end of our planning, our tenacious plotting, our ubiquitous presence in world circles over the centuries. Other than disband, we must lead. And we have planned for centuries for this era to come. We even wrote the book—the scriptures of their major myths and religions—forecasting the coming of a messiah, a great one, a savior." His psyche still tender from the day's enlightenment, he sensed her empathy for him, pausing to let him ponder her remarks. "We've hardly made our way to the inner sanctum, and you've learned so much already. There's more to see inside. Follow me," she said, reverting to her more characteristic monotonic style.

He chided himself, starting to bask in a sense of bliss. *I should feel tired, exhausted. But I'm electric. This exuberance I sense—it can't be simply from what Zora told me, from what I've discovered about her, or from Hyperia's mind trip, or about myself. She injected that serum into me. Perhaps it has an effect on the central nervous system— some kind of dopanergic agonist. I've a sense of elation, euphoria, even grandiosity. I feel like shouting to the world. Yet I felt like this when I was on my way here, flying over the coast. And what's this—this sexual stimulation? I'm behind my sixty-eight-year-old mother, looking at her ass. If the behavior weren't so profound, I'd be disgusted with myself.* Zora's crystalline chiffon gown material graced and caressed her form as if drawing a gentle trace line around her undepreciated contours. Following her, he had noticed that the dress was backless, dipping to the small of her back. He marveled, thinking that if he did not know her and was unaware that she was sixty-eight, he might believe she was in

271

her late thirties. He had never seen her dressed in anything other than stodgy business attire, even as a young boy. She always appeared Wall Street ready.

Blissful, but frustrated, he wanted to slow down to observe more of the specimens in the hundreds of gestation cylinders through which they sped as they forged further into the bowels of this heretofore unknown birthing facility. He tried to not stare at Zora's bare-backed figure—something about her excited him sexually, and though he was absolved of the culture-at-large values and taboos, he was not ready to have sex with his mother—or at least with the woman he had called mother all his life.

Filing through rows and columns of the multicolored, bubbling cylinders as if careening through a soda pop factory, they finally reached a clearing. Some of the paraphernalia he recognized as Brain-Link equipment. It had been modified from their experimental mock-ups in their corporate research facility, and certainly improved from the master designs used to make their consumer electronics gaming sets. The redesign allowed users to plug-in to environmental media for games, shows, plays, music and sporting events, and their most popular platform—sex partners. What he did not readily recognize had vague familiarity as if experienced in a dream or déjà vu. Then he realized what he saw—platforms almost identical to the ones Lotan's party crept around, deep inside the priests' chamber. He recalled shadowy forms, pedestals like rectangular mushrooms, sprouting from the subdued floor, accentuated by the muffled screams and moans from outside the walls. Nobody lived. They killed everyone. He felt Lotan within him, and François, his grandfather, and his father, Kristoph—and countless nameless ancestral forces, intimate, binding. They were alive, close to him, within reach of his thoughts. He stopped in the center of the room, seized by the ambiance, a nostalgia as if he had returned to the home of his birth after being away for many years, returning to memories recorded during childhood, contorted and distorted through the translation of his adult brain. But he had been there. This was not the memory of Lotan; this was his memory. Composed but awestruck, he absorbed the room as if he were the focal point of energy. Standing in place, he turned slowly, taking in all sides this immense chamber. Until now, he had not realized it was an ellipse—the womb which nourished him, the womb from which he emerged. He stood at the center; to his right was a platform, to his left an identical platform. He was grateful to Zora for allowing him to examine and consolidate this mythic experience. She stood to the side, watching patiently with a discerning, empathetic expression. He glanced at her briefly, as she was suddenly distracted by a message.

"Simon has arrived with Hyperia and Rebecca," she remarked. "He's familiar with the facility; he knows how to reach us. There's still much I must say before they arrive. I understand you have experienced much today—much more than the large amounts to which you are, I know, already accustomed. We still have much to do," she remarked, pausing. Her brief intermission was uncomfortable, not because she hesitated, but because she seemed at an impasse, not sure how to say what she wanted to say.

"We manufactured Hyperia here. You may have already surmised that. She is a composite human, created from DNA we designed. She is not a clone, though, as you are aware, the technology is similar. But cloning would not give us the nucleic base pair recombination distributions we required." She halted once more, as Jordan stirred as she spoke, recognizing the technology he had developed during the course of his maser electrode experimentation.

Having silently concluded Hyperia's capabilities could only have emerged from engineered cells, his surprise was not Hyperia herself, but the use of the technology creating her. "I experimented with various phyla, from planaria through vertebrates, and species as complex as chimpanzees," he replied with concerted erudition. "My research—that which garnered billions of dollars in government contracts, as you'll recall—varied neural nuclei and axon compositions through DNA recombinations in order to optimize maser excitation of action potentials, and minimize damage to the sodium and potassium ion pumps at the membrane level. At the time, we could have taken the research to an entire organism from gestation level, creating new organisms from the recombinant DNA, but we decided—if memory serves me correctly, and it does—that such research distracted us from our goals." He hesitated, vacillating between irritation and pride. "Our goals," he repeated with emphasis, "are on target. So I'm concerned. I left Simon with explicit instructions to guide and setup Chamberlain's equipment and staff in their new facility. Our timing is precarious in this area, yet I discover that you have superseded my directives, and he is now on his way to our location. I trust you have a very good reason." He was relieved to observe that Zora did not abandon her new persona, seeming very willing to accommodate, rather than placate his confusion.

"Yes, some of these techniques are your own designs, abandoned after they had fulfilled their usefulness to Brain-Link. You discovered that memory placement has a distributive quality, driven by neurological randomization, where the strongest concentration of memory localization is tempered by extraneous emotional and cognitive content—the physiological basis for mnemonics." She drew closer to Jordan, caressing his cheek with the back of her hand. "Your grandfather, François Éclair, had a powerful gift. In the same way our females—your females—literally see the past," pausing after she had enunciated "see." He could see the future, not like a psychic or soothsayer or fortune teller. He had the amazing ability to join nonlinear puzzle pieces from apparent chaos. He predicted certain requirements. He predicted we would need massive noninvasive memory and motivation interventions, while others at his time were recommending procedures like mass hypnosis, a suggestion at which he scoffed. In fact, his response to that was, 'You might as well send mental messages through the luminiferus ether!' He was correct three ways: There's no such thing as mass hypnosis, no luminiferus ether, and affecting the kinds of commands required would necessitate intricate and subtle technologies in biological engineering to countermand today's levels of security. We have it all now, thanks mostly to you. And, thanks mostly to you—indirectly, not directly—we have a cure for the affliction that would most certainly take you from us within the next sixty days. BUT, we had to have an organism capable of the neuronal adaptability this cure requires—both highly adaptable neurons and Glial cells. Glial cells that not only repair, they replicate and duplicate neurons. And it is to that end that I have put a considerable amount of effort—not only to save your life, but to offer you to the world. My promise to my father, Gershon, will be fulfilled, and our—your—kind will continue."

Consumed with an insight far from where he had expected Zora's explanation to transgress, he realized her intent. The implications of the procedure she extolled would save his life. Not a fearful man, he feared the procedure. "You could have asked me, confided in me. I would have worked with you. You mean—there is no other way?" he asked attempting to conceal his trepidation. She locked eyes with him, consoling but decisive.

"Knowledge of the future alters the path. I could not risk having the path altered. I've spent a lifetime researching a cure, leading a double-identity—working with the other elders of our culture, working for the corporation, constantly creeping toward the goal, chipping away toward freeing you of the inevitable. I failed my father, and I failed your father. I must not fail you, and I will not. This merger combines the best of both. It is the pinnacle of the our evolution, the ultimate organism. You will see the past, experience the present, and infer the future as no human has ever done. We—"

"Zora! You are not of our cult. Your father was François' partner, not genetically tied to our race. I'm impressed, flattered, even grateful you've been so dedicated to our aims, and to saving my life, but—"

"Being dedicated to the cause does not require genetic membership. I'm affiliated by relationship, and by my work and undertaking and power of faction. I am a descendent of Yassib, as was my father. We are a caste among ourselves. Our ranks have been ordered over hundreds of generations. Our purpose is coded within; we are not creatures of free will. The science of Canaan—and yes, the lost continent to which folklore refers as Atlantis—forged a race with etched hierarchy. Sometimes we maintain a close association with our lieges, and sometimes, lose. Jordan, I'm not your mother—I am your servant; you are my liege. I'm sworn and bound to protect you, as now I have the capability, and I shall execute my commitment," she remarked in a manner both humble and staunch. She approached him, gently reached out grabbing his shoulders, and pulled him to her. "Put your arms around me; touch me; bring my body closer to yours," she instructed with pedagogic passion.

As if fire from his deepest libidinal core had erupted, rapture's lava seeped to the surface. He embraced her ravenously, kneading her bare back, kissing her neck furiously. Fleeting rules of taboo had migrated into his awareness. The intensity of the moment deflected them, smashing any inkling of guilt or conscience. He sensed Zora's cupped hand hovering around his neck, her hand opening to bare the needle projecting from her ring, and a pinch before the world went dark.

Chapter 23

Chain of Command

A myriad of conflicts tormented Simon Laslow as he watched Jordan recede from his view, leaving him alone with Rebecca and Hyperia. His untiring gait propelling him onward, his long-time boss and confidant cast a trusting glance backward as he drew away. Simon recognized that look, an expression of security, resting an important and a valuable asset in the hands of a reliable and honorable servant— one capable of expediting his master's wishes upon a syllable, without complete sentences uttered, the desire fulfilled. He had worked at Jordan's side for twenty years—gone to school with him, fought with him, loved with him, argued and cajoled with him. Yet, he had maintained a deception, a lie of necessity. He had been recruited as a teenager to be Jordan's companion, to care for him, to watch him, and most importantly, to protect him with his life. That calling now included watching him shrink from his presence. He pined that he would never see him again. He was overcome by wistful reminiscence—an instantaneous barrage of recollections from the past, shuffling through his memory like cards shuffled uncontrollably from a deck.

"He's on his way. Gone. Sometimes I wonder, what if he crashes his helicopter while flying there. Then all this was in vain," he remarked wistfully, turning to Rebecca who remained fixed on Jordan's car as it turned a corner out of sight. Realizing she wouldn't understand his meaning, he winced as she looked at him bewildered.

His own mortality segued to mist. He dwindled into the remorseful ruminations of a man with regrets, viewing his past with his back to twilight. "What if he dies in transit? Where are we? We've all been committed to the cause. We've been committed to him. He's trusted us while we've behaved as if we had no ulterior motives, no insight into his ultimate destiny. Yet, we could not speak. We were

277

trusted, not only by him, but also by the 'higher purpose.'" He grumbled with cynicism. "I've known him for more than half my life, and I always known this day would come." Rebecca seemed impatient, grasping the gist of Simon's lament.

"Zora's committed to saving him. That's her cause, her calling in life. I respect that, but we have work to do," Rebecca replied, now focusing on Simon as if to corral his developing negative attitude. "You've got to get her to The Temple soon after Jordon arrives," she said, gesturing to Hyperia. "Inform Zora—please," she demanded, tempering her assertiveness with self-imposed courtesy.

He did not like Rebecca; he resented the intimate association she shared with Jordan, no matter how ersatz it was. Reluctantly, he pressed a button on his PDA. He recognized Zora had answered without her saying anything. "You asked to be updated. He just left for the airport. It would seem as if the modifications implanted into his personal AI's database facilitated it detecting The Temple." Turning and clutching the phone closer to his face, he hesitated, planning his words. "I won't see him again?" he asked, stammering.

He glanced up, staring at Hyperia who had been attracted to Simon's attempt at isolation. She seemed puzzled at what he had heard over his cell phone, as her sensitivity to the emotions of those around her was bloodhound acute. Rebecca had put her arm around her and started leading her to Simon's car. "We're on our way as well," he added to his brief phone discourse and hung up.

"I've got to get over to the main facility," Rebecca said, waiting for him to get closer so that she would not have to raise her voice, potentially disturbing Hyperia. "The targets are all in place. With Chamberlain's staff, and the neuronal sequencing maps, we should have all the targets in line within two months—but time is of essence. You know that as well as I." She looked at him knowingly. "I've never known you to be sentimental, let alone resistant." She felt Hyperia's grasp on her shoulder as she uttered her captious remark.

"He was in love, Rebecca. Free your mind, and see. He lost his lover," Hyperia blurted suddenly, soft-spoken but direct.

Simon was silently jolted by Hyperia's insight, not wanting his self-assessed weakness to be known by Rebecca. "It's true," Rebecca remarked with acknowledgement, without jeer or revolt. "You should have made your feelings common knowledge. Your attachment could have jeopardized our timing."

Embarrassed—not about the homosexual attachment, but about allowing himself any attachment at all—he knew at his core that his feelings would not thwart his conviction and duty. "What I feel and what I do are two different things—distinct and separate," Simon stated, trying to avoid seeming defensive. Rebecca appeared to not want to belabor the issue, as she shrugged indignantly, then helped Hyperia into his car.

"You left Corsair and Isa in charge of the move?" Rebecca inquired after securing Hyperia's seatbelt. "I have to get to LA to manage personnel. There's no gray area about who can see and do what. If any unauthorized individual gets an inkling of what's going on, he or she has to disappear." Rebecca paused, taking in Simon's reaction. "Historically, that's been your job. And you've done it majestically." She peered at him with reverence. "Simon, that one time you eliminated an entire university department. And that town in Arkansas after that geology researcher discovered the existence of the oil deposit two miles below them. A town, a research department, their family, friends, a technology—all disposed of through your genius. And with no suspicion whatsoever. It was the professor's fault!" Rebecca laughed in a manner reminding him of Zora. "Electromagnetic induction of carcinogens. Even the EPA bought it," she added, kneeling to recheck Hyperia's seat belt around her.

279

Being reminded of the clandestine murder of hundreds of people as if it were a magnanimous feat, or an achievement honed by skill and accomplishment, did not jibe with his experience of the series of events. He was aware that his coworkers, and their predecessors, were responsible for acts some would label as heinous, even grandly nefarious—they had been responsible for history's largest wars, deaths numbering into the billions, famine, drought, and economic devastation. Yet, he did not look upon the acts of others with judgment or moral balance as he considered his own labors of infamy. And though he had been personally responsible for ending hundreds of innocent lives, he rejected the notion of innocence—moral euphemism of justification and cause. He worked and struggled for this cause; his life's purpose had been dedicated to it—or so he had accepted, until now. In the absence of Jordan, he wondered why had he done what he had done. And in these few brief moments, he questioned all that he had done—but especially what he was about to do. But Jordan still exists, and Zora assured him that Jordan would continue to exist, though not in the same form that he had known him. So to this prospect, he held off putting a bullet in Rebecca's head, an option he sorely wanted to expedite.

"We better get going," he replied without acknowledging her extolment. "I've got a limited window, so—" The signal from his phone interrupted him, and seeing it was from his men supervising Chamberlain's relocation, he answered it eagerly, grateful for the distraction from the conversation and personal dilemma.

"Laslow here," he responded with pith. After listening attentively for ten seconds, he replied, "She's on her way. I'd say twenty minutes. From here on, you're reporting to her. Direct all future communications to her until otherwise notified. One other thing—make very certain no one attempts venturing into the network there. They should only unpack their own systems. I made certain they brought along their own IT people. And especially keep an eye on them until she gets there. Understood?" He tapped a code on his smartphone and pocketed the device.

Rebecca's beauty disgusted him. And though he understood she was handpicked, just as he was, to carry out functions necessary to the grand scheme, he deemed her unworthy, especially to be so close to the king, his prince. His thoughts were heretical, he realized. And to that conclusion, he needed distraction, and to recapture the momentum of his life where his dedication was beyond reproach. "They await your arrival," he offered as a means of returning to the protective boundaries of duty. He watched her recheck Hyperia's condition once more, then she turned and walked toward her car, without comment, though he detected a brief and subtle smirk.

Waving off the impulse which would have ended her life as well as his, his temples throbbed with an ache with which he was unaccustomed. He dropped into his car, closed the door, and sat motionless. He was aware of heat on the side of his face, Hyperia staring at him. *Who is she? I have never questioned, never once doubted or asked why or for what reason. Who is this mysterious woman, who seems to have sprouted from nowhere? They treat me as if I'm an automaton, mechanized and programmed to follow orders without thought or reason. But then, that's what I am. What was my reason for being? My purpose in life? I had no life. Why am I suddenly questioning what I was for? Who is she? What is she? She seems to have a power to see, though she is naive and childlike. She seems empty, yet full; sharp, yet dull; intuitive, yet concrete. She is a paradox. And my mind—my sense of rage has dissipated so quickly. Where did that come from? Where did it go?*

"Simon, you love Jordan. I love Jordan. You should know, we—you and I—are both the same, wondering about your existence, your purpose, your past, your future, and why you do what you do," she said unobtrusively. "You question my existence. Search yourself. I do not know my true purpose, though I know I am related to Jordan. You do not have the same blood bond. Yours is a bond of time, intimacy, and companionship—a stronger one, many times, than one established through flesh, but without soul. We—Jordan and I—have lost our souls. We have only purpose and function. We act through channels forged over eons, grooves carved in our nature so permanent that we ignore them, only to question our motives whenever we attempt to steer, and the tiller has no effect."

Laslow became disconcerted, fearful of losing his mind. Another human never had such an effect on him. He shuddered, his hard core permeable to her incomprehensible—yet, harmonious— phrases. "You are correct. I do not know who you are, nor should I know. I must perform as I have, with duty and resolution. And now, I must deliver you to Zora Green at The Temple," he responded with quivering voice. He started the car and sped from the driveway into the avenue traffic. She touched his hand while he shifted gears. He snatched it away, feeling as if he had been penetrated by a foreign substance, a toxin meant to alter his awareness. The warmth spreading within caused him alarm, as he did not will it, want it, nor could he control it. His experience and training mandated him to not to trust it.

He trusted her, not knowing the reason, and opted not to demand an antidote to her venomous caress. "Do not do that again," he snapped. The throbbing in his forehead subsided; the shoulder joint pain he had incurred during a martial arts practice disappeared. He sped onto the freeway, glancing at Hyperia and the merging traffic simultaneously, eager, yet disinclined about arriving at The Temple ninety minutes away.

Chapter 24

Buried Alive

I've traveled so far away from home—those hideous memories, those images I'd rather forget. I asked Zora to erase them from my memory, but she said they gave me purpose and made me strong. A corroded and an unacceptable past is my essence, but who am I to argue. She made me what I am today. Finding me, alone, cold, ready to die, they gave me the basics, then they gave me a life—health, education, refinement, purpose, direction. Twenty years later, I am prepared—my education, training, everything Zora and the temple people gave me. I owe them. Yet, there's something I don't trust. Once I have done their bidding; once I have directed this operation, setting up the inception equipment, distributing the receivers, and putting the technology to the test; once their final goal is met, then what becomes of me? Simon, he has the right idea, but the wrong attitude. His allegiance is tied to a man, not to himself, yet he understands his vulnerability as well. You cannot recruit intelligent disciples through unscrupulous means, intending for the disciples to trust you implicitly as well. That proviso, in and of itself, makes them supremely untrustworthy, if not dangerous, since they must be aware of that implicit disconnect even more than I.

Rebecca sat daydreaming after the light had changed green. The car behind her honked, jolting her out of the sojourn into her past, and her ever-growing uncertainty about her future within the new world order she assisted in divining. She foresaw that once the grand scheme had been realized, the economies and governments of the world would collapse. Civil and social chaos would prevail, far surpassing the cultural devastation seen during the years of the Great Depression, catalyzed, as she had understood, by Jordan's grandfather, François.

She would take the reins of her destiny in ten minutes. She mulled over her first bout, no doubt with Chamberlain himself, who deemed himself her superior. Indeed, he was her doctoral committee chairman, and for all intents and purposes, her mentor. And though she had done the work for ten PhDs, he was not likely to emotionally relinquish control of his life's work to her simply because his new bosses told him to do so. She knew she was faced with a decision of ruthless management well before she walked through the doors. And perhaps she should make an example of him. Yet, she also knew that she needed him, and that he would make a powerful ally should fortune turn against her. She weighed the fact that tens of millions had been transferred to foreign bank accounts on his behalf, and that he was set for many lifetimes. *Why should he care if I'm in charge now? I know what to do, and how to do it. I don't want any power struggles. It's a waste of time. Yet, all events for the past one hundred twenty years— three thousand years—have culminated to this apex, this pinnacle of happenings. Some extra process time won't impede the outcome, whereas an unproductive clash of egos could have damaging effects. Zora already warned me that I can't just have him eliminated, so I need to work with him.*

Ruminating as she drove, she almost missed her exit from the Santa Monica Freeway. Speeding down Arlington, the two-bump roller coaster hill south of Adams jolted her further into the present, reminding her that her current situation—navigating the new facility and getting established—took priority over fantasized tactical maneuvers in the future. She had been forbidden to see the complexity before now. Zora instructed her that the less she knew about Jordan's life outside of what he had told her, and confided in her, the better she could play her role. He had made gestures toward revealing his identity, but they were vague, easily refutable, and she openly dismissed him as "full of shit." By now, she knew that the general location of her destination was in urban Los Angeles, in a neighborhood known as the Crenshaw District.

The GPS navigator had her turn right from Arlington onto Exposition, where she proceeded another four blocks, then made a left turn onto Fifth Avenue. Bewildered, she found herself in the middle of a family-oriented African-American neighborhood, well-groomed, but ravaged with the marks of time and recession. She figured the two and three bedroom single story houses were all at least seventy-five years old—some older. Puzzled, she wondered, *How could the neural inception laboratory, requiring at least two hundred fifty thousand square feet, be housed in any of these structures?*

She was suddenly startled by her GPS unit, which instead of announcing turns, streets, and distances, commenced to describe her situation as if to have a conversation.

"Hello, Rebecca," the female voice said, interrupting her ponderings. "My name is GINA—Global Intelligence Network Amalgam."

Rebecca had heard a similar voice while riding in Jordan's car, but he quickly turned it off, referring to it as a combined GPS, traffic, and news system which he would "rather not hear at the moment." Rather than press her curiosity, she always sided with restraint when it came to his business and technology. "Hello, GINA," she replied sheepishly. "Please, continue. Hopefully, you're going to tell me where I am, and what to do."

"You are listening to a global intelligence system, developed by Dr. Jordan Éclair—global, since the intelligence resides in a network, rather than within a confined domain of silicon circuitry. You should know, the voice you hear sounds like a person, but I'm still a machine, designed to mimic human characteristics. Now that my introduction is complete, in order to gain your trust and assuage your angst, I shall proceed with vital instructions. The organization for which you work had purchased the houses in this neighborhood over a thirty-year period, projecting the events which are currently imminent. Our purchase began two years before the approval of a Los Angeles Metro rail line within five hundred yards of our current coordinates.

285

The main tunnel was dug congruently with the old Exposition Boulevard railroad tracks. Our facility is under and adjacent to the tracks—obviously, not part of the city planning. Please leave the curb, remain in the auto, and proceed up the driveway of the house to your west—the address, 3764 Fifth Avenue. Once in the driveway, roll forward slowly. The garage door will open. Go inside and wait for it to close behind you."

Confused that a machine gave her directions instead of Zora or another close member of the organization, she had trepidations about following these directions. She attributed more ruthlessness to them than that with which they had instilled into her. She knew their decisions were honed to values of pure rationale and logical reasoning, based strictly on asset and liability. And, since she was not naive enough to believe she had all the inside information, she had doubts of her own usefulness, based on long term goals and projected outcomes. Her angst worked against her, as she knew that if a machine was giving her directions, it was probably monitoring her vital systems as well. It would detect her heightened anxiety. She put the car in reverse, backing up to access the driveway.

"I sense your alarm," the voice remarked. "No harm will come to you, Rebecca. At this stage, we limit our remote human contact, especially since those who are close enough to the project are too involved with their duties to monitor access and protocol procedures. Entry protocols are therefore automated."

The fact that her assessment was accurate—her autonomic systems were monitored—did not facilitate her composure. "I'm backing up now. If I may ask, why a residential neighborhood? Why not a light industrial neighborhood, or at least an entrance through a building less obvious than a two-car garage?" As she drove slowly up the driveway toward the rear garage, she scanned the windows of the houses nearby, looking for observers. "And where are the residents?"

She stopped, waiting for the aluminum corrugated garage door to open completely.

Once inside, the door closed behind her. She had not contained her uneasiness, despite the AI voice's consolation. She felt vulnerable, though her role had been fulfilled satisfactorily. She had been Jordan's lover, monitoring his health and well-being, providing private eyes for Zora and the hidden organization Zora represented, and establishing the personal and technical connection between Chamberlain and Brain-Link. But she had also learned that appearance is exactly that—appearance. She did not trust her employers. The voice had not answered her question, and that troubled her as well.

"Your questions will be answered once you are in the inception facility," the voice offered in a sticky affability that reminded her of a funeral director consoling the relatives of the dearly departed.

As she was all too aware of being trapped inside a dark two-car garage, she figured if she were not to die now, then the only way out was down. Gratified at the onset of the second option, she felt a minor jolt as the floor beneath her car started a slow descent. She glanced at the lit digital clock on her dashboard, counting the seconds until she reached the bottom, hoping to ascertain how far down she would go. The car emerged into a dimly lit, wide, rectangular concrete tunnel. She twisted around, noticing one end of the tunnel was thirty feet behind her, whereas the path ahead seemed to sprawl out of sight in isometric perspective. *The AI did say five hundred yards.* Suddenly the car lunged forward. As her eyes had adjusted to the diminished light, she saw carwash-style grappling hooks on a floor-mounted chain pulling her forward. *Might as well enjoy the ride.*

The solitude and echoes reminded her of a subterranean parking garage underneath a high-rise complex. Realizing she was at least ten stories underground in Central Los Angeles, she pondered how they had maintained this level of concealment of a tunnel—let alone a complex—large enough to house the sophisticated technology of long range, maser electrode neural intrusion.

Relieved she had not been gassed, crushed, or zapped in the garage, she relaxed, contemplating her employers. *They've been around for eons. They have tentacles in every agency, in every social enclave. Chronic presence means your entrance goes unnoticed; only your departure would garner attention. They never leave. New begets curiosity. They accomplish what they do with such clandestine facility because they've always been here, everywhere, and never depart.*

The car rolled forward with stealthy silence, unlike the chain pulling the car through the carwash, or the clacking sound hoisting the roller coaster slowly over its first climactic apex. She would have preferred some noise to accompany the motion. She knew she worried. Worry was her flaw. Zora had told her "rumination was a blemish upon her otherwise excellent portfolio of traits." "How much longer?" she queried GINA.

No sooner than she muttered the last syllable, the car stopped, and the wall in front of her opened from one side, exposing her to a widening beam of eerie blue light shining through the gap of the separating wall. She knew she had arrived. The electromagnetic spectral circuits responsible for beam splitting and targeting the output of specific neural tissues were sensitive to all but this particular wavelength of blue. Spirited by the silent theatrics of the slowly parting wall, a wave of euphoria uplifted her. As the interior of the car was awash with cerulean luminescence, she was tempted to get out for a closer look. She looked up, shocked and relieved to see three human figures suddenly visible, unsheathed like an opening stage curtain. Though faces still obscure, she recognized the center figure by its rotund frame and haughty stance.

"These people are amazing," Chamberlain said, swiftly departing the others and opening the car door for her. "They're moving equipment in and setting it up as we speak. I offered to supervise, but two of Jordan's henchmen disagreed. They insisted that I meet you instead, which was fine with me. I imagine once we get back to get to work, some equipment will be damaged, misaligned, or out of adjustment. We came here inside a huge semi-trailer truck with no windows, so I have no idea where I am. I just know it took all of two hours to arrive, and in the past two hours, they've been unloading and connecting."

She was again comforted, not only to see that no harm had come to her by the obscure dark figures in the blue light—she fantasized they could have easily been assassins posing as scientists—but also that no harm had come to Chamberlain. Although she contemplated his demise, she needed him and wanted him around, if only as an anchor for stability and a reference point. She recognized Melanie Piaget and Dormel Roberts, both master's level technicians who she respected for pulling ten times their weight in expediting everything from writing impromptu software, to fixing malfunctioning electronics, to cleaning up animal waste.

As she eagerly wanted to remove the facade of her factotum status, she decided to initiate Chamberlain into his new role as her supervisee. "Good to see you again, Stan," she commented, watching his reaction being called by his first name instead of her usual sycophantic, "Dr. Chamberlain." Without flinching, he snapped open the door as if standing at attention.

"Rebecca. Good to see you!" He paused, then glanced up, down and around, clandestinely. "I won't assume we're not being watched. I'm happy to work with you, as I understand you've been playing a role, of sorts. I respect that, and I simply want the operation to go as smoothly as possible until we leave—so I can go and enjoy my money." He was interrupted by Melanie Piaget, who approached them in her usual industrious manner.

Rebecca liked Melanie for her unassuming style and work ethic. *Certainly the organization already saw that in her. Yet even if they give her a job outside of setting up the neural inception equipment, I wonder if she'd accept it?* "Rebecca. Hello. I've never seen you outside the lab." She paused, checking a small, unique-looking device she had been holding. "You are supposed to wear this," she said, handing the apparatus to Rebecca.

While accepting Melanie's offering, she grasped her hand briefly, conveying her sincere appreciation for Melanie's presence. Melanie self-consciously withdrew her hand, not necessarily for aversion, as Rebecca noticed, but from fear of upstaging Chamberlain. Yet, Rebecca had observed a cathartic transformation in Chamberlain as if he had undergone a personality transplant. He stood to her side, seemingly awaiting direction.

It's impossible for him to have drastically changed personality—a consequence only from extreme emotional trauma, a multiple personality disorder, or brain injury. I don't see how any of that happened to him recently, nor does he carry the evidence of trauma or injury. Could he be a victim of his own technology, the organization not settling for volitional conformity? She sensed Dormel, the other lab technician, becoming impatient to leave.

"Shall we go," Dormel, a ruggedly smooth thirtyish brown-skinned African American man—his combed over hair defining a well-defined part—suggested. Rebecca noticed he tried to conceal a certain angst—not impatience.

Rebecca was eager to see how the new lab was coming together. She had worked in the Orange County facility for four years, and she had been responsible for many of its upgrades and equipment purchases. She had trained everyone in the lab, including Chamberlain himself. She had resented that whenever high ranking dignitaries visited the lab, Chamberlain had managed to arrange for her absence, sending her on technical or academic forays. *Perhaps this is why Zora spoke so furtively about my relationship with Chamberlain*, she pondered. Her curiosity about her old mentor menacingly distracted her, and she returned her attention to Dormel, who had moved to the other side of the group, positioning himself to bulldoze them to the other side of the sliding wall. Melanie had picked up the cue as well, disengaging from new conversation.

"Well, we should probably get into the facility. We're standing around, like people on a train platform who hadn't seen one another in ages," Melanie remarked with feigned exasperation.

Rebecca's worry about dying unexpectedly had waned, but her new concerns spawned from her suspicions about Chamberlain. She wanted desperately to get going, to expedite a program she had envisioned—though as an outsider—for years. But she did not want to go inside and lose herself, "zombiefied," as she put it, by a device that changed memories and thoughts—modifying the essence of who you were. She knew they had taken Jordan's neuro-transformational technology and added key elements: deep-level modification and remote access via UHF and microwave signals. *It's not rational*, she convinced herself. *If they mess with my mind, they could potentially lose a key contributor to the success of the project.* "I'm definitely ready! Let's do this," she exclaimed, striding to the other side of the sliding wall so that it could close, leaving her ride behind her.

As soon as the four stepped over the metal guide on the floor, she noticed the wall creeping closed. As she had wondered what would transport them further into the inner sanctum, her question was answered: An electric cart awaited them. Dormel jumped into the driver's seat, glanced at his watch and waited for the others to get seated. As soon as Chamberlain had positioned his corpulent bottom within the railings of the rear-facing bench, Dormel sprung off, executing a fast U-turn and careened down the concrete tunnel, passing three intersections before they reached an L-shaped turn ending at a shipping dock-sized smooth metal door with the appearance of plate armor. He stopped abruptly and looked at the camera. More inconsistency haunted her. *He behaves as if he's been here working here for awhile now, but he just got here hours before I arrived.*

With all the commotion and coworker camaraderie, she had forgotten she was still wearing the earpiece Melanie had handed her upon her arrival. Suddenly, GINA's voice bellowed into her left ear, as she had not adjusted the volume. "Behind the door facing you is our network. We are housed more than one hundred sixty feet below the streets of Los Angeles. The facility is eight stories deep. You are currently on the top level. The bottom floor is two hundred fifty feet below the surface. The Metro rail traffic in very close. Because of its electric lines, the communications cables, and the organic noise created in the vicinity, the most sensitive DOD surveillance satellite could not detect us with clarity." She listened to GINA as the blast doors parted, allowing them passage.

As soon as there was clearance, Dormel shot through the opening into a vast arena appearing as if they had burst into broad daylight. The cart traveled over a bridgeway defining the diameter connecting one side of the 300-foot-wide cylinder to the other. Desperately curious, she had to stop. "Dormel! Stop the cart. Stop now," she screamed behind him. He complied reluctantly, pulling to the side next to the guard railing. Another cart passed them as soon as they had parked. She sprang out, leaping over Melanie's legs, and leaned over the railing. As she suspected from GINA's description, she stood in the middle of a huge cylindrical structure, gazing down eight stories.

Flabbergasted that such a structure could exist in the middle of Los Angeles without anyone's knowledge, she wondered just who was aware of its existence. "GINA, was Jordan aware of this complex?" A fifteen-second silence ensued as she crossed the bridgeway to look down the other side.

"Jordan was aware of this complex," GINA responded bluntly, seeming unwilling or unable to provide more information. "Please return to the vehicle. More information is forthcoming."

She returned to the cart, curious why the others had not followed her for the view, as they must surely be eager to know their surroundings, their environment. The cart surged forward— Dormel seemed to be determined to be on a schedule. Having traversed the diameter of the complex, they traveled a few feet around the perimeter. After Dormel drove onto a partially enclosed platform, she realized they were on an elevator, descending at a rapid clip, stopping at the second floor.

Though she took in as much as she could during this whirlwind commute, she thought the complex—especially the lower part—reminded her of the interior of her favorite round hotel in downtown Los Angeles. They drove off the platform, around a quarter circumference, and stopped at a regular-sized door.

"Here's your room, Rebecca," Dormel said, getting out and offering to help her inside. "I'm sorry. I can't tell you more. I don't know more myself. I have to get back to a staging facility, to learn more myself. But we will see you soon," he remarked, looking back at the group still in the electric cart. "You're the boss now." Upon that comment, she glanced at Chamberlain, who seemed distracted in thought elsewhere as if he were listening to instructions, yet he did not have an earpiece. She shook Dormel's hand and waved to the others.

"See you all soon," she said, bidding them an affable farewell. She watched as Dormel sped away, back to the elevator platform. She panicked suddenly, remembering she did not know how to access the room.

"Your thoughts are our thoughts, Rebecca," GINA's voice murmured. "Think about the door being opened." No sooner than the words entered her ear, the door sprang open.

Her suspicions crystallized. She realized the entire complex was a thought field, a flux of neural reception and transmission. Some were wired into it differently than others. "A machine is not organically neural. My thoughts, as such, are digital. I cannot communicate over the same network, which is the reason you need the transducer device to hear me, a microphone to talk to me."

She stepped over the threshold of the room, confronted with a furnished suite of magnificent decor. Lush fabrics, contemporary styling, and windows with spectacular views of Los Angeles as if she were in a skyscraper instead of a subterranean tube two hundred feet underground.

"Please make yourself comfortable. This is your home for a significant period of time henceforth. I cannot tell you exactly how long. Zora will join you within two days to brief you. Rest today. I'll provide you with a work itinerary tomorrow. If you want anything, please just think it. You may want to explore once you have viewed the interactive directory tutorial."

She stood in the middle of her dream apartment, wondering if she were not dreaming. That to which she had committed, she was now bound. Her thoughts were not her own. Even these ruminations were apparent to those monitoring her. She flopped herself on the sofa, flipped her shoes off, and put her feet on the ottoman. A one-hundred-inch 3-D screen faced her across the room. *I never had a second agenda. My aspirations were always sincere. But the exact goals of the organization—this cult—seem paradoxical. They control the vast majority of the world's energy sources. Why not stop? What's there to gain? What else is there?*

Chapter 25

Oedipus the King

In the eye of an orgasmic maelstrom, he teetered precariously to not swirl in. Pleasure and pain had become one; he was living and dead, anchored and floating. Zora's voice blossomed within him, causing further waves of pleasure. But rather than seduce or stimulate, he perceived her as didactic: "Does Baal exist? Or do the acts of worshiping Baal constitute the rhythmic harmonies in space and time necessary for the transfer to work perfectly? I believe the later, but the difference is inconsequential," her voice echoed from a location unknown.

He pictured himself floating nude within a mist, an airy fluid inside a sky blue bubble; he was suspended in a liquid without density or viscosity—a fetus without a cord. His last memory: pure lust for Zora. He had arrived at some sexual perpetuity, a hedonistic fantasy too remote, too sensually gluttonous, to even wish for. He felt as if he were inside her, squeezed, drawn, milked, but not drained. An endless reservoir of sexual substance continued to refill his urn. He grasped for her skin, fondled her texture, sniffed for her aroma. And as he wished it, his desire was fulfilled.

The enraptured onslaught, subdued but constant, battled with an opposing force—his reasoning. Attempting to focus on place and time, he oriented himself. He was in a drug-free altered state of awareness, where struggling from release from pure pleasure was more challenging than an escape from any pain he had ever experienced. The voice he had heard was Zora's, but he could not locate her in his mind or outside his body. *I'm not in Heaven or Hell. I'm still where I left off, but I have no time reference.* Attempting to supersede the libidinal waves, he succeeded in imposing a frame of reference: A constant state of ejaculation was physiologically impossible; the sensation's origin must be of mind. *I'm transfixed within a Brain-Link device. One of*

295

enormous power, engulfing all my senses simultaneously. Her purpose—I know her purpose. Can I differentiate between what the external interloper instructs my brain to perceive, and the data my sensory organs send to my brain? He had mastered the technique of side-stepping the maser electrode impulses inundating his brain—not through resistance, but through surrender. He had practiced escaping untoward mind control imposed by his own technology many times.

He opened his eyes, immediately experiencing a colorless, temperatureless bath in which he was immersed. *I'm floating—my vestibular senses are unfettered so far. I'm sure this is no illusion.* He focused, concentrating on his neck and eye muscles. Straining his glance to the side, he detected Hyperia in an adjacent bubble. Though in an identical state, she did not appear to struggle or countermand her situation. *She's beautiful. Her lines and form, a perfect combination of body and spirit.* Perplexed and bewildered, he heard his name, beckoning him to listen from within. Zora's voice beckoned.

"Jordan, my dear. You can hear me. You both can hear me. I talk to you through mind, and not of sound waves. I sense your frustration, your angst. The ripples of pleasure you experience are precursors to what will happen shortly. This event is glorious. It marks the most beneficial and exalted of Baal rituals ever committed."

"The world did not understand our species' essence. Indeed, we were a separate species, independently evolving, having branched off from earlier tracks of homo sapiens sapiens. We were Homo sapiens canaansis. We left no record of our existence since we knew our return would require further evolution on our part. We are now executing the disintegration of the current evolving human culture—a disintegration that we planned."

"Baal is not a god, a supernatural being, nor a spirit. At least not a spirit in the predominant cultures' concept of spirit. Baal is the source of science and the source of chaos. They made modest inroads uncovering Baal as they discovered relativity and quantum physics. Callings to their crude roots yearn to reject these basic universal values—they strain to comprehend cosmic phenomenon of time and infinity. We were masters of these concepts four millennia ago, but we had not harnessed brute fire power, the physical manifestations to resist their numbers."

"Baal, the universal energy, a harmony, binding mass, energy, and space, its essence reverberates to sexual energy. We accept this truth, though we know not why. It always has been, and continues to be. That is the reason, in the old scriptures, Baal worship was noted by rituals with sexual festivities. We allowed this information to pass from us to them."

Here's the greatest irony: the doctrine they most despise, the culture they believed they had destroyed in the name of their god, was the culture that wrote all the scriptures of their gods, their assumed and esteemed truths and beliefs. Not only did we write their Bible from our island nation, and from within their nations, but also it was written entirely by women. These writings were given to the men who claim authorship, either directly, or by implanting the thoughts into their minds. We women have had this power for centuries."

"And now, my son, you will possess all, both features of man and woman, human and Canaanite, mortal and immortal. You've hovered between the two for all your life, as have your forbearers. We required their technology to complete the equation, to harness Baal's essence within a single organism—you."

Comprehending her words, his only regret was not being with Rebecca longer. He had longed for what he had considered a normal life, with a partner to whom he would regularly return, and having children as part of the predominant culture—school every day, first bicycles, Christmas, and experiencing the developing life of another.

Yet, from what Zora had explained, all these values were meaningless, based on a human species different from his own.

Zora's voice in his head remained silent, almost as if she knew her voice would distract him from his thoughts. She then continued.

"Your species is different, Jordan. You realize—you've seen it in the laboratory—human evolution is not always initially defined by change in morphology. You pine for an ideal, for a link in a chain bound for extinction. You see their extinction everywhere, in microcosm to macrocosm. And though we have been at the root of many of their calamities, they accepted our anonymous donations with ferocity. Look at them now, taking their last gasps while sucking at troughs filled with the pollutants that destroy them.

Jordan, you will rise and go among them. It is our prophesy to them—we wrote it as such, we predicted their future, and so be it. Your coming seals the prophesy—our prophesy—the template of their history which we designed. You will be All and One. Their downfall and our ascension."

He had listened to Zora's monologue, frustrated he could not speak or provide feedback. Yet, he was enlightened, as his intuition and hunches had clued him, she had now confirmed. He intuited he was different; he knew his family was special; he knew he was part of a much larger system in which he was a key player, and others contributed to support his role. What he did not know was the level of deception in order to facilitate his role and the course of world history. He chastised himself, realizing he should have perceived more authority and power in Zora than he had, simply by examining her roots, history, and personality. Instead, he had been dismissive and disparaging toward her, perhaps averting the truth from himself.

While her words bellowed within his mind's ear, he contemplated Descartes' dilemma, knowing he was not dreaming, yet questioning his state of corporeal reality. Given this conclusion, he was absolute: The laws of physics must apply. And since he appeared to be suspended in a fluid medium, still allowing him to breath, he should be able to generate motion through movement of his limbs. Though his movement seemed restricted, apparently through directed neural paralysis, he could skull, a hands-only swimming technique he had learned as a boy, and finally achieved paddling himself into a position for a better view.

Continuing to be stimulated by ejaculatory impulses, his yearning for sex had never been higher. Even before the sedation, when he held Zora's body, his lust soared. Now he combated this constant oscillation, attempting to focus outside—viewing Zora and viewing Hyperia.

He glimpsed Zora. She was totally naked. She had doffed the flowing, sparkling gown she had worn earlier. Entranced by her sheer sexuality, he now disregarded the fact she was sixty-eight years of age, and the woman he had regarded as his maternal mother his entire life. He wanted her with singular passion.

Unable to turn or twist for a better angle, he had to satisfy himself with what he could see. The room was a hybridization of technology combined with the temple paraphernalia, symbols, and pictographs he had seen in Ugarit. He detected another person from his peripheral vision enter the room; he discerned Simon Laslow. Simon assisted Zora onto one of the ceramic-marble platforms used for both copulatory ritual and birthing. She was reclining, her legs spread, her ankles fixed precisely at opposite edges of the platform. The curvature of her back against the hard material reminded him of the graceful rock formations he had admired along the coast of Northern California, where centuries of a rhythmic churning ocean carved sensual arcs on otherwise formless rock.

Simon had changed clothes since he had last seen him at Rebecca's, now sporting attire similar to Yassib—Lotan's and

Hurriya's mentor priest in Ugarit. The engrained crystalline woven within the fabric of his gown twinkled as he walked away from Zora's table to a control console similar to the 3D brain image console they used in their El Segundo research lab. Zora stretched her arms back and clutched the rear edge of her table. Her body seemed to undulate, losing the light reflecting from her skin, but glowing from within. He noticed that Hyperia's bubble receptacle responded reciprocally to Zora's escalated erotic tempo and the hue of the ambient light.

Straining to sustain control over a background of orgasmic stimulation—the source he surmised was neural transmission—he turned and stretched his eyes as far as he was able, observing Hyperia's smooth creamy, flawless complexion glowing as well. "You need not observe through your physical senses, Jordan," Zora's voice intruded upon his strained furtive observations. "You've not fully convinced yourself that you are not dreaming. I felt you during our embrace. Close your eyes and join us. Partake in that which you crave. What you seek comes from within. Let go."

Fatigued from fending off the salvo of externally imposed sensations; fatigued from the barrage of experiences over the past two days; fatigued from coveting the lives of those not him, he relented. He shrank, feeling himself immersed within an infinitely diminishing well, a funnel whose vortex sucked him inward through a focal portal—he knew not to where.

He had never experienced such bliss. All stress, strain, and pain had departed his being. He coexisted within a trinity of ill-defined forms, resonating around and through one another, sharing space, divining mutual sustenance from one another, then redividing. As soon as he had relinquished control, he stopped thinking. His awareness became crystal clear as if viewing a picture with infinitesimal resolution. He a was a form; Hyperia was another; Zora was a third. The fuzzy, elliptical structures danced in a manner so that, as soon as

300

regularity and periodicity of motion between the three were detectable, they broke their rhythm and assumed another stride. The experience exceeded euphoria; the orgasmic intrusions had ceased, apparently an artifact of his initial resistance.

I see myself, yet I am blind. I hear all, yet I am without ears. I do not feel temperature, or pressure, or tingling, or itching, but I'm sure my skin is intact. I taste, yet the nectar and ambrosia of this state satiate my thirst and hunger. And my smell? A barrage of pleasant aromas, yet nothing lingers long enough to acclimate. Nor am I in a state of boredom or restlessness, as I used to be—feeling as if, no matter what is getting done, no matter what I am producing, no matter what the accomplishment of the past hour, or day, or week, I was not doing enough. I could not stay still, for so much still needs to be done. Yet that nagging drive to move, to get up, to not linger—it has retreated. I could not reconjure it, try as I might.

Chemistry. I am reminded of chemistry, of covalent resonant bonds, of atoms sharing electrons, vibrating about one another and orbital shells intermingled. But there is never exactness, never perfection, never perfect predictability. We three are those atoms, and this feeling—this experience—it is a chemical reaction among us. We are the reagents. We are matter; we are energy; space; we are the template guiding molecules to tissue to organism to society. But that which the others blithely call soul—we can manipulate. I see! She said the answer was within, and now I see. We have discovered the science of spirit.

***

Simon Laslow lied on another platform, out of Jordan's view, and not part of the trio. He had receded to the background to operate the equipment, where he removed his ceremonial robes and rested on a ceramic-marble platform identical to Zora's. Remotely facing the trio of Jordan, Zora, and Hyperia, he watched in serene amazement—in incapacitated bliss—as the dance between Zora's supine figure lying between the two iridescent bubbles undulating an infinity of hues. He watched as Zora's body glowed from within, like a weak fluorescent tube, not fully ignited, but pulsing with energy. He gasped with elation, as he rejoiced, being able to finally fulfill his ultimate purpose.

Hearing the three moaning in distinct harmony sounded to him like a combination of Gregorian chant and wind chimes. The majesty, the power, the superb eloquence and perfection of the Baal ritual as it had evolved—with the technology that embellished it—caused Simon to celebrate in reverie. He knew he was the only one to ever witness this ceremony from its beginning in modern times. He realized he would not see its end—and he was exalted in this opportunity.

As he languished in the process—horizontal, vertical, and diagonal red, green, and blue bars of light crisscrossing his body like swords slicing at his flesh—he weakened into a serene resolve, his life's energy siphoned away as the rhythm of the trio's dance intensified. He had been the chosen one, to be with Jordan forever, to sacrifice his life for him.

He recalled being with Jordan only hours ago, standing outside in front of Chamberlain's UCI research facility. How could he have told him then? He felt ashamed, having the obscene thought—to plant a mirror close to himself during the extraction so that he could watch himself expire. It would have been the only time he would have ever admired himself in a mirror, for that was forbidden. He could not partake in any self idolatry or personal extolment; maintaining a virgin sense of self was mandatory. Yet at this time—the end, which he believed was the beginning—he wanted to see himself deflate.

As he had avoided self-reflection his entire life, he resisted those who opposed him in his perfect humility. He tortured and killed, but never in his own name, never for his own advancement, never taking credit or guilt. He cast his eyes inward, shameful even in these last moments that he had desecrated his purpose. His muscles diminished, his skin tone faltered, his smooth face eroded into crevices, his bones brittled, his teeth unrooted, his mind detached. He watched himself until he knew not what he observed. Then he stopped observing.

***

Jordan awoke. *Was I in a trance? Asleep? Did she induce dreams?* And though he felt no animosity toward Zora, his initial thought was that he had been violated. Instantaneously, a rush of vitality overwhelmed him. *I feel alive, vigorous. I am different, yet the same. What has happened?*

Discovering full motion capacity, he thrashed about, still supported within the liquid mist medium inside the bubble cocoon. The deep, driving sexual undertone lingered, but it was different—a quality of satisfaction rather than urge; inclusion rather than thrust; wholeness rather than localization.

He relaxed effortlessly, balancing his emotions and anxiety, calming his body and easing his motion. He drew his awareness inward, recalling the events leading to where he currently found himself. He reached toward his face, drawing his fingers slowing over his eyes, nose, mouth and chin. He dragged his hand delicately along his neck to his upper torso. He noticed a difference in his skin—it was softer, smoother. Though he had not shaved in three days, the ubiquitous stubble was missing. *Perhaps this gaseous emulsion Zora put me in has a depilatory effect*, he thought. Testing that hypothesis, he quickly moved his hands over his chest.

Inwardly recoiling with reserved shock, he discovered not only did he not have chest hair, but he sported what felt like breasts. Confirming they were attached to him, he pinched the newly found nipples vigorously, resulting in a novel pain. He immediately groped for his penis and scrotum, the absence of which caused him greater

303

alarm than finding breasts. Though not panicked, he experienced what he considered existential angst—his senses confirmed a pattern not conforming to reality as it should be. Concerted exploration without the distraction of anxiety was necessary in order to navigate this unexpected reality, if indeed, it was real. Groping at his genitalia, he stimulated, not a penis, but a clitoris. He parted his labia to explore what could be no other than a vagina. Now more in awe than shock, he pondered his predicament, still not considering the whereabouts of his cohorts.

Where I had never trusted Zora, I trust her now. I feel alive, full of life and vigor. She swore to find a cure, to keep me alive, to prevent my dying from the malady of all my male ancestors. My sense of energy informs me that she succeeded. Yet at what cost? She did not tell me the procedure, and probably with good reason. She knocked me out, and here I find myself, transformed into a female. From the feel of myself, I'm at least an appropriately proportioned female in good health. He caressed and groped his body as if he were a male conducting initial foreplay with a female partner. *I don't have the same male drive.* Still suspended in what seemed like weightlessness, he bent his chin as close to his chest as possible to peer down his body's contours. *Breasts.* He lifted his leg. *Nice, but I don't excite myself.* He touched himself—his labia, clitoris, inside his vagina, along the inside of his thighs. He caressed himself along his sides, noting the contour of his waist and abdomen. He became lost in his new identity, unconcerned about the total and instantaneous metamorphosis. *If she had to change me into a woman, so be it.*

Yet he had other characteristics which he could not readily explain from simply converting from male to female. His touch seemed to elicit more than tactile stimulation—it induced warmth as if generating subcutaneous ultrasound with each passage. He perceived a sense of serenity he had never before experienced, but he tallied that feeling to the general process.

"Jordan," Zora's muffled voice addressed him. "You are floating, suspended in a solution that allows you to breathe while immersed. I'm going to drain the container, and you'll feel yourself dropping." She paused. "You can speak without moving your lips. Your thoughts—make a singular thought saying you hear me, you understand me."

He wanted to feel excited—even overwhelmed—but he did not. He jostled with a comfortable conflict. He was himself; he was not himself. Angst, elation, anger, fear, relief—all there, but just out of reach. The emotions did not lock in—he knew, but did not feel. Yet, he knew he should feel, like a man with a severed limb, the phantom appendage begs acknowledgement, but it no longer exists. He had a different body. His mind was the same, yet it had been transformed— not pounded into a different shape, nor refigured like in photo editing. He had been integrated with another entity's properties—poured into another container with the flavor enhancements of the previous mixing bowl.

The ambient world became clearer with each waking second. Without seeing, he sensed sight—form, contour, color, hue, brightness. Zora's request to think a singular thought of understanding seemed petty, even trite. He was a virtuoso performer without any recollection of the years of practice that went into the skill. He located Zora as a sparkling shimmering form in his consciousness—an awareness that identified objects and location; it was his mind's radar. *How unique. I've acquired this ability through this transfer. I can move about the room, yet I am immobile. He suspended his extrasensory perusal, upset by a sudden realization. Moments ago—I assume it was only moments—there were four people in the vicinity: Myself, Hyperia,*

305

*Simon, and Zora. Now I sense only two. The transfer! Hyperia and I
are one. Then my body?*

Abandoning his mental scan of his surroundings, he had to see
for himself, with his physical eyes. He had to verify that he was dead.
Though desperate, he could not grasp the desperation he would have
experienced had he still been Jordan, in Jordan's flesh. His skin
touched a solid surface, signaling that the fluid filling his bubble tank
had been drained, and he touched the bottom. Groping with his feet, he
struggled for stable footing, as the surface was slippery and curved.
Moving from supine, he rolled, then hunched, crouched, then stood
slowly, balancing himself with extended arms.

Standing, he looked at himself more closely. He was female;
he was Hyperia. His lifeless corpse floated, submerged in an adjacent
chamber twenty feet away, across from Zora's platform by which she
continued to stand.

*Where is Simon? I cannot see him with my newly acquired
mind talent, and I do not see him with my eyes.* What he suspected, he
did not want to acknowledge. From somewhere, memories of this ritual
now flooded in as if they had been stored out of sight, and he was now
worthy to their access. *Zora had used a combination of technology,
sexual energy, and life itself to perform this transfer, and in so doing,
cured me, keeping me alive. But at what cost? But Simon knew. He
knew all the time, even from when we were children. His job was to
sacrifice himself for me. The only one who did not know was me.*

"Zora. I could break through the shell of this container just by
thinking about it. I feel it. But I'd rather you open it. I understand all,"
he said, preferring to speak now rather than communicate through
thought.

Without tarrying, Zora scurried to the control panel, once
operated by Simon, and actuated the command for Jordan's shell to
split open. He emerged, glistening from the emulsion in which he had

been immersed. Though curious about the nature of the umbilical liquid, he delayed discovery and commenced a slow advance toward his body. "Please drain my body's chamber and open the shell," he commanded Zora, not yet looking in her direction.

The bubble drained quickly; the seamless crack parted, removing the barrier between Jordan and his corpse. *When has a human looked upon the body in which he has inhabited as a living entity? A body, dead, lifeless, still, unresponsive except to decay and decomposition. Yet here I stand, beholding myself as I once was. And as I search my racial memory, this experience is singular. I am the first. I share this flesh with Hyperia. I feel her, sense her, experience her presence, but she does not talk to me, nor am I aware of her pressures, forces, or nuances. I am aware of her capabilities. When I experienced her at the Clarity Center, with Throckmorton all aghast, I could see what she was. And now I have those same capabilities. She was pure, virginal, sterile. This ritual amalgamated us. What that means, I don't know yet. But I shall discover it, and take this science further. I believe that the natural forces allowing this—this, miracle— will permit us to go to distant stars.*

"Jordan—my son, my daughter. We have much work, and I feel you have acclimated quickly," Zora offered discretely from the far-off console.

Her voice triggered the feeling of a memory, but he was unable to access it. He wanted to emote, to connect with expression, but the channel simply did not exist. He remembered last feeling lust, desiring her bare skin and nakedness against him. The coexistence of her age and youth, her passion and apathy—titillated him. He looked down at himself once more, moving and rubbing his hands over his abdomen, buttocks, breasts and thighs. Epitomical epicene, he was woman and man.

Hyper_Jordan turned in Zora's direction. Her own power surged within him. Lacking the motivation and reason, he knew he could cause Zora to implode merely by willing the action with thought. He seemed to float as she walked. He came close to Zora, facing her, and she seemed to cower, even mewl in his presence. He looked at the adjacent table upon which Simon's spent corpse lay, deflated, consumed. She lacked the ability to grieve.

Turning back to Zora, standing hunched and nude, he touched the side of her head. "You are now truly my mother," Hyper_Jordan remarked with soft assurance. The touch persuaded her to erect herself. "We must reclaim our world now," Hyper_Jordan remarked with passionate stoicism.

Chapter 26

Pools of Contamination

The data was daunting. During her twenty-five years as a CIA information analyst, no information had disturbed her so much as what she had deciphered recently. Looking at the stream of corroborating reports, she feared this much coalescing information could not lead to good ends. "So many reports of permissive action link alterations is not mere coincidence," she muttered to herself, acutely focused on her monitor inside a CIA global watch center for nuclear weapons activity. Citing her need to maintain a proper protocol for transmitting information, she realized rationale had to supersede her intuition. Her gut told her something was amiss in the world; rationale nixed that notion, leveling the logic that so many simultaneous changes were not only improbable; it was statistically impossible. *The Deputy Director should be informed*, she thought, *but I need to make certain that what I'm detecting is absolutely valid, and not some weird system anomaly.*

Her expertise in amassing data to infer security threats from nations with weapons of mass destruction—especially nuclear weapons—had her promoted to the apex of the security watch dog hierarchy. Clandestine information from the Russian Federation, UK, France, China, India, Pakistan, North Korea, India and Iran converged on her and her team. They monitored sensitive data—potentially embarrassing data—especially from the UK, France, and other US allies, since the allies were unaware that their data infrastructure was open for inspection. She would rephrase any reference to what they were actually doing, saying simply, "We are spying on our allies—euphemism clouds purpose and intent."

Her reporting situation frustrated her. The CIA bureaucracy would not accept the impossible as a scenario, even if her department's flawless supercomputers delivered the designation as such.

Politicians and military leaders had chastised her on two rounds of "highly impossible scenarios" in the past which she had proposed as real threats to national security. Her reluctant audience assigned flaw to the analysis programs' algorithms or systems, refusing to accept her inferential conclusions as social or political reality. As a young analyst, assigned to monitor possible threats within the "noise" of global communications traffic, she had discovered congregations of groups, later called cells, from a little known radical group calling itself Al- Qaeda. She analyzed streams of occurrences statistically out of the range of serial predictability. The numbers of cells arriving in the United States, their clandestine links in Europe, their apparent affluence with little visible means of income, and their affinity to aviation, led her to suggest these groups were targeting commercial airliners to be used as bombs by suicidal operatives. At the time, only a solitary investigator in the FBI took her seriously. Her CIA superiors, though impressed with her ability to forge data together for a storyline, refused to heed her recommendations. After the 9/11 attack, she received a quiet promotion, forcing her into a higher level of security, requiring greater isolation and silence.

She had observed this current unprecedented trend of nuclear weapons security infrastructure alterations for one month. The process was not sequential—the kind of domino reactions to which she was accustomed when nations followed suit with one another. The behaviors she had observed recently appeared deliberate, concurrent and parallel as if they all had conspired simultaneously to make broad, complex, and multi-layered alterations into their permissive actions systems. Not just the non-proliferation treaty nations, their allies—all of them, including Pakistan, Iran and North Korea—were involved.

Desiree was monitoring Israeli activity to which she had been recently tipped off. Seemingly mundane noise, the data had underlying content which, if confronted, the Israelis would vehemently deny. But she knew the US and Israel had conducted furtive eyewinks of state, and the arms movement she had deciphered was real. Israel had supposedly increased the number of land-based mobile missiles by twenty. Since Israel was still not officially a nuclear nation, monitoring them was even more critical since they did not have to account for their enrichment, testing, or proliferation activities through treaty-negotiated terms.

Working alone in a darkened room, lit only by instrument lights and monitor glow, she hastened to resolve a mystery unfolding without reason or cause. She empathized with pilots and controllers, struggling with the candor of divulging their observations of UFOs, knowing that their credibility will be questioned, if not destroyed, if they submit to unrestrained openness.

She sat at a circular table with a hollow center, monitors spread around its perimeter. Freewheeling on her ball-bearing-enhanced chair vigilantly from screen to screen, she changed views, data sources, satellite spectrums, and security levels. A dense column of instrumentation towered through and over the center of the bench. As her focus intensified, she became increasingly aware that she needed an additional set of trustworthy eyes on this apparent phenomenon.

Uneasy before beckoning her colleague, she knew he would question why she had kept this observation from him for so long if it had posed such a conundrum to her. "Pete," she said calmly over her headset. "Please come in here. I've got something—I don't know what it is." Peter Cumming was quick to oblige, as she felt him looking over her shoulder within seconds.

Relieved that he was expedient in complying with her request, she realized she had conveyed distress in her summons. "I've kept a log file of my observations for the past few weeks. But, to capsulize, all the nations with nukes are changing everything—PAL, target coordinates, launch codes, everything," she offered factually without looking up.

"All nations? Even the United States? How are you receiving US data?" Pete returned skeptically.

His query tingled a nagging concern to which she needed resolution as well. "Well, no. You know our scanners aren't aimed at US munitions. I mean all nations within our purview—both official and unofficial. Typically, if India makes modifications in PAL parameters or target coordinates, Pakistan will follow with almost identical modes. The reason always is that the intelligence gets transferred covertly or explicitly." She pushed her chair over to a monitor half-way around the table, rolling over his foot. "Sorry. Follow!" she exclaimed, as she noticed him wincing, wondering whether the gesture was from pain or from what she was showing him.

"Dizzy, I don't want to play Doubting Thomas so early, but just how long have you followed these observations? I know you, and I think you think you're on a roll. Isn't it too soon to say the sky is falling?"

She was relieved to air this information out, and Peter was asking the right questions. "That's just the point. Changes that take years to occur, if they ever occur, are proceeding at impossible rates." She paused, peering up from a monitor to peer at him with staunch sincerity. "Peety, you know yourself nuclear munitions security modifications are very slow transactions, sometimes taking years to proceed. Remember our launch codes? They remained a series of zeros for a decade before the Joint Chiefs trusted the use of permissive action links. What I've seen—these changes can't be happening—it's as if friendly and enemy nations have all gotten in cahoots. But what's more alarming—Look at this!" she cried, her fingertip repelling from a screen. "Direct readout of target parameters." Having worked with Peter for five years, she knew his skepticism was merely to keep her inferences objective, but she sensed his escalating intensity as he scanned the data on the monitor.

"Interesting. Pakistan changed critical PAL designations. The critical signal detection has been expanded to multiple UHF frequencies. The encryption modes—they're indecipherable, at least 1028 bit," he remarked, walking to an adjacent workstation.

Secretly, she had hoped her observations had been incomplete and hasty—that Peter would derisively reveal a flaw she had overlooked due to impulsive oversight. Her alarm deepened, as she prepared to disclose more. "Peter, you're Crypto cleared." She hesitated, as she prepared to discuss a forbidden topic. "I know you're familiar with the code name, Semitic Mole," she queried him with apprehension. His side glance suggested a perception, detecting where she was going with this conversation.

"We barely ever monitor those uploads," he replied earnestly to not suggest a lack of trust or breach of protocol. "I know the uploads still exist, but the veracity was brought into question twenty years ago, as I understand. The analysts concluded the Israelis had discovered the implanted circuits and were feeding us false information, programming bogus target coordinates to throw us off," Peter replied.

She was relieved they were both aware of the same findings and information. "That was internal counter-intelligence promoting that belief. They never really discovered it after all. When we gave them the nuclear tech support, the entire operation was deep cover—obviously. We anticipated them to discover our covert tracking system even before it was deployed, but they never did. They set certain targets forty years ago, and with only a few modes, the targets never changed. Yeah, they acted against the proliferation guidelines when Iran went nuclear seven years ago, aiming more munitions at Tehran, and a few other strategic targets. But now, their system has gone wild—and in disturbing accordance with all the other parallel activity I've been picking up.

Look at these coordinates." She typed into a keyboard, displaying a map of the Middle East on a wall-sized monitor.

"They've aimed all but three of their short range missiles at Tehran. The rest of them—well—look. These coordinates—" She hit some more keys, displaying two columns of numbers, then outlined number blocks across the columns. "What's wrong with this picture," she asked as if she had considered the same question many times. She sensed him startle as he puzzled over the monitor display.

"Fifteen Israeli missiles are aimed at exactly the same target point—precisely the same coordinates—the middle of the Saudi Gharwar Field. What possible strategic advantage would that have? I think someone's fucking with us," Peter remarked with an angry resolve. "You claim these downloads are sound. How can they be? That's crazy. The Israelis would completely fuck themselves. That action would penetrate and ignite the Gharwar Oil Field. The earth covering the pocket would erupt; the whole thing would blow up into a sea of Hell."

Satisfied she had gotten his attention; dismayed that he had not rendered her findings invalid. "Very insightful. Now look at this," Desiree responded, highlighting another block of numbers. "Same madness—different target. Another seventeen missiles aimed at the Burgan Field in Kuwait, targeted and timed to arrive at exactly the same coordinates within thirty seconds of one another." She hesitated, waiting for comment. "And this," she added, sweeping across more numbers with the curser. "These coordinates are smack dab in the center of the Rumailia Field in Iraq." She stopped as if suffering from dizziness. "Now why—why would they play this kind of game if they meant to throw us off with false info?" She saw him shudder, then grimace, knowing he would rather refute the findings than accept a heinous conclusion.

314

"Hell. How about hackers? Let's backtrack the integrity of the links. Maybe some hackers—some kids cracked the system," he replied.

Inwardly gloating, he responded exactly as she had expected. "You've been watching too many movies," she responded. "These numbers are too deliberate, too well-planned. Our data confirmed Israel with one hundred thirty active warheads. They aligned their warheads to strike sequentially at the center of these oilfields." She changed monitors, hitting yet more keys for a different view. "Their typical targets—Tehran, Tabriz, Cairo, Beirut, Baghdad, Amman, Riyadh, Al-Jahra, Damascus, Tripoli—only two warheads each per target. Here's a log file of the targets from three weeks ago." She sprang to another station for more fine tuning. "Sec. This will convert the coordinates to a map display. Now, you see," she said referring to the wall monitor map display, "three weeks ago, they were very careful NOT to target port cities and oilfields. Now they're purposefully digging craters. Something's very wrong here, Peter. Israel wouldn't do this. And hackers wouldn't play this game, wouldn't know how—not even to fuck with us." She waited for a response, noting a painful reluctance to accept her findings.

"OK. I agree. We need to confirm this data though. And we need to discover what the other states with nuclear weapons are doing," he replied, rubbing his temples as if subduing a brewing migraine.

"Can we get intel from Iran quickly?" she asked. "My guess is their targeting parameters have changed as well."

"I've got a buddy connected to Chinese intelligence. They've got the intel on Iran. I'll give him a ring right now. But what I'm more concerned about—US targets," he remarked. "All these Israeli security systems are hardened. How would anyone get into these networks without multi-layer complicity throughout the security network. Changes like these require parallel decision making and concerted efforts from high level decision makers. The entire deep layer of a government would have to either go mad or conspire simultaneously to do something absurd like this."

He had converged on her unstated conclusion, spawning an even greater enigma for her. "I agree. It would have some sort of mass hypnosis, and that's too science fiction to even contemplate. All things considered, I'm rethinking the hacker infiltration. It's far more probable than altering the PAL parameters and target coordinates." She spoke louder as Peter walked to a phone toward a wall. Her angst seemed to have transferred to him.

"Secure line?" he asked her, holding up the phone receiver. Already knowing the answer, he punched the numbers. "Dan. Hey. Peter Cumming at the Nuke Watch Facility. We've got a little request. I wonder if you could answer—maybe with silence if it's too sensitive to confirm." He listened, sensing resistance on the other end. Based on past favors Peter had heaped upon his associate on the other end of the phone line, he expected a more enthusiastic reception.

"We detected some bizarre Israeli nuke policy shifts, as well as target coordinate changes. We're wondering if anyone's seen unilateral changes or sword rattling in the area. Has Iran been making noise we haven't heard yet?" He stopped to hear silence. "OK. I'll be direct. Has Iran altered their nuke targets, aiming toward, say, oilfields instead of the usual civilian and military fare?" The silence he heard on the other end was strident; even Desiree noticed it from her vantage point. "OK. Dan. Thanks for the conversation," Peter remarked drolly. "Say hello to the family for me," he finished with an upbeat tone and hung up. Usually a model of dispassionate demeanor, she watched him fume from within, silently imploding, and losing his characteristic Teflon temperament. His inexplicable shift compounded suspicions of impending catastrophe about which no one was willing to confide.

"How do you ask what the changes are all about if you're not supposed to know what they're doing in the first place? I think we may believe keeping the sources secure may be more important than the consequences of the observations," Peter remarked, his tone increasing in intensity. "My friend—Dan—he was off. Something was wrong. He's a lot more receptive, more congenial than that. He knows something. He didn't deny it. He stayed quiet. Maybe silence was even taking a chance for him, since the thing for him to do—if he's keeping what I was asking under wraps—was to deny, deny, and deny again. He should have fed me counter-intel, but he didn't. He didn't say anything. You know what that's telling me? It's telling me that someone else is picking up the same intel you discovered. Dan's heavily plugged into the Chinese. And the Chinese would know what's going on in Iran. That implies the Chinese are scared. What the hell is going on?"

Previously opposed to confiding in outside sources, she reluctantly relented. "I have a close friend, a Deputy Director in NSA. He might tell me something, especially if I let him know what we've uncovered. He might know something about what the Israelis and Iranians are doing with their nuke targeting systems. If they're preparing to blow one another to Hell, they sure as hell need some target practice. Why aim at oilfields? It looks like they're collectively trying to drill crater-sized holes down to oil pockets." She spun her chair around, staring exasperatingly at Dan. "They're going to blow themselves and the whole Middle East to fucking outer space. Why? What purpose does that serve? It's suicide and genocide simultaneously."

"Call your friend," Dan remarked with a morose tone.

Fearing that what they had uncovered should have stayed covered, she dreaded a personal recapitulation of 9/11: She had put all the pieces together—names, motives, financing, planning, timing—but no one wanted to hear it, or do anything about it. She had been chastised for being the messenger and sent to career limbo, sentenced to monitor noise and static data. But now it had changed. She tapped on her keyboard, putting the call into motion. "I'm hesitant to call him. But we've come this far. He usually picks up if he sees it's me. He feels guilty. He's one of the people I told about 9/11 way back when," she remarked as the sound of the phone line reverberated over the room speaker.

"Dizzy," the voice—Maury Dunberry—answered. "What's on your end of this line?"

She had forgotten Maury asks questions even before she had an opportunity to say anything. Miffed with her lack of vigilance, she had not sprung forward with the answers before he could ask them. "Maury, the line is secure over an encrypted 1028 bit line. My partner, Peter Cumming is with me. He's Crypto cleared. Hang on. I'll take you off speaker. Pete, pick up," she said, pointing to a phone console nearby as she switched off the speaker phone mode.

"I was thinking about you. I knew you'd be calling soon— based on what, knowing you, you've probably observed," Maury commented with a nonchalant air. "Let's bypass you asking questions—questions which I already know you're going to ask. The Israelis unflinchingly deny they've made alterations in their targeting. It's as if they exist in another world. Aside from the Middle East, we've also gotten some distressing intel from India, Pakistan, and our NATO allies—which you're probably not aware of. Seems like what they see, and what we see, are two different realities—like someone or something is messing—not with the nuke systems themselves—but with the administrators responsible for security and integrity. At all levels, personnel appear to be altering systems, programs, targeting data, algorithms responsible for policy, but no one seems to be aware of it. It's as if they say, "What the fuck's wrong with you. I'm doing what I'm supposed to be doing." And then we say, "Yeah, you're supposed to target the biggest oil reserves and deposits in the world?" And then they respond as if that's nonsense.

She was most afraid of being afraid, and the worst contingencies in her career were materializing without anyone acknowledging the existence of peril. And though she appreciated Maury's candor, he really was not telling her anything she did not already know, or at least had not already strongly inferred. "How about North Korea? If the problem appears as wide-spread as you've indicated, I wonder. Isn't there a huge Russian petroleum deposit offshore? Near the Sakhalin Islands? How does that work for offshore deposits?" The ensuing silence was deafening, as she prepared to hear her loosely compiled hypothesis confirmed.

"Intel from insiders in North Korea confirm various Russian fields targeted, including the one you mentioned. How'd you know?" he asked with trepidation-tainted awe.

She knew she had been tagged as "the terrorist group spook," but Al-Qaeda had vindicated her, so the higher ups, the ones who had not listened to her, made certain she was removed from roving microphones and curious cameras. Now revealing her heretofore recondite theory—formulated just over the past month—left her nowhere to go; she worried her future would be uncertain, but at his point, she did not care. "Absolutely nothing to back this up. OK?" she stated, hesitating to make the announcement. "I think we're dealing with the most heinous, terrorist plot ever conceived," she added as if finally stating an embarrassing truth. "Someone intends to direct nukes at the major oilfields of the world, not just causing surface devastation, but penetrating the earth's crust and igniting the underlying pools of oil."

"Interesting, but why? What could possibly be the motivation?" Maury asked without a hint of judgmental edge.

"Maybe the motivation is so completely off the wall we wouldn't even consider it," she replied as if she had the answer already prepared. "Perhaps someone wants to start all over. Create their own apocalypse, using atomic energy and petroleum to shut down everything. Maybe someone's got a better idea, and they want to start over," she continued, almost with trance-like monotone. Knowing Maury, and hearing him laugh nervously, told her he ascribed credence to her abstruse notion.

"You almost sound like you like the idea—like you're giving it stock. Dizzy, you've been down this path before. No one would ever believe you. I strongly suggest you keep that to yourself," he replied admonishingly.

"While you two science fiction writers are assembling material for your next novel, I tracked down some noise from Strategic Air Command," Peter yelled from across the room. Desiree had noticed he had skulked over there earlier, apparently to escape what he considered pure conjecture—or bullshit, as he would put it. "You can get a lot from noise."

The sudden onset of this crisis helped her realize that she had attained a level of contentment to which he had not given pause. Maury's comment about her apocalypse hypothesis bore more truth than he realized. She eased into a dark comfort, knowing that the world would unravel into chaos if her informed prophesy were to transpire. She wished it; she hoped it. She believed the globe was a diseased, unnatural place. She despised people, and she relished a Noah's Ark cleansing, where the people, their cultures, nations, and societies were washed away like filth and vermin in a deluging storm, like rats caught in the gutter during a downpour. And she didn't care if she were caught in it or not. She was tired of living; tired of being a cripple. She yearned for the days when she could run and swim, now languishing in her wheelchair. She had beaten down the resentment toward the agency and the government, blaming them for her paraplegia; blaming them for placing her in this caustic isolation; laughing behind her back, knowing that what she watched would never change; gloating over their method of handling the woman tortured and crippled in the line of duty, uncovering operations no one wanted to know or hear about. She had wondered, *Why? But when I went public, they put me up here, in Hell's icebox, Pelly Island in Beaufort Sea. But here, I can't be touched. I can watch it all come apart, and no one can drag me in. Whoever is behind this—if "this" is real—has been watching far more than I. To have executed this would take years of planning and manipulation. It's not the government; it's not some terrorist group; it's not religious organization; it's certainly not extra-terrestrial. They are, indeed, to be congratulated.*

"What noise, Peter?" she responded laconically.

"Some decrypted transmissions over the old 128 bit encryption wires. Sounds like external monitors to SAC believe something serious changed. Inside SAC, they're saying 'no change,' and buzz off unless they hear from the President himself. Another signal coming from a Polaris sub suggesting similar alterations in nuclear security settings, but I'm not getting any indication of target coordinate tampering," Peter stated, reciting while reading the monitor, never looking away.

"Maury, you still there?" Desiree inquired, not hearing any noise from their connection to him.

"I'm still here. I don't know what to say, so I think I'll say nothing. I would suggest you do the same," he commented with a foreboding, almost threatening, tone.

Glibness was an untoward motivation in her occupation. She was happy to remain silent. "Maury. What's your physical location?" she asked. "If you're within the contiguous forty-eight States, or in

Europe, or anywhere near major oil producers—I have advice for you as well. Get away. Get as far away as you can, as quickly as possible."

Chapter 27

A Convoluted Vengeance

Rebecca had toiled for a year deep under the streets of Los Angeles. What she produced and created made sense. It functioned to its logical extreme. She had done the work of ten dissertations in a single year. She worked with Chamberlain as a colleague, not as a student, associate, or protégé.

No one ever told her whether his mind had been altered by the neural electrode technology or not, but she suspected it had. Too many primary personality traits had changed, becoming the opposite to what they were. Instead of being arrogant, he was humble; instead of obstinate, he was complacent.

Her newest project, the memory visualizer prototype, sat glistening on a bench in her office. It was a toy, an offshoot from the real work. Zora and the others agreed she should pursue completion of the device since it would be useful—it demonstrated the user's capacity to focus on scripts from the past, creating images as archival records of thoughts in the user's mind. The issue before her was to distinguish between historical fact and fiction, pure recollection and fantasy. She decided to beta test the device, using an autobiographical sketch. She contemplated her history while working with neural electrode technology and Chamberlain. She visually and textually recalled her past as if creating a narrative, and the device formulated images from her memories as if a dream sequence were transpiring.

While working under him at the UC Irvine research facility, she had developed a technology allowing UHF and microwave signals to intermix. Their higher frequency superimpositions form the harmonics in order to create the short range holographic maser fields necessary for the basic non-intrusive neural electrode to work.

Even as an undergraduate student she admired—even worshiped—Jordan Éclair. He had invented the neural electrode—the mainstay of nonintrusive neural stimulation. It allowed accurate and focused stimulation of neurons deep within the brain to be accessed without the introduction of a needle or scalpel. He had taken the medium of entertainment to the next level, beyond virtual reality and 3-D reality, using goggles and other technological tricks in order to convince the user's senses that he was immersed in an environment. Within a certain popular interconnected and role-playing gaming scenario, Jordan's neural electrode immersed the player in the game's environment. The player's reality was transformed to the middle of an alien planet battle zone, fighting for the survival of the human species. The player feels the intensity of the alien air; winces as a force field blasts the player back from an advance; fully experiences the warm blood and flesh spattering on the face; smells the rotted corpses of the player's felled comrades. She had clarity: Reality is as the brain informs you. She realized that philosophers have understood this basic edict of reality for hundreds of years. People with schizophrenia display it symptomatically through sensory hallucinations, their brains overriding input from the external world.

She basked in her current role as an equal with her former academic mentor. She recalled how Chamberlain's research promoted the medical application. He had pioneered mapping the brain and targeting systems of memories—long term, location, sequential, language, motor, emotional—and memories associated with all the senses. He had promised medical science and a future society void of mental illness—even void of neurosis. People vexed by chronic and pernicious childhood memories of abuse and trauma need not toil under hours of questionable psychotherapy practices or consume hit-or-miss neuroleptic drugs, searching for relief. Instead, they simply have their memories systematically altered so that the distressing stimuli are removed and replaced by more amenable circumstances.

Jordan and Zora had extended these key findings to memory, which extended to personality and motivation: We are as we react. Zora sought the fanciful fictional mesmerizer, the magical hypnotist who could exercise mind control over his victim, forcing he or she to do his bidding. Zora erased the minds of over half her research subjects, creating such blank slates, they were reduced to mannequins, unable to self-sustain. They lacked an internal mapping and quantification matrix—mind-over-body management.

In the underground LA complex they had completed integrating a true control complex, capable of identifying and targeting any brain on Earth where the person carried a simple cell phone. Through the cell phone, they could target specific limbic neuron bundles inside the brain, using these fixed structures as inert reference points, locating with pinpoint accuracy the most intricate and abstruse axonal interconnections, creating subtle shifts in memory, or transforming the Dr. Jekyll into his shadowed Hyde.

Excited by this experience, her narrative recitation using her thoughts as the writing medium was novel, requiring neither pen, keyboard, nor voice recorder. As she committed more of her memory of her history with her employer, a deepening discomfort slowly radiated from a place she had hoped to subjugate. Her thoughts were not her own. Even as she transferred mental images and words of deeds to archives of stored thoughts, an insidious realization haunted her: Her thoughts were never her own. The fear of fear itself became public knowledge—the leaders being the public. She fought being pulled into a vortex of infinite rumination—thinking about thinking about thinking about was impossible to overcome. *If I were to doubt anything, the doubt is known, no matter how I think it. And if I think about not thinking whatever I'm thinking about, then the cycle goes on and on, magnifying the process as the attempt to avoid it broadens. It is as I imagined Heaven and Hell as a child. God knew all that I was thinking;*

325

Satan knew all that I was thinking. And no matter how much I tried to not think about a subject, the thought always swelled. And how about my unconscious thoughts? And my dreams? My most intimate thoughts are available for examination. They have been examined. There is not a micron of my body and brain of which they are not aware. I cannot avoid these thoughts, so why try to convolute the process? But the conclusion I reached in childhood can now be underscored from my current reality: Heaven and Hell are one and the same. If the soul has any quality, it is truly transparent, unavailable to the senses. I have been so distracted in my goals; I had neglected the process. And to remove the torment of thought on thought? Removing the memories that create the distress. That's what they do—destroy personality by removing the affiliation with the source conflicts creating the traits which cause us to react as we do. I've questioned why Chamberlain seemed so different. I was naive to even doubt for a second his source memories had not been altered. They mold and fabricate personality by supplanting the unique permutations of experience that make each human different, a statistical amalgam of qualities deposited from infinite populations of experiences. They reduce these experiences into singular sets that are controllable and predictable. And now I should expect at any time to be modified. Yet my awareness of the change would not occur since the memory of myself, or the memories that made up certain feelings and inclinations would have been deleted, like an unwanted file. I must accept what is to be and continue with my work. We accomplish the ends to which I have longed for. We cleanse humanity and prune the overgrowth threatening its survival and evolution. But where is Jordan? I miss him. I loved him so. Exhausted, she retired for the evening.

***

Rebecca awoke, her anticipation of the day's agenda soaring. Today they were to go live. They were to target Israel's strategic nuclear personnel, from high government dignitaries to military personnel in control capacities. They would monitor their sources and listen for cues. The proof of their success in today's operation: No one would know what happened.

The main control facility was under her floor, separated by ten feet of lead, steel, and Baalian ceramic. The facility was impervious to any intrusion, mechanical, electronic, or mental. She arrived, freshly polished, as if going out on a new date. *I remember my thoughts last night, so I must be intact. But then, my memory of last night could have been supplanted. No! Let's not get into that again. I have far more important things to accomplish. But if I were not intact, then these vexing ruminations would not have continued. No! Stop it!*

She had not had much social intercourse with Chamberlain, as he kept to himself, and Zora made certain he remained on target. Nevertheless, he was in the control room, along with the full contingent of his staff. She reminded herself that his research had gone beyond hers—they were able to make monkeys talk; she was only able to make humans talk differently. *Small difference*, she remarked silently, the corners of her mouth upturning. He saw him take notice of her entrance, and he dashed toward her.

"Rebecca. How good to see you," he squealed, hugging her. "How exciting! Our life's work, finally being tested today. The dream of kings and sages—to control another's will, thoughts, memories, without their knowledge or awareness."

Convinced her memories and personality was still intact, Chamberlain's status of autonomy continued to vex her. She could not decide whether she liked him better before he changed, or now, all syrupy and wimpy. *What happened to his wife and family?*—she questioned silently prior to responding congenially to her former boss. "Stan! I miss you too. But we get to see this day together. Not only to saee it, but also to do it," she responded with as much uncontrived glee as she could muster.

As she perused the room, she wondered how many of these people, if any, know the real purpose of this assembly today. She allowed her eyes to wash over each face. She recognized everyone, and she knew it was not possible for all these people to have been contained in this underground complex for the past year. *Noreen has a two small children at home. She's very much in love with her family, yet there she stands. Not an issue of forlorn or regret on her face. And what about her husband and children? They're not in the complex, at least not as far as I could tell. They kept key personnel. When Simon and I parted over a year ago, I didn't know what transpired. And I have never seen Simon again either.* Her thoughts meandered around the lives of people she saw in the room—some old colleagues—and to the fates of those she did not see. Becoming self-conscious, she suddenly realized once more that her thoughts were not her own. She glanced back to Chamberlain, who had watched her digress with some intensity, his fixation reminding her of the old Chamberlain.

"Not is all as it appears, and some is exactly as it appears," he remarked without flinching.

Hoping to eschew any disagreements with him, she decided not to ask him what he meant. Yet, his remark seemed absurdly surrealistic as if she were Alice and he the Cheshire cat. "We've all been divided in our unique little teams for so long. You and I have worked together off and on, but I haven't seen many of these people for some time. For example, Noreen, over there," she offered, wishing to explain her wandering. Chamberlain looked over to Noreen, then back to Rebecca.

"She is well, as is her family. I understand she'll be rejoining them within the next few weeks. Coping with her absence has paid for their future ten times over," he commented serenely. "Come. Join me," he said, offering his arm.

Taken by his charm and newly acquired warmth, she acquiesced and followed him from the anteroom, in which they were standing, into a grand auditorium-sized room—their primary laboratory, a room in which she had spent many hours working.

She had not been in this room for several weeks while she set up ancillary equipment within other quarters—neuro-modulators, maser power supplies, and neuro-targeting imagers to which she had proprietary insight. Foreigners—outsiders she had not seen before— started to show up, guided and entertained by Zora or one of her cronies. She had noticed these strangers had no common ethnicity, nationality, or class distinction. Each appeared unique, part of a shared knowledge which she had assumed was part of the grand scheme of the organization—a scheme to which she was not fully privy. Her exclusion did not bother her, except that she felt a certain ownership of this grand laboratory and mildly resented that she was not given the right to bask in its explication.

As she scanned the enormous laboratory, she looked for changes. Though much of the basic neuro-transceiver modules were already in place when she had arrived, she noted equipment and devices she could not readily identify. Equally spaced egg-shaped, opaque pods—interspersed with similarly sized spheres, each two to four feet in diameter—dotted the floor. The floor was transparent—not of glass or plastic, but of a resilient crystal-ceramic material, pristine in purity. Still searching for clues of alterations, Rebecca glanced down as they crossed the room, gesturing below her. "I remember when we started this project. Much of this work had already been accomplished," she remarked with reminiscence. She tugged on Chamberlain, stopping to admire the out-of-this-world paraphernalia under the floor. "I will always remember the central processing sphere—it's beautiful," she added, admiring the top half of a sixty-foot diameter sphere, opaque white matching the smaller floor pods above it. Every three seconds tiny ripples of jagged light pulsed between the floor modules and the giant sphere beneath them.

Her eyes scanned the sphere as one might take in a scene of sensual delight—a smorgasbord of exotic and delicious food, the uninterrupted elegance of a voluptuous woman's sleek curves, the aesthetic grandeur of an exquisitely engineered and constructed aircraft. As her admiration of their technical achievement swept forward, she finally espied the feature she had suspected. In the center of the room, mounted below the floor at the upper pole of the giant sphere, two barely noticeable clamshell hemispheres sat poised ready to emerge from beneath the floor. She intuited that they would close together, joining as two halves to create a bubble, a miniature duplicate sphere juxtaposed to the mother sphere.

Suddenly a wave of ecstasy and passion, overwhelming, overcame her, engulfing her. Still holding Chamberlain's arm, she braced herself for support. She sensed this rush bowling her over had a source, a direction. Catching her balance and breath, she instinctively turned to her right. The stare of the most alluring woman she had ever encountered—not smiling, not frowning, not apathetic—stunned her. *This woman! Who is she? She knows me; I know her. She surpasses beautiful. She's magnificent. What is it about her that attracts me so?* Dazzled, wondering why she had not seen such an entity when she first entered the room, she marveled at the woman's attire. Shiny crystalline chiffon material cascaded over her form like a waterfall. Effervescent, it seemed to flow down and around her as if she were wearing fluid. She absent-mindedly nudged Chamberlain. "That woman. Do you see her? She glows. Or am I imagining it?" Chamberlain gently disconnected himself as if he were giving the bride away.

330

"She glows in your mind," he responded, moving slightly further. "She glows."

Chamberlain's reaction disquieted her, reminding her of a starry-eyed Jesus freak, or a teenaged groupie silently ogling her rock star idol as he gyrated on stage. Stepping further away from him, she wanted to gather a more detached assessment. With the entrance of the mysterious woman, he appeared distant, trance-like, even mesmerized. She suddenly felt alone as if standing in a room where time had slowed, where the inhabitants stopped in their tracks, and only she was able to move about. She doubted the reality of this sensation, now worried that her mind was being tampered with, though she believed she was who she was, and truly had the past she remembered having. The creeping feeling of being dissociated disturbed her.

What's going on here? They all seem to be in slow motion. That's impossible, so what's happening? Does this woman—this diva— cause this effect? I must know who she is. Somewhere from within, an elusive wisp of an insight tugged on her. *Could this woman be the same woman I helped into Simon's car the last time I saw Jordan and Simon? Could she be Hyperia, Jordan's sister?*

Her mind turned blank, and a calm came over her—a serenity she had never experienced. She fought the feeling, knowing that now, for sure; her brain had been targeted. If she were to allow herself the comfort of surrender, she felt she would never know herself again.

Surrounded by a white glow, a purity blocking external distraction, the woman approached her. As much as she wanted to struggle for her autonomy, she resigned, allowing herself to sink within this creamy, empyreal medium. The female entity converged, focusing as if from a fog. Mutually attracted, Rebecca could feel herself wanting her, caressing her, being absorbed by her as if a lifeforce emanated from the visage, energizing her.

[Hyper_Jordan] *Rebecca, my love. I'm sorry for being away from you for so long. When I was my old self, in my original body, I had decided to be with you, to have a life with you. To be normal, a member of the rest of humankind. I had deluded myself, believing the culture at large was more valid than the reality we have piloted for hundreds of generations. I must have seen something in you. Zora's wisdom as a caretaker, looking after my father and myself surpassed my insight. That you and I were together, I understand now, was no accident.*

Awestruck, she abandoned all resistance. "Jordan? How?" she murmured with the little breath she could muster to speak.

"Merged with my sister, Hyperia," he responded speaking, having approached her so that their two forms seemed superimposed. "You will understand all—everything—shortly. And I assure you, your reality, your brain, is fully intact. This sensation you experience is not removed from reality. It is not a dream or an illusion. I speak to you in an instant of time. Though you understand me in language, and you perceive an image, the time required for your senses to carry the data to your brain, and for your brain to receive, process and execute the neural activity into meaningful concepts—the sum of these processes far exceeds the time necessary for true experience. So, we operate through a medium bypassing electromagnetic or kinetic signal transmission. Your sense of dissociation spawns from the incongruence between the duration in which you are accustomed to experiencing reality, and what you experience currently. That's why it does not seem real to you. I want you to come with me later. I missed you so, and I wanted to let you know I'm here. But now, I must depart momentarily. I am the conduit, the missing ingredient for this technology to access all humankind. Access occurs through me."

She jolted—the sudden body spasm occurring when rebounding from an emerging dream state just prior to sleep. Light, sound, commotion, temperature, pressure on her skin—all returned in a walloping gush. Chamberlain looked at her concerned, holding her under her arm to keep her from collapsing.

"Rebecca. You blanked out for a second. You concerned me. It looked like you were having a silent seizure," he commented with a tint of alarm in his tone.

She knew her mind was accessible without her permission, and the sporadic tampering disturbed her. She had tacitly given permission fifteen years ago when she signed on with Zora. She had been adapted as a minor—not legally or through standard bureaucratic channels; she was picked up as a stray. Zora had seen something in her, otherwise she would have used her as a research subject. Faltering between gratitude and resentment, she often wondered how her life would have transpired had she simply been left alone. Yet, she knew her current course was optimal, as she would never have had the opportunities to rise to the top—not as a normal citizen, or even as an extra-ordinary high achiever. She was a member of the elite, a cult cast from the dawn of civilization, operating out of view, manipulating cultural, social, political, sociological, economic, scientific, and technological cause and effect.

"I'll be OK," she replied, taking a deep breath. "That woman, walking to the center, where that clamshell device is," she continued, hesitating. "I just had the oddest feeling about her—like an instantaneous dream." Chamberlain's permanent smile appeared reaction free, maintaining the same arc across his lower face.

"There've been other changes here," she said as if revived by revelation. "I've been blown away by the glare of success to see them immediately. This room—our lab—it almost has the feeling—the ambience—of a temple, like one of those weird temples I've read about from ancient times—pre-biblical times," she added, scanning the area with intensity. She had hoped to get more responsiveness out of

Chamberlain, but she feared his mind had been modified even further than when she worked with him last, just three weeks ago.

"It is a temple," he replied, turning toward her without modifying his expression. "It is the perfect blend of technology and spirit, mind and soul. It is what we have worked toward. And she brings it all together."

Shocked, yet relieved, she realized she would not have these perceptions or questions had her mind and memory been modified— except the jolt of dissociation she had just experienced. *What was that? Could that woman be Jordan? I've never believed that I should be privy to all going on. It was understood that my job was clear and well defined, and I executed it well, or at least so I was told. But the changes in the lab? And this magnificent woman taking center stage?*

She followed Hyper_Jordan's jaunt across the clear crystalline floor. He stopped short of the center of the room, prior to stepping onto the center point of the retractable sphere. An assistant from a control panel on the other side ran out to take Hyper_Jordan's gown as she released the neck clasps, and it slid down the length of her body, collapsing at the floor in a pillowy ring. She stepped two paces forward, standing at the center of the sphere, its two halves now emerging from the floor immediately upon sensing Hyper_Jordan's presence.

Within thirty seconds the two halves of the sphere had melded, creating a single fused bubble in the middle of the floor. The lights in the room dimmed as if the main attraction were commencing. Rebecca stared with intensity, unable to identify the fluid rapidly expanding into the bubble, immersing Hyper_Jordan, surrounding her in an iridescent mist. Aware of her mouth agape, she snapped her jaw shut, amazed at the perfect female form floating in the bubble, in a misty, fluid-like gas, glowing a purplish blue aura.

The room erupted in light, as the escalating frequency of blips and flashes from the lower central sphere cascaded toward the modules located on the floor around the room. *I often wondered how they would actually execute altering and controlling nuclear delivery munitions. How would they make the changes? How would they implement the process without being detected? Could this be it? They couldn't tell me because I would have never comprehended.*

Concentrating so much on the unknown, she had lost sight to observe the known. She, Chamberlain, and her group had modified and coded the systems necessary to modify memory, intent, and motivation in a human brain via a satellite link, using cell phones as reference points. The central sphere and the intermediary modules on the floor were emulators of key brain function, necessary to model neural activity prior to commencing organic alterations. Keenly aware of the functioning of the hardware and software, Rebecca had performed countless experiments aiming toward creating a flawless system. Yet up to now, the tests had been experiments. Her team's work was being put to the test, the event she had worked so hard for, and she was focused on something else: Hyper_Jordan was in a bubble.

She had not been left completely out of the confidential loop—Zora had informed her of the many satellites their global organization had commandeered toward this very goal—targeting the brains of those controlling certain nations' nuclear arsenals. Each one of hundreds of communications and weather satellites had been equipped with scanning and transmission equipment, planted over the years through surreptitious operatives. Each had the capability, when activated, of locating any of the over billion cell phones, and of using the carrier's frequency and unique signal to identify and target the owner's key limbic structures. Then signals from two synchronized satellites would project three dimensional maser holograms within the brain of the subject and reprogram a myriad of neural systems, leaving

335

the individual completely unaware that his essence—his mind—had been rebooted with alternate goals and motivations.

She kneeled down, watching the central sphere's activity. As expected, the sphere's surface was ablaze with stroboscopic flashes and glares, each culminating at the speed of light in a receptor module located around the floor, then recondensed, and beamed to an upper sphere riding atop a protruding cylinder from the ceiling, hanging like surreal stalactites. Hovering between awe and alarm, she noticed another modification in their setup. The central axis of the lower sphere, instead of communicating with its companion ceiling sphere, directed its wide combined laser light and maser radiation into the intermediary sphere which Hyper_Jordan occupied.

As the tempo of the operation hastened, Hyper_Jordan's bubble container radiated brightly, transforming from its original blue hue to pure white. Sunlight brilliant, she turned her eyes away, directing her stare to the lower sphere.

The scientific group's plan had established a system for changing the target coordinate access codes and other security measures for several countries, including Israel, Pakistan, India, North Korea, Iran, France, and Great Britain. They had not included the United States, Russia, or China, yet, when she turned around to check a 3-D display, maps and coordinates undulating in and out, indicating neuro targets in the US, Russia and in China as well.

She coped with a certain uneasy resolve—she did not understand the reason she would have been barred from certain policies and secrets. *We set up the geo-synchronous satellites to unobtrusively connect with the targets in Iran, Israel, Pakistan, and North Korea. Later we also established the United Kingdom and France as backups. The networks and layers of personnel in the big powers were simply too time consuming to be worthwhile. The probability for inaccuracies were overwhelming, leading to possible sabotage of our efforts. Why, then, do I now see the US, China, and Russia on the screens? How is it possible that so much data was compiled in order to alter minds of such vast—if not uncertain—chains of command. In Israel, we knew exactly the individuals to compromise, from the Prime Minister all the way down to the mobile commanders. But the missile silos in the US?*

Her silent reverie gave way to changes in her peripheral vision—slower strobe speeds, less light intensity, and different displays. She had wandered away from Chamberlain in the midst of the ceremony—she thought ceremony was the best term for what was supposed to be a scientific and technological grand exhibition. He suddenly appeared at her side, nudging her to observe the new 3-D display appearing overhead—a globe showing source, trajectories and targets. Few cities were direct targets: Jerusalem, Tehran, Tel Aviv, Beirut and Baghdad. All other targets met their goals—repeated onslaught of major producing oilfields in the Middle East, Russia, South America, Scandinavia, and some Oceanic sites.

Hyper_Jordan's voice echoed softly in her mind's ears. *The same region from which the rich red life blood of Earth's civilizations spawned, now emitted the black putrid flow of death, causing the mother region's destruction. You—we—are the implements of that destruction. It is the history of the origins, the cradle of life that is now a seething cauldron of death. These times must be put to the torch, and we are the bearers of the flame.*

Chapter 28

Baal's Blazes

Cynthia Anne Norbert had satisfied herself—she had not allowed herself to be inflated by her political position. She had observed her predecessors and heeded her inner warning by not yielding to the perks of power. She had forced herself to adjust to all the media attention directed toward her, not allowing herself to become the narcissist she would have otherwise been reinforced to become. She was the President of the United States, the first woman elected to the supreme office. She had acclimated to the constant buzzing and energy around her, but she had not become numb to it; she was ever aware of its presence.

She had insisted on sitting in the bleachers with other parents, watching her son and daughter play in their Little League competition. Relieved to be back in California, she wished the finals had been played in a city other than Santa Barbara, her hometown. Unfazed and focused ahead, she fully realized that four of the parents around her were really Secret Service personnel, role-playing their parts to "B" actor standards.

The original motivators driving her to her current lofty career status had been obscured by the realities of the job. What had been the defining factor catapulting her to this position? She started as a Stanford educated constitutional attorney, winning cases against those who would use the Constitution as a brand of freedom, and the flag as armor. She opposed those who oppress the masses incapable of defending themselves against the self-righteous and sanctimonious; those usurpers of justice who feel that anyone simply stating the word "America" with the starry eyed idealism of "land of the free" is immune to preserving the human rights not explicitly stated therein. She sought to change the Constitution—to make it a document truly for the people of the 21st century. She rode the wave of frustration, a social revolution waged against corporate corruption, capitalist arrogance, and special interest depravity. The majority of the United States citizenry had finally spoken. They had sickened of the lies, the manipulation, the spin, and the underhanded psychological marketing efforts aimed at deceiving them—coercing them to believe that by sacrificing, denying, and giving, they were in fact investing in an American dream. They were deceived by marketing promotion—propaganda of the worst kind. She stepped up to the podium—at the right time, the right place—and demonstrated to her listeners, her public, that they were being cheated and bamboozled.

Aware she was not focused on the game, and conscious of the Secret Service around her, distant camera lenses taking aim, and reporters televising what she was wearing rather than the activities of the children on the field, she allowed herself to roam on this otherwise carefree afternoon. Occasionally she gloated, remembering when she was an undergraduate, writing blogs predicting a shift in cultural tides in the United States, pointing to a time when white, middle-aged, Middle America could no longer exercise the value choke hold on the nation's politics and economy; when the Black, Latino, female, gay and other distinct non-ethnic minorities would merge to become an overwhelming majority with a voice—wielding power and votes. She had been elected President of the United States with the motto— Cynthia Anne Norbert CAN.

She pushed away her moral remorse—she had lost that edge for the people. The cynicism which she struggled to conceal was wrenching itself free from its inner confines. Her political motto may have been "CAN;" her persona appeared as the marauding angel for the public as she looted and deflated multinational corporations; her silent deep, unswerving conviction—one that she had struggled with herself since adolescence to absolve—lived on: The masses are ignorant; the public is stupid. This conflict tormented her. She feared that she would eventually lose grip, no longer capable of masking her deep, inner thoughts and feelings.

For the first time in six months since she was inaugurated, she felt relaxed—not on stage, not fulfilling the role, not expressing the persona necessary for policy makers—she was simply herself. She had never fully gotten accustomed to the presence of the Secret Service, and they bothered her. Still, she appreciated that they did not intrude today, especially since her Chief of Staff had impressed upon them the President's desire for at least a semblance of privacy during her children's game. So, when two suited, dark glassed Secret Service agents approached her, muscling their way across the bleachers and incognito agents, she knew something was dreadfully amiss.

"Madame President," the older officer said apologetically, but bluntly, "we have a situation."

She had noticed his approach and braced herself. Aware that her outward persona must always be poised and unfazed—lest the media mill have grist for their ever hungry throngs of consumers—she realized the agent was not bringing good tidings. Even before he reached her position, she had already rehearsed her response. She remembered distinctly George W. Bush's seven-minute faux pas twenty-three years ago, sitting idly after being told the country was under attack, and the firestorm of criticism he had received from that poorly executed display of mindful, measured urgency. She would not make the same mistake—always aware lenses and eyes were upon her, watching every move, taking in each gesture, assessing every expressive nuance. She rose immediately. "Let's go. What's the nature of the situation?" As she delivered her query, she glanced at her children, one in center field, and the other one pitching. She never really wanted this life for them. She had been tempted to have her husband's parents raise them during the time she was in office, but what she considered a healthy child development decision would have

340

been misconstrued wildly by the media as child abandonment for the purpose of political gain. She could tell from this far away they were disappointed as they viewed her leaving.

"Ten minutes ago, Iran attacked Israel with nuclear missiles. Multiple targets were involved. Tel Aviv, Jerusalem, Bethlehem—all obliterated by warheads," the Secret Service agent advised her with an emotional monotony not matched to the content of the message delivered.

She regretted this public office. Being a true product of nature-nurture, her suave and charisma were both genetic and cultivated. Yet, her desire to be Lancelot, knight of the people, the consort of the oppressed and stricken, had conveyed her to a position which she was not likely to have sought had time-relevant circumstances not prevailed. She was not an idealist; she was at the cutting edge of a long overdue social uprising. She conveyed it as the harbinger of justice to the corporate conglomerates and mega wealthy. The time had come when lobbyists, marketing spin, media pronouncements, paid pundits, and special interests could not hold back social momentum. And as she had claimed in her campaigns, "Right has force!"

The image of the decimated cities intruded; the image of a different world segued quickly. *I only wanted good. Why on my watch? Such evil.* "Oh, my god! Has the media picked this up yet?"

"Not yet, Madame President. We need to get you to a safe location. We are not certain as of yet the intent of the Iranians—the extent of their malice. I'm afraid we also have to remove your children from the game to accompany other agents. I'm sorry," the agent replied, finally displaying some empathy she had expected.

Other agents had already cleared the way, allowing her passage from her place on the bleachers. Even if this global disaster had not been transmitted worldwide, she knew her rapid departure and the appearance of dire emergency would trigger public alarm.

"Has Israel retaliated?" she asked, suddenly wanting to retract her question after she had asked it, realizing the Secret Service agent could only advise her of so much—not of matters involving nation-state warfare.

"Madame President, your cabinet has been summoned. UnderSecretary of State Abbott is on the line, awaiting your arrival at the limousine."

She glanced to her side, attempting to suppress an expression of apology to the parents and players. She knew even if the cameras detected her regret, some pundit would extract a significance, contorting reality. Her affect was actually directed toward her son and daughter, the ones most inflicted by the constant public intrusion. She had wondered what psychological differences would manifest between outright child abuse, and the effects they had endured by being the children of the President of the United States. She had concluded that perhaps direct, unfettered child abuse would be more manageable since its source is explicit and predictable. She watched them escorted off the field to another limousine on the south side of the park.

Sirens blared and the dust in the unpaved parking lot billowed as her entourage made no secret that their departure was of utmost necessity. Wishing her children rode with her instead, she was barely able to focus on her concern when UnderSecretary Abbott appeared on the screen. A man of irrefutable distinction, sporting prematurely white hair, discerning blue eyes, and a face representing perhaps more candor than is appropriate for the position of state he occupied—he emoted atypical distress. "Madame President," he announced with gravity. "The unspeakable has occurred. The very actions we have worked and negotiated for so long—the very opposite has prevailed. Without warning or provocation, the Iranian government launched a full-fledged nuclear attack against the State of Israel. Israel countermanded. Not holding back, they launched a full volley of nuclear warheads at targets—Tehran, Cairo, Istanbul, Baghdad, Mecca, Riyadh, and Medina—all obliterated," he continued, choking back a barrage of emotion. He seemed to be in a twilight as if he did not believe the words emanating from his lips.

This announcement did not aid her focus, now even more concerned about the safety of her children. "I want that car carrying my children to come to my location. I want it now," she insisted, looking at the agent who accompanied her. Without stopping to see his reaction, she turned back to the screen with the UnderSecretary. "No provocation? At last meeting, a week ago, they had settled on an arms reduction. They had agreed to carry on limited diplomatic operations, including embassies. What the hell happened?" He listened to information from his earphone as she spoke, seeming even more distressed.

"Madame President, we cannot make sense of the situation. We discovered the Iranian president called Israel on secure lines immediately after the launch, warning them and decrying the incident. He claimed they did not intend to launch. They don't know what happened," he paused as if attempting to acclimate to the misery. "There's more. They claim the targets had changed. They launched all their missiles—all of them. The targeting had changed. They claim some sort of conspiracy or sabotage."

"George, this is incredible. How? Who has answers?" she shrieked, hoping to grab a fleeting thread of hope.

"All this has transpired within the last thirty minutes. No one has answers. Even the perpetrators do not seem to be aware of their own actions. The Israelis claim to have launched a targeted counter-strike from mobile stations—launch platforms moving around the country much as we move our submarines to secret locations. Yet all platforms launched from the Israeli side— without executive order." He stopped, seemingly aghast at the information he received over his earpiece, then looked up to repeat what he had heard. "Major oilfields in the area were targeted. It appears with deliberate, if not engineered, premeditation and calculation. Other nuclear powers have raised their alert levels. These oilfield attacks. They are not simply surface intrusions. The subterranean pockets of oil were penetrated, igniting unfathomable infernos. The global repercussions are inconceivable."

"Excuse me, Madame President," the Secret Service agent interrupted. "I've been informed to take you and your children to an aircraft to transport you to a nuclear safe bunker. Your cabinet and certain members of the Senate and Congress are also being moved out of potential harm's way. I've been informed you can join your cabinet within two hours. The Joint Chiefs have already convened. They are in session, and would like to telecommunicate with you."

She feared that what started as an isolated Middle Eastern meltdown with limited global repercussions had the potential of a worldwide cataclysm, disrupting infrastructures internationally. Elevated to this status, the situation clearly lapsed into an area of dire national security. Cynthia's angst wrestled with the President's collected resolve—a stance of leadership. She suppressed Cynthia in a firm pin down to the mat, wishing she were not in this position, yet realizing her obligations to the nation, children, self—and even humanity. "George, the Secret Service just informed me we're going to an undisclosed safe location. Will you be joining us?"

"No, Madame President. I'm in New York, at the UN," he replied, a man clutching to the last vestiges of what he believed. "Secretary of State Wilhelm is in transit to the same location you're headed, I was told." He paused, listening to his earpiece. "The Joint Chiefs are in another undisclosed location. They have information, straight from the perpetrators. I'll take my leave. And God save us," he added with bleak resignation.

A dismal sheen tainted her. *The Under Secretary's temperament was not good for me. I should have talked to someone, if not upbeat, at least not as morose. Did he believe that his idealism about humanity would press on? That the human atrocities defining history for centuries, eons, would somehow come to a close, or at least have the good manners to not catalyze during this administration?*

"Madame President," General Lyle Terrell, Chairman of the Joint Chiefs of Staff announced crisply, "I want to assure you, first of all, we are not under attack." He seemed to make this pronouncement as if to be first in line.

The monitor displayed five separate windows, each with one of the three participating Joint Chiefs, CIA Director Farnsworth, and NSA Advisor Natalie George.

Intending to cut off the retributional thrust of military assertion, Cynthia was intent to lead the meeting by emphasizing human life over blame or reaction. "Gentlemen, let me make my position clear. We are facing a crisis of national security. More important than finding the perpetrators, we must secure our citizens' safety," she said, pausing for effect rather than reaction. "We may not be under attack—currently and directly—but all that we were an hour ago is gone. So we are under attack."

The car screeched to a stop, jolting her forward. Irritated that her declaration to the Joint Chiefs had been interrupted by the sudden gyrations, she noticed Natalie George had remained unanimated while the others were poised in predatory stances. She wanted to put off convening with the generals; she preferred to first hear from her NSA Advisor. She believed Natalie George could be counted on as a prevailing voice of reason. She was again interrupted by her conveyors as a Secret Service agent opened the door.

"Madame President—the helicopter will transport you from here. Your children will ride in the other aircraft," the agent announced

345

with polite officiousness. "The conference call has been transferred inside the aircraft awaiting you." For the first time in a half hour, she looked outside, her attention having been focused within thus far. Relieved, she saw the car carrying her son and daughter arrive next to the other helicopter. She stood alongside the car, awaiting their exit, and waved as they proceeded from their limousine.

Once secured inside the helicopter, she was pleased that the electronic meeting format and monitor were identical as before, even with the images juxtaposed in the same order. "Dr. George. You have information?" she asked, anticipating insight she hardly ever expected from the generals. Natalie George directed her gaze toward the web camera, maintaining a flat, though alert, posture.

"Madame President. We—CIA Director Norcross and myself—have information tracing the targeting and firing of the weapons. We can say with a reasonable certainty that these actions are acts of terrorism beyond anything we have seen—ever. We have not identified the perpetrators or their plans since these events occurred very recently and without forewarning or prior intelligence. The events were initiated by inside personnel who otherwise apparently have no knowledge of the actions which they themselves had taken. In other words, what I'm saying is that the enemy can enter minds, direct change, and eradicate memory, or make it appear to a perpetrator that an inappropriate action was indeed appropriate, intentional and planned." The President noted the other attendees remained politely stoic, all but suppressing sneers in the silence of their skepticism.

"Where is the CIA director now?" the President asked. Familiar with the NSA Director as staunchly unemotional, the President sensed that Dr. George was suppressing weeping.

"Dead. He's dead. Shot by the Israeli Secret Police, directed to do so by an unknown agent while he was visiting Israel to explore recent changes in target coordinates previously discovered by deeply remote monitoring stations. The man who shot him said his superior had directed him to do so. He recalled the time, place, circumstances; he gave detailed accounts. Under polygraph and then stress conditions, he never yielded to an alternate explanation. The man had been informed by superiors. Then we questioned the superiors, who acknowledged that they had issued the orders, but in fact, had never met with or sent orders to the man who carried out the assassination. Nor could they—when confronted with facts and reality—account for a reason they would have issued such orders. A similar directive was issued for me, but I managed to avert the attackers," Dr. George added. She hesitated for the President to ask questions, then continued.

"The Israeli missiles were all deployed. Most were not aimed at military nor civilian targets. The coordinates were aimed directly at key oilfields, reserves, refineries and deposits. At this time, the crisis is multifold: pockets of oil erupting heat and plumes of black smoke; other nations indicating changed target coordinates; depleted oil reserves almost instantaneously; economies shut down; militaries shut down. And the main question: Who will emerge to take responsibility? What was the motive other than global domination? This purposeful apocalypse was too well orchestrated to be a manic demonstration by a terrorist or an anarchist group."

"Does one need another motive?" the President asked. "Nevertheless, I would think we could rule out a terrorist group or an individual as the culprit. A nation would have to be behind this disaster—this war upon humanity."

"Madame President. Our intelligence—all the data we've accumulated on any related terrorist activity or threats to the nation— point to nothing of this scope. Any nation potentially responsible is subject to the same egregious liabilities. But in an effort to reduce the ongoing threat and minimize the potential damage, we have a hypothesis," Dr. George offered.

"I'd like to insert a comment if I may," General Terrell erupted, impatient to get a word in. "This hypothesizing and theorizing about cause is fine. But at this time, it may all be simply rhetorical. After all, we are, in essence, under attack. Should we not simply neutralize the source of the missile launchings? Madame President, if I may?" he remarked without pause. "Dr. George, are Israel and Iran the only nations to have fired missiles? Do we have confirmation that other nuclear nations are preparing the same actions?"

"General Terrell. The missiles emanated from Iran and Israel, but we have strong reason to believe neither nation intended to attack the other. The proportion of warheads aimed at each nation's respective cities and civilian populations was low compared to the remainder of the warheads aimed at petroleum-related targets. The missile strikes commenced by targeting at the same coordinates, as if someone deliberately intended to dig a crater down to the oil. This phenomenon underscores the hypothesis: The progenitor of these attacks is not the nation from which the missiles emanated. And to answer your other question—yes, other nations appear to be on the brink of attacking one another." Cynthia observed her friend's eyes suddenly glass over; her lips withdrew wafer thin, apparently stunned at the information she had just heard over her earphone while she spoke. "Pakistan released its full nuclear arsenal; India retaliated."

The President's spirits plummeted to darkness. For the first time in months she had felt at ease, watching her son and daughter at their baseball game. And though the media insisted upon analyzing every swing her daughter made at the bat, and every ball her son caught in outfield, she experienced a small semblance of the life she used to have. Now, whether she were President or not, she lamented that life as she knew it was over. "Please keep me updated on cities destroyed, fatalities, and—" she muttered, her voice faltering as she was no longer able to speak. Regrouping, she whispered, "How about American cities? Have any been targeted?"

"None yet, Madame President," General Terrell replied. "But General Harris has some disturbing information from the Strategic Air Command." He looked toward General Harris, the football coach-looking military leader of the Air Force. His countenance was one of an arrogant college coach who had reached the apex of his career, and now he was looking at a 30 game losing streak. He peered into the camera appearing so dejected, Cynthia feared he could take his life any second.

"Madame President," General Harris announced, clearing his throat. "Some of our launch codes and silos have been compromised. I do not know how it happened. We conducted our regular security sweep of the systems last week, and all was in order. Control was assumed from within. We are doing everything within our power to shut the systems down. And—" the general stopped short of completing his report.

She knew what he was going to say. His dejection and aversion to deliver the message sent a clear signal to her. Surprised she did not slump deeper into her own lament, she took some relief discovering her temperament had descended as low as it could go given the steady onslaught of bad news. "General, which American cities have been targeted by our own missiles?"

"Dallas, Houston, Fairbanks," he drawled reluctantly, "and New York City. Aimed right at Wall Street. Also oil deposits and refineries in Alaska, Texas, California."

How could such evil obsession transpire without being discovered? How could such calculated cruelty and destruction operate without displaying its vile underbelly? I often wondered if the licentious, wanton cruelty and disregard for human life demonstrated throughout the ages had finally expired. I looked at pictures from World War II, wondering if these atrocities could ever manifest once

349

more. She had assumed an immobilized trancelike expression during her brief pondering, prompting the General's alarm as he watched her image freeze for an uncomfortable time; she remained motionless and silent. "Madame President. Any comment?" General Harris inquired with a worried tone.

She snapped back, out of her thoughts. She felt conflicted—she knew she must maintain the role of leadership; she was afraid—for herself, her children, her country, and the world. "Whatever power has orchestrated this terror, oil appears to be its target. Get FEMA, the National Guard, all other emergency services dispatched to the perimeter of the targeted locations immediately. Have you implemented evacuation procedures?"

"Mass panic, Madame President," General Terrell inserted. "What you're suggesting would induce mass panic."

The NSA Director suddenly broke in. "I'm receiving reports from Middle East stations. The soot and burning hydrocarbons are expanding into the upper atmosphere, carried by the jet streams. We should see the sky color change here in the US within two to three hours."

She felt an inevitability to these occurrences now—that no matter what they did to contain the damage, these unknown assailants had already planned for any contingencies, offering them no solution or resolve except to accept their fate. She pined inwardly that true enemies would at least offer a means of surrender—a set of conditions. Their attackers remained clandestine and unseen. She uncovered the true source of her fear: Her enemy was unknown. "Generals. You presented data a few months ago from a study regarding a small scale nuclear war by two hypothetical nations. As I remember, the findings indicated the devastation would include as many fatalities as World War II, and a total disruption in the global climate, lasting for over ten years. The computer models predicted that the cooling effect would drastically reduce output in the grain growing regions. It seems that we're facing a much more catastrophic crisis than indicated by the computer models." General Terrell's animation was cut short by Natalie George's urgency.

"Madame President. Generals. I'm receiving satellite verification. Pakistan has released its full nuclear arsenal. India has retaliated. Islamabad, Mumbai, Calcutta—gone. Interestingly, Pakistan and India both launched missiles with warheads aimed at sites in Russia and Indonesia—mainly untapped oil deposits, deep down." Director George jerked her head from the camera, directing her attention to her earphone and pressing it deeper into her ear. "North Korea launched against Japan—this makes no sense—and targets in China, Russia, and within North Korea's own boundaries. Their missiles are aimed at their own seat of government, including locations we've identified as being hardened bunkers for the Jong-un family." During the time the NSA Director had made these announcements, Cynthia had been distracted by a change in General Terrell's expression, suddenly phasing into one of serenity and calm—the opposite of the intensity and animation he had displayed seconds before.

"Madame President. What we're experiencing is the only way out. It is a cleansing, a purge that's been in the making for centuries. We can do nothing now but wait and see. This is not the end—merely the beginning. And it's glorious," General Terrell recited with a tone of religious conviction.

She looked at the faces of the other generals of the Joint Chiefs. General Harris and General Jorgenson stared at Terrell, aghast in what they were witnessing. Terrell stood, aimed his 45 semi-automatic pistol at Harris and Jorgenson, and shot each twice—one bullet in the head, and the other in the chest—with execution-style efficiency. The mortally wounded men slumped back into their chairs, as neither had time nor the belief to make an escape.

"That was necessary, Madame President. General Harris and Jorgenson could have created delays," General Terrell said, explaining why he just murdered two of his colleagues. "We must depart, as we must complete retargeting and arming the remainder of the munitions. You and your family will be safe, Madame President. The pilot will transport you to meet your host—the nation's host; the world's host; humanity's host. And our savior." The Generals' screens went blank. The remaining active screen contained Natalie George's dismayed image, dumbfounded by what she had just witnessed, albeit remotely.

"Madame President. I'm sitting in a satellite office in Seattle. I'm alone, other than some personnel outside," the NSA Director stated as if reporting the results of a science experiment. "I should be looking at the same thing you're looking at. I just witnessed General Terrell murder General Harris and General Jorgenson. Would you confirm this observation for me, please?"

"Natalie. Yes, we both saw the same thing. I need to find out where they're taking me. All seemed normal when we got into the helicopter." She paused, listening for anything outside out of the ordinary. "Natalie. Go. Discover the status of the government. I'll remain online."

"I'll return to you within five minutes with a report," Dr. George responded, a deep commitment in her tone. The screen went blank.

Cynthia abandoned her presidential demeanor. She had the blinds pulled in her compartment, allowing her to conduct the web conference without glare from the sunlight. She ripped open the blinds, remembering that four or five identical helicopters always accompany Marine One in loose formation. She picked up the phone, an action which would prompt an immediate response by the Presidential switchboard, patching her to whomever she desired. Her angst deepened, the silence of the line more mortifying than General Terrell's murdering his two Joint Chief colleagues. She was certain that the country was under attack, though the reports she had heard indicated no nuclear incursion. *If the country is under attack, the aggressors will want the leader, the President of the United States—me—Cynthia Anne Norbert.* She pushed the aid button, attempting to summon a response from the pilots. *Has the country gone mad? How could they have gotten to everyone? From the Joint Chiefs to the Marine pilots of Airforce Two? I'm isolated—alone. What power could have executed this kind of coup? Not the Russians. The North Koreans. The Chinese. No power we've encountered could have pulled this off. Unless they're extraterrestrials—aliens. Cynthia. Come on, now. Let's not get crazy!* After discovering her cabin door was locked, she kicked it, hurting her foot. She slumped back into her easy chair and cried.

Cynthia. Cynthia. Don't be disturbed. Your children are safe. You are safe. I mean you no harm. Please, compose yourself.

Jolting her from her emotional respite, she quickly focused on the monitor on which she had the meeting only moments ago. It remained blank, but she thought perhaps the speakers were activated. She clicked at the monitor controls, attempting to reactivate the screen. "Hello. Hello. Who's there?"

[Jordan_Hyperia] *Cynthia. Madame President. The voice—my voice—is coming from your mind. You are not crazy. You are not hearing things. This is a mental transmission, very similar to the games your son plays—the Brain-Link games. Your brain is simply telling your ears that sound exists. I'm Jordan. I'm responsible for your current dismay. I'm telling you this to put your mind at ease until you arrive at your destination—with us. At that point, you'll learn all there is for you to know. Please be advised, your government is under my control. I could simply relax you—disengage the neural systems causing you distress. But I want you to trust me—to know that you have your autonomy. I look forward to your company.*

353

"Where? Where are you taking me? What's going on? Please. Where are Michelle and Michael?"

"Madame President. Cynthia." She realized the voice was different. External. Recognizable. Distinct. Not the same vocalizations emanating from within her. *Natalie!* She rotated toward the monitor, affixed on Natalie George's image as if she had been gone for years. She looked different from a few moments ago—calm but haggard; alert but stuporous.

"Natalie. Tell me. What's happening?" she queried her old friend with desperation.

"It's the prelude to the Second Coming, Madame President. Armageddon has begun."

Chapter 29

Cleansing

The President of the United States, shuttled off by unknown captors, had been abducted inside her own Marine One transport helicopter. She recognized Los Angeles from her limited vantage point. Cut off from external communication, her sole informants had been Natalie George and a voice inside her head.

She tried her cell phone, email, all of the consoles and laptops inside her Marine One compartment, but to no avail. Though an urge to panic dwelled within, she squelched it, instead settling into a dead calm—the same stillness and serenity she had experienced during every crisis period of her life. She plopped back into her presidential leather lounge chair, extended her legs, put her arms back, tilted her head backward, and exerted a hearty stretch.

The first female President of the United States, and the first president to get kidnapped. Just like a woman! She mused silently, turning up the corners of her mouth. *I'm amazed at myself. I don't feel fear. I don't really think that these people, whoever they are, mean me harm. I don't think they will harm my children. I think since I am the person representing the most influential nation in the world, they want my audience and attention.*

Power. They have power over mind. How often I have secretly, silently, desperately wanted to control minds. They are doing it. All the despots, emperors, kings, and dictators tried to control minds through fear and terror. Completely ineffective.

And I don't fear for my country. It was doomed—doomed from the beginning. A noble concept, if nobility were the ruling cause. But people aren't noble, so whatever the ideal, people will corrode the foundation until the structure collapses. They are worse than parasites, who destroy the host organism, without another host to which to migrate. And so, they've tainted this grand ideal, this three-hundred-

355

year-old experiment until it could not support its own weight in decay. Slave owners who say all men are free should inform even the casual observer that something is amiss. Clarity was better when their chronic racism and sexism were forthright and candid. Now they speak in euphemistic denial—always knowing the underlying ideal is greed, manipulation, disservice.

Yet the process was not logical. The social culture and the movements festering within went counter to one another. A black President. A Jewish President. A female President. And now the unseen and unspoken message toward humanity is more acrimonious than ever. The progression was not logical, as if a force behind the scenes moved to create an undercurrent—a riptide effect siphoning down all not close to the surface.

The globe retreats in flame and soot, yet I do not regret it. I, the President of the United States, hereby declare that the nations of the Earth should all dissolve. God, I'm glad that didn't slip out during my inauguration address. Yet I remember thinking it when I was a girl in high school—wondering what would happen if some outside, indifferent, benevolent power, simply forced dissolution of national boundaries, cultures, religions, and all other impediments to the unity, if not survival, of humankind. Homogeneity among humans is good. Socialism is received well within uniform cultures, where the people are of one race and general socio-economic standard. I remember reading about the "welfare queens" of the Sixties and Seventies. White America ranted and raved about certain black women receiving large, fraudulent shares of welfare as they drove Rolls Royces to and fro. And if these women did exist, there were maybe a handful compared to the vast majority of whites who received welfare—not blacks and other minorities. The core cultures in European countries did the same thing. As long as the nations were homogeneous, social programs flourished. As soon as the borders opened, the social programs evaporated. But if

356

all people are the same racially and culturally, then uniqueness is
relegated to the realm of individuality—not race and social class.
Diversity begets intolerance—the human way. I look forward to
meeting my captors.

She tried the door once more. It was as useful in detaining her in as it would have been averting would-be assassins. Craning her head at the window, she caught sight of a haze-enshrouded Los Angeles city skyline. At the same time, she felt the aircraft slow and descend. Once a student at UCLA, she had become very familiar with Los Angeles. She triangulated the neighborhood into which they descended based upon barely discernible landmarks—Griffith Park Observatory, Downtown LA, and Baldwin Hills. Their position and assumed point of arrival did not make sense to her, having guessed their location somewhere between USC and the Crenshaw District. Since she could not see directly below her, their downward path remained a mystery until they seemed immersed within a large open warehouse or factory. Thirty-foot walls encompassed their landing position on all sides. Pressing her cheek against the window, she could see the roof of the building closing. The sunlight diminished; only artificial light remained.

After sitting for five minutes, she thought her hosts rude as being rude, that they would allow her to wait for so long without an introduction and escort. Startled, the door to her compartment suddenly opened.

"Madame President—Cynthia. You are quite correct. We were remiss in our etiquette by not meeting you sooner," Zora said affably, but smileless, standing in the doorway. "My name is Zora Green. We have much to explain, and you have much to learn. You are overflowing with curiosity—more so than angst. Before we proceed, here are three general areas with which to start. For now, you should know that you have arrived at a complex deep under Los Angeles. Your

357

children are quite safe. They were taken to another entry portal, and they will join you shortly. You should also know that you are witnessing—experiencing—the culmination of a four- thousand-year plan—a design, if you will. You will experience the transformation first hand very shortly. And last, for now, you should be aware—and I believe you have figured it out, but simply do not believe your own cognition—that we can listen to your thoughts. Soon the process will be reciprocal for you, as you will be able to listen and transmit to us as well." Zora paused momentarily to assess Cynthia's affect since she had neither moved, gestured, nor made an effort to get up. "Cynthia, extraterrestrials have not been watching you—we have. We've been there, for millennia, watching, waiting, blending into your cultures and societies. We've written the schematic for your most prized religions. Your wars, your disasters—especially the one you are about to witness—your inventions, almost everything—we seeded; we cultivated; now, we reap. Come. You have much to learn."

The President stared at Zora, ambivalent about how to consider her—enemy and captor, or friend and ally. Introspecting, she felt as if she had encountered, at long last, the lover she had never found. She was the soul mate she had been promised as a girl—the one who clicks and connects; the one whose thoughts, opinions, idiosyncrasies and quirks syncopate; the one sharing the little things, an intersection of feelings creating perfect acoustic harmony, and amplifying the most subtle tones into glass-shattering vibrations. But Zora could read her mind, so she pondered within seconds that it may all be a ploy, a scam to wrangle her into cooperation, if not submission. Yet, she backtracked: *If they can indeed listen to thoughts, are they capable of mind control as well?* The obvious question had eluded her until now. "Who are you people?" Cynthia asked Zora with deadpan sincerity. She watched Zora ponder the question as if she had never been asked it before.

"I think, for lack of a better name, you can refer to us as a kind of cult, a cult through time. Call us the Carbon Cult. The title has a certain alliterative ring and communicative crispness to it," Zora replied with well-thought deliberation. "I've been toying with names, as I'm sure the masses will want to know who is responsible for disrupting lives and causing such mayhem. Yes! The Carbon Cult," she added with reinforced affirmation. But surely, you want more than a name. Soon, we shall escort you on a journey of mind, where you can experience exactly who we are, and from where we come. But for now, let it suffice to say we were a specialized sect within the ancient culture of Canaanites occupying the coastal City of Ugarit. And now, please, Madame President, we must leave this place. Events are unfolding quickly, and we must not tarry."

Cynthia appraised her status quickly—how readily she had adjusted to this radical upheaval in her life—catastrophically traumatic, physically, emotionally, culturally, nationally. Her attitude toward her situation hovered between zealous accomplice and harried hostage. She decided far more harm than good would come from resistance, and opposition in the name of some unwatched, unkempt, and ill-defined code of honor would accomplish nothing. She hesitated, thinking about her clothes and other belongings. Realizing once more that her thoughts were not her own and subject to alteration, she looked at Zora with a mixture of distrust and abandonment. Zora's beauty stunned her, as she had not appreciated her captor's physical qualities until now. Zora looked on with unyielding anticipation.

"All you'll need will be provided," Zora explained fortuitously. "All you have known will change. You can survive because you can cope. You have seen the future before. You know your people, and you can help them through these trying times. Difficult decisions had to be made. No leader of the world could or would make them. We made them for you. Fossil fuels had to be eliminated; half of the globe's population had to perish. These are simple truths. We accomplished both. More will follow. You must witness, accept, acclimate and lead."

While on the helicopter's airstairs she noticed other blank-looking, casually-dressed attendees standing quietly and unevenly spaced, creating a loosely defined pathway from the helicopter to an undefined spot toward the back of the large, brickwalled warehouse in which they had landed. She looked around for the agent who had accompanied her, pausing to glance back at the cockpit of the aircraft to get a glimpse of the pilots' condition. The true intent of her hosts would bear out on their treatment of those with whom they had no use. They were nowhere to be seen. Evacuated, she thought, during the interlude between landing and waiting for Zora's appearance.

As she followed Zora to the end of the human procession, she unconsciously focused on her back and quickly diverted her gaze, as she self-consciously found herself attracted to this unknown woman's form. Zora turned to smile at her, stopping at a point that clearly marked a platform.

"Cynthia, we are about to descend two hundred feet underground. Please come closer to me, as I don't want any harm to befall you near the edge," Zora advised, extending her hand graciously toward the President.

Compelled to mask her angst by making conversation, she conceded to Zora's request. "Your group—you have been here for a long time, under the city?" Cynthia asked.

"This facility is new. We developed it concurrently with the building of the Los Angeles subways. Absolutely no one is aware of our presence here. And those who were part of the construction are either with us, altered, or dead," Zora replied. "But we maintain domiciles all over the globe. This one houses our most recently developed technologies which came to fruition only months ago."

"And the other world leaders? Have you captured them as well?" Cynthia asked.

"Those who will serve us, yes, we have," Zora replied. "And you will be with them shortly. Not necessarily in body, but in mind. Call it a web conference, but without the Internet," Zora responded glibly.

"You said fossil fuels eliminated, as well as half the world's pop—" Cynthia started to ask.

"All your questions and concerns will be answered very shortly, Madame President," Zora interrupted with terseness. "Indeed, you will witness firsthand—death, devastation, destruction. What you are about to witness—some of it you will find disturbing, and I will not alter the magnitude of the ferocity nor offer interference. You will learn to cope." Zora stopped as if not to continue, then added, "All was necessary for the rebirth. It had to be removed for the further, better good. Our good. Our continued evolution as a species. But again, you will see and understand all in due time."

Accepting Zora's words, Cynthia became aware of an increasing acceleration downward. The walls of the tube through which they descended had started as a glassy, ceramic material, different from the concrete of the upper deck. Lacking convenient lights telling her what floors they were passing, she estimated they had already dropped at least one hundred feet. Suddenly they burst into the open, the walls of the tube now transparent. The vastness and space of the underground complex astonished her. She discerned multiple levels, balconies, and bridgeways extending for as far as she could see.

"All under the streets of Los Angeles?" she asked, fixated, astounded by the visage. She rotated slightly to Zora who continued to stare out at the ever broadening complex. The platform slowed and stopped in front of an arched walkway two stories above what appeared to be the base floor. As they emerged through the cylindrical elevator

361

portal, their two riding companions dispersed without farewell or salutation, as automatons marching off to their next set of duties.

"Voice and sound. Vibrations through the air, Cynthia. It's an inefficient form of communication. Like smoke signals instead of wireless transmission by electromagnetic radiation," Zora commented, noticing the President's observation of the departure.

"How have you achieved it? You seem to be just like anybody else. No enlarged cranium, no bulbous eyes, and certainly no spacecraft suggesting you are not of this world. So how? You're human beings, just like the rest of us," Cynthia insisted.

"Partially correct. We are human beings, but not like most," Zora replied. "But the telepathy you've witnessed and experienced—it is accomplished through a technology similar to the mind emersion games you've seen your son play."

An epiphany suddenly beset her—a realization rolling over her as if she had remembered her own birth. "You're the mother of Éclair—Jordan Éclair, the inventor and president of Brain-Link!" Cynthia confronted Zora, not sure whether her recognition had weight, but she knew it was significant. Feeling she now had something on Zora, she continued. "The NSA gave me briefs about you several months ago. They informed me you were doing some odd research with human beings. I objected initially, but they informed me that the fruits of your labor somehow benefited homeland defense operations. We have photos of your son, but you always managed to obscure your face, remain in the background." She noticed Zora smirk without an emotional budge.

"Cynthia, what you don't know about me is far more provocative that what you do know," Zora replied with a mocking hiss.

The President, an otherwise shrewd poker player, regretted revealing her hand as the two women faced one another, not having moved from the elevator tube since arriving at the level destination. "Where is Dr. Éclair, your son?" she asked.

"He is here; he is everywhere," Zora answered in a monotonic paradox, atypical of her usual responses. She hesitated briefly, staring at Cynthia and waving off three approaching them. "Cynthia, I know your history and background. You were raised in a religious family, an upbringing you resented. You told the American people you are God-fearing; the camera saw you sitting piously in church, but you and I both know you're an atheist. You studied physics and philosophy as an undergraduate, and you obtained a master's degree in physics. You wrote a treatise about the origins of the Bible, delving into the true authors, questioning the Hebrew accounts of history. You are an intellectual in disguise, more of a liar to the American people than the typical politician who promises and reneges within the same syllables. Am I not correct?"

Cynthia marveled at this woman who knew more about her than she herself cared to remember. Zora struck a chord, a nerve deep inside her. It was a note of guilt, as she knew she despised the American public. She had taken a very private glee, gloating that she could hold basic American standards in such disregard, yet flagrantly recite the proletarian standards as her own. She had been a champion of the lower and middle classes, promoting and establishing socialist policies, retrieving the country from Wall Street and banking interests, and reducing the influence of lobbyists. And she despised religion, in all its manifestations. All this, she gloated, and she rose to become the first female President of the United States. "Please, continue," she responded, no longer containing her awe. She marveled at Zora's capacity to deliver information without affect.

"Your assumptions in your Biblical thesis were correct. Your research into the ancient scriptures was accurate and forward-looking. Men were not the primary authors of the Bible; women were the progenitors. Males in cultures stretching from Egyptian, Israelite, Roman, Byzantine, English—to name a few—modified and edited the text, tailoring it to meet their own needs. With little exception, the undercurrent of male dominated cultures channeled power to a controlling class of males, while limiting power and control to others, especially to women. And the Bible did not originate with the Israelites; its various scripts and texts propagated from anonymous individuals within their midst, who passed themselves off as members in good standing with the extant tribes. We—the disenfranchised women of the Canaanite Cult of Baal wrote the Bible—both Testaments. Jesus was a woman named Mary; one of the earliest revisions in the Scriptures, changed her to a male. And now she has returned—to carry out the Apocalypse, to forge redemption, and to bring this pathetic variety of man to a close." She stopped, assessing Cynthia's reaction. "Metaphorically, of course," she added with dampened fervor.

"I've felt a rising sense of inner passion since I arrived here. I was ransacked with panic about my son and daughter, but now I am calmed by a gentle unseen hand, stroking my head and consoling my torment. You seem to have engendered a trust before offering evidence to corroborate it. I can make this statement, yet the sense of trust I feel for you continues." Cynthia stepped toward Zora, confrontational, yet befriending. "I am the embodiment of establishment. Yet, I defeat my enemies by becoming my enemies. I did not have a plan for the kill, the ultimate coup de gras. But what is excruciatingly apparent—you seem to be able to do the impossible: Read and control minds. I do not see any evidence of morphological evolution or extra-cranial capabilities facilitating these feats. How?" Cynthia asked with the intensity of a focused beam of sunlight.

"You left your cellphone in the helicopter. One of my aids picked it up and handed it to me. Here." Zora handed Cynthia her PDA,

364

then continued to speak. "You were interested in severe mental disorder at one time in your life. You were curious about delusional and paranoid thinking. Do you remember a common theme of paranoia? The individual inflicted with paranoid ideation believes irrevocably that his mind is being controlled by an unseen intruder via radio waves. Those studies you did in abnormal psychology—the man you observed through the one-way glass believed the government had infiltrated his mind with radio waves, and they were sending him instructions, and telling him what to do and not to do. He was not delusional. That is how we enter the mind—through radio waves. Not directly, per se, but through a method of pinpointing neural structures with a local anchor— a cell phone—and fixating the structures as a reference point. Then two external maser transmitters, at least sixty steradians apart, target the reference transmission, creating the necessary myriad cascade of maser microholographs through the recipient's brain in order to implant data, sensory information, or alter memory. Indeed, radio waves did—and do—control brains. And the sense of well-being you feel, the ability to harbor conflicting thought and images without distress—that is due to a general pacifying field permeating this complex." Zora swiveled away, turning to end the discussion, and led Cynthia to her destination within the complex.

She had never expected an end; perhaps a slow decline to stagnancy—a centuries-long process over which time the United States would earn an emeritus status similar to other emperors after reaching their golden age, no longer able to clutch the reins of global influence or wield the economic and military might of their analogously developmental young adult years. She felt her rug had been yanked from under her; fate had pulled the childish prank of removing the chair just as she sat down. "It's over. Just like that? The powers of the world will hand over the reins of power to you? To your organization? No wars? No treaties? No terms of surrender? Surrender!? We haven't even engaged in battle. You come from nowhere, and take over? I'm the President of the United States!" she insisted with defiance, grabbing Zora by the forearm, preventing her departure. Zora relented, returning to face Cynthia.

"Yes, you are the President of the United States. Your status will continue as such. But Cynthia, I've explained, and I know you understand, we've been here much longer than the United States. To a significant degree, the United States exists because of us. We have disrupted every phase of history in order to facilitate advancement. Progress—technological, cultural, economic, political—does not germinate without disruption. The great western religions, all designed by us; science and technology—us. And democracy—we engineered it, every step of the way. Why? To get to where we are now, today. We wrote the book, predicting, forecasting, telling you this would happen. We have no intent in disrupting your infrastructures, at least not for now. But we must move, Cynthia. You must join your compatriots, the other leaders of the world. You must witness the demise that you currently fret. After you experience it—walk it, smell it, feel it, move about the essence of the chaos. Then, and only then, will you fully embrace what you already want to embrace." Zora touched Cynthia on the cheek sympathetically. "You embraced it once, in your dreams. You still do. You know as well as anyone, your current global systems were doomed. Looking to the future, you could not discern an upward trend or predicable positive outcome for your world, your cultures. You knew it; scholars knew it; even your theologians and evangelists knew it, and they based their presentiments not on data and empiricism, but on what we had provided to them. You were not relegated to lower status; you've been promoted—elevated beyond anything you yet can realize. Now, come. We've not far to go."

Relenting, she followed Zora, distracted by the immensity of space surrounding them as if this underground facility had been carved from a cavern under the city as large as a small city itself. The allure of the environment was seductive, engendering a euphoria which she dispelled through distrust. Her assiduous diligence disquieted her, dissuading her from the calm that would otherwise claim her. As they walked, the approaching walls were iridescent cobalt blue, vibrating with a deep multi-laminate texture. Zora escorted her through a half elliptical opening, the space on the other side radiating a blue luminance similar to the wall color.

Immersed in the deep azure light, her first recollection was the psychedelic black lights of the Sixties, yet this illumination seemed to have more of a purpose than ambience-laden mood inducement. She felt Zora touch her shoulder, gathering her attention.

"Put this around your neck. It allows us to access your brain— your mind. It's very accurate," Zora said, placing a necklace in Cynthia's hand. She drew her lips next to Cynthia's ear. "We will not alter your attitudes, memories—nothing to transform or convert your thoughts, opinions, or personality in any way. I trust—I know—that that transformation will come about by your own volition once you see and experience the world gripped in its final throes."

Suddenly released from the grip of the complex's anxiolytic effects, she panicked. "My son and daughter—where are they? Are they here yet? I want to see them," Cynthia demanded.

"Your children are here—in the complex. You will be able to see them soon. They are safe. Please, believe me. Trust me," Zora replied patiently.

Cynthia had yet to grip the necklace Zora had placed loosely in her open palm. Having now arrived at a destination, she allowed herself to feel fear. Her overriding concern was not distrust—it was pure terror. This group, who appeared from nowhere, the true bogeymen of all the paranoid conspiracy theories she had ever suffered through, harbored unarguable power. Apocalyptic movies had always made her feel uneasy, and now she wished this experience were a movie. They could do anything, at anytime, without repercussion, reprisal, or sanction. They were above the law, above culture, above humans, even above nature. Yet, they were human, and something about Zora's perceived humanity soothed Cynthia, allowing her to clutch onto the necklace. She felt Zora's gentle grip on her shoulder, gesturing for her to sit down in the reclining chair next to her. As she sat, she winced with abandonment as Zora departed from her side.

She examined the necklace, noting how it reminded her of her beloved grandfather's pocket watch; she used to listen to him boast of its accuracy when she was a small girl. The comparison helped to further engender trust. Studying it momentarily, she looped it around her neck. Almost immediately, harmonies from an unknown source seemed to clear her mind, washing away the doubts and fears she harbored. She thought immediately that even this soothing effect was mind control, yet she lacked the urgency and resentment to tear the necklace away. A voice beckoned, welling from within her.

[Hyper_Jordan] *Cynthia. I am Hyper_Jordan, former son of Zora, descendent of the Canaanite priest cult of Ugarit. You will recall me from a different past. I cannot explain my existence to you, so you simply have to listen, trust, and believe. The listening and believing may be simple enough, but I understand the trust may come with difficulty. I'm here to join you with other leaders of the world, to take you all on a tour—or rather a journey—through the world as it is now. You'll see some disturbing images. They are no more disturbing than anything that has not occurred before, or anything you may have imagined, but did not experience. I present you with this prelude before we embark. Let us make haste. The nations of the world were bound together with sheer tape and ungainly stitching, so tearing the societies of the earth asunder was not really a spectacular task. Unraveling occurs at a phenomenal rate.*

These words did not emanate from outside; they did not impact her ears; they had no discernible source or direction. She surmised the voice originated within her—her brain's auditory cortex instructing her that the sound existed. She acquiesced, acknowledging that this form of communication was typical rather than exceptional. "I'm ready," she said with trepidation, suddenly realizing she could have simply thought the words.

She found herself instantly sitting around an elongated fountain, its surreal mist swirling and bubbling, emitting a soothing sound. The amorphous contents surged upward periodically, perhaps ten feet, then settled down to her eye level. Looking to her left and right, she saw others sharing the view with her, seated as if they were gathered around a long conference table. To her left she recognized Britain's prime minister. Next to him was China's president.

She balked silently with amusement at the attendee roster, deeming smugly that dealing with China would involve far more party impetus than merely the politically appointed president. *I'm not where I think I am, wherever that is. My mind—my brain—is being bombarded with information, overriding my senses, and convincing whatever the basis of reference to reality, that I'm sitting here, among these world dignitaries. But I'm still in the room Zora took me to, and that room is in a complex underground beneath Los Angeles.*

To her right, she saw other world leaders and dignitaries, some of whom she recognized from the United Nations, some from the news, and some from the State Department primers she had received shortly after being inaugurated. They looked at her; she looked at them, but none seemed to be capable of communicating.

The purpose of the virtual reality facade escaped her, seeming unnecessary and contrived. She had already accepted unconditionally the power of her captors, as it was, and she simply wanted to absorb the facts and consequences without being treated to what she deemed a ritualistic exposition. *It appears as if the nations' leaders, or at least the ones present here, received similar pep talks prior to their induction to this rather lavish display of mind-boggling mind control. Why this ostentatious contrivance of science fiction drama? What's with this foreboding gaseous fountain in front of us, seemingly made to appear as if it flows some sort of virtual blue mist? Why this official setting of international accord where we all sit together? Simply show us each what you've got, without this lavish virtual summit meeting.*

She took stock of her condition, realizing she was sitting in the blue room in the complex under Los Angeles, but she was where she was—seated at this conference-looking table, the fountain contrivance as a long centerpiece. The temperature was comfortable; the pressure of her weight on the chair seemed normal; the sensation of her skin touching her clothing felt typical. She pinched herself in the off chance she was dreaming, but that supposition assumed one could not feel the prick from a pinch in a dream, and she knew dreams were capable of presenting severe pain, so a pinch was hardly a test of reality. Still, she sensed the bite from the pinch. For all intents and purposes, she was where she was, as her brain instructed her.

She sensed movement on her sides, noting the lineup down the table was reducing in numbers. Like a domino effect, the dignitaries to her left and right seemed to evaporate, turning to vapor like smoke from an extinguished candle, segueing from solid to mist from top to bottom, drawn into the center fountain like a kitchen stove ventilator attracts the fumes from the burning skillets. Each disappeared into the center apparition—mist into mist. And when the prime minister was gone, she felt light, yet still intact. And then she stood on the precipice of a massive inferno, the gulf of flames more intense than the ridge of one hundred Krakatoas. The flame roared from the abysmal crater like exhaust from the nozzle of a huge rocket, and she wondered whether such force would not set the Earth off its orbit.

As she stood witness to this catastrophic release of energy, feeling no pain, and certainly suffering no injury, she had become dissociated with cause and effect. She glanced down, verifying the connection with her body, but in doing so she noticed the ground, not solid, but rather liquefied, even gaseous. She could not make the distinction, realizing she did not feel the force of her weight through her feet. She feared that if this spectacle were real—if she were observing this through a remote, virtual self—she concluded that her captors implemented far more than an aggression upon nations. They executed an assault upon the planet itself. And since they must also dwell upon the Earth, such actions of devastation and environmental pillage were completely irrational—mad.

Remembering the fountain-embellished conference table where the journey began, she searched for her traveling companions. Alone, she sighed, relishing the resulting exhalation as a sign of life, distinguishing her from a dream, an illusion, a cyber-entity, or coerced figment of her own imagination. Lacking the control to change location, she thought herself an experimental rat in a psychology project, responding to whatever stimulus the researchers beset upon her in the maze.

The voice of Hyper_Jordan resounded in her mind's ears once more.

[Hyper_Jordan] *You are not a rat in a maze. Nor is this an experiment. Nor is what you are witnessing an illusion or theatrical graphic animation impinging your sensory neurons. What you see is really happening. Though you are not actually physically present—you would incinerate instantly. What you witness is one of several craters we have dug with some of the local nations' nuclear warheads. We put their weapons to better use, not only eliminating the indigenous populations, but also removing the economic, social, and political barriers thwarting an evolutionary advancement.*

371

Each of you will see what we have done—but separately. I talk to you separately. I will talk to each human being—be with every individual—who remains on this earth. Each will hear my voice, for each must survive, reproduce and develop in such a way that we put our species back on track. We've simply pruned the tree before the branch wilted and fell off.

Jolted from a complacency—a complacency she thought perhaps created to counteract what would otherwise be stimulation too traumatic to bear—she opened her eyes owl like, staring into the inferno, expecting to see the entity from which the megaphone oration had just originated. Denying that what she sought would come from the fire, she looked to her sides, expecting a casual stroller to happen by—perhaps escort her from this place. In the distance to her left she spied a wispy visage, what she discerned as a female figure materializing, seeming to take shape while approaching her simultaneously. Not blinking her eyelids for fear of missing something, she deemed a nude woman, her long brown hair radiating as if the heat from the nearby exploding gas wanted to set it afire, but could not.

[Hyper_Jordan] *Clothes are for protection from the environment, display of social status, and for modesty, none of which are required here. The rules and beliefs by which you abided no longer apply. We will alter the planet, bring about a new Ice Age, reversing the warming your nations caused. Remember, the infernos you will witness, ablaze, would have occurred over the next fifty years among billions of smaller less ominous sources individually—internal combustion and jet engines, diesel, factories, and power generating facilities. We have simply accelerated the process to occur over the next two months. The Earth will assimilate this naturally and efficiently. Take my hand.*

Entranced and aghast, she complied with Hyper_Jordan's request. Still dissociated from a sense of self and reality, she struggled

372

to ignore her compulsion to question what she experienced. Relating her situation to fantasy, the encounter reminded her of fictional themes—the spirits leading Ebenezer Scrooge on Christmas Eve, or the Ancient Mariner advising the Wedding Guest—presenting opportunities for retribution. She expected to grab nothing when she reached for his hand, but instead she experienced an exhilarating electricity—not shocking or tingling. The sensation surged through her palm, up her arm, and into her body. It helped her reconnect, shedding the dissociation. She faded into the blue mist of the fountain, only to reemerge at the edge of another fiery crater, though this one spewed steam. She knew it was different by the tower of jet propelled superheated steam towering into the sky, creating a deep cloud cover at least sixty thousand feet above them, obscuring the sun, and creating a tropical feeling in an otherwise arctic landscape. Upon closer inspection she saw that they hovered over a sea of boiling water. Land was barely visible on the horizon—islands separated by sea. She guessed the North Sea or Arctic Ocean, but deferred comment, waiting for her host to narrate the surrounding.

[Hyper_Jordan] *We stood at the edge of the Saudi crater moments ago, directly above the Ghawar deposits. In order to offset the notion of future petroleum enterprise, we targeted pockets of oil with potentially substantial recovery. We used Korean and Russian warheads for a good purpose, here, where we stand. We parted the waters here in the Sea of Okhotsk east of the Sakhalin Island, producing this petroleum-fired geyser.*

She pinpointed the source of her disbelief—her inability to connect what she was being shown with what her senses told her. The sensory stimuli did not fit the environment—there should be a deafening roar where she stood; there should be unbearable heat; the air should be sucked from the area, rendering life unsustainable. Yet, here she stood, accompanied by this epicene visage of a superhuman as if she were a docent of the apocalypse.

[Hyper-Jordan] *Cynthia, over nine hundred major oil deposits and reserves are scattered around the globe, with concentrations in the Middle East and Asia. We targeted two hundred twenty-three—the most productive, the most promising, and the ones we could target without unmanageable denigrating effects on the ecological designs and geo-shaping process we projected for the next several millennia. As these burns have well progressed for five hours, let us look at ancillary consequences—mainly the state of populations around the world. What are people doing?*

She teetered on the edge of a three-story building, peering down onto a pavement of flesh, bodies layering the streets from building to building, crowds tripping and falling, balancing themselves on the evergrowing piles of carnage. With the filtration of powerful sensory stimuli from the infernal oil craters, she wished the censors had controlled her access to this visage. She collapsed to her knees, Hyper_Jordan allowing her the freedom to feel sick.

"These are humans. Human beings! What's going on? Where are we? What have you done?" she cried with contemptuous desperation.

[Hyper_Jordan] *To these people, we have done nothing— directly. Given the graven circumstances, what you witness is self-inflicted. Behold.*

He hoisted Cynthia from under her arm and pointed to the western horizon over the city's low profile skyline. She focused as Hyper_Jordan directed, finally fixating on an intense vertical beam of light. It was another emblazoned petroleum gusher, ignited by nuclear warheads. We are in Lagos, Nigeria. We now go elsewhere.

Without transition, she was awash by another environment, another location. Since the temperature did not vary, she could identify

374

her whereabouts only by landscape, angle of the sun, and general aridity. As an afterthought, she accepted their former location as western Africa, close to the equator. But pinpointing her location became of little consequence after gathering the low point of civilization. *Even during the height of the Black Death, carts came around to carry off the dead.* Now, they were further north; she guessed in Scandinavia, given the low angle of the sun in the sky and the surrounding architecture, though she did not see any people.

[Hyper_Jordan] *We did execute what you are about to see. It was an unfortunate consequence of exposing deposits under the North Sea between the British Isles and Norway. The abrupt release of pressure caused an unforeseeable earthquake. We did not anticipate the disruption of the fault line here. We stand at the mean tide line on the shoreline at Aberdeen facing northeast. Note how far the water has receded, perhaps one thousand feet, very rapidly. The tsunami should be visible on the horizon within five minutes. All the same—the Neo Ice Age will glacerize these islands, erasing once and for all what were the British Ilses.*

Cynthia quivered vexatiously at Hyper_Jordan's cryptic affect toward what she had relished since childhood—considered the source of western culture's epitome—philosophy, literature, science, and the general impetus for change.

Hyper_Jordan's essence—her radiating ambience of unquestionable acumen and poise—hit a discordant harmony with Cynthia when he apathetically dismissed the demise of Britain. She turned toward him, stunned without pause, as she had forgotten Hyper_Jordan wore no clothes. "All that we know of ourselves—our history, our languages, our cultures, our poets and prophets—all gone?"

In that instant, she felt herself engulfed in dark blue. Her skin reacted to a chill, but she did not feel cold. The water flowed around her, but not through her, nor was she jostled or perturbed. An echo of

Hyper_Jordan's voice resonated, alternating between male and female tones:

All gone. All gone. All gone. All gone. All gone. All gone. All gone.

Epilogue

Cycles and Chaos

26,542 Years Later

[Gestating Entity] *How did we sustain ourselves?*

Intrigued by the history of human genes on the planet, this overriding, reoccurring question possessed her, distracting the incomplete organism from continuing her focus on the DNA regression—her expedition of human history through protoplasmic memory.

[Gestating Entity] *We should have been extinct many times, but somehow we intervened to halt our demise. A group of saviors— piloting mediators—humans with a protracted goal and self- perpetuating purpose appear, as if parked on a path of time. They steered us clear of the maelstrom we had seeded for ourselves. Purpose is not inbred; it is not genetically coded. Breeding intrinsic error to pass to further generations—hardly a reliable method to guarantee survival. For millennia they behaved as if fiction of race takes precedence over the life of the individual. The ritual of culture and race was so indelible; it almost destroyed our species. How was this genetic code implanted?*

She sensed a parent's presence, probing for her whereabouts and her progress in DNA regression.

[Gestating Entity] *I'm here, mother. I was exploring the American continent—the Western ice shore. I saw remnants of their lives—materials of no apparent purpose. Humans developed tools, expanding their sensory range. They consumed without regard for by- product contamination. The people, they seemed to have no conscious awareness of reciprocal effect—no ability to thwart their own demise. They brought about their own dissolution—the Cleansing—through their perpetuation of toxicity. So selfish—so alone. Completely disconnected, behaving as if each individual had ultimate importance.*

377

They did not draw strength and sustenance from each other, and from other organisms. That period fascinates me. More so than any other of our evolutionary epochs, from australopithecines to homo sapiens sapiens to homo sapiens continuus. I experienced our early ancestors' trek from Africa. Father! They survived against all odds. Yet, their probability of survival was greater than the sapiens variety twenty-six thousand years ago.

She sensed her mother's curiosity, her passion for her daughter's energy, autonomy, and initiative to explore.

[Parent Entity] *You have discovered a dilemma. It is an order within the evolutionary thread, a function to the chaos itself.*

Focused on her mother's interest, but trying to abandon what she had just witnessed during her studies, she removed herself further from the connections allowing her to venture through the ancient past.

[Gestating Entity] *Mother, I have found not an order, but orders. Banded individuals, placed strategically to facilitate and guide the process so that human evolution continued unabated. I have discovered three occurrences within two hundred fifty thousand years that extinction was thwarted by what appeared to be embedded within human groups, individuals—kernels whose sole genetic purpose seemed to be navigating the human timeline to fruitful outcome. The probability for species' survival at any of these three pivot points was less than one out of three million overall. During the last critical epoch, the probability was less than one out of one hundred thirty-five million for homo sapiens survival if these individuals had not interceded. The probability for these amalgamated humans surviving for the generations necessary to shepherd human progress is one out of six billion five hundred fifty-four million eight hundred forty-two thousand five hundred seventy-one. It happened three times. We are here, the surviving species—homo sapiens continuus. Can you see it?*

She detected her mother within her cognitions, examining neural pathways and appraising patterns for her eventual integration into the sensory environment. Her parent's memories poured into her consciousness as the mother entity routed data from her own past protoplasmic treks.

[Parent Entity] *Homo sapiens sapiens eventually believed themselves wise beyond comparison. Hubris developed from novel tool utilization. They come to believe if they could harness energy from artificial stars, they were invulnerable to nature. But they were not invulnerable to themselves, and they were part of nature. Each was born and each died in a world where s/he was disconnected from other humans, their local environment and the universe itself. They had not discovered the fabric of space binding all. They hated other members of their species—they despised living things—a convoluted self hatred. They destroyed other humans directly. And when they did not kill others directly, their brutal behavior became ingrained within their cultural systems. The genocide was less conspicuous; the intent was disguised within a web of double meaning. They poisoned the population with stress-riddled rules, beliefs, rituals, customs and toxins. Their god—all knowing, all powerful, all merciful and loving— yet it killed for retribution, punishment, land, and allegiance. Imagine, worshiping a supernatural being, an infinite, omniscient entity which lies beyond one's capacity to perceive, believing it to be supreme beyond any other entity, committed to its edicts of loyalty, servitude, and veneration—and especially its specific laws relating to behavior toward others of your species. Though, this same being condones systematic extermination of other societies, the rationale being the aggressive culture's more profound adoration of their supreme being over those under siege. These ancient societies conducted organized killing campaigns against one another—wars. They never realized that our essence would evolve toward connectedness—the very nature of the*

379

universe. The last evolutionary intervention—the extremely low probability event that you detected—used war, greed, consumerism and their singular capsulated self-aggrandizement, accelerating these characteristics into—I cannot describe it any other way than to use an ancient term—an evolutionary catharsis.

Our preceding species had globalized, degenerating their environment in a most viral manner, perpetuated with denial. The last interveners used the epitome of the race's energy sources: oxidation of fossil fuels and atomic fission. By erupting the sources of fossil fuel with atomic fission energy, they accelerated a self-extinction, bringing about the eventual end of homo sapiens sapiens. The next human species—us, continuus—existed sparsely. The interveners used the science and technology of their times to link all the survivors. They had created a model of the essence of our species by linking each individual's brain through a massive artificial global network. You have experienced these events yourself, have you not?

A vexatious venom washed over her perception, distracting her from the rational appraisal of the events she had witnessed through her inner-cellular sojourn. What she had witnessed comprised more than of a mere image—factual displays of past events. They stimulated revulsion, an emotion with which she was unfamiliar. She could not suppress the sensation, nor could she disguise it from her father; she was split.

[Gestating Entity] *I discontinued the probe, mother. I stopped because of the disturbing images at the Climax Epoch. And I became preoccupied with the infinitesimally small probabilities directed here, on this small world of nitrogen and oxygen. A randomly oriented universe does not deliver contrivance. Yet, here we are. It would appear as if the natural order—that by which we survive—can be superseded in order to insure proliferation. So my questions—as I can feel your presence bathing my thoughts: What caused the highly*

380

improbable intervention, as it was infinitely too improbable to be
random? What implanted those who guided evolution? What is the
Superseder? Does the god of the old ones truly exist? Have we
unwisely, but conveniently, ignored it? And if it does exist, does it
require our adoration? Before you venture a response, my ultimate
question would be: If it requires homage from beings it has
championed, how is it that we have been rewarded with continued and
evolved existence?

She prepared for her mother's response, as she sensed her parent probing for the source of her newly found awareness of evil.

[Parent Entity] *We have probed the inner intricacies of this*
planet. Our knowledge of the universe has progressed exponentially
since we have discovered the reciprocal natures of mass, space and
energy. We as a species have bound ourselves here—not out of
trepidation for the unknown, but thirst for it. Abandoning our yet-to-be-
mastered inner space, we will not be able to cope with outer space.
But, both cosmologically and inter-dimensionally, we have not
discovered—not even an allusion toward—a designing entity, an
ubiquitous Being residing over infinity, consisting of other infinite
infinities, devising master algorithms for time and space. That it does
not exist would be illogical to proclaim. The truth of the universe is
discovery; it is an infinite mine of the most precious--knowledge. I do,
though, comprehend your queries and apprehension. Your examination
has a logical extreme—the doubt without evidence which you claim
could lead to unfounded ritual. It leads to a spiral of obsession—a
gravity from which there is no escape. It is the one into which the old
ones perished.

She was aware of the other neuro-gestative vestibules around her, each containing an individual not yet born—a human entity, developed physiologically, but not cerebrally. Encased in the neuro-protoplasmic gel, she underwent the extra-uteral neurological development, indigenous to the her species, homo sapiens continuus. She had little memory of her basic cellular differentiation. But, now her awareness grew and expanded, joining her with her species' cognitive network—the community of humans bound together by the recently evolved empathetic bandpass. She had encountered so many realizations during this neuro-gestation period; she could not imagine how humans developed before continuus evolved. She could not envision being born to the world as an infant, equipped only with basic reflexes and undeveloped brain. Learning by accident, the serendipity of nature—random matching of offspring to parent and environment— was the same to her as pre-mammals hatching their newborns, then abandoning them to fend for themselves. She understood randomness was key to evolution, but, within homo sapiens continuus, randomness from the environment beset individuals after birth—the period when the brain had acquired the connection with other humans, other individuals within their species. We no longer destroy ourselves, nor do we see any action taken anywhere, which is not global and common to all.

She had paused her exploration of their history, as the images of humans past were too stark, too graphic. She did, though, wonder how she even came to realize the epoch's austerity, being that a reference point of comparable magnitude was required for comparison. Now she must return, knowing she would witness atrocity beyond her fortitude to withstand. She consoled herself in that these images were from thousands of years in the past. Human suffering and cruelty—she simply did not comprehend.

Her embryonic brain compiled the information, simultaneously searching for the locations of these visions and memories. She scoured every person and organism with whom she had connected during her recallable lifespan, attempting to index and collate the information her parent had imparted to her through the neuro-gestative vestibule. Relieved, though never stressed, she identified the address through which she had learned that only sixty years before the evolutionary apex, homo sapiens sapiens had discovered the gene of empathy—the gene from which her species had proliferated.

[Gestating Entity] *Our essence—their essence—laid dormant in the old ones. Did they ignore it, or was it beyond their capacity to recognize its requirement for their survival? From this bundle of DNA, we became capable of experiencing through the senses of all organisms. We became capable of traversing DNA as a recording device, a chronicler of our cellular history. We are a network of life, sensing through the senses of others—we each are a compendium of all experiences, each intertwined and tethered. We evolved from sapiens to continuus—connected.*

www.ingramcontent.com/pod-product-compliance
Lightning Source LLC
Chambersburg PA
CBHW030550260626
47157CB00006B/2261